TALES FROM THE
PERILOUS REALM

Works by J.R.R. Tolkien
THE HOBBIT
LEAF BY NIGGLE
ON FAIRY-STORIES
FARMER GILES OF HAM
THE HOMECOMING OF BEORHTNOTH
THE LORD OF THE RINGS
THE ADVENTURES OF TOM BOMBADIL
THE ROAD GOES EVER ON (WITH DONALD SWANN)
SMITH OF WOOTTON MAJOR

Works published posthumously
SIR GAWAIN AND THE GREEN KNIGHT, PEARL AND SIR ORFEO*
THE FATHER CHRISTMAS LETTERS
THE SILMARILLION*
PICTURES BY J.R.R. TOLKIEN*
UNFINISHED TALES*
THE LETTERS OF J.R.R. TOLKIEN*
FINN AND HENGEST
MR BLISS
THE MONSTERS AND THE CRITICS & OTHER ESSAYS*
ROVERANDOM
THE CHILDREN OF HÚRIN*
THE LEGEND OF SIGURD AND GUDRÚN*
THE FALL OF ARTHUR*
BEOWULF: A TRANSLATION AND COMMENTARY*
THE STORY OF KULLERVO
THE LAY OF AOTROU AND ITROUN
BEREN AND LÚTHIEN*
THE FALL OF GONDOLIN*

The History of Middle-earth – by Christopher Tolkien
I THE BOOK OF LOST TALES, PART ONE
II THE BOOK OF LOST TALES, PART TWO
III THE LAYS OF BELERIAND
IV THE SHAPING OF MIDDLE-EARTH
V THE LOST ROAD AND OTHER WRITINGS
VI THE RETURN OF THE SHADOW
VII THE TREASON OF ISENGARD
VIII THE WAR OF THE RING
IX SAURON DEFEATED
X MORGOTH'S RING
XI THE WAR OF THE JEWELS
XII THE PEOPLES OF MIDDLE-EARTH

* Edited by Christopher Tolkien

TALES FROM THE PERILOUS REALM

BY

J.R.R. Tolkien

Illustrated by Alan Lee

HarperCollins*Publishers*

HarperCollins*Publishers*
1 London Bridge Street
London SE1 9GF

HarperCollins*Publishers*
Macken House, 39/40 Mayor Street Upper
Dublin1
D01 C9W8 Ireland

Published by HarperCollins*Publishers* 2008

17

This collection first published in Great Britain
by HarperCollins*Publishers* 1997

Farmer Giles of Ham first published 1949
Copyright © The J.R.R. Tolkien Copyright Trust 1949
The Adventures of Tom Bombadil first published 1961
Copyright © The J.R.R. Tolkien Copyright Trust 1962
Leaf By Niggle first published in *Tree and Leaf* 1964
Copyright © The Tolkien Trust 1964
Smith of Wootton Major first published 1967
Copyright © The Tolkien Trust 1967
Roverandom first published 1998
Copyright © The Tolkien Trust 1998

Introduction © Tom Shippey 2008
Illustrations and Afterword copyright © Alan Lee 2008

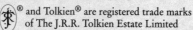

® and Tolkien® are registered trade marks
of The J.R.R. Tolkien Estate Limited

ISBN 978 0 00 728059 9

Set in Stempel Garamond

Printed and bound in the UK using 100%
renewable electricity at CPI Group (UK) Ltd

MIX
Paper | Supporting
responsible forestry
FSC™ C007454
www.fsc.org

This book is produced from independently certified FSC™ paper
to ensure responsible forest management.

For more information visit: www.harpercollins.co.uk/green

CONTENTS

Introduction by Tom Shippey   ix

Roverandom   1
Farmer Giles of Ham   99
The Adventures of Tom Bombadil   167
Smith of Wootton Major   243
Leaf by Niggle   283

Appendix
On Fairy-stories   313

Afterword by Alan Lee   401

FAERIE is a perilous land, and in it are pitfalls for the unwary and dungeons for the overbold . . . The realm of fairy-story is wide and deep and high and filled with many things: all manner of beasts and birds are found there; shoreless seas and stars uncounted; beauty that is an enchantment, and an ever-present peril; both joy and sorrow as sharp as swords. In that realm a man may, perhaps, count himself fortunate to have wandered, but its very richness and strangeness tie the tongue of a traveller who would report them. And while he is there it is dangerous for him to ask too many questions, lest the gates should be shut and the keys be lost.

J.R.R. Tolkien[1]

[1] From *On Fairy-Stories*, a lecture given on 8 March 1939. The full text is reproduced at the end of this book.

INTRODUCTION

We do not know when Tolkien began to turn his thoughts to the Perilous Realm of Faërie. In his essay "On Fairy-stories", to be found at the end of this book, he admits that he took no particular interest in tales of that kind as a child: they were just one of many interests. A "real taste" for them, he says, "was wakened by philology on the threshold of manhood, and quickened to full life by war". This seems to be strictly accurate. The first of his works to take an interest in fairies, that we know of, is a poem called "Wood-sunshine", written in 1910, when Tolkien was eighteen and still at King Edward's School in Birmingham. By the end of 1915, the year in which he took his Oxford degree and immediately joined the army to fight in the Great War, he had written several more, some of them containing major elements of what would be his developed Faërie mythology. By the end of 1917, most of which he spent in military hospital or waiting to be passed fit for active service once more, he had written the first draft of tales which would sixty years later be published in *The Silmarillion*, and much of Middle-earth, as also of Elvenhome beyond it, had taken shape in his mind.

What happened then is a long story, about which we now know a great deal more than we did, but once again it was summed up concisely and suggestively by Tolkien himself, in the story "Leaf by Niggle". It is generally accepted that this has a strong element of self-portrait about it, with Tolkien the writer – a confirmed "niggler", as he said himself – transposed as Niggle the painter. Niggle, the story tells us, was busy on all kinds of pictures, but one in particular started to grow on him. It began as just a single leaf, but then it became a tree, and the tree grew to be a Tree, and behind it a whole country started to open out, with "glimpses of a forest marching over the land, and of mountains tipped with snow". Niggle, Tolkien wrote, "lost interest in his other pictures; or else he took them and tacked them on to the edges of his great picture".

Once again this is an accurate account of what Tolkien can be seen doing in the 1920s, 1930s, and 1940s. During those thirty years he kept working at variants of "Silmarillion" stories, writing occasional poems, often anonymously, and making up other stories, not always written down and sometimes told initially only to his children. *The Hobbit* started life as one of these, set in Middle-earth, but to begin with connected only tangentially with the Elvish history of the Silmarils: it was, to use the modern term, a spin-off. *The Lord of the Rings* was a further spin-off, this time from *The Hobbit*, and initially motivated by Tolkien's publisher's strong desire for a *Hobbit*-sequel. But what Tolkien started to do, just like Niggle, was to take things he had written before and start "tacking them on to the edges". Tom Bombadil, who had begun as the name for a child's toy, got into print in 1934 as the hero of a poem, and then became perhaps the most mysterious figure in the world of *The Lord of the Rings*. That work also drew in other poems, some of them comic, like Sam Gamgee's "Oliphaunt" rhyme, first published in 1927, others grave and sad, like the version Strider gives on Weathertop of the tale of Beren and Lúthien, again going back to a poem published in 1925, and based on a story written even earlier.

Quite what was the "leaf" of Tolkien's original inspiration, and what he meant by "the Tree", we cannot be sure, though the "forest marching over the land" does sound very like the Ents. But the little allegory makes one further point which corroborates what Tolkien said elsewhere, and that is that "fairy-stories", whoever tells them, are not about fairies so much as about Faërie, the Perilous Realm itself. Tolkien indeed asserted there are not many stories actually *about* fairies, or even about elves, and most of them – he was too modest to add, unless they were written by Tolkien himself – were not very interesting. Most good fairy-stories are about "the *aventures* of

men in the Perilous Realm or upon its shadowy marches",
a very exact description once again of Tolkien's own tales
of Beren on the marches or borders of Doriath, Túrin
skirmishing around Nargothrond, or Tuor escaping from
the Fall of Gondolin. Tolkien remained strongly ambiva-
lent about the very notion of "fairy". He disliked the
word, as a borrowing from French – the English word is
"elf" – and he also disliked the whole Victorian cult of
fairies as little, pretty, ineffective creatures, prone to being
co-opted into the service of moral tales for children, and
often irretrievably phony. Much of his essay "On Fairy-
Stories", indeed (published in 1945 in a memorial volume
for Charles Williams, and there expanded from a lecture
given in 1939 in honour of Andrew Lang the fairy-tale
collector) is avowedly corrective, both of scholarly termi-
nology and of popular taste. Tolkien thought he knew
better, was in touch with older, deeper, and more powerful conceptions than the Victorians knew, even those as
learned as Andrew Lang.

However, while he had no time for fairies, Tolkien was
all for Faërie itself, the land, as Bilbo Baggins puts it, of
"dragons and goblins and giants", the land where one may
hear of "the rescue of princesses and the unexpected luck
of widow's sons". The stories and poems in this book
show Tolkien trying out various approaches to perilous
realms of one kind or another, all of them suggestive, original, independent. They represent, one may say, the pictures Niggle did *not* "tack on to the edges of his great

picture". They hint tantalisingly at directions which might have been explored further, like the later unwritten history of Farmer Giles's Little Kingdom. And they give quite different views of Tolkien's inspiration, spread over a period of at least forty years, and extending from maturity to old age. Also, as it happens, we know a good deal about how each of them came into being.

Roverandom, not published till 1998, began more than seventy years earlier as a story with a single limited purpose: to console a little boy for the loss of his toy dog. In September 1925 the Tolkien family, father, mother, and three sons, John (aged eight), Michael (aged five), and baby Christopher, went on holiday to the seaside town of Filey in Yorkshire. Michael at that time was very attached to a small toy dog, which went everywhere with him. He and his father and elder brother went down to the beach, he put it down to play, but when they went back for it they couldn't find it: the dog was white with black spots, and on a white shingle beach it was invisible. They looked for it without success that day and the next, and then a storm wrecked the beach and made further search impossible. To cheer Michael up, Tolkien invented a story in which toy Rover was *not* a toy, but a real dog turned into a toy by an angry wizard; the toy then met a friendly wizard on the beach, who sent him off on various quests in order to become a real dog again, and be reunited with his one-time owner, the boy called "Two". Like all Tolkien's stories, this grew in the telling, being written down, with several of Tolkien's own illustrations, probably around Christmas 1927, and reaching final shape at about the same time as *The Hobbit*, in 1936.

Besides the beach at Filey, where Rover meets the sand-wizard Psamathos, *Roverandom* has three main settings, the light side of the Moon, where the Man in the Moon has his tower, the dark side, where sleeping children come down the moon-path to play in the valley of dreams, and the undersea kingdom of the mer-king, where the angry wizard Artaxerxes has gone to take up a position as Pacific Atlantic Magician, or PAM. Both in the Moon and under the sea Rover is befriended by a moon-dog, or a mer-dog, both called Rover, which is why he has to take the name Roverandom. The three of them get into continual scrapes, teasing the Great White Dragon on the Moon, and stirring up the Sea-serpent on the ocean-bed, whose writhings send a storm like the one that scattered the shingle at Filey, while Roverandom is carried by the great whale Uin across the Shadowy Seas and beyond the Magic Isles to within sight of Elvenhome itself and the light of Faery – the nearest Tolkien comes to attaching this story to his greater mythology. "I should catch it, if this was found out!", says Uin, diving hastily, and we hear no more of what would be Valinor.

"Catch it!" captures the tone of this early and humorous piece. The little dogs' adventures are playful, the animals who transport them, Mew the gull and Uin the whale, are no worse than condescending, and even the three wizards who make an appearance are good-natured or, in the case of Artaxerxes, something less than competent. Nevertheless there are hints of things older and darker and deeper. The Great White Dragon the dogs tease on the Moon is also the White Dragon of England in the Merlin legend, forever at war with the Red Dragon of the Welsh; the Sea-serpent recalls the Midgard Serpent who will be the death of Thor on the day of Ragnarok; mer-dog Rover remembers a Viking master who sounds very like the famous King Olaf Tryggvason. There is myth, and legend, and even history, in *Roverandom*. Nor did Tolkien forget that even for children there must be suggestions of peril in the Perilous Realm. The dark side of the Moon has black spiders, as well as grey ones ready to pickle little dogs for their larders, while on the white side "there were sword-flies, and glass-beetles with jaws like steel-traps, and pale unicornets with stings like spears … And worse than the insects were the shadowbats", not to mention, on the way back from the valley where the children go in dreams, "nasty creepy things in the bogs" that without the Man in the Moon's protection "would otherwise have grabbed the little dog quick". There are sea-goblins too, and a whole list of calamities caused by Artaxerxes tipping out his spells. Already Tolkien had grasped the effect of suggestion, of stories not told, of beings and powers (like the Necromancer in *The Hobbit*) held just out of sight. Whatever logic may say, time spent on details, even when they lead nowhere, is not all simply "niggling".

Humour is also the dominant tone of "Farmer Giles of Ham", but it is humour of a different sort, more adult and even scholarly. Once again, this story began as a tale told impromptu to Tolkien's children: his eldest son John remembered being told a version of it as the family sheltered under a bridge from a storm, probably after they moved to Oxford in 1926. (One of the major scenes in the story is the dragon Chrysophylax coming out from under a bridge to rout the king and his army.) In the first written version, the narrator is "Daddy", and a child interrupts to ask what is a "blunderbuss". The tale was steadily expanded, reaching its final shape when it was read to an Oxford student society in January 1940, and was eventually published in 1949.

The first joke lies in the title, for we have two of them, one in English and one in Latin. Tolkien pretends to have translated the story out of Latin, and in his "Foreword" imitates a kind of scholarly introduction, which is thoroughly patronising. The imaginary editor despises the imaginary narrator's Latin, sees the tale as useful mainly for explaining place-names, and raises a snobbish eyebrow at those deluded people who "may find the character and adventures of its hero attractive in themselves". But the tale takes its revenge. The editor shows his approval of "sober annals" and "historians of the reign of Arthur", but the "swift alternations of war and peace" he mentions come from the start of the romance of *Sir Gawain and the Green Knight*, as marvellous and unhistorical a source as one could hope to find. As the story indicates, the truth is that the "popular lays" which the editor sneers at are much more reliable than the scholarly commentary imposed on them. All through *Farmer Giles*, the old and the traditional defeat the learned and new-fangled. The "Four Wise Clerks of Oxenford" define a blunderbuss, and their definition is that of the great *Oxford English Dictionary* with (in Tolkien's day) its four successive editors. Giles's blunderbuss, however, defies the definition and works just the same. "Plain heavy swords" are "out of fashion" at the king's court, and the king gives one away to Giles as being of no value: but the sword is "Tailbiter" (or if one insists on using Latin, "Caudimordax"), and Giles is heartened by having it, even in the face of dragons, because of his love of the old tales and heroic songs which have gone out of fashion too.

Gone out of fashion, maybe, but not gone away. All his life Tolkien was fascinated by survivals: words and phrases and sayings, even stories and rhymes, which came from a prehistoric past but which had been passed on by word of mouth, quite naturally, often garbled and generally unrecognized, right down to modern common experience. Fairy-stories are an obvious example, kept in being for centuries not by scholars but by old grannies and nursemaids. Nursery-rhymes too. Where do they come from? Old King Cole figures in Tolkien's "Foreword" (suitably transferred to scholarly pseudo-history), and Chrysophylax quotes "Humpty Dumpty" when he comes out from under the bridge. Two more nursery-rhymes were rewritten as the "Man in the Moon" poems in *Tom Bombadil*. Riddles are survivals as well, told by Anglo-Saxons (we still have more than a hundred of them), and by modern schoolchildren. And then there are popular sayings, always open to revision – "Sunny Sam" the blacksmith inverts a couple of them in *Farmer Giles*, as does Bilbo in *The Lord of the Rings*, with his "All that is gold does not glitter" – but never dying out. And the commonest types of survival are names, of people and of places. They often descend from remote antiquity, their meaning is often forgotten, but they are still overpower-ingly present. Tolkien was convinced that old heroic names hung on even in names associated with his own family, and one inspiration for *Farmer Giles* must be the urge to "make sense" of the local Buckinghamshire place-names of Tame and Worminghall.

Myths are the greatest of survivals, though, and the most important revenge in *Farmer Giles* is the revenge of the mythical on the everyday. For who is to say which is which? It is the young and silly dragons who conclude "So knights are mythical! ... We always thought so." It is the silly over-civilised court which prefers sweet and sticky Mock Dragon's Tail to Real Tail. The courtiers' descendants (Tolkien implies) will eventually substitute their feeble imitations for the real thing even in fantasy – just like Nokes the Cook in *Smith of Wootton Major*, with his sad diminished idea of the Fairy Queen and Faërie itself. Giles deals firmly and fairly with king and court and dragon alike, though we should not forget the assistance he receives from the parson – a scholar who makes up for all the others – and from the story's unsung heroine, the grey mare. She knew what she was doing all the time, even when she sniffed at Giles's unnecessary spurs. He didn't need to pretend to be a knight.

The Adventures of Tom Bombadil also owe their existence to prompting from Tolkien's family. In 1961 his Aunt Jane Neave suggested to him that he might bring out a little book with Tom Bombadil in it, which people like her could afford to buy as Christmas presents. Tolkien responded by collecting a clutch of poems he had already written at different times over the preceding forty years or more. Most of the sixteen had been printed, sometimes in very obscure publications, in the 1920s and 1930s, but Tolkien took the opportunity in 1962 to revise them thoroughly. By this time *The Lord of the Rings* had appeared, and was already well-known, and Tolkien did what Niggle had done with his earlier pictures: he put these early compositions into the overall frame of his greater one. Once again he used the device of the scholarly editor, this time someone who has access to the Red

Book of Westmarch, the hobbit-compilation from which *The Lord of the Rings* was supposed to have been drawn, and who has decided this time to edit not the main story but the "marginalia" – the things which medieval scribes in reality often wrote round the edges of their more official works.

This device allowed Tolkien to put in poems which were clearly just jokes, like no. 12, "Cat", written as late as 1956 for his granddaughter Joanna; or poems which had no connection with Middle-earth, like no. 9, "The Mewlips", originally printed in *The Oxford Magazine* for 1937 and there sub-titled "Lines Induced by Sensations When Waiting for an Answer at the Door of an Exalted Academic Person"; or poems which did have such a connection, but one which now made Tolkien uneasy. No. 3, "Errantry", for instance, had been first written at least thirty years before, and had then been revised to become a song sung by Bilbo in *The Lord of the Rings*, but the names in it did not fit Tolkien's increasingly developed Elvish languages. Editor-Tolkien accordingly explains that while the poem is Bilbo's, he must have written it not long after his retirement to Rivendell, at a time when he did not know much about Elvish tradition. By the time Bilbo composed the *Lord of the Rings* version, he knew better, though Strider still thinks he should have left well alone. Several other poems, like nos. 7 and 8, the two troll-poems, or no. 10, "Oliphaunt", are ascribed to Sam Gamgee, which helps to account for their non-serious nature. Nos. 5 and 6, the two "Man in the Moon" poems, both of them dating back to 1923, confirm Tolkien's interest in nursery-rhymes: they are, in Tolkien's imagination, the old complete poems of which modern children's rhymes are garbled descendants, and the kind of thing that would have been popular in his imaginary Shire.

The first two and last three poems in the collection however show Tolkien working more deeply and more seriously. No. 1, the title poem, had also been published in *The Oxford Magazine*, in 1934, but no. 2, "Bombadil Goes Boating", may date back even further. Like Roverandom, Bombadil had begun as the name of one of the Tolkien children's toys, but had soon established himself as a kind of image of the English countryside and the country-folk and their enduring traditions, powerful, indeed masterful, but uninterested in exercising power. In both poems Tom is continually threatened, seriously by Barrow-wight, jokingly by otter-lad and by the hobbits who shoot arrows into his hat, or else teased by the wren and the kingfisher, and again by the hobbits. He gives as good as he gets, or better, but while the first poem ends on a note of triumph and contentment, the second ends on a note of loss: Tom will not come back.

The last three poems are all heavily reworked from earlier originals, and have become thematically much darker. "The Hoard" (going back to 1923) describes what Tolkien in *The Hobbit* would call "dragon-sickness", the greed and possessiveness which successively overpowers

elf and dwarf and dragon and hero and leads all of them –
like Thorin Oakenshield in *The Hobbit* and the elf-king
Thingol "Greycloak" in *The Silmarillion* – to their deaths.
"The Last Ship" shows Tolkien balanced between two
urges, on the one hand the wish to escape mortality and
travel to the Undying Lands like Frodo, and on the other
the sense that this is not only impossible, but ultimately
unwelcome: the right thing to do is to turn back and live
one's life, like Sam Gamgee. Right it may be, but as Arwen
finds, if there is no way to reverse it that choice is bitter.
Finally, "The Sea-Bell" reminds us why the Perilous
Realm is perilous. Those who have travelled to it, like the
speaker of the poem, know they will not be allowed to
stay there, but when they come back, they are overwhelmed by a sense of loss. As Sam Gamgee says of
Galadriel, the inhabitants of Faërie may mean no harm,
but they are still dangerous for ordinary mortals. Those
who encounter them may never be the same again. In
Tolkien's editorial fiction, though the speaker should not
be identified with Frodo himself, the hobbit-scribe who
called the poem "Frodos Dreme" was expressing the fear
created in the Shire by the dimly-understood events of the
War of the Ring, as also (in reality) Tolkien's own sense of
loss and age.

These themes become stronger in Tolkien's last published story, *Smith of Wootton Major*. This began with a
request from a publisher, in 1964, that Tolkien should write

a preface to a new illustrated edition of the story "The Golden Key", by the Victorian author George MacDonald. (Tolkien had praised the story in his essay "On Fairy-Stories" nearly twenty years before.) Tolkien agreed, began work on the preface, and got a few pages into it when he started to illustrate his argument about the unexpected power of Faërie with a story about a cook trying to bake a cake for a children's party. But at that point he broke off the preface, which was never resumed, and wrote the story instead. A developed version was read to a large audience in Oxford on 28 October 1966, and the story was published the following year.

Its title is almost aggressively plain, even more so than *Farmer Giles of Ham*, and Tolkien himself noted that it sounded like an old-fashioned school story. The name "Wootton", however, though perfectly ordinary in England, has a meaning, as all names once did. It means "the town in the wood", and the second sentence confirms that it was "deep in the trees". Woods and forests were important for Tolkien, recurring from Mirkwood to Fangorn, and one of their recurrent (and realistic) features is that in them people lose their bearings and their way. One feels this is true of the inhabitants of Wootton Major, or many of them: a bit smug, easily satisfied, concerned above all with food and drink – not entirely bad qualities, but limited. To this Smith is an exception. At the children's party which the village holds every twenty-four years he swallows a star, and this star is his passport into Faërie (or

Faery, as Tolkien spells it here). The story follows Smith's life, recounting some of his visions and experiences in Faërie, but also takes us through repeated festivals till the time when Smith has to give up the star, and allow it to be baked into a cake for some other child to succeed him. Smith knows when he leaves Faërie for the last time that "his way now led back to bereavement". He is in the same position, if with more acceptance, as the narrator of "The Sea-bell". The story is "a farewell to Fairyland".

This does not mean that Smith has been a failure. His passport to the Other World has made him a better person in this one, and his life has done something to weaken what Tolkien called, in a commentary on his own story, "the iron ring of the familiar" and the "adamantine ring of belief", in Wootton, that everything worth knowing is known already. The star is also passed on, in an unexpected way, and will continue to be. Nevertheless the power of the banal remains strong, and the main conflict in the story lies between Alf – an emissary from Faërie into the real world, as Smith is a visitor in the opposite direction – and his predecessor as Master Cook to the village, whose name is Nokes. Nokes sums up much of what Tolkien disliked in real life. It is sad that he has such a limited idea himself of Faërie, of whatever lies beyond the humdrum world of the village deep among the trees, but it is inexcusable that he denies that there can be any more imaginative one, and tries to keep the children down to his own level. Sweet and sticky is his idea of a cake, insipidly pretty is his idea of fairies. Against this stand Smith's visions of the grim elf-warriors returning from battles on the Dark Marches, of the King's Tree, the wild Wind and the weeping birch, the elf-maidens dancing. Nokes is daunted in the end by his apprentice Alf, revealed as the King of Faërie, but he never changes his mind. He gets the last word in the story, most of the inhabitants of Wootton are happy to see Alf go, and the star passes out of Smith's family and into Nokes's. If Smith and Alf and Faërie have had an effect, it will take a while to show. But that may be just the way things are.

The way they are in *this* world, that is. In "Leaf by Niggle" Tolkien presents his vision of a world elsewhere, one with room in it for Middle-earth and Faërie and all other hearts' desires as well. Nevertheless, although it presents a "divine comedy" and ends with world-shaking laughter, the story began in fear. Tolkien reported in more than one letter that the whole story came to him in a dream and that he wrote it down immediately, at some time (reports vary) between 1939 and 1942. This is the more plausible in that it is so obvious what kind of a dream it was: an anxiety-dream, of the kind we all get. Students with an exam to take dream that they have overslept and missed it, academics due to make a presentation dream they have arrived on the podium with nothing to read and nothing in their heads, and the fear at the heart of "Leaf by Niggle" is clearly that of *never getting finished*. Niggle knows he has a deadline – it is obviously death, the journey we all have to take – he has a painting he desperately wants to finish, but he puts things off and puts things off, and when he finally buckles down to it, first there is a call on his time he cannot refuse, and then he gets sick, and then an Inspector turns up and condemns his painting as scrap, and as he starts to contest this the Driver turns up and tells him he must leave now with no more than he can snatch up. He leaves even that little bag on the train, and when he turns back for it, the train has gone. This kind of one-thing-after-another dream is all too famil-iar. The motive for it is also easy to imagine, in Tolkien's case. By 1940 he had been working on his "Silmarillion" mythology for more than twenty years, and none of it had been published except for a scattering of poems and the "spin-off" *The Hobbit*. He had been writing *The Lord of the Rings* since Christmas 1937, and it too was going slowly. His study was full of drafts and revisions. One can guess also that, like most professors, he found his many adminis-trative duties a distraction, though Niggle (and perhaps Tolkien) is guiltily aware that he is easily distracted, and not a good manager of his time.

Concentration and time-management are what Niggle has to learn in the Workhouse, which most critics have identified as a version of Purgatory. His reward is to find that in the Other World, dreams come true: there before him is his Tree, better than he had ever painted it and better even than he had imagined it, and beyond it the Forest and the Mountains that he had only begun to imagine. And yet there is room for more improvement, and to make it Niggle has to work with his neighbour Parish, who in the real world had seemed only another distraction. What becomes their joint vision is recognized as therapeutically valuable even by the Voices who judge people's lives, but even then it is only an introduction to a greater vision mortals can only guess at. But everyone has to start somewhere. As the Fairy Queen says in *Smith*, "Better a little doll, maybe, than no memory of Faery at all", and better Faery than no sense of anything beyond the mundane world of everyday.

"Leaf" after all has two endings, one in the Other World and one in the world which Niggle left. The Other World ending is one of joy and laughter, but in the real world hope and memory are crushed. Niggle's great painting of the Tree was used to patch a hole, one leaf of it went to a museum, but that too was burned down and Niggle was entirely forgotten. The last words ever said about him are "never knew he painted", and the future seems to belong to people like Councillor Tompkins, with his views on practical education and – remember that this is a story of at latest the early 1940s – the elimination of undesirable elements of Society. If there is a remedy for us, Tolkien says, stressing that Niggle uses the word "quite literally", it will be "a gift". Another word for "gift" is "grace".

"Leaf by Niggle" ends, then, both with what Tolkien in "On Fairy-Stories" calls "dyscatastrophe . . . sorrow and failure", and with what he regards as the "highest function" of fairy-story and of *evangelium*, the "good news" or Gospel beyond it, and that is "eucatastrophe", the "sudden joyous 'turn'", the "sudden and miraculous grace", which one finds in Grimm, in modern fairy-tale, and supremely in Tolkien's own "Tales of the Perilous Realm". In the Middle English poem *Sir Orfeo*, which Tolkien edited in 1943-4 (in an anonymous pamphlet of which, characteristically, hardly any copies survive), the barons comfort the steward who has just been told his lord is dead, "and telleth him hou it geth, / It is no bot of mannes deth". That's the way it goes, they say, there's no help for it, or as Tolkien rendered the last line in his posthumously-published translation of 1975, "death of man no man can mend". The barons are compassionate, well-intentioned, and above all sensible: that *is* the way things go. But the poem proves them wrong, just this once, for Orfeo is alive, and has rescued his queen from captivity in Faërie as well. We find the same "turn" in *The Lord of the Rings*, as Sam, who has lain down to die on Mount Doom after the destruction of the Ring, wakes to find himself alive, rescued, and faced by the resurrected Gandalf. There is joy in the Perilous Realm, and on its Dark Marches too, all the stronger for the real-life sorrows and losses which it challenges and surmounts.

TOM SHIPPEY

ROVERANDOM

I

Once upon a time there was a little dog, and his name was Rover. He was very small, and very young, or he would have known better; and he was very happy playing in the garden in the sunshine with a yellow ball, or he would never have done what he did.

Not every old man with ragged trousers is a bad old man: some are bone-and-bottle men, and have little dogs of their own; and some are gardeners; and a few, a very few, are wizards prowling round on a holiday looking for something to do. This one was a wizard, the one that now walked into the story. He came wandering up the garden-path in a ragged old coat, with an old pipe in his mouth, and an old green hat on his head. If Rover had not been so busy barking at the ball, he might have noticed the blue feather stuck in the back of the green hat, and then he would have suspected that the man was a wizard, as any other sensible little dog would; but he never saw the feather at all.

3

When the old man stooped down and picked up the ball – he was thinking of turning it into an orange, or even a bone or a piece of meat for Rover – Rover growled, and said:

'Put it down!' Without ever a 'please'.

Of course the wizard, being a wizard, understood perfectly, and he answered back again:

'Be quiet, silly!' Without ever a 'please'.

Then he put the ball in his pocket, just to tease the dog, and turned away. I am sorry to say that Rover immediately bit his trousers, and tore out quite a piece. Perhaps he also tore out a piece of the wizard. Anyway the old man suddenly turned round very angry and shouted:

'Idiot! Go and be a toy!'

After that the most peculiar things began to happen. Rover was only a little dog to begin with, but he suddenly felt very much smaller. The grass seemed to grow monstrously tall and wave far above his head; and a long way away through the grass, like the sun rising through the trees of a forest, he could see the huge yellow ball, where the wizard had thrown it down again. He heard the gate click as the old man went out, but he could not see him. He tried to bark, but only a little tiny noise came out, too small for ordinary people to hear; and I don't suppose even a dog would have noticed it.

So small had he become that I am sure, if a cat had come along just then, she would have thought Rover was a mouse, and would have eaten him. Tinker would. Tinker was the large black cat that lived in the same house.

4

At the very thought of Tinker, Rover began to feel thoroughly frightened; but cats were soon put right out of his mind. The garden about him suddenly vanished, and Rover felt himself whisked off, he didn't know where. When the rush was over, he found he was in the dark, lying against a lot of hard things; and there he lay, in a stuffy box by the feel of it, very uncomfortably for a long while. He had nothing to eat or drink; but worst of all, he found he could not move. At first he thought this was because he was packed so tight, but afterwards he discovered that in the daytime he could only move very little, and with a great effort, and then only when no one was looking. Only after midnight could he walk and wag his tail, and a bit stiffly at that. He had become a toy. And because he had not said 'please' to the wizard, now all day long he had to sit up and beg. He was fixed like that.

After what seemed a very long, dark time he tried once more to bark loud enough to make people hear. Then he tried to bite the other things in the box with him, stupid little toy animals, really only made of wood or lead, not enchanted real dogs like Rover. But it was no good; he could not bark or bite.

Suddenly someone came and took off the lid of the box, and let in the light.

'We had better put a few of these animals in the window this morning, Harry,' said a voice, and a hand came into the box. 'Where did this one come from?' said the voice, as the hand took hold of Rover. 'I don't remember seeing this one before. It's no business in the three-penny box, I'm sure. Did you ever see anything so real-looking? Look at its fur and its eyes!'

'Mark him sixpence,' said Harry, 'and put him in the front of the window!'

There in the front of the window in the hot sun poor little Rover had to sit all the morning, and all the afternoon, till nearly tea-time; and all the while he had to sit up and pretend to beg, though really in his inside he was very angry indeed.

'I'll run away from the very first people that buy me,' he said to the other toys. 'I'm real. I'm not a toy, and I won't be a toy! But I wish someone would come and buy me quick. I hate this shop, and I can't move all stuck up in the window like this.'

'What do you want to move for?' said the other toys. 'We don't. It's more comfortable standing still thinking of nothing. The more you rest, the longer you live. So just shut up! We can't sleep while you're talking, and there are hard times in rough nurseries in front of some of us.'

They would not say any more, so poor Rover had no one at all to talk to, and he was very miserable, and very sorry he had bitten the wizard's trousers.

I could not say whether it was the wizard or not who sent the mother to take the little dog away from the shop. Anyway, just when Rover was feeling his miserablest, into the shop she walked with a shopping-basket. She had seen Rover through the window, and thought what a nice little dog he would be for her boy. She had three boys, and one was particularly fond of little dogs, especially of little black and white dogs. So she bought Rover, and he was screwed up in paper and put in her basket among the things she had been buying for tea.

Rover soon managed to wriggle his head out of the paper. He smelt cake. But he found he could not get at it; and right down there among the paper bags he growled a little toy growl. Only the shrimps heard him, and they asked him what was the matter. He told them all about it, and expected them to be very sorry for him, but they only said:

'How would you like to be boiled? Have you ever been boiled?'

'No! I have never been boiled, as far as I remember,' said Rover, 'though I have sometimes been bathed, and that is not particularly nice. But I expect boiling isn't half as bad as being bewitched.'

'Then you have certainly never been boiled,' they answered. 'You know nothing about it. It's the very worst thing that could happen to anyone – we are still red with rage at the very idea.'

Rover did not like the shrimps, so he said: 'Never mind, they will soon eat you up, and I shall sit and watch them!'

After that the shrimps had no more to say to him, and he was left to lie and wonder what sort of people had bought him.

He soon found out. He was carried to a house, and the basket was set down on a table, and all the parcels were taken out. The shrimps were taken off to the larder, but Rover was given straight away to the little boy he had been bought for, who took him into the nursery and talked to him.

Rover would have liked the little boy, if he had not been too angry to listen to what he was saying to him. The little boy barked at him in the best dog-language he could manage (he was rather good at it), but Rover never tried to answer. All the time he was thinking he had said he would run away from the first people that bought him, and he was wondering how he could do it; and all the time he had to sit up and pretend to beg, while the little boy patted him and pushed him about, over the table and along the floor.

At last night came, and the little boy went to bed; and Rover was put on a chair by the bedside, still begging until it was quite dark. The blind was down; but outside the moon rose up out of the sea, and laid the silver path across the waters that is the way to places at the edge of the world and beyond, for those that can walk on it. The father and mother and the three little boys lived close by the sea in a white house that looked right out over the waves to nowhere.

When the little boys were asleep, Rover stretched his tired, stiff legs and gave a little bark that nobody heard except an old wicked spider up a corner. Then he jumped from the chair to the bed, and from the bed he tumbled off onto the carpet; and then he ran away out of the room and down the stairs and all over the house.

Although he was very pleased to be able to move again, and having once been real and properly alive he could jump and run a good deal better than most toys at night, he found it very difficult and dangerous getting about. He was now so small that going downstairs was almost like jumping off walls; and getting upstairs again was very tiring and awkward indeed. And it was all no use. He found all the doors shut and locked, of course; and there was not a crack or a hole by which he could creep out. So poor Rover could not run away that night, and morning found a very tired little dog sitting up and pretending to beg on the chair, just where he had been left.

The two older boys used to get up, when it was fine, and run along the sands before their breakfast. That morning when they woke and pulled up the blind, they saw the sun jumping out of the sea, all fiery-red with clouds about his head, as if he had had a cold bathe and was drying himself with towels. They were soon up and dressed; and off they went down the cliff and onto the shore for a walk – and Rover went with them.

Just as little boy Two (to whom Rover belonged) was leaving the bedroom, he saw Rover sitting on the chest-of-drawers where he had put him while he was dressing.

'He is begging to go out!' he said, and put him in his trouser-pocket.

But Rover was not begging to go out, and certainly not in a trouser-pocket. He wanted to rest and get ready for the night again; for he thought that this time he might find a way out and escape, and wander away and away, until he came back to his home and his garden and his yellow ball on the lawn. He had a sort of idea that if once he could get back to the lawn, it might come all right: the enchantment might break, or he might wake up and find it had all been a dream. So, as the little boys scrambled down the cliff-path and galloped along the sands, he tried to bark and struggle and wriggle in the pocket. Try how he would, he could only move a very little, even though he was hidden and no one could see him. Still he did what he could, and luck helped him. There was a handkerchief in the pocket, all crumpled and bundled up, so that Rover was not very deep down, and what with his efforts and the galloping of his master, before long he had managed to poke out his nose and have a sniff round.

Very surprised he was, too, at what he smelt and what he saw. He had never either seen or smelt the sea before, and the country village where he had been born was miles and miles from sound or snuff of it.

Suddenly, as he was leaning out, a great big bird, all white and grey, went sweeping by just over the heads of the boys, making a noise like a great cat on wings. Rover was so startled that he fell right out of the pocket onto the soft sand, and no one heard him. The great bird flew on and away, never noticing his tiny barks, and the little boys walked on and on along the sands, and never thought about him at all.

At first Rover was very pleased with himself.

'I've run away! I've run away!' he barked, toy barking that only other toys could have heard, and there were none to listen. Then he rolled over and lay in the clean dry sand that was still cool from lying out all night under the stars.

But when the little boys went by on their way home, and never noticed him, and he was left all alone on the empty shore, he was not quite so pleased. The shore was deserted except by the gulls. Beside the marks of their claws on the sand the only other footprints to be seen were the tracks of the little boys' feet. That morning they had gone for their walk on a very lonely part of the beach that they seldom visited. Indeed it was not often that anyone went there; for though the sand was clean and yellow, and the shingle white, and the sea blue with silver foam in a little cove under the grey cliffs, there was a queer feeling there, except just at early morning when the sun was new. People said that strange things came there, sometimes even in the afternoon; and by the evening the place was full of mermen and mermaidens, not to speak of the smaller sea-goblins that rode their small sea-horses with bridles of green weed right up to the cliffs and left them lying in the foam at the edge of the water.

Now the reason of all this queerness was simple: the oldest of all the sand-sorcerers lived in that cove, *Psamathists* as the sea-people call them in their splashing language. Psamathos Psamathides was this one's name, or so he said, and a great fuss he made about the proper pronunciation. But he was a wise old thing, and all sorts of strange folk came to see him; for he was an excellent magician, and very kindly (to the right people) into the bargain, if a bit crusty on the surface. The mer-folk used to laugh over his jokes for weeks after one of his midnight parties. But it was not easy to find him in the daytime. He liked to lie buried in the warm sand when the sun was shining, so that not more than the tip of one of his long ears stuck out; and even if both of his ears were showing, most people like you and me would have taken them for bits of stick.

It is possible that old Psamathos knew all about Rover. He certainly knew the old wizard who had enchanted him; for magicians and wizards are few and far between, and they know one another very well, and keep an eye on one another's doings too, not always being the best of friends in private life. At any rate there was Rover lying in the soft sand and beginning to feel very lonely and rather queer, and there was Psamathos, though Rover did not see him, peeping at him out of a pile of sand that the mermaids had made for him the night before.

But the sand-sorcerer said nothing. And Rover said nothing. And breakfast-time went by, and the sun got high and hot. Rover looked at the sea, which sounded cool, and then he got a horrible fright. At first he thought that the sand must have got into his eyes, but soon he saw that there could be no mistake: the sea was moving nearer and nearer, and swallowing up more and more sand; and the waves were getting bigger and bigger and more foamy all the time.

The tide was coming in, and Rover was lying just below the high-water mark, but he did not know anything about that. He grew more and more terrified as he watched, and thought of the splashing waves coming right up to the cliffs and washing him away into the foaming sea (far worse than any soapy bathing-tub), still miserably begging.

That is indeed what might have happened to him; but it did not. I dare say Psamathos had something to do with it; at any rate I imagine that the wizard's spell was not so strong in that queer cove, so close to the residence of another magician. Certainly when the sea had come very near, and Rover was nearly bursting with fright as he struggled to roll a bit further up the beach, he suddenly found he could move.

His size was not changed, but he was no longer a toy. He could move quickly and properly with all his legs, daytime though it still was. He need not beg any more, and he could run over the sands where they were harder; and he could bark – not toy barks, but real sharp little fairy-dog barks equal to his fairy-dog size. He was so delighted, and he barked so loud, that if you had been there, you would have heard him then, clear and far-away-like, like the echo of a sheep-dog coming down the wind in the hills.

And then the sand-sorcerer suddenly stuck his head out of the sand. He certainly was ugly, and about as big as a very large dog; but to Rover in his enchanted size he looked hideous and monstrous. Rover sat down and stopped barking at once.

'What are you making such a noise about, little dog?' said Psamathos Psamathides. 'This is my time for sleep!'

As a matter of fact all times were times for him to go to sleep, unless something was going on which amused him, such as a dance of the mermaids in the cove (at his invitation). In that case he got out of the sand and sat on a rock to see the fun. Mermaids may be very graceful in the water, but when they tried to dance on their tails on the shore, Psamathos thought them comical.

'This is my time for sleep!' he said again, when Rover did not answer. Still Rover said nothing, and only wagged his tail apologetically.

'Do you know who I am?' he asked. 'I am Psamathos Psamathides, the chief of all the Psamathists!' He said this several times very proudly, pronouncing every letter, and with every *P* he blew a cloud of sand down his nose.

Rover was nearly buried in it, and he sat there looking so frightened and so unhappy that the sand-sorcerer took pity on him. In fact he suddenly stopped looking fierce and burst out laughing:

'You are a funny little dog, Little Dog! Indeed I don't remember ever having seen another little dog that was quite such a little dog, Little Dog!'

And then he laughed again, and after that he suddenly looked solemn.

'Have you been having any quarrels with wizards lately?' he asked almost in a whisper; and he shut one eye, and looked so friendly and so knowing out of the other one that Rover told him all about it. It was probably quite unnecessary, for Psamathos, as I told you, probably knew about it beforehand; still Rover felt all the better for talking to someone who appeared to understand and had more sense than mere toys.

'It was a wizard all right,' said the sorcerer, when Rover had finished his tale. 'Old Artaxerxes, I should think from your description. He comes from Persia. But he lost his way one day, as even the best wizards sometimes do (unless they always stay at home like me), and the first person he met on the road went and put him on the way to Pershore instead. He has lived in those parts, except on holidays, ever since. They say he is a nimble plum-gatherer for an old man – two thousand, if he is a day – and extremely fond of cider. But that's neither here nor there.' By which Psamathos meant that he was getting away from what he wanted to say. 'The point is, what can I do for you?'

'I don't know,' said Rover.

'Do you want to go home? I am afraid I can't make you your proper size, at least not without asking Artaxerxes' permission first, as I don't want to quarrel with him at the moment. But I think I might venture to send you home. After all, Artaxerxes can always send you back again, if he wants to. Though of course he might send you somewhere much worse than a toyshop next time, if he was really annoyed.'

Rover did not like the sound of this at all, and he ventured to say that if he went back home so small, he might not be recognized, except by Tinker the cat; and he did not very much want to be recognized by Tinker in his present state.

'Very well!' said Psamathos. 'We must think of something else. In the meantime, as you are real again, would you like something to eat?'

Before Rover had time to say 'Yes, please! YES! PLEASE!' there appeared on the sands in front of him a little plate with bread and gravy and two tiny bones of just the right size, and a little drinking-bowl full of water with drink puppy drink written round it in small blue letters. He ate and drank all there was before he asked: 'How did you do that? – Thank you!'

He suddenly thought of adding the 'thank you', as wizards and people of that sort seemed rather touchy folk. Psamathos only smiled; so Rover lay down on the hot sand and went to sleep, and dreamed of bones, and of chasing cats up plum-trees only to see them change into wizards with green hats who threw enormous plums like marrows at him. And the wind blew gently all the time, and buried him almost over his head in blown sand.

That is why the little boys never found him, although they came down into the cove specially to look for him, as soon as little boy Two found he was lost. Their father was with them this time; and when they had looked and looked till the sun began to get low and tea-timish, he took them back home and would not stay any longer: he knew too many queer things about that place. Little boy Two had to be content for some time after that with an ordinary threepenny toy dog (from the same shop); but somehow, though he had only had him such a short while, he did not forget his little begging-dog.

At the moment, however, you can think of him sitting down very mournful to his tea, without any dog at all; while far away inland the old lady who had kept Rover and spoiled him, when he was an ordinary, proper-sized animal, was just writing out an advertisement for a lost puppy – 'white with black ears, and answers to the name of Rover'; and while Rover himself slept away on the sands, and Psamathos dozed close by with his short arms folded on his fat tummy.

2

When Rover woke up, the sun was very low; the shadow of the cliffs was right across the sands, and Psamathos was nowhere to be seen. A large seagull was standing close by looking at him, and for a moment Rover was afraid that he might be going to eat him.

But the seagull said: 'Good evening! I have waited a long time for you to wake up. Psamathos said that you would wake about tea-time, but it is long past that now.'

'Please, what are you waiting for me for, Mr Bird?' asked Rover very politely.

'My name is Mew,' said the seagull, 'and I'm waiting to take you away, as soon as the moon rises, along the moon's path. But we have one or two things to do before that. Get up on my back and see how you like flying!'

Rover did not like it at all at first. It was all right while Mew was close to the ground, gliding smoothly along with his wings stretched out stiff and still; but when he shot up into the air, or turned sharp from side to side, sloping a different way each time, or stooped sudden and steep, as if he was going to dive into the sea, then the little dog, with the wind whistling in his ears, wished he was safe down on the earth again.

He said so several times, but all that Mew would answer was: 'Hold on! We haven't begun yet!'

They had been flying about like this for a little, and Rover had just begun to get used to it, and rather tired of it, when suddenly 'We're off!' cried Mew; and Rover very nearly was off. For Mew rose like a rocket steeply into the air, and then set off at a great pace straight down the wind. Soon they were so high that Rover could see, far away and right over the land, the sun going down behind dark hills. They were making for some very tall black cliffs of sheer rock, too sheer for anyone to climb. At the bottom the sea was splashing and sucking at their feet, and nothing grew on their faces, yet they were covered with white things, pale in the dusk. Hundreds of sea-birds were sitting there on narrow ledges, sometimes talking mournfully together, sometimes saying nothing, and sometimes slipping suddenly from their perches to swoop and curve in the air, before diving down to the sea far below where the waves looked like little wrinkles.

This was where Mew lived, and he had several people to see, including the oldest and most important of all the Blackbacked Gulls, and messages to collect before he set out. So he set Rover down on one of the narrow ledges, much narrower than a doorstep, and told him to wait there and not to fall off.

You may be sure that Rover took care not to fall off, and that with a stiff sideways wind blowing he did not like the feeling of it at all, crouching as close as he could against the face of the cliff, and whimpering. It was altogether a very nasty place for a bewitched and worried little dog to be in.

At last the sunlight faded out of the sky entirely, and a mist was on the sea, and the first stars showed in the gathering dark. Then above the mist, far out across the sea, the moon rose round and yellow and began to lay its shining path on the water.

Soon after, Mew came back and picked up Rover, who had begun to shiver miserably. The bird's feathers seemed warm and comfortable after the cold ledge on the cliff, and he snuggled in as close as he could. Then Mew leapt into the air far above the sea, and all the other gulls sprang off their ledges, and cried and wailed good-bye to them, as off they sped along the moon's path that now stretched straight from the shore to the dark edge of nowhere.

Rover did not know in the least where the moon's path led to, and at present he was much too frightened and excited to ask, and anyway he was beginning to get used to extraordinary things happening to him.

As they flew along above the silver shimmer on the sea, the moon rose higher and grew whiter and more bright, till no stars dared stay anywhere near it, and it was left shining all alone in the eastern sky. No doubt Mew was going by Psamathos' orders to where Psamathos wanted him to go, and no doubt Psamathos helped Mew with magic, for he certainly flew faster and straighter than even the great gulls ordinarily fly, even straight down the wind when they are in a hurry. Yet it was ages before Rover saw anything except the moonlight and the sea below; and all the time the moon got bigger and bigger, and the air got colder and colder.

Suddenly on the edge of the sea he saw a dark thing, and it grew as they flew towards it, until he could see that it was an island. Over the water and up to them came the sound of a tremendous barking, a noise made up of all the different kinds and sizes of barks there are: yaps and yelps, and yammers and yowls, growling and grizzling, whickering and whining, snickering and snarling, mumping and moaning, and the most enormous baying, like a giant bloodhound in the backyard of an ogre. All Rover's fur round his neck suddenly became very real again, and stood up stiff as bristles; and he thought he would like to go down and quarrel with all the dogs there at once – until he remembered how small he was.

'That's the Isle of Dogs,' said Mew, 'or rather the Isle of Lost Dogs, where all the lost dogs go that are deserving or lucky. It isn't a bad place, I'm told, for dogs; and they can make as much noise as they like without anyone telling them to be quiet or throwing anything at them. They have a beautiful concert, all barking together their favourite noises, whenever the moon shines bright. They tell me there are bone-trees there, too, with fruit like juicy meat-bones that drops off the trees when it's ripe. No! We are not going there just now! You see, you can't be called exactly a dog, though you are no longer quite a toy. In fact Psamathos was rather puzzled, I believe, to know what to do with you, when you said you didn't want to go home.'

'Where are we going to, then?' asked Rover. He was disappointed at not having a closer look at the Isle of Dogs, after he heard of the bone-trees.

'Straight up the moon's path to the edge of the world, and then over the edge and onto the moon. That's what old Psamathos said.'

Rover did not like the idea of going over the edge of the world at all, and the moon looked a cold sort of place. 'Why to the moon?' he asked. 'There are lots of places on the world I have never been to. I never heard of there being bones in the moon, or even dogs.'

'There is at least one dog, for the Man-in-the-Moon keeps one; and since he is a decent old fellow, as well as the greatest of all the magicians, there are sure to be bones for the dog, and probably for visitors. As for why you are being sent there, I dare say you will find that out in good time, if you keep your wits about you and don't waste time grumbling. I think it is very kind of Psamathos to bother about you at all; in fact I don't understand why he does. It isn't like him to do things without a good big reason – and you don't seem good or big.'

'Thank you,' said Rover, feeling crushed. 'It is very kind of all these wizards to trouble themselves about me, I am sure, though it is rather upsetting. You never know what will happen next, when once you get mixed up with wizards and their friends.'

'It is very much better luck than any yapping little pet puppy-dog deserves,' said the seagull, and after that they had no more conversation for a long while.

The moon got bigger and brighter, and the world below got darker and farther off. At last, all of a sudden, the world came to an end, and Rover could see the stars shining up out of the blackness underneath. Far down he could see the white spray in the moonlight where waterfalls fell over the world's edge and dropped straight into space. It made him feel most uncomfortably giddy, and he nestled into Mew's feathers and shut his eyes for a long, long time.

When he opened them again the moon was all laid out below them, a new white world shining like snow, with wide open spaces of pale blue and green where the tall pointed mountains threw their long shadows far across the floor.

On top of one of the tallest of these, one so tall that it seemed to stab up towards them as Mew swept down, Rover could see a white tower. It was white with pink and pale green lines in it, shimmering as if the tower were built of millions of seashells still wet with foam and gleaming; and the tower stood on the edge of a white precipice, white as a cliff of chalk, but shining with moonlight more brightly than a pane of glass far away on a cloudless night.

There was no path down that cliff, as far as Rover could see; but that did not matter at the moment, for Mew was sailing swiftly down, and soon he settled right on the roof of the tower, at a dizzy height above the moon-world that made the cliffs by the sea where Mew lived seem low and safe.

To Rover's great surprise a little door in the roof immediately opened close beside them, and an old man with a long silvery beard popped his head out.

'Not bad going, that!' he said. 'I've been timing you ever since you passed over the edge – a thousand miles a minute, I should reckon. You are in a hurry this morning! I'm glad you didn't bump into my dog. Where in the moon has he got to now, I wonder?'

He drew out an enormously long telescope and put it to one eye.

'There he is! There he is!' he shouted. 'Worrying the moonbeams again, drat him! Come down, sir! Come down, sir!' he called up into the air, and then began to whistle a long clear silver note.

Rover looked up into the air, thinking that this funny old man must be quite mad to whistle to his dog up in the sky; but to his astonishment he saw far up above the tower a little white dog on white wings chasing things that looked like transparent butterflies.

'Rover! Rover!' called the old man; and just as our Rover jumped up on Mew's back to say 'Here I am!' – without waiting to wonder how the old man knew his name – he saw the little flying dog dive straight down out of the sky and settle on the old man's shoulders.

Then he realised that the Man-in-the-Moon's dog must also be called Rover. He was not at all pleased, but as nobody took any notice of him, he sat down again and began to growl to himself.

The Man-in-the-Moon's Rover had good ears, and he at once jumped onto the roof of the tower and began to bark like mad; and then he sat down and growled: 'Who brought that other dog here?'

'What other dog?' said the Man.

'That silly little puppy on the seagull's back,' said the moon-dog.

Then, of course, Rover jumped up again and barked his loudest: 'Silly little puppy yourself! Who said that you could call yourself Rover, a thing more like a cat or a bat than a dog?' From which you can see that they were going to be very friendly before long. That is the way, anyhow, that little dogs usually talk to strangers of their own kind.

'O fly away, you two! And stop making such a noise! I want to talk to the postman,' said the Man.

'Come on, tiny tot!' said the moon-dog; and then Rover remembered what a tiny tot he was, even beside the moon-dog who was only small, and instead of barking something rude he only said: 'I would like to, if only I had some wings and knew how to fly.'

'Wings?' said the Man-in-the-Moon. 'That's easy! Have a pair and be off!'

Mew laughed, and actually threw him off his back, right over the edge of the tower's roof! But Rover had only gasped once, and had only begun to imagine himself falling and falling down like a stone onto the white rocks in the valley miles below, when he discovered that he had got a beautiful pair of white wings with black spots (to match himself). All the same, he had fallen a long way before he could stop, as he wasn't used to wings. It took him a little while to get really used to them, though long before the Man had finished talking to Mew he was already trying to chase the moon-dog round the tower. He was just beginning to get tired by these first efforts, when the moon-dog dived down to the mountain-top and settled at the edge of the precipice at the foot of the walls. Rover went down after him, and soon they were sitting side by side, taking breath with their tongues hanging out.

'So you are called Rover after me?' said the moon-dog.

'Not after you,' said our Rover. 'I'm sure my mistress had never heard of you when she gave me my name.'

'That doesn't matter. I was the first dog that was ever called Rover, thousands of years ago – so you must have been called Rover after me! I *was* a Rover too! I never would stop anywhere, or belong to anyone before I came here. I did nothing but run away from the time I was a puppy; and I kept on running and roving until one fine morning – a very fine morning, with the sun in my eyes – I fell over the world's edge chasing a butterfly.

'A nasty sensation, I can tell you! Luckily the moon was just passing under the world at the moment, and after a terrible time falling right through clouds, and bumping into shooting stars, and that sort of thing, I tumbled onto it. Slap into one of the enormous silver nets that the giant grey spiders here spin from mountain to mountain I fell, and the spider was just coming down his ladder to pickle me and carry me off to his larder, when the Man-in-the-Moon appeared.

'He sees absolutely everything that happens on this side of the moon with that telescope of his. The spiders are afraid of him, because he only lets them alone if they spin silver threads and ropes for him. He more than suspects that they catch his moonbeams – and that he won't allow – though they pretend to live only on dragonmoths and shadowbats. He found moonbeams' wings in that spider's larder, and he turned him into a lump of stone, as quick as kiss your hand. Then he picked me up and patted me, and said: "That was a nasty drop! You had better have a pair of wings to prevent any more accidents – now fly off and amuse yourself! Don't worry the moonbeams, and don't kill my white rabbits! And come home when you feel hungry; the window is usually open on the roof!"

'I thought he was a decent sort, but rather mad. But don't you make that mistake – about his being mad, I mean. I daren't really hurt his moonbeams or his rabbits. He can turn you into dreadfully uncomfortable shapes. Now tell me why you came with the postman!'

'The postman?' said Rover.

'Yes, Mew, the old sand-sorcerer's postman, of course,' said the moon-dog.

Rover had hardly finished telling the tale of his adventures when they heard the Man whistling. Up they shot to the roof. There the old man was sitting with his legs dangling over the ledge, throwing envelopes away as fast as he opened the letters. The wind took them whirling off into the sky, and Mew flew after them and caught them and put them back into a little bag.

'I've just been reading about you, Roverandom, my dog,' he said. '(Roverandom I call you, and Roverandom you'll have to be; can't have two Rovers about here.) And I quite agree with my friend Samathos (I'm not going to put in any ridiculous *P* to please him) that you had better stop here for a little while. I have also got a letter from Artaxerxes, if you know who that is, and even if you don't, telling me to send you straight back. He seems mighty annoyed with you for running away, and with Samathos for helping you. But we won't bother about him; and neither need you, as long as you stay here.

'Now fly off and amuse yourself. Don't worry the moonbeams, and don't kill my white rabbits, and come home when you are hungry! The window on the roof is usually open. Good-bye!'

He vanished immediately into thin air; and anybody who has never been there will tell you how extremely thin the moon-air is.

'Well, good-bye, Roverandom!' said Mew. 'I hope you enjoy making trouble among the wizards. Farewell for the present. Don't kill the white rabbits, and all will yet be well, and you will get home safe – whether you want to or not.'

Then Mew flew off at such a pace that before you could say 'whizz!' he was a dot in the sky, and then had vanished. Rover was now not only turned into toy-size, but his name had been altered, and he was left all alone on the moon – all alone except for the Man-in-the-Moon and his dog.

Roverandom – as we had better call him too, for the present, to avoid confusion – didn't mind. His new wings were great fun, and the moon turned out to be a remark-ably interesting place, so that he forgot to ponder any more why Psamathos had sent him there. It was a long time before he found out.

In the meanwhile he had all sorts of adventures, by himself and with the moon-Rover. He didn't often fly about in the air far from the tower; for in the moon, and especially on the white side, the insects are very large and fierce, and often so pale and so transparent and so silent that you hardly hear or see them coming. The moonbeams only shine and flutter, and Roverandom was not frightened of them; the big white dragon-moths with fiery eyes were much more alarming; and there were sword-flies, and glass-beetles with jaws like steel-traps, and pale unicornets with stings like spears, and fifty-seven varieties of spiders ready to eat anything they could catch. And worse than the insects were the shadowbats.

Roverandom did what the birds do on that side of the moon: he flew very little except near at home, or in open spaces with a good view all round, and far from insect hiding-places; and he walked about very quietly, especially in the woods. Most things there went about very quietly, and the birds seldom even twittered. What sounds there were, were made chiefly by the plants. The flowers – the whitebells, the fairbells and the silverbells, the tinklebells and the ringaroses; the rhymeroyals and the pennywhistles, the tintrumpets and the creamhorns (a very pale cream), and many others with untranslatable names – made tunes all day long. And the feather-grasses and the ferns – fairy-fiddlestrings, polyphonies, and brasstongues, and the cracken in the woods – and all the reeds by the milk-white ponds, they kept up the music, softly, even in the night. In fact there was always a faint thin music going on.

But the birds were silent; and very tiny most of them were, hopping about in the grey grass beneath the trees, dodging the flies and the swooping flutterbies; and many of them had lost their wings or forgotten how to use them. Roverandom used to startle them in their little ground-nests, as he stalked quietly through the pale grass, hunting the little white mice, or snuffing after grey squirrels on the edges of the woods.

The woods were filled with silverbells all ringing softly together when he first saw them. The tall black trunks stood straight up, high as churches, out of the silver carpet, and they were roofed with pale blue leaves that never fell; so that not even the longest telescope on earth has ever seen those tall trunks or the silverbells beneath them. Later in the year the trees all burst together into pale golden blossoms; and since the woods of the moon are nearly endless, no doubt that alters the look of the moon from below on the world.

But you must not imagine that all of Roverandom's time was spent creeping about like that. After all, the dogs knew that the Man's eye was on them, and they did a good many adventurous things and had a great deal of fun. Sometimes they wandered off together for miles and miles, and forgot to go back to the tower for days. Once or twice they went up into the mountains far away, till looking back they could see the moon-tower only as a shining needle in the distance; and they sat on the white rocks and watched the tiny sheep (no bigger than the Man-in-the-Moon's Rover) wandering in herds over the hillsides. Every sheep carried a golden bell, and every bell rang each time each sheep moved a foot forward to get a fresh mouthful of grey grass; and all the bells rang in tune, and all the sheep shone like snow, and no one ever worried them. The Rovers were much too well brought-up (and afraid of the Man) to do so, and there were no other dogs in all the moon, nor cows, nor horses, nor lions, nor tigers, nor wolves; in fact nothing larger on four feet than rabbits and squirrels (and toy-sized at that), except just occasionally to be seen standing solemnly in thought an enormous white elephant almost as big as a donkey. I haven't mentioned the dragons, because they don't come into the story just yet, and anyway they lived a very long way off, far from the tower, being all very afraid of the Man-in-the-Moon, except one (and even he was half-afraid).

Whenever the dogs did go back to the tower and fly in at the window, they always found their dinner just ready, as if they had arranged the time; but they seldom saw or heard the Man about. He had a workshop down in the cellars, and clouds of white steam and grey mist used to come up the stairs and float away out of the upper windows.

'What does he do with himself all day?' said Roverandom to Rover.

'Do?' said the moon-dog. 'O he's always pretty busy – though he seems busier than I have seen him for a long time, since you arrived. Making dreams, I believe.'

'What does he make dreams for?'

'O! for the other side of the moon. No one has dreams on this side; the dreamers all go round to the back.'

Roverandom sat down and scratched; he didn't think the explanation explained. The moon-dog would not tell him any more all the same: and if you ask me, I don't think he knew much about it.

However, something happened soon after that, that put such questions out of Roverandom's mind altogether for a while. The two dogs went and had a very exciting adventure, much too exciting while it lasted; but that was their own fault. They went away for several days, much farther than they had ever been before since Roverandom came; and they did not bother to think where they were going. In fact they went and lost themselves, and mistaking the way got farther and farther from the tower when they thought they were getting back. The moon-dog said he had roamed all over the white side of the moon and knew it all by heart (he was very apt to exaggerate), but eventually he had to admit that the country seemed a bit strange.

'I'm afraid it's a very long time since I came here,' he said, 'and I'm beginning to forget it a bit.'

As a matter of fact he had never been there before at all. Unawares they had wandered too near to the shadowy edge of the dark side, where all sorts of half-forgotten things linger, and paths and memories get confused. Just when they felt sure that at last they were on the right way home, they were surprised to find some tall mountains rising before them, silent, bare, and ominous; and these the moon-dog made no pretence of ever having seen before. They were grey, not white, and looked as if they were made of old cold ashes; and long dim valleys lay among them, without a sign of life.

Then it began to snow. It often does snow in the moon, but the snow (as they call it) is usually nice and warm, and quite dry, and turns into fine white sand and all blows away. This was more like our sort. It was wet and cold; and it was dirty.

'It makes me homesick,' said the moon-dog. 'It's just like the stuff that used to fall in the town where I was a puppy – on the world, you know. O! the chimneys there, tall as moon-trees; and the black smoke; and the red furnace fires! I get a bit tired of white at times. It's very difficult to get really dirty on the moon.'

This rather shows up the moon-dog's low tastes; and as there were no such towns on the world hundreds of years ago, you can also see that he had exaggerated the length of time since he fell over the edge a very great deal too. However, just at that moment, a specially large and dirty flake hit him in the left eye, and he changed his mind.

'I think this stuff has missed its way and fallen off the beastly old world,' he said. 'Rat and rabbit it! And we seem to have missed our way altogether, too. Bat and bother it! Let's find a hole to creep in!'

It took some time to find a hole of any sort, and they were very wet and cold before they did: in fact so miserable that they took the first shelter they came to, and no precautions – which are the first things you ought to take in unfamiliar places on the edge of the moon. The shelter they crawled into was not a hole but a cave, and a very large cave too; it was dark but it was dry.

'This is nice and warm,' said the moon-dog, and he closed his eyes and went off into a doze almost immediately.

'Ow!' he yelped not long afterwards, waking straight up dog-fashion out of a comfortable dream. 'Much too warm!'

He jumped up. He could hear little Roverandom barking away further inside the cave, and when he went to see what was up, he saw a trickle of fire creeping along the floor towards them. He did not feel homesick for red furnaces just then; and he seized little Roverandom by the back of his little neck, and bolted out of the cave as quick as lightning, and flew up to a peak of stone just outside.

There the two sat in the snow shivering and watching; which was very silly of them. They ought to have flown off home, or anywhere, faster than the wind. The moon-dog did not know everything about the moon, as you see, or he would have known that this was the lair of the Great White Dragon – the one that was only half-afraid of the Man (and scarcely that when he was angry). The Man himself was a bit bothered by this dragon. 'That dratted creature' was what he called him, when he referred to him at all.

All the white dragons originally come from the moon, as you probably know; but this one had been to the world and back, so he had learned a thing or two. He fought the Red Dragon in Caerdragon in Merlin's time, as you will find in all the more up-to-date history books; after which the other dragon was Very Red. Later he did lots more damage in the Three Islands, and went to live on the top

35

of Snowdon for a time. People did not bother to climb up while that lasted – except for one man, and the dragon caught him drinking out of a bottle. That man finished in such a hurry that he left the bottle on the top, and his example has been followed by many people since. A long time since, and not until the dragon had flown off to Gwynfa, some time after King Arthur's disappearance, at a time when dragons' tails were esteemed a great delicacy by the Saxon Kings.

Gwynfa is not so far from the world's edge, and it is an easy flight from there to the moon for a dragon so titanic and so enormously bad as this one had become. He now lived on the moon's edge; for he was not quite sure how much the Man-in-the-Moon could do with his spells and contrivances. All the same, he actually dared at times to interfere with the colour-scheme. Sometimes he let real red and green flames out of his cave when he was having a dragon-feast or was in a tantrum; and clouds of smoke were frequent. Once or twice he had been known to turn the whole moon red, or put it out altogether. On such uncomfortable occasions the Man-in-the-Moon shut himself up (and his dog), and all he said was 'That dratted creature again'. He never explained what creature, or where he lived; he simply went down into the cellars, uncorked his best spells, and got things cleared up as quick as possible.

Now you know all about it; and if the dogs had known half as much they would never have stopped there. But stop they did, at least as long as it has taken me to explain about the White Dragon, and by that time the whole of him, white with green eyes, and leaking green fire at every joint, and snorting black smoke like a steamer, had come out of the cave. Then he let off the most awful bellow. The mountains rocked and echoed, and the snow dried up; avalanches tumbled down, and waterfalls stood still.

That dragon had wings, like the sails that ships had when they still were ships and not steam-engines; and he did not disdain to kill anything from a mouse to an emperor's daughter. He meant to kill those two dogs; and he told them so several times before he got up into the air. That was *his* mistake. They both whizzed off their rock like rockets, and went away down the wind at a pace that Mew himself would have been proud of. The dragon came after them, flapping like a flapdragon and snapping like a snapdragon, knocking the tops of mountains off, and setting all the sheep-bells ringing like a town on fire. (Now you see why they all had bells.)

Very luckily, down the wind was the right direction. Also a most stupendous rocket went up from the tower as soon as the bells got frantic. It could be seen all over the moon like a golden umbrella bursting into a thousand silver tassels, and it caused an unpredicted fall of shooting stars on the world not long after. If it was a guide to the poor dogs, it was also meant as a warning to the dragon; but he had got far too much steam up to take any notice.

So the chase went fiercely on. If you have ever seen a bird chasing a butterfly, and if you can imagine a more than gigantic bird chasing two perfectly insignificant butterflies among white mountains, then you can just begin to imagine the twistings, dodgings, hairbreadth escapes, and the wild zigzag rush of that flight home. More than once, before they got even half way, Roverandom's tail was singed by the dragon's breath.

What was the Man-in-the-Moon doing? Well, he let off a truly magnificent rocket; and after that he said 'Drat that creature!' and also 'Drat those puppies! They will bring on an eclipse before it is due!' And then he went down into the cellars and uncorked a dark, black spell that looked like jellified tar and honey (and smelt like the Fifth of November and cabbage boiling over).

At that very moment the dragon swooped up right above the tower and lifted a huge claw to bat Roverandom – bat him right off into the blank nowhere. But he never did. The Man-in-the-Moon shot the spell up out of a lower window, and hit the dragon splosh on the stomach (where all dragons are peculiarly tender), and knocked him crank-sideways. He lost all his wits, and flew bang into a mountain before he could get his steering right; and it was difficult to say which was most damaged, his nose or the mountain – both were out of shape.

So the two dogs fell in through the top window, and never got back their breath for a week; and the dragon slowly made his lopsided way home, where he rubbed his

nose for months. The next eclipse was a failure, for the
dragon was too busy licking his tummy to attend to it.
And he never got the black sploshes off where the spell hit
him. I am afraid they will last for ever. They call him the
Mottled Monster now.

3

The next day the Man-in-the-Moon looked at Roverandom and said: 'That was a narrow squeak! You seem to have explored the white side pretty well for a young dog. I think, when you have got your breath back, it will be time for you to visit the other side.'

'Can I come too?' asked the moon-dog.

'It wouldn't be good for you,' said the Man, 'and I don't advise you to. You might see things that would make you more homesick than fire and chimney-stacks, and that would turn out as bad as dragons.'

The moon-dog did not blush, because he could not; and he did not say anything, but he went and sat down in a corner and wondered how much the old man knew of everything that went on, and everything that was said, too. Also for a little while he wondered what exactly the old man meant; but that did not bother him long – he was a lighthearted fellow.

As for Roverandom, when he had got his breath back,

a few days later, the Man-in-the-Moon came and whistled for him. Then down and down they went together; down the stairs, and into the cellars which were cut inside the cliff and had small windows looking out of the side of the precipice over the wide places of the moon; and then down secret steps that seemed to lead right under the mountains, until after a long while they came into a completely dark place, and stopped, though Roverandom's head went on turning giddily after the miles of corkscrewing downwards.

In complete darkness the Man-in-the-Moon shone palely all by himself like a glow-worm, and that was all the light they had. It was quite enough, though, to see the door by – a big door in the floor. This the old man pulled up, and as it was lifted darkness seemed to well up out of the opening like a fog, so that Roverandom could no longer see even the faint glimmering of the Man through it.

'Down you go, good dog!' said his voice out of the blackness. And you won't be surprised to be told that Roverandom was not a good dog, and would not budge. He backed into the furthest corner of the little room, and set his ears back. He was more frightened of that hole than of the old man.

But it was not any good. The Man-in-the-Moon simply picked him up and dropped him plump into the black hole; and as he fell and fell into nothing, Roverandom heard him calling out, already far above him: 'Drop straight, and then fly on with the wind! Wait for me at the other end!'

That ought to have comforted him, but it did not. Roverandom always said afterwards that he did not think even falling over the world's edge could be worse; and that anyway it was the nastiest part of all his adventures, and still made him feel as if he had lost his tummy whenever he thought of it. You can tell he is still thinking of it when he cries out and twitches in his sleep on the hearthrug.

All the same, it came to an end. After a long while his falling gradually slowed down, until at last he almost stopped. The rest of the way he had to use his wings; and it was like flying up, up, through a big chimney – luckily with a strong draught helping him along. Jolly glad he was when he got at last to the top.

There he lay panting at the edge of the hole at the other end, waiting obediently, and anxiously, for the Man-in-the-Moon. It was a good while before he appeared, and Roverandom had time to see that he was at the bottom of a deep dark valley, ringed round with low dark hills. Black clouds seemed to rest upon their tops; and beyond the clouds was just one star.

Suddenly the little dog felt very sleepy; a bird in some gloomy bushes nearby was singing a drowsy song that seemed strange and wonderful to him after the little dumb birds of the other side to which he had got used. He shut his eyes.

'Wake up, you doglet!' called a voice; and Roverandom bounced up just in time to see the Man climbing out of the hole on a silver rope which a large grey spider (much larger than himself) was fastening to a tree close by.

The Man climbed out. 'Thank you!' he said to the spider. 'And now be off!' And off the spider went, and was glad to go. There are black spiders on the dark side, poisonous ones, if not as large as the monsters of the white side. They hate anything white or pale or light, and especially pale spiders, which they hate like rich relations that pay infrequent visits.

The grey spider dropped back down the rope into the hole, and a black spider dropped out of the tree at the same moment.

'Now then!' cried the old man to the black spider.

'Come back there! That is my private door, and don't you forget it. Just make me a nice hammock from those two yew-trees, and I'll forgive you.

'It's a longish climb down and up through the middle of the moon,' he said to Roverandom, 'and I think a little rest before they arrive would do me good. They are very nice, but they need a good deal of energy. Of course I could take to wings, only I wear 'em out so fast; also it would mean widening the hole, as my size in wings would hardly fit, and I'm a beautiful rope-climber.

'Now what do you think of this side?' the Man continued. 'Dark with a pale sky, while tother was pale with a dark sky, eh? Quite a change, only there is not much more real colour here than there, not what I call real colour, loud and lots of it together. There are a few gleams under the trees, if you look, fireflies and diamond-beetles and ruby-moths, and such like. Too tiny, though; too tiny like all the bright things on this side. And they live a terrible life of it, what with owls like eagles and as black as coal, and crows like vultures and as numerous as sparrows, and all these black spiders. It's the black-velvet bob-owlers, flying all together in clouds, that I personally like least. They won't even get out of *my* way; I hardly dare give out a glimmer, or they all get tangled in my beard.

'Still this side has its charms, young dog; and one of them is that nobody and no-doggy on earth has ever seen it before – when they were awake – except you!'

Then the Man suddenly jumped into the hammock, which the black spider had been spinning for him while he was talking, and went fast asleep in a twinkling.

Roverandom sat alone and watched him, with a wary eye for black spiders too. Little gleams of firelight, red, green, gold, and blue, flashed and shifted here and there beneath the dark windless trees. The sky was pale with strange stars above the floating wisps of velvet cloud. Thousands of nightingales seemed to be singing in some other valley, faint beyond the nearer hills. And then Roverandom heard the sound of children's voices, or the echo of the echo of their voices coming down a sudden soft-stirring breeze. He sat up and barked the loudest bark he had barked since this tale began.

'Bless me!' cried the Man-in-the-Moon, jumping up wide awake, straight out of the hammock onto the grass, and nearly onto Roverandom's tail. 'Have they arrived already?'

'Who?' asked Roverandom.

'Well, if you didn't hear them, what did you yap for?' said the old man. 'Come on! This is the way.'

They went down a long grey path, marked at the sides with faintly luminous stones, and overhung with bushes. It led on and on, and the bushes became pine-trees, and the air was filled with the smell of pine-trees at night. Then the path began to climb; and after a time they came to the top of the lowest point in the ring of hills that had shut them in.

Then Roverandom looked down into the next valley; and all the nightingales stopped singing, like turning off a tap, and children's voices floated up clear and sweet, for they were singing a fair song with many voices blended to one music.

Down the hillside raced and jumped the old man and the dog together. My word! the Man-in-the-Moon could leap from rock to rock!

'Come on, come on!' he called. 'I may be a bearded billy-goat, a wild or garden goat, but you can't catch me!' And Roverandom had to fly to keep up with him.

And so they came suddenly to a sheer precipice, not very high, but dark and polished like jet. Looking over, Roverandom saw below a garden in twilight; and as he looked it changed to the soft glow of an afternoon sun, though he could not see where the soft light came from that lit all that sheltered place and never strayed beyond. Grey fountains were there, and long lawns; and children everywhere, dancing sleepily, walking dreamily, and talking to themselves. Some stirred as if just waking from deep sleep; some were already running wide awake and laughing: they were digging, gathering flowers, building tents and houses, chasing butterflies, kicking balls, climbing trees; and all were singing.

'Where do they all come from?' asked Roverandom, bewildered and delighted.

'From their homes and beds, of course,' said the Man.

'And how do they get here?'

'That I ain't going to tell you at all; and you'll never find out. You are lucky, and so is anyone, to get here by any way at all; but the children don't come by your way, at any rate. Some come often, and some come seldom, and I make most of the dream. Some of it they bring with them, of course, like lunch to school, and some (I am sorry to say) the spiders make – but not in this valley, and not if I catch 'em at it. And now let's go and join the party!'

The cliff of jet sloped steeply down. It was much too smooth even for a spider to climb – not that any spider ever dared try; for he might slide down, but neither he nor anything else could get up again; and in that garden were hidden sentinels, not to mention the Man-in-the-Moon, without whom no party was complete, for they were his own parties.

And he now slid bang into the middle of this one. He just sat down and tobogganed, swish! right into the midst of a crowd of children with Roverandom rolling on top of him, quite forgetting that he could fly. Or could have flown – for when he picked himself up at the bottom he found that his wings had gone.

'What's that little dog doing?' said a small boy to the Man. Roverandom was going round and round like a top, trying to look at his own back.

'Looking for his wings, my boy. He thinks he has rubbed them off on the toboggan-run, but they're in my pocket. No wings allowed down here, people don't get out of here without leave, do they?'

'No! Daddy-long-beard!' said about twenty children all at once, and one boy caught hold of the old man's beard and climbed up it onto his shoulder. Roverandom expected to see him turned into a moth or a piece of india-rubber, or something, on the spot.

But 'My word! you're a bit of a rope-climber, my boy!' said the Man. 'I'll have to give you lessons.' And he tossed the boy right up into the air. He did not fall down again; not a bit of it. He stuck up in the air; and the Man-in-the-Moon threw him a silver rope that he slipped out of his pocket.

'Just climb down that quick!' he said; and down the boy slithered into the old man's arms, where he was well tickled. 'You'll wake up, if you laugh so loud,' said the Man, and he put him down on the grass and walked off into the crowd.

Roverandom was left to amuse himself, and he was just making for a beautiful yellow ball ('Just like my own at home,' he thought) when he heard a voice he knew.

'There's my little dog!' it said. 'There's my little dog! I always thought he was real. Fancy him being here, when I've looked and looked all over the sands and called and whistled every day for him!'

As soon as Roverandom heard that voice, he sat up and begged.

'My little begging dog!' said little boy Two (of course); and he ran up and patted him. 'Where have you been to?'

But all Roverandom could say at first was: 'Can you hear what I'm saying?'

'Of course I can,' said little boy Two. 'But when mummy brought you home before, you wouldn't listen to me at all, although I did my best bark-talk for you. And I don't believe you tried to say much to me either; you seemed to be thinking of something else.'

Roverandom said how sorry he was, and he told the little boy how he had fallen out of his pocket; and all about Psamathos, and Mew, and many of the adventures he had had since he was lost. That is how the little boy and his brothers got to know about the odd fellow in the sand, and learned a lot of other useful things they might otherwise

48

have missed. Little boy Two thought that 'Roverandom' was a splendid name. 'I shall call you that too,' he said. 'And don't forget that you still belong to me!'

Then they had a game with the ball, and a game of hide-and-seek, and a run and a long walk, and a rabbit-hunt (with no result, of course, except excitement: the rabbits were exceedingly shadowy), and much splashing in the ponds, and all kinds of other things one after another for endless ages; and they got to like one another better and better. The little boy was rolling over and over on the dewy grass, in a very bed-timish light (but no one seems to mind wet grass or bed-time in that place), and the little dog was rolling over and over with him, and standing on his head like no dog on earth ever has done since Mother Hubbard's dead dog did it; and the little boy was laughing till he — vanished quite suddenly and left Roverandom all alone on the lawn!

'He's waked up, that's all,' said the Man-in-the-Moon, who suddenly appeared. 'Gone home, and about time too. Why! it's only a quarter of an hour before his breakfast time. He'll miss his walk on the sands this morning. Well, well! I am afraid it's our time to go, too.'

So, very reluctantly, Roverandom went back to the white side with the old man. They walked all the way, and it took a very long time; and Roverandom did not enjoy it as much as he ought to have done. For they saw all kinds of queer things, and had many adventures – perfectly safe, of course, with the Man-in-the-Moon close at hand. That was just as well, as there were lots of nasty creepy things in the bogs that would otherwise have grabbed the little dog quick. The dark side was as wet as the white side was dry, and full of the most extraordinary plants and creatures, which I would tell you about, if Roverandom had taken any particular notice of them. But he did not; he was thinking of the garden and the little boy.

At last they came to the grey edge, and they looked past the cinder valleys where many of the dragons lived, through a gap in the mountains to the great white plain and the shining cliffs. They saw the world rise, a pale green and gold moon, huge and round above the shoulders of the Lunar Mountains; and Roverandom thought: 'That is where my little boy lives!' It seemed a terrible and enormous way away.

'Do dreams come true?' he asked.

'Some of mine do,' said the old man. 'Some, but not all; and seldom any of them straight away, or quite like they were in dreaming them. But why do you want to know about dreams?'

'I was only wondering,' said Roverandom.

'About that little boy,' said the Man. 'I thought so.' He then pulled a telescope out of his pocket. It opened out to an enormous length. 'A little look will do you no harm, I think,' he said.

Roverandom looked through it – when he had managed at last to shut one eye and keep the other open.

He saw the world plainly. First he saw the far end of the moon's path falling straight onto the sea; and he thought he saw, faint and rather thin, long lines of small people sailing swiftly down it, but he could not be quite sure. The moonlight quickly faded. Sunlight began to grow; and suddenly there was the cove of the sandsorcerer (but no sign of Psamathos – Psamathos did not allow himself to be peeped at); and after a while the two little boys walked into the round picture, going hand in hand along the shore. 'Looking for shells or for me?' wondered the dog.

Very soon the picture shifted and he saw the little boys' father's white house on the cliff, with its garden running down to the sea; and at the gate he saw – an unpleasant surprise – the old wizard sitting on a stone smoking his pipe, as if he had nothing to do but watch there for ever, with his old green hat on the back of his head and his waistcoat unbuttoned.

'What's old Arta-what-d'you-call-him doing at the gate?' Roverandom asked. 'I should have thought he had forgotten about me long ago. And aren't his holidays over yet?'

'No, he's waiting for you, my doglet. He hasn't forgotten. If you turn up there just now, real or toy, he'll put some new bewitchment on you pretty quick. It isn't that he minds so much about his trousers – they were soon mended – but he is very annoyed with Samathos for interfering; and Samathos hasn't finished making his arrangements yet for dealing with him.'

Just then Roverandom saw Artaxerxes' hat blown off by the wind, and off the wizard ran after it; and plain to see, he had a wonderful patch on his trousers, an orange-coloured patch with black spots.

'I should have thought that a wizard could have managed to patch his trousers better than that!' said Roverandom.

'But he thinks he has managed it beautifully!' said the old man. 'He bewitched a piece off somebody's window-curtains; they got fire insurance, and he got a splash of colour, and both are satisfied. Still, you are right. He is failing, I do believe. Sad after all these centuries to see a man going off his magic; but lucky for you, perhaps.' Then the Man-in-the-Moon closed the telescope with a snap, and off they went again.

'Here are your wings again,' he said when they had reached the tower. 'Now fly off and amuse yourself! Don't worry the moonbeams, don't kill my white rabbits, and come back when you feel hungry! – or have any other sort of pain.'

Roverandom at once flew off to find the moon-dog and tell him about the other side; but the other dog was a bit jealous of a visitor being allowed to see things which he could not, and he pretended not to be interested.

'Sounds a nasty part altogether,' he growled. 'I'm sure I don't want to see it. I suppose you'll be bored with the white side now, and only having me to go about with, instead of all your two-legged friends. It's a pity the Persian wizard is such a sticker, and you can't go home.'

Roverandom was rather hurt; and he told the moon-dog over and over again that he was jolly glad to be back at the tower, and would never be bored with the white side. They soon settled down to be good friends again, and did lots and lots of things together; and yet what the moon-dog had said in bad temper turned out to be true. It was not Roverandom's fault, and he did his best not to show it, but somehow none of the adventures or explorations seemed so exciting to him as they had done before, and he was always thinking of the fun he had in the garden with little boy Two.

They visited the valley of the white moon-gnomes (moonums, for short) that ride about on rabbits, and make pancakes out of snowflakes, and grow little golden apple-trees no bigger than buttercups in their neat orchards. They put broken glass and tintacks outside the lairs of some of the lesser dragons (while they were asleep), and lay awake till the middle of the night to hear them roar with rage – dragons often have tender tummies, as I have told you already, and they go out for a drink at twelve midnight every night of their lives, not to speak of between-whiles. Sometimes the dogs even dared to go spider-baiting – biting webs and setting free the moon-beams, and flying off just in time, while the spiders threw lassoes at them from the hill-tops. But all the while Roverandom was looking out for Postman Mew and

News of the World (mostly murders and football-matches, as even a little dog knows; but there is sometimes something better in an odd corner).

He missed Mew's next visit, as he was away on a ramble, but the old man was still reading the letters and news when he got back (and he seemed in a mighty good humour too, sitting on the roof with his feet dangling over the edge, puffing at an enormous white clay-pipe, sending out clouds of smoke like a railway-engine, and smiling right round his round old face).

Roverandom felt he could bear it no longer. 'I've got a pain in my inside,' he said. 'I want to go back to the little boy, so that his dream can come true.'

The old man put down his letter (it was about Artaxerxes, and very amusing), and took the pipe out of his mouth. 'Must you go? Can't you stay? This is so sudden! So pleased to have met you! You must drop in again one day. *Dee*lighted to see you any time!' he said all in a breath.

'Very well!' he went on more sensibly. 'Artaxerxes is arranged for.'

'How??' asked Roverandom, really excited again.

'He has married a mermaid and gone to live at the bottom of the Deep Blue Sea.'

'I hope she will patch his trousers better! A green seaweed patch would go well with his green hat.'

'My dear dog! He was married in a complete new suit of seaweed green with pink coral buttons and epaulettes of sea-anemones; and they burnt his old hat on the beach!

Samathos arranged it all. O! Samathos is very deep, as deep as the Deep Blue Sea, and I expect he means to settle lots of things to his liking this way, lots more than just you, my dog.

'I wonder how it will turn out! Artaxerxes is getting into his twentieth or twenty-first childhood at the moment, it seems to me; and he makes a lot of fuss about very little things. Most obstinate he is, to be sure. He used to be a pretty good magician, but he is becoming bad-tempered and a thorough nuisance. When he came and dug up old Samathos with a wooden spade in the middle of the afternoon, and pulled him out of his hole by the ears, the Samathist thought things had gone too far, and I don't wonder. "Such a lot of disturbance, just at my best time for sleeping, and all about a wretched little dog": that is what he writes to me, and you needn't blush.

'So he invited Artaxerxes to a mermaid-party, when both their tempers had cooled down a bit, and that is how it all happened. They took Artaxerxes out for a moonlight swim, and he will never go back to Persia, or even Pershore. He fell in love with the rich mer-king's elderly but lovely daughter, and they were married the next night.

'It is probably just as well. There has not been a resident Magician in the Ocean for some time. Proteus, Poseidon, Triton, Neptune, and all that lot, they've all turned into minnows or mussels long ago, and in any case they never knew or bothered much about things outside the

Mediterranean – they were too fond of sardines. Old Niord retired a long while ago, too. He was of course only able to give half his attention to business after his silly marriage with the giantess – you remember she fell in love with him because he had clean feet (so convenient in the home), and fell out of love with him, when it was too late, because they were wet. He's on his last legs now, I hear; quite doddery, poor old dear. Oil-fuel has given him a dreadful cough, and he has retired to the coast of Iceland for a little sunshine.

'There was the Old Man of the Sea, of course. He was my cousin, and I'm not proud of it. He was a bit of a burden – wouldn't walk, and always wanted to be carried, as I dare say you have heard. That was the death of him. He sat on a floating mine (if you know what I mean) a year or two ago, right on one of the buttons! Not even *my* magic could do anything with that case. It was worse than the one of Humpty Dumpty.'

'What about Britannia?' asked Roverandom, who after all was an English dog; though really he was a bit bored with all this, and wanted to hear more about his own wizard. 'I thought Britannia ruled the waves.'

'She never really gets her feet wet. She prefers patting lions on the beach, and sitting on a penny with an eel-fork in her hand – and in any case there is more to manage in the sea than waves. Now they have got Artaxerxes, and I hope he will be of use. He'll spend the first few years trying to grow plums on polyps, I expect, if they let him; and that'll be easier than keeping the mer-folk in order.

'Well, well, well! Where was I? Of course – you can go back now, if you want to. In fact, not to be too polite, it's time you went back as soon as possible. Old Samathos is your first call – and don't follow my bad example and forget your Ps when you meet!'

Mew turned up again the very next day, with an extra post – an immense number of letters for the Man-in-the-Moon, and bundles of newspapers: *The Illustrated Weekly Weed*, *Ocean Notions*, *The Mer-mail*, *The Conch*, and *The Morning Splash*. They all had exactly the same (exclusive) pictures of Artaxerxes' wedding on the beach at full moon, with Mr Psamathos Psamathides, the well-known financier (a mere title of respect), grinning in the background. But they were nicer than our pictures, for they were at least coloured; and the mermaid really did look beautiful (her tail was in the foam).

The time had come to say good-bye. The Man-in-the-Moon beamed on Roverandom; and the moon-dog tried to look unconcerned. Roverandom himself had rather a drooping tail, but all he said was: 'Good-bye, pup! Take care of yourself, don't worry the moonbeams, don't kill the white rabbits, and don't eat too much supper!'

'Pup yourself!' said the moon-Rover. 'And stop eating wizards' trousers!' That was all; and yet, I believe, he was always worrying the old Man-in-the-Moon to send him on a holiday to visit Roverandom, and that he has been allowed to go several times since then.

After that Roverandom went back with Mew, and the Man went back into his cellars, and the moon-dog sat on the roof and watched them out of sight.

4

There was a cold wind blowing off the North Star when they got near the world's edge, and the chilly spray of the waterfalls splashed over them. It had been stiffer going on the way back, for old Psamathos' magic was not in such a hurry just then; and they were glad to rest on the Isle of Dogs. But as Roverandom was still his enchanted size, he did not enjoy himself much there. The other dogs were too large and noisy, and too scornful; and the bones of the bone-trees were too large and bony.

It was dawn of the day after the day after tomorrow when at last they sighted the black cliffs of Mew's home; and the sun was warm on their backs, and the tips of the sand-hillocks were already pale and dry, by the time they alighted in the cove of Psamathos.

Mew gave a little cry, and tapped with his beak on a bit of wood lying on the ground. The bit of wood immediately grew straight up into the air, and turned into Psamathos' left ear, and was joined by another ear, and quickly followed by the rest of the sorcerer's ugly head and neck.

'What do you two want at this time of day?' growled Psamathos. 'It's my favourite time for sleep.'

'We're back!' said the seagull.

'And you've allowed yourself to be carried back on his back, I see,' Psamathos said, turning to the little dog.

'After dragon-hunting I should have thought you would have found a little flight back home quite easy.'

'But please, sir,' said Roverandom, 'I left my wings behind; they didn't really belong to me. And I should rather like to be an ordinary dog again.'

'O! all right. Still I hope you have enjoyed yourself as "Roverandom". You ought to have done. Now you can be just Rover again, if you really want to be; and you can go home and play with your yellow ball, and sleep on arm-chairs when you get the chance, and sit on laps, and be a respectable little yap-dog again.'

'What about the little boy?' said Rover.

'But you ran away from him, silly, all the way to the moon, I thought!' said Psamathos, pretending to be annoyed and surprised, but giving a merry twinkle out of one knowing eye. 'Home I said, and home I meant. Don't splutter and argue!'

Poor Rover was spluttering because he was trying to get in a very polite 'Mr P-samathos'. Eventually he did.

'P-P-Please, Mr P-P-P-samathos,' he said, most touch-ingly. 'P-Please p-pardon me, but I have met him again;

and I shouldn't run away now; and really I belong to him, don't I? So I ought to go back to him.'

'Stuff and nonsense! Of course you don't and oughtn't! You belong to the old lady that bought you first, and back you'll have to go to her. You can't buy stolen goods, or bewitched ones either, as you would know, if you knew the Law, you silly little dog. Little boy Two's mother wasted sixpence on you, and that's an end of it. And what's in dream-meetings anyway?' wound up Psamathos with a huge wink.

'I thought some of the Man-in-the-Moon's dreams came true,' said little Rover sadly.

'O! did you! Well that's the Man-in-the-Moon's affair. *My* business is to change you back at once into your proper size, and send you back where you belong. Artaxerxes has departed to other spheres of usefulness, so we needn't bother about him any more. Come here!'

He took hold of Rover, and he waved his fat hand over the little dog's head, and hey presto — there was no change at all! He did it all over again, and still there was no change.

Then Psamathos got right up out of the sand, and Rover saw for the first time that he had legs like a rabbit. He stamped and ramped, and kicked sand into the air, and trampled on the seashells, and snorted like an angry pug-dog; and still nothing happened at all!

'Done by a seaweed wizard, blister and wart him!' he swore. 'Done by a Persian plum-picker, pot and jam him!'

he shouted, and kept on shouting till he was tired. Then he sat down.

'Well, well!' he said at last when he was cooler. 'Live and learn! But Artaxerxes is most peculiar. Who could have guessed that he would remember you amidst all the excitement of his wedding, and go and waste his strongest incantation on a dog before going on his honeymoon – as if his first spell wasn't more than any silly little puppy is worth? If it isn't enough to split one's skin.

'Well! I don't need to think out what is to be done, at any rate,' Psamathos continued. 'There is only one possible thing. You have got to go and find him and beg his pardon. But my word! I'll remember this against him, till the sea is twice as salt and half as wet. Just you two go for a walk, and be back in half an hour when my temper's better!'

Mew and Rover went along the shore and up the cliff, Mew flying slowly and Rover trotting along very sad. They stopped outside the little boys' father's house; and Rover even went in at the gate, and sat in a flower-bed under the boys' window. It was still very early, but he barked and barked hopefully. The little boys were either still fast asleep or away, for nobody came to the window. Or so Rover thought. He had forgotten that things are different on the world from the back-garden of the moon, and that Artaxerxes' bewitchment was still on his size, and the size of his bark.

After a little while Mew took him mournfully back to the cove. There an altogether new surprise was waiting for him. Psamathos was talking to a whale! A very large whale, Uin the oldest of the Right Whales. He looked like a mountain to little Rover, lying with his great head in a deep pool near the water's edge.

'Sorry I couldn't get anything smaller at a moment's notice,' said Psamathos. 'But he is very comfortable!'

'Walk in!' said the whale.

'Good-bye! Walk in!' said the seagull.

'Walk in!' said Psamathos; 'and be quick about it! And don't bite or scratch about inside; you might give Uin a cough, and that you would find uncomfy.'

This was almost as bad as being asked to jump into the hole in the Man-in-the-Moon's cellar, and Rover backed away, so that Mew and Psamathos had to push him in. Push him they did, too, without a coax; and the whale's jaws shut to with a snap.

Inside it was very dark indeed, and fishy. There Rover sat and trembled; and as he sat (not daring even to scratch his own ears) he heard, or thought he heard, the swish and beating of the whale's tail in the waters; and he felt, or thought he felt, the whale plunge deeper and downer towards the bottom of the Deep Blue Sea.

But when the whale stopped and opened his mouth wide again (delighted to do so: whales prefer going about trawling with their jaws wide open and a good tide of food coming in, but Uin was a considerate animal) and Rover peeped out, it was deep, altogether immeasurably deep, but not at all blue. There was only a pale green light;

and Rover walked out to find himself on a white path of sand winding through a dim and fantastic forest.

'Straight along! You haven't far to go,' said Uin.

Rover went straight along, as straight as the path would allow, and soon before him he saw the gate of a great palace, made it seemed of pink and white stone that shone with a pale light coming through it; and through the many windows lights of green and blue shone clear. All round the walls huge sea-trees grew, taller than the domes of the palace that swelled up vast, gleaming in the dark water. The great indiarubber trunks of the trees bent and swayed like grasses, and the shadow of their endless branches was thronged with goldfish, and silverfish, and redfish, and bluefish, and phosphorescent fish like birds. But the fishes did not sing. The mermaids sang inside the palace. How they sang! And all the sea-fairies sang in chorus, and the music floated out of the windows, hundreds of mer-folk playing on horns and pipes and conches of shell.

Sea-goblins were grinning at him out of the darkness under the trees, and Rover hurried along as fast as he could – he found his steps slow and laden deep down under the water. And why didn't he drown? I don't know, but I suppose Psamathos Psamathides had given some thought to it (he knows much more about the sea than most people would think, even though he never sets toe in it, if he can help it), while Rover and Mew had gone for a walk, and he had sat and simmered down and thought of a new plan.

Anyway Rover did not drown; but he was already wishing he was somewhere else, even in the whale's wet inside, before he got to the door: such queer shapes and faces peered at him out of the purple bushes and the spongey thickets beside the path that he felt very unsafe indeed. At last he got to the enormous door – a golden archway fringed with coral, and a door of mother-of-pearl studded with sharks' teeth. The knocker was a huge ring encrusted with white barnacles, and all the barnacles' little red streamers were hanging out; but of course Rover could not reach it, nor could he have moved it anyway. So he barked, and to his surprise his bark came quite loud. The music inside stopped at the third bark, and the door opened.

Who do you think opened it? Artaxerxes himself, dressed in what looked like plum-coloured velvet, and green silk trousers; and he still had a large pipe in his mouth, only it was blowing beautiful rainbow-coloured bubbles instead of tobacco-smoke; but he had no hat.

'Hullo!' he said. 'So you've turned up! I thought you would get tired of old P-samathos' (how he snorted over that exaggerated *P*) 'before long. He can't do quite everything. Well, what have you come down here for? We are just having a party, and you're interrupting the music.'

'Please, Mr Arterxaxes, I mean Ertaxarxes,' began Rover, rather flustered and trying to be very polite.

'O never mind about getting it right! I don't mind!' said the wizard rather crossly. 'Get on to the explanation, and make it short; I've no time for long rigmaroles.' He had become rather full of his own importance (with strangers), since his marriage to the rich mer-king's daughter, and his appointment to the post of Pacific and Atlantic Magician (the PAM they called him for short, when he was not present). 'If you want to see me about anything pressing, you had better come in and wait in the hall; I might find a moment after the dance.'

He closed the door behind Rover and went off. The little dog found himself in a huge dark space under a dimly-lighted dome. There were pointed archways curtained with seaweed all round, and most of them were dark; but one of them was full of light, and music came loudly through it, music that seemed to go on and on for ever, never repeating and never stopping for a rest.

Rover soon got very tired of waiting, so he walked along to the shining doorway and peeped through the curtains. He was looking into a vast ballroom with seven domes and ten thousand coral pillars, lit with purest magic and filled with warm and sparkling water. There all the golden-haired mermaids and the darkhaired sirens were dancing interwoven dances as they sang – not dancing on their tails, but wonderful swim-dancing, up and down, as well as to and fro, in the clear water.

Nobody noticed the little dog's nose peeping through the seaweed at the door, so after gazing for a while he crept inside. The floor was made of silver sand and pink butterfly shells, all open and flapping in the gently swirling water, and he had picked his way carefully among them for some way, keeping close to the wall, before a voice said suddenly above him:

'What a sweet little dog! He's a land-dog, not a sea-dog, I'm sure. How could he have got here – such a tiny mite!'

Rover looked up and saw a beautiful mer-lady with a large black comb in her golden hair, sitting on a ledge not far above him; her regrettable tail was dangling down, and she was mending one of Artaxerxes' green socks. She was, of course, the new Mrs Artaxerxes (usually known as Princess Pam; she was rather popular, which was more than you could say for her husband). Artaxerxes was at the moment sitting beside her, and whether he had the time or not for long rigmaroles, he was listening to one of his wife's. Or had been, before Rover turned up. Mrs Artaxerxes put an end to her rigmarole, and to her sock-mending, as soon as she caught sight of him, and floating down picked him up and carried him back to her couch. This was really a window-seat on the first floor (an indoors window) – there are no stairs in sea-houses, and no umbrellas, and for the same reason; and there is not much difference between doors and windows, either.

The mer-lady soon settled her beautiful (and rather capacious) self comfortably on her couch again, and put Rover on her lap; and immediately there was an awful growl from under the window-seat.

'Lie down, Rover! Lie down, good dog!' said Mrs Artaxerxes. She was not talking to our Rover, though; she was talking to a white mer-dog who came out now, in

67

spite of what she said, growling and grumbling and beating the water with his little web-feet, and lashing it with his large flat tail, and blowing bubbles out of his sharp nose.

'What a horrible little thing!' the new dog said. 'Look at his miserable tail! Look at his feet! Look at his silly coat!'

'Look at yourself,' said Rover from the mer-lady's lap, 'and you won't want to do it again! Who called you Rover? – a cross between a duck and a tadpole pretending to be a dog!' From which you can see that they took rather a fancy to one another at first sight.

Indeed, they soon made great friends – not quite such friends, perhaps, as Rover and the moon-dog, if only because Rover's stay under the sea was shorter, and the deeps are not such a jolly place as the moon for little dogs, being full of dark and awful places where light has never been and never will be, because they will never be uncovered till light has all gone out. Horrible things live there, too old for imagining, too strong for spells, too vast for measurement. Artaxerxes had already found that out. The post of PAM is not the most comfortable job in the world.

'Now swim away and amuse yourselves!' said his wife, when the dog-argument had died down and the two animals were merely sniffing at one another. 'Don't worry the fire-fish, don't chew the sea-anemones, don't get caught in the clams; and come back to supper!'

'Please, I can't swim,' said Rover.

68

'Dear me! What a nuisance!' she said. 'Now Pam!' – she was the only one so far that called him this to his face – 'here is something you can really do, at last!'

'Certainly, my dear!' said the wizard, very anxious to oblige her, and pleased to be able to show that he really had some magic, and was not an entirely useless official (limpets they call them in sea-language). He took a little wand out of his waistcoat-pocket – it was really his fountain-pen, but it was no longer any use for writing: mer-folk use a queer sticky ink that is absolutely no use in fountain-pens – and he waved it over Rover.

Artaxerxes was, in spite of what some people have said, a very good magician in his own way (or Rover would never have had these adventures) – rather a minor art, but still needing a deal of practice. Anyway after the very first wave Rover's tail began to get fishy and his feet to get webby, and his coat to get more and more like a mackintosh. When the change was over, he soon got used to it; and he found swimming a good deal easier to pick up than flying, very nearly as pleasant, and not so tiring – unless you wanted to go down.

The first thing he did, after a trial swim round the ballroom, was to bite at the other dog's tail. In fun, of course; but fun or not, there was nearly a fight on the spot, for the mer-dog was a bit touchy-tempered. Rover only saved himself by making off as fast as possible; nimble and quick he had to be, too. My word! there was a chase, in and out of windows, and along dark passages, and round pillars, and out and up and round the domes; till at last the mer-dog himself was exhausted, and his bad temper too, and they sat down together on the top of the highest cupola next to the flag-pole. The mer-king's banner, a seaweed streamer of scarlet and green, spangled with pearls, was floating from it.

'What's your name?' said the mer-dog after a breathless pause. 'Rover?' he said. 'That's my name, so you can't have it. I had it first!'

'How do you know?'

'Of course I know! I can see you are only a puppy, and you have not been down here hardly five minutes. I was enchanted ages and ages ago, hundreds of years. I expect I'm the first of all the dog Rovers.

'My first master was a Rover, a real one, a sea-rover who sailed his ship in the northern waters; it was a long ship with red sails, and it was carved like a dragon at the prow, and he called it the Red Worm and loved it. I loved him, though I was only a puppy, and he did not notice me much; for I wasn't big enough to go hunting, and he didn't take dogs to sail with him. One day I went sailing without being asked. He was saying farewell to his wife; the wind was blowing, and the men were thrusting the Red Worm out over the rollers into the sea. The foam was white about the dragon's neck; and I suddenly felt that I should not see him again after that day, if I didn't go too.

I sneaked on board somehow, and hid behind a water-barrel; and we were far at sea and the landmarks low in the water before they found me.

'That's when they called me Rover, when they dragged me out by my tail. "Here's a fine sea-rover!" said one. "And a strange fate is on him, that turns never home," said another with queer eyes. And indeed I never did go back home; and I have never grown any bigger, though I have grown much older – and wiser, of course.

'There was a sea-fight on that voyage, and I ran up on the fore-deck while the arrows fell and sword clashed upon shield. But the men of the Black Swan boarded us, and drove my master's men all over the side. He was the last to go. He stood beside the dragon's head, and then he dived into the sea in all his mail; and I dived after him.

'He went to the bottom quicker than I did, and the mermaids caught him; but I told them to carry him swift to land, for many would weep, if he did not come home. They smiled at me, and lifted him up, and bore him away; and now some say they carried him to the shore, and some shake their heads at me. You can't depend on mermaids, except for keeping their own secrets; they're better than oysters at that.

'I often think they really buried him in the white sand. Far away from here there lies still a part of the Red Worm that the men of the Black Swan sank; or it was there when last I passed. A forest of weed was growing round it and over it, all except the dragon's head; somehow not even barnacles were growing on that, and under it there was a mound of white sand.

'I left those parts long ago. I turned slowly into a sea-dog – the older sea-women used to do a good deal of witchcraft in those days, and one of them was kind to me. It was she that gave me as a present to the mer-king, the reigning one's grandfather, and I have been in and about the palace ever since. That's all about me. It happened hundreds of years ago, and I have seen a good deal of the high seas and the low seas since then, but I have never been back home. Now tell me about you! I suppose you don't come from the North Sea by any chance, do you? – we used to call it England's Sea in those days – or know any of the old places in and about the Orkneys?'

Our Rover had to confess that he had never heard before of anything but just 'the sea', and not much of that. 'But I have been to the moon,' he said, and he told his new friend as much about it as he could make him understand.

The mer-dog enjoyed Rover's tale immensely, and believed at least half of it. 'A jolly good yarn,' he said, 'and the best I have heard for a long time. I have seen the moon. I go on top occasionally, you know, but I never imagined it was like that. But my word! that sky-pup has got a cheek. Three Rovers! Two's bad enough, but three's impossible! And I don't believe for a moment he is older than I am; if he is a hundred yet, I should be mighty surprised.'

He was probably quite right too. The moon-dog, as you noticed, exaggerated a lot. 'And anyway,' went on the mer-dog, 'he only gave himself the name. Mine was given me.'

'And so was mine,' said our little dog.

'And for no reason at all, and before you had begun to earn it any way. I like the Man-in-the-Moon's idea. I shall call you Roverandom, too; and if I were you I should stick to it – you never do seem to know where you are going next! Let's go down to supper!'

It was a fishy supper, but Roverandom soon got used to that; it seemed to suit his webby feet. After supper he suddenly remembered why he had come all the way to the bottom of the sea; and off he went to look for Artaxerxes. He found him blowing bubbles, and turning them into real balls to please the little mer-children.

'Please, Mr Artaxerxes, could you be bothered to turn me – ' began Roverandom.

'O! go away!' said the wizard. 'Can't you see I can't be bothered? Not now, I'm busy.' This is what Artaxerxes said all too often to people he did not think were important. He knew well enough what Rover wanted; but he was not in a hurry himself.

So Roverandom swam off and went to bed, or rather roosted in a bunch of seaweed growing on a high rock in the garden. There was the old whale resting just underneath; and if anyone tells you that whales don't go down to the bottom or stop there dozing for hours, you need not let that bother you. Old Uin was in every way exceptional.

'Well?' he said. 'How have you got on? I see you are still toy-size. What's the matter with Artaxerxes? Can't he do anything, or won't he?'

'I think he can,' said Roverandom. 'Look at my new shape! But if ever I try to get onto the matter of size, he keeps on saying how busy he is, and he hasn't time for long explanations.'

'Umph!' said the whale, and knocked a tree sideways with his tail – the swish of it nearly washed Roverandom off his rock. 'I don't think that PAM will be a success in these parts; but I shouldn't worry. You'll be all right sooner or later. In the meanwhile there are lots of new things to see tomorrow. Go to sleep! Good-bye!' And he swam off into the dark. The report that he took back to the cove made old Psamathos very angry all the same.

The lights of the palace were all turned off. No moon or star came down through that deep dark water. The green got gloomier and gloomier, until it was all black, and there was not a glimmer, except when big luminous fish went by slowly through the weeds. Yet Roverandom slept soundly that night, and the next night, and several nights after. And the next day, and the day after, he looked for the wizard and couldn't find him anywhere.

One morning when he was beginning already to feel quite a sea-dog and to wonder if he had come to stay there for ever, the mer-dog said to him: 'Bother that wizard!

Or rather, don't bother him! Give him a miss today. Let's go off for a really long swim!'

Off they went, and the long swim turned into an excursion lasting for days. They covered a terrific distance in the time; they were enchanted creatures, you must remember, and there were few ordinary things in the seas that could keep up with them. When they got tired of the cliffs and mountains at the bottom, and of the racing runs in the middle heights, they rose up and up and up, right through the water for a mile and a bit; and when they got to the top, no land was to be seen.

The sea all round them was smooth and calm and grey. Then it suddenly ruffled and went dark in patches under a little cold wind, the wind at dawn. Swiftly the sun looked up with a shout over the rim of the sea, red as if he had been drinking hot wine; and swiftly he leaped into the air and went off for his daily journey, turning all the edges of the waves golden and the shadows between them dark green. A ship was sailing on the margin of the sea and the sky, and it sailed right into the sun, so that its masts were black against the fire.

'Where's that going to?' asked Roverandom.

'O! Japan or Honolulu or Manila or Easter Island or Thursday or Vladivostok, or somewhere or other, I suppose,' said the mer-dog, whose geography was a bit vague, in spite of his hundreds of years of boasted prowlings. 'This is the Pacific, I believe; but I don't know which part – a warm part, by the feel of it. It's rather a large piece of water. Let's go and look for something to eat!'

When they got back, some days later, Roverandom at once went to look for the wizard again; he felt he had given him a good long rest.

'Please, Mr Artaxerxes, could you bother – ' he began as usual.

'No! I could not!' said Artaxerxes, even more definitely than usual. This time he really was busy, though. The Complaints had come in by post. Of course, as you can imagine, all kinds of things go wrong in the sea, that not even the best PAM in the ocean could prevent, and some of which he is not even supposed to have anything to do with. Wrecks come down plump now and again on the roof of somebody's sea-house; explosions occur in the sea-bed (O yes! they have volcanoes and all that kind of nuisance quite as badly as we have) and blow up somebody's prize flock of goldfish, or prize bed of anemones, or one and only pearl-oyster, or famous rock and coral garden; or savage fish have a fight in the highway and knock mer-children over; or absent-minded sharks swim in at the dining-room window and spoil the dinner; or the deep, dark, unmentionable monsters of the black abysses do horrible and wicked things.

The mer-folk have always put up with all this, but not without complaining. They liked complaining. They used of course to write letters to *The Weekly Weed*, *The Mer-mail*, and *Ocean Notions*; but they had a PAM now, and they wrote to him as well, and blamed him for *everything*, even if they got their tails nipped by their own pet lobsters. They said his magic was inadequate (as it sometimes was) and that his salary ought to be reduced (which was true but rude); and that he was too big for his boots (which was also near the mark: they should have said slippers, he was too lazy to wear boots often); and they said lots besides to worry Artaxerxes every morning, and especially on Mondays. It was always worst (by several hundred envelopes) on Mondays; and this was a Monday, so Artaxerxes threw a lump of rock at Roverandom, and he slipped off like a shrimp from a net.

He was jolly glad when he got out into the garden to find that he was still unchanged in shape; and I dare say if he had not removed himself quick the wizard would have changed him into a sea-slug, or sent him to the Back of Beyond (wherever that is), or even to Pot (which is at the bottom of the deepest sea). He was very annoyed, and he went and grumbled to the sea-Rover.

'You'd better give him a rest till Monday is over, at any rate,' advised the mer-dog; 'and I should miss out Mondays altogether, in future, if I were you. Come and have another swim!'

After that Roverandom gave the wizard such a long rest that they almost forgot about one another – not quite: dogs don't forget lumps of rock very quickly. But to all appearances Roverandom had settled down to become a permanent pet of the palace. He was always off somewhere with the mer-dog, and often the mer-children came along as well. They were not as jolly as real, two-legged children in Roverandom's opinion (but then of course Roverandom did not really belong to the sea, and was not a perfect judge), but they kept him happy; and they might have kept him there for ever and have made him forget little boy Two in the end, if it had not been for things that happened later. You can make up your mind whether Psamathos had anything to do with these events, when we come to them.

There were plenty of these children to choose from, at any rate. The old mer-king had hundreds of daughters and thousands of grandchildren, and all in the same palace; and they were all fond of the two Rovers, and so was Mrs Artaxerxes. It was a pity that Roverandom never thought of telling her his story; she knew how to manage the PAM in any mood. But in that case, of course, Roverandom would have gone back sooner and missed many of the sights. It was with Mrs Artaxerxes, and some of the mer-children that he visited the Great White Caves, where all the jewels that are lost in the sea, and many that have always been in the sea, and of course pearls upon pearls, are hoarded and hidden.

They went too, another time, to visit the smaller seafairies in their little glass houses at the bottom of the sea. The sea-fairies seldom swim, but wander singing over the bed of the sea in smooth places, or drive in shell-carriages harnessed to the tiniest fishes; or else they ride astride little green crabs with bridles of fine threads (which of course don't prevent the crabs from going side-ways, as they always will); and they have troubles with the sea-goblins that are larger, and ugly and rowdy, and do nothing except fight and hunt fish and gallop about on sea-horses. Those goblins can live out of the water for a long while, and play in the surf at the water's edge in a storm. So can some of the sea-fairies, but they prefer the calm warm nights of summer evenings on lonely shores (and naturally are very seldom seen in consequence).

Another day old Uin turned up again and gave the two dogs a ride for a change; it was like riding on a moving mountain. They were away for days and days; and they only turned back from the eastern edge of the world just in time. There the whale rose to the top and blew out a fountain of water so high that a lot of it was thrown right off the world and over the edge.

Another time he took them to the other side (or as near as he dared), and that was a still longer and more exciting journey, the most marvellous of all Roverandom's travels, as he realised later, when he was grown to be an older and a wiser dog. It would take the whole of another story, at least, to tell you of all their adventures in Uncharted Waters and of their glimpses of lands unknown to geography, before they passed the Shadowy Seas and reached the great Bay of Fairyland (as we call it) beyond the Magic Isles; and saw far off in the last West the Mountains of Elvenhome and the light of Faery upon the waves.

Roverandom thought he caught a glimpse of the city of the Elves on the green hill beneath the Mountains, a glint of white far away; but Uin dived again so suddenly that he could not be sure. If he was right, he is one of the very few creatures, on two legs or four, who can walk about our own lands and say they have glimpsed that other land, however far away.

'I should catch it, if this was found out!' said Uin. 'No one from the Outer Lands is supposed ever to come here; and few ever do now. Mum's the word!'

What did I say about dogs? They don't forget ill-tempered lumps of rock. Well then, in spite of all these varied sight-seeings and these astonishing journeys, Roverandom kept it in his underneath mind all the time. And it came back into his upper mind, as soon as ever he got back home.

His very first thought was: 'Where's that old wizard? What's the use of being polite to him! I'll spoil his trousers again, if I get half a chance.'

He was in that frame of mind when, after trying in vain to have a word alone with Artaxerxes, he saw the magician go by, down one of the royal roads leading from the palace. He was of course too proud at his age to grow a tail or fins or learn to swim properly. The only thing he did like a fish was to drink (even in the sea, so he must have been thirsty); he spent a lot of time that might have been employed on official business conjuring up cider into large barrels in his private apartments. When he wanted to get about quickly, he drove. When Roverandom saw him, he was driving in his express – a gigantic shell shaped like a cockle and drawn by seven sharks. People got out of the way quick, for the sharks could bite.

'Let's follow!' said Roverandom to the mer-dog; and follow they did; and the two bad dogs dropped pieces of rock into the carriage whenever it passed under cliffs. They could nip along amazingly fast, as I told you; and they whizzed ahead, hid in weed-bushes and pushed anything loose they could find over the edge. It annoyed the wizard intensely, but they took care that he did not spot them.

Artaxerxes was in a very bad temper before he started, and he was in a rage before he had gone far, a rage not unmixed with anxiety. For he was going to investigate the damage done by an unusual whirlpool that had suddenly appeared – and in a part of the sea that he did not like at all; he thought (and he was quite right) that there were nasty things in that direction that were best left alone. I dare say you can guess what was the matter; Artaxerxes did. The ancient Sea-serpent was waking, or half thinking about it.

He had been in a sound sleep for years, but now he was turning. When he was uncoiled he would certainly have reached a hundred miles (some people say he would reach from Edge to Edge, but that is an exaggeration); and when he is curled up there is only one cave other than Pot (where he used to live, and many people wish him back there), only one cave in all the oceans that will hold him, and that is very unfortunately not a hundred miles from the mer-king's palace.

When he undid a curl or two in his sleep, the water heaved and shook and bent people's houses and spoilt their repose for miles and miles around. But it was very stupid to send the PAM to look into it; for of course the Sea-serpent is much too enormous and strong and old and idiotic for any one to control (primordial, prehistoric, autothalassic, fabulous, mythical, and silly are other adjectives applied to him); and Artaxerxes knew it all only too well.

Not even the Man-in-the-Moon working hard for fifty years could have concocted a spell large enough or long enough or strong enough to bind him. Only once had the Man-in-the-Moon tried (when specially requested), and at least one continent fell into the sea as a result.

Poor old Artaxerxes drove straight up to the mouth of the Sea-serpent's cave. But he had no sooner got out of his carriage than he saw the tip of the Sea-serpent's tail sticking out of the entrance; larger it was than a row of gigantic water-barrels, and green and slimy. That was quite enough for him. He wanted to go home at once before the Worm turned again – as all worms will at odd and unexpected moments.

It was little Roverandom that upset everything! He did not know anything about the Sea-serpent or its tremendousness; all he thought about was baiting the ill-tempered wizard. So when a chance came – Artaxerxes was standing staring stupid-like at the visible end of the serpent, and his steeds were taking no particular notice of anything – he crept up and bit one of the sharks' tails, for fun. For fun! What fun! The shark jumped straight forward, and the carriage jumped forward too; and Artaxerxes, who had just turned round to get into it, fell on his back. Then the shark bit the only thing it could reach at the moment, which was the shark in front; and that shark bit the next one; and so on, until the last of the seven, seeing nothing else to bite – bless me! the idiot, if he did not go and bite the Sea-serpent's tail!

The Sea-serpent gave a new and very unexpected turn! And the next thing the dogs knew was being whirled all over the place in water gone mad, bumping into giddy fishes and spinning sea-trees, scared out of their lives in a cloud of uprooted weeds, sand, shells, slugs, periwinkles, and oddments. And things got worse and worse, and the serpent kept on turning. And there was old Artaxerxes, clinging on to the reins of the sharks, being whirled all over the place too, and saying the most dreadful things to them. To the sharks, I mean. Luckily for this story, he never knew what Roverandom had done.

I don't know how the dogs got home. It was a long, long time before they did, at any rate. First of all they were washed up on the shore in one of the terrible tides caused by the Sea-serpent's stirrings; and then they were caught by fishermen on the other side of the sea and jolly nearly sent to an Aquarium (a disgusting fate); and then having escaped that by the skin of their feet they had to get all the way back themselves as best they could through perpetual subterranean commotion.

And when at last they got home there was a terrible commotion there too. All the mer-folk were crowded round the palace, all shouting at once:

'Bring out the PAM!' (Yes! they called him that publicly, and nothing longer or more dignified.) 'Bring out the PAM! BRING OUT THE PAM!'

And the PAM was hiding in the cellars. Mrs Artaxerxes found him there at last, and made him come out; and all the mer-folk shouted, when he looked out of an attic-window:

'Stop this nonsense! STOP THIS NONSENSE! STOP THIS NONSENSE!'

And they made such a hullabaloo that people at all the seasides all over the world thought the sea was roaring louder than usual. It was! And all the while the Sea-serpent kept on turning, trying absentmindedly to get the tip of his tail in his mouth. But thank heavens! he was not properly and fully awake, or he might have come out and shaken his tail in anger, and then another continent would have been drowned. (Of course whether that would have been really regrettable or not depends on which continent was taken and which you live on.)

But the mer-folk did not live on a continent, but in the sea, and right in the thick of it; and very thick it was getting. And they insisted that it was the mer-king's business to make the PAM produce some spell, remedy, or solution to keep the Sea-serpent quiet: they could not get their hands to their faces to feed themselves or blow their noses, the water shook so; and everybody was bumping into everybody else; and all the fish were seasick, the water was so wobbly; and it was so turbid and so full of sand that everyone had coughs; and all the dancing was stopped.

Artaxerxes groaned, but he had to do something. So he went to his workshop and shut himself up for a fortnight, during which time there were three earthquakes, two submarine hurricanes, and several riots of the mer-people. Then he came out and let loose a most prodigious spell (accompanied with soothing incantation) at a distance from the cave; and everybody went home and sat in cellars waiting – everybody except Mrs Artaxerxes and her unfortunate husband. The wizard was obliged to stay (at a distance, but not a safe one) and watch the result; and Mrs Artaxerxes was obliged to stay and watch the wizard.

All the spell did was to give the Serpent a terrible bad dream: he dreamed that he was covered all over with barnacles (very irritating, and partly true), and also being slowly roasted in a volcano (very painful, and unfortunately quite imaginary). And that woke him!

Probably Artaxerxes' magic was better than was supposed. At any rate, the Sea-serpent did not come out – luckily for this story. He put his head where his tail was, and yawned, opened his mouth as wide as the cave, and snorted so loud that everyone in the cellars heard him in all the kingdoms of the sea.

And the Sea-serpent said: 'Stop this NONSENSE!'

And he added: 'If this blithering wizard doesn't go away at once, and if he ever so much as paddles in the sea again, I shall COME OUT; and I shall eat him first, and then I shall knock everything to dripping smithereens. That's all. Good night!'

And Mrs Artaxerxes carried the PAM home in a fainting fit.

When he had recovered – and that was quick, they saw to that – he took the spell off the Serpent, and packed his bag; and all the people said and shouted:

'Send the PAM away! A good riddance! That's all. Good-bye!'

And the mer-king said: 'We don't want to lose you, but we think you ought to go.' And Artaxerxes felt very small and unimportant altogether (which was good for him). Even the mer-dog laughed at him.

But funnily enough, Roverandom was quite upset. After all, he had his own reasons for knowing that Artaxerxes' magic was not without effect. And he had bitten the shark's tail, too, hadn't he? And he had started the whole thing with that trouser-bite. And he belonged to the Land himself, and felt it was a bit hard on a poor land-wizard being baited by all these sea-folk.

Anyway he came up to the old fellow and said: 'Please, Mr Artaxerxes – !'

'Well?' said the wizard, quite kindly (he was so glad not to be called PAM, and he had not heard a 'Mister' for weeks). 'Well? What is it, little dog?'

'I beg your pardon, I do really. Awfully sorry, I mean. I never meant to damage your reputation.' Roverandom was thinking of the Sea-serpent and the shark's tail, but (luckily) Artaxerxes thought he was referring to his trousers.

'Come, come!' he said. 'We won't bring up bygones. Least said, soonest mended, or patched. I think we had both better go back home again together.'

'But please, Mr Artaxerxes,' said Roverandom, 'could you bother to turn me back into my proper size?'

'Certainly!' said the wizard, glad to find somebody that still believed he could do anything at all. 'Certainly!

But you are best and safest as you are, while you are down here. Let's get away from this first! And I am really and truly busy just now.'

And he really and truly was. He went into the work-shops and collected all his paraphernalia, insignia, symbols, memoranda, books of recipes, arcana, apparatus, and bags and bottles of miscellaneous spells. He burned all that would burn in his waterproof forge; and the rest he tipped into the back-garden. Extraordinary things took place there afterwards: all the flowers went mad, and the vegetables were monstrous, and the fishes that ate them were turned into sea-worms, sea-cats, sea-cows, sea-lions, sea-tigers, sea-devils, porpoises, dugongs, cephalopods, manatees, and calamities, or merely poisoned; and phantasms, visions, bewilderments, illusions, and hallucinations sprouted so thick that nobody had any peace in the palace at all, and they were obliged to move. In fact they began to respect the memory of that wizard after they had lost him. But that was long afterwards. At the moment they were clamouring for him to depart.

When all was ready Artaxerxes said good-bye to the mer-king – rather coldly; and not even the mer-children seemed to mind very much, he had so often been busy, and occasions of the bubbles (like the one I told you about) had been rare. Some of his countless sisters-in-law tried to be polite, especially if Mrs Artaxerxes was there; but really everybody was impatient to see him going out of the gate, so that they could send a humble message to the Sea-serpent:

'The regrettable wizard has departed and will return no more, Your Worship. Pray, go to sleep!'

Of course Mrs Artaxerxes went too. The mer-king had so many daughters that he could afford to lose one without much grief, especially the tenth eldest. He gave her a bag of jewels and a wet kiss on the doorstep and went back to his throne. But everybody else was very sorry, and especially Mrs Artaxerxes' mass of mer-nieces and mer-nephews; and they were also very sorry to lose Roverandom too.

The sorriest of all and the most downcast was the mer-dog: 'Just drop me a line whenever you go to the seaside,' he said, 'and I will pop up and have a look at you.'

'I won't forget!' said Roverandom. And then they went.

The oldest whale was waiting. Roverandom sat on Mrs Artaxerxes' lap, and when they were all settled on the whale's back, off they started.

And all the people said: 'Good-bye!' very loud, and 'A good riddance of bad rubbish' quietly, but not too quietly; and that was the end of Artaxerxes in the office of Pacific and Atlantic Magician. Who has done their bewitchments for them since, I don't know. Old Psamathos and the Man-in-the-Moon, I should think, have managed it between them; they are perfectly capable of it.

5

The whale landed on a quiet shore far, far away from the cove of Psamathos; Artaxerxes was most particular about that. There Mrs Artaxerxes and the whale were left, while the wizard (with Roverandom in his pocket) walked a couple of miles or so to the neighbouring seaside town to get an old suit and a green hat and some tobacco, in exchange for the wonderful suit of velvet (which created a sensation in the streets). He also purchased a bath-chair for Mrs Artaxerxes (you must not forget her tail).

'Please, Mr Artaxerxes,' began Roverandom once more, when they were sitting on the beach again in the afternoon. The wizard was smoking a pipe with his back against the whale, looking happier than he had done for a long while, and not at all busy. 'What about my proper shape, if you don't mind? And my proper size, too, please!'

'O very well!' said Artaxerxes. 'I thought I might just have had a nap before getting busy; but I don't mind.

Let's get it over! Where's my — ' And then he stopped short. He had suddenly remembered that he had burnt and thrown away all his spells at the bottom of the Deep Blue Sea.

He really was dreadfully upset. He got up and felt in his trouser-pockets, and his waistcoat-pockets, and his coat-pockets, inside and out, and he could not find the least bit of magic anywhere in any of them. (Of course not, the silly old fellow; he was so flustered he had even forgotten that it was only an hour or two since he had bought his suit in a pawnbroker's shop. As a matter of fact it had belonged to, or at any rate had been sold by, an elderly butler, and he had gone through the pockets pretty thoroughly first.)

The wizard sat down and mopped his forehead with a purple handkerchief, looking thoroughly miserable again. 'I really am very, very sorry!' he said. 'I never meant to leave you like this for ever and ever; but now I don't see that it can be helped. Let it be a lesson to you not to bite the trousers of nice kind wizards!'

'Ridiculous nonsense!' said Mrs Artaxerxes. 'Nice kind wizard, indeed! There is no nice or kind or wizard about it, if you don't give the little dog back his shape and size at once – and what's more I shall go back to the bottom of the Deep Blue Sea, and never come back to you again.'

Poor old Artaxerxes looked almost as worried as he did when the Sea-serpent was giving trouble. 'My dear!' he said. 'I'm very sorry, but I went and put my very strongest anti-removal spell-preserver on the dog – after Psamathos began to interfere (drat him!) and just to show him that he can't do everything, and that I won't have sand-rabbit wizards interfering in my private bit of fun – and I quite forgot to save the antidote when I was clearing up down below! I used to keep it in a little black bag hanging on the door in my workshop.

'Dear, dear me! I am sure you'll agree that it was only meant to be a bit of fun,' he said, turning to Roverandom, and his old nose got very large and red with his distress.

He went on saying 'dear, dear, deary me!' and shaking his head and beard; and he never noticed that Roverandom was not taking any notice, and the whale was winking. Mrs Artaxerxes had got up and gone to her luggage, and now she was laughing and holding out an old black bag in her hand.

'Now stop waggling your beard, and get to business!' she said. But when Artaxerxes saw the bag, he was too surprised for a moment to do anything but look at it with his old mouth wide open.

'Come along!' said his wife. 'It is your bag, isn't it? I picked it up, and several other little oddments that belonged to *me*, on the nasty rubbish heap you made in the garden.' She opened the bag to peep inside, and out jumped the wizard's magic fountain-pen wand, and also a cloud of funny smoke came out, twisting itself into strange shapes and curious faces.

Then Artaxerxes woke up. 'Here, give it to me! You're wasting it!' he cried; and he grabbed Roverandom by the scruff of his neck, and popped him kicking and yapping into the bag, before you could say 'knife'. Then he turned the bag round three times, waving the pen in the other hand, and —

'Thank you! That'll do nicely!' he said, and opened the bag.

There was a loud bang, and lo! and behold! there was no bag, only Rover, just as he had always been before he first met the wizard that morning on the lawn. Well, perhaps not just the same; he was a bit bigger, as he was now some months older.

It is no good trying to describe how excited he felt, or how funny and smaller everything seemed, even the oldest whale; nor how strong and ferocious Rover felt. For just one moment he looked longingly at the wizard's trousers; but he did not want the story to begin all over again, so, after he had run a mile in circles for joy, and nearly barked his head off, he came back and said 'Thank you!'; and he even added 'Very pleased to have met you', which was very polite indeed.

'That's all right!' said Artaxerxes. 'And that's the last magic I shall do. I'm going to retire. And *you* had better be getting home. I have no magic left to send you home with, so you'll have to walk. But that won't hurt a strong young dog.'

So Rover said good-bye, and the whale winked, and Mrs Artaxerxes gave him a piece of cake; and that was the last he saw of them for a long while. Long, long afterwards, when he was visiting a seaside place that he had never been to before, he found out what had happened to them; for they were there. Not the whale, of course, but the retired wizard and his wife.

They had settled in that seaside town, and Artaxerxes, taking the name of Mr A. Pam, had set up a cigarette and chocolate shop near the beach – but he was very, very careful never to touch the water (even fresh water, and that he found no hardship). A poor trade for a wizard, but he did at least try to clear up the nasty mess that his customers made on the beach; and he made a good deal of money out of 'Pam's Rock', which was very pink and sticky. There may have been the least bit of magic in it, for children liked it so much they went on eating it even after they had dropped it in the sand.

But Mrs Artaxerxes, I should say Mrs A. Pam, made much more money. She kept bathing-tents and vans, and gave swimming lessons, and drove home in a bath-chair drawn by white ponies, and wore the mer-king's jewels in the afternoon, and became very famous, so that no one ever alluded to her tail.

In the meanwhile, however, Rover is plodding down the country lanes and highways, going along following his nose, which is bound to lead him home in the end, as dogs' noses do.

'All the Man-in-the-Moon's dreams don't come true, then – just as he said himself,' thought Rover as he padded along. 'This was evidently one that didn't. I don't even know the name of the place where the little boys live, and that's a pity.'

The dry land, he found, was often as dangerous a place for a dog as the moon or the ocean, though much duller. Motor after motor racketed by, filled (Rover thought) with the same people, all making all speed (and all dust and all smell) to somewhere.

'I don't believe half of them know where they are going to, or why they are going there, or would know it if they got there,' grumbled Rover as he coughed and choked; and his feet got tired on the hard, gloomy, black roads. So he turned into the fields, and had many mild adventures of the bird and rabbit sort in an aimless kind of way, and more than one enjoyable fight with other dogs, and several hurried flights from larger dogs.

And so at last, weeks or months since the tale began (he could not have told you which), he got back to his own garden gate. And there was the little boy playing on the lawn with the yellow ball! And the dream had come true, just as he had never expected!!

'There's Roverandom!!!' cried little boy Two with a shout.

And Rover sat up and begged, and could not find his voice to bark anything, and the little boy kissed his head, and went dashing into the house, crying: 'Here's my little begging dog come back large and real!!!'

* * *

He told his grandmother all about it. How was Rover to know that he had belonged to the little boys' grandmother all the while? He had only belonged to her a month or two, when he was bewitched. But I wonder how much Psamathos and Artaxerxes had known about it?

The grandmother (very surprised indeed as she was at her dog's return looking so well and not motor-smashed or lorry-flattened at all) did not understand what on earth the little boy was talking about; though he told her all he knew about it very exactly, and over and over again. She gathered with a great deal of trouble (she was of course just the wee-est bit deaf) that the dog was to be called Roverandom and not Rover, because the Man-in-the-Moon said so ('What odd ideas the child has, to be sure'); and that he belonged not to her after all but to little boy Two, because mummy brought him home with the shrimps ('Very well, my dear, if you like; but I thought I bought him from the gardener's brother's son').

I haven't told you all their argument, of course; it was long and complicated, as it often is when both sides are right. All that you want to know is that he *was* called Roverandom after that, and he *did* belong to the little boy, and went back, when the boys' visit to their grandmother was over, to the house where he had once sat on the chest-of-drawers. He never did *that* again, of course. He lived sometimes in the country and sometimes, most of the time, in the white house on the cliff by the sea.

He got to know old Psamathos very well, never well enough to leave out the P, but well enough, when he was grown up to a large and dignified dog, to dig him up out of the sand and his sleep and have many and many a chat with him. Indeed Roverandom grew to be very wise, and had an immense local reputation, and had all sorts of other adventures (many of which the little boy shared).

But the ones I have told you about were probably the most unusual and the most exciting. Only Tinker says she does not believe a word of them. Jealous cat!

THE END

FARMER GILES OF HAM

**Aegidii Ahenobarbi Julii Agricole de Hammo
Domini de Domito
Aule Draconarie Comitis
Regni Minimi Regis et Basilei
mira facinora et mirabilis exortus**

or in the vulgar tongue
*The Rise and Wonderful Adventures
of Farmer Giles, Lord of Tame
Count of Worminghall and
King of the Little Kingdom*

FOREWORD

Of the history of the Little Kingdom few fragments have survived; but by chance an account of its origin has been preserved: a legend, perhaps, rather than an account; for it is evidently a late compilation, full of marvels, derived not from sober annals, but from the popular lays to which its author frequently refers. For him the events that he records lay already in a distant past; but he seems, nonetheless, to have lived himself in the lands of the Little Kingdom. Such geographical knowledge as he shows (it is not his strong point) is of that country, while of regions outside it, north or west, he is plainly ignorant.

An excuse for presenting a translation of this curious tale, out of its very insular Latin into the modern tongue of the United Kingdom, may be found in the glimpse that it affords of life in a dark period of the history of Britain, not to mention the light that it throws on the origin of some difficult place-names. Some may find the character and adventures of its hero attractive in themselves.

The boundaries of the Little Kingdom, either in time or space, are not easy to determine from the scanty evidence. Since Brutus came to Britain many kings and realms have come and gone. The partition under Locrin, Camber, and Albanac, was only the first of many shifting divisions. What with the love of petty independence on the one hand, and on the other the greed of kings for wider realms, the years were filled with swift alternations of war and peace, of mirth and woe, as historians of the reign of Arthur tell us: a time of unsettled frontiers, when men might rise or fall suddenly, and song-writers had abundant material and eager audiences. Somewhere in those long years, after the days of King Coel maybe, but before Arthur or the Seven Kingdoms of the English, we must place the events here related; and their scene is the valley of the Thames, with an excursion north-west to the walls of Wales.

The capital of the Little Kingdom was evidently, as is ours, in its south-east corner, but its confines are vague. It seems never to have reached far up the Thames into the West, nor beyond Otmoor to the North; its eastern borders are dubious. There are indications in a fragmentary legend of Georgius son of Giles and his page Suovetaurilius (Suet) that at one time an outpost against the Middle Kingdom was maintained at Farthingho. But that situation does not concern this story, which is now presented without alteration or further comment, though the original grandiose title has been suitably reduced to *Farmer Giles of Ham.*

FARMER GILES OF HAM

Ægidius de Hammo was a man who lived in the midmost parts of the Island of Britain. In full his name was Ægidius Ahenobarbus Julius Agricola de Hammo; for people were richly endowed with names in those days, now long ago, when this island was still happily divided into many kingdoms. There was more time then, and folk were fewer, so that most men were distinguished. However, those days are now over, so I will in what follows give the man his name shortly, and in the vulgar form: he was Farmer Giles of Ham, and he had a red beard. Ham was only a village, but villages were proud and independent still in those days.

Farmer Giles had a dog. The dog's name was Garm. Dogs had to be content with short names in the vernacular: the Book-latin was reserved for their betters. Garm could not talk even dog-latin; but he could use the vulgar tongue (as could most dogs of his day) either to bully or to brag or to wheedle in. Bullying was for beggars and trespassers, bragging for other dogs, and wheedling for his master. Garm was both proud and afraid of Giles, who could bully and brag better than he could.

The time was not one of hurry or bustle. But bustle has very little to do with business. Men did their work without it; and they got through a deal both of work and of talk. There was plenty to talk about, for memorable events occurred very frequently. But at the moment when this tale begins nothing memorable had, in fact, happened in Ham for quite a long time. Which suited Farmer Giles down to the ground: he was a slow sort of fellow, rather set in his ways, and taken up with this own affairs. He had his hands full (he said) keeping the wolf from the door: that is, keeping himself as fat and comfortable as his father before him. The dog was busy helping him. Neither of them gave much thought to the Wide World outside their fields, the village, and the nearest market.

But the Wide World was there. The forest was not far off, and away west and north were the Wild Hills, and the dubious marches of the mountain-country. And among other things still at large there were giants: rude and uncultured folk, and troublesome at times. There was one giant in particular, larger and more stupid than his fellows. I find no mention of his name in the histories, but it does not matter. He was very large, his walking-stick was like a tree, and his tread was heavy. He brushed elms aside like tall grasses; and he was the ruin of roads and the desolation of gardens, for his great feet made holes in them as deep as wells; if he stumbled into a house, that was the end of it. And all this damage he did wherever he went, for his head was far above the roofs of houses and left his feet to look after themselves. He was near-sighted and also rather deaf. Fortunately he lived far off in the Wild, and seldom visited the lands inhabited by men, at least not on purpose. He had a great tumbledown house away up in the mountains; but he had very few friends, owing to his deafness and his stupidity, and the scarcity of giants. He used to go out walking in the Wild Hills and in the empty regions at the feet of the mountains, all by himself.

One fine summer's day this giant went out for a walk, and wandered aimlessly along, doing a great deal of damage in the woods. Suddenly he noticed that the sun was setting, and felt that his supper-time was drawing near; but he discovered that he was in a part of the country that he did not know at all and had lost his way. Making a wrong guess at the right direction he walked and he walked until it was dark night. Then he sat down and waited for the moon to rise. Then he walked and walked in the moonlight, striding out with a will, for he was anxious to get home. He had left his best copper pot on the fire, and feared that the bottom would be burned. But his back was to the mountains, and he was already in the lands inhabited by men. He was, indeed, now drawing near to the farm of Ægidius Ahenobarbus Julius Agricola and the village called (in the vulgar tongue) Ham.

It was a fine night. The cows were in the fields, and Farmer Giles's dog had got out and gone for a walk on his own account. He had a fancy for moonshine, and rabbits. He had no idea, of course, that a giant was also out for a walk. That would have given him a good reason for going out without leave, but a still better reason for staying quiet in the kitchen. At about two o'clock the giant arrived in Farmer Giles's fields, broke the hedges, trampled on the crops, and flattened the mowing-grass. In five minutes he had done more damage than the royal fox-hunt could have done in five days.

Garm heard a thump-thump coming along the river-bank, and he ran to the west side of the low hill on which the farmhouse stood, just to see what was happening. Suddenly he saw the giant stride right across the river and tread upon Galathea, the farmer's favourite cow, squashing the poor beast as flat as the farmer could have squashed a blackbeetle.

That was more than enough for Garm. He gave a yelp of fright and bolted home. Quite forgetting that he was out without leave, he came and barked and yammered underneath his master's bedroom window. There was no answer for a long time. Farmer Giles was not easily wakened.

'Help! help! help!' cried Garm.

The window opened suddenly and a well-aimed bottle came flying out.

'Ow!' said the dog, jumping aside with practised skill. 'Help! help! help!'

Out popped the farmer's head. 'Drat you, dog! What be you a-doing?' said he.

'Nothing,' said the dog.

'I'll give you nothing! I'll flay the skin off you in the morning,' said the farmer, slamming the window.

'Help! help! help!' cried the dog.

Out came Giles's head again. 'I'll kill you, if you make another sound,' he said. 'What's come to you, you fool?'

'Nothing,' said the dog; 'but something's come to you.'

'What d'you mean?' said Giles, startled in the midst of his rage. Never before had Garm answered him saucily.

'There's a giant in your fields, an enormous giant; and he's coming this way,' said the dog. 'Help! help! He is trampling on your sheep. He has stamped on poor Galathea, and she's as flat as a doormat. Help! help! He's bursting all your hedges, and he's crushing all your crops. You must be bold and quick, master, or you will soon have nothing left. Help!' Garm began to howl.

'Shut up!' said the farmer, and he shut the window. 'Lord-a-mercy!' he said to himself; and though the night was warm, he shivered and shook.

'Get back to bed and don't be a fool!' said his wife. 'And drown that dog in the morning. There is no call to believe what a dog says; they'll tell any tale, when caught truant or thieving.'

'May be, Agatha,' said he, 'and may be not. But there's something going on in my fields, or Garm's a rabbit. That dog was frightened. And why should he come yammering in the night when he could sneak in at the back door with the milk in the morning?'

'Don't stand there arguing!' said she. 'If you believe the dog, then take his advice: be bold and quick!'

'Easier said than done,' answered Giles; for, indeed, he believed quite half of Garm's tale. In the small hours of the night giants seem less unlikely.

Still, property is property; and Farmer Giles had a short way with trespassers that few could outface. So he pulled on his breeches, and went down into the kitchen and took his blunderbuss from the wall. Some may well ask what a blunderbuss was. Indeed, this very question, it is said, was put to the Four Wise Clerks of Oxenford, and after thought they replied: 'A blunderbuss is a short gun with a large bore firing many balls or slugs, and capable of doing execution within a limited range without exact aim. (Now superseded in civilised countries by other firearms.)'

However, Farmer Giles's blunderbuss had a wide mouth that opened like a horn, and it did not fire balls or slugs, but anything that he could spare to stuff in. And it did not do execution, because he seldom loaded it, and never let it off. The sight of it was usually enough for his purpose. And this country was not yet civilised, for the blunderbuss was not superseded: it was indeed the only kind of gun that there was, and rare at that. People preferred bows and arrows and used gunpowder mostly for fireworks.

Well then, Farmer Giles took down the blunderbuss, and he put in a good charge of powder, just in case extreme measures should be required; and into the wide mouth he stuffed old nails and bits of wire, pieces of broken pot, bones and stones and other rubbish. Then he drew on his top-boots and his overcoat, and he went out through the kitchen garden.

The moon was low behind him, and he could see nothing worse than the long black shadows of bushes and trees, but he could hear a dreadful stamping-stumping coming up the side of the hill. He did not feel either bold or quick, whatever Agatha might say; but he was more anxious about his property than his skin. So, feeling a bit loose about the belt, he walked towards the brow of the hill.

Suddenly up over the edge of it the giant's face appeared, pale in the moonlight, which glittered in his large round eyes. His feet were still far below, making holes in the fields. The moon dazzled the giant and he did not see the farmer; but Farmer Giles saw him and was scared out of his wits. He pulled the trigger without thinking, and the blunderbuss went off with a staggering bang. By luck it was pointed more or less at the giant's large ugly face. Out flew the rubbish, and the stones and the bones, and the bits of crock and wire, and half a dozen nails. And since the range was indeed limited, by chance and no choice of the farmer's many of these things struck the giant: a piece of pot went in his eye, and a large nail stuck in his nose.

'Blast!' said the giant in his vulgar fashion. 'I'm stung!' The noise had made no impression on him (he was rather deaf), but he did not like the nail. It was a long time since he had met any insect fierce enough to pierce his thick skin; but he had heard tell that away East, in the Fens, there were dragonflies that could bite like hot pincers. He thought that he must have run into something of the kind.

'Nasty unhealthy parts, evidently,' said he. 'I shan't go any further this way tonight.'

So he picked up a couple of sheep off the hill-side, to eat when he got home, and went back over the river, making off about nor-nor-west at a great pace. He found his way home again in the end, for he was at last going in the right direction; but the bottom was burned off his copper pot.

As for Farmer Giles, when the blunderbuss went off it knocked him over flat on his back; and there he lay looking at the sky and wondering if the giant's feet would miss him as they passed by. But nothing happened, and the stamping-stumping died away in the distance. So he got up, rubbed his shoulder, and picked up the blunderbuss. Then suddenly he heard the sound of people cheering.

Most of the people of Ham had been looking out of their windows; a few had put on their clothes and come out (after the giant had gone away). Some were now running up the hill shouting.

The villagers had heard the horrible thump-thump of the giant's feet, and most of them had immediately got under the bed-clothes; some had got under the beds. But Garm was both proud and frightened of his master. He thought him terrible and splendid, when he was angry; and he naturally thought that any giant would think the same. So, as soon as he saw Giles come out with the blunderbuss (a sign of great wrath as a rule), he rushed off to the village, barking and crying:

'Come out! Come out! Come out! Get up! Get up! Come, and see my great master! He is bold and quick. He is going to shoot a giant for trespassing. Come out!'

The top of the hill could be seen from most of the houses. When the people and the dog saw the giant's face rise above it, they quailed and held their breath, and all but the dog among them thought that this would prove a matter too big for Giles to deal with. Then the blunderbuss went bang, and the giant turned suddenly and went away, and in their amazement and their joy they clapped and cheered, and Garm nearly barked his head off.

'Hooray!' they shouted. 'That will learn him! Master Ægidius has given him what for. Now he will go home and die, and serve him right and proper.' Then they all cheered again together. But even as they cheered, they took note for their own profit that after all this blunderbuss could really be fired. There had been some debate in the village inns on that point; but now the matter was settled. Farmer Giles had little trouble with trespassers after that.

When all seemed safe some of the bolder folk came right up the hill and shook hands with Farmer Giles. A few – the parson, and the blacksmith, and the miller, and one or two persons of importance – slapped him on the back. That did not please him (his shoulder was very sore), but he felt obliged to invite them into his house. They sat round in the kitchen drinking his health and loudly praising him. He made no effort to hide his yawns, but as long as the drink lasted they took no notice. By the time they had all had one or two (and the farmer two or three), he began to feel quite bold; when they had all had two or three (and he himself five or six), he felt as bold as his dog thought him. They parted good friends; and he slapped their backs heartily. His hands were large, red, and thick; so he had his revenge.

Next day he found that the news had grown in the telling, and he had become an important local figure. By the middle of the next week the news had spread to all the villages within twenty miles. He had become the Hero of the Countryside. Very pleasant he found it. Next market day he got enough free drink to float a boat: that is to say, he nearly had his fill, and came home singing old heroic songs.

At last even the King got to hear of it. The capital of that realm, the Middle Kingdom of the island in those happy days, was some twenty leagues distant from Ham, and they paid little heed at court, as a rule, to the doings of rustics in the provinces. But so prompt an expulsion of a giant so injurious seemed worthy of note and of some

little courtesy. So in due course – that is, in about three
months, and on the feast of St Michael – the King sent a
magnificent letter. It was written in red upon white parch-
ment, and expressed the royal approbation of 'our loyal
subject and well-beloved Ægidius Ahenobarbus Julius
Agricola de Hammo'.

The letter was signed with a red blot; but the court
scribe had added:

**Ego Augustus Bonifacius Ambrosius Aurelianus Antoni-
nus Pius et Magnificus, dux rex, tyrannus, et Basileus
Mediterranearum Partium, subscribo;**

and a large red seal was attached. So the document was
plainly genuine. It afforded great pleasure to Giles, and
was much admired, especially when it was discovered that
one could get a seat and a drink by the farmer's fire by
asking to look at it.

Better than the testimonial was the accompanying gift.
The King sent a belt and a long sword. To tell the truth the
King had never used the sword himself. It belonged to the
family and had been hanging in his armoury time out of
mind. The armourer could not say how it came there, or
what might be the use of it. Plain heavy swords of that
kind were out of fashion at court just then, so the King
thought it the very thing for a present to a rustic. But
Farmer Giles was delighted, and his local reputation
became enormous.

Giles much enjoyed the turn of events. So did his dog. He never got his promised whipping. Giles was a just man according to his lights; in his heart he gave a fair share of the credit to Garm, though he never went as far as to mention it. He continued to throw hard words and hard things at the dog when he felt inclined, but he winked at many little outings. Garm took to walking far afield. The farmer went about with a high step, and luck smiled on him. The autumn and early winter work went well. All seemed set fair – until the dragon came.

In those days dragons were already getting scarce in the island. None had been seen in the midland realm of Augustus Bonifacius for many a year. There were, of course, the dubious marches and the uninhabited mountains, westward and northward, but they were a long way off. In those parts once upon a time there had dwelt a number of dragons of one kind and another, and they had made raids far and wide. But the Middle Kingdom was in those days famous for the daring of the King's knights, and so many stray dragons had been killed, or had returned with grave damage, that the others gave up going that way.

It was still the custom for Dragon's Tail to be served up at the King's Christmas Feast; and each year a knight was chosen for the duty of hunting. He was supposed to set out upon St Nicholas' Day and come home with a dragon's tail not later than the eve of the feast. But for many years now the Royal Cook had made a marvellous confection, a Mock Dragon's Tail of cake and almond-paste, with cunning scales of hard icing-sugar. The chosen knight then carried this into the hall on Christmas Eve, while the fiddles played and the trumpets rang. The Mock Dragon's Tail was eaten after dinner on Christmas Day, and everybody said (to please the cook) that it tasted much better than Real Tail.

That was the situation when a real dragon turned up again. The giant was largely to blame. After his adventure he used to go about in the mountains visiting his scattered relations more than had been his custom, and much more than they liked. For he was always trying to borrow a large copper pot. But whether he got the loan of one or not, he would sit and talk in his long-winded lumbering fashion about the excellent country down away East, and all the wonders of the Wide World. He had got it into his head that he was a great and daring traveller.

'A nice land,' he would say, 'pretty flat, soft to the feet, and plenty to eat for the taking: cows, you know, and sheep all over the place, easy to spot, if you look carefully.'

'But what about the people?' said they.

'I never saw any,' said he. 'There was not a knight to be seen or heard, my dear fellows. Nothing worse than a few stinging flies by the river.'

'Why don't you go back and stay there?' said they.

'Oh well, there's no place like home, they say,' said he.

'But maybe I shall go back one day when I have a mind. And anyway I went there once, which is more than most folk can say. Now about that copper pot.'

'And these rich lands,' they would hurriedly ask, 'these delectable regions full of undefended cattle, which, way do they lie? And how far off?'

'Oh,' he would answer, 'away east or sou'east. But it's a long journey.' And then he would give such an exaggerated account of the distance that he had walked, and the woods, hills, and plains that he had crossed, that none of the other less long-legged giants ever set out. Still, the talk got about.

Then the warm summer was followed by a hard winter. It was bitter cold in the mountains and food was scarce. The talk got louder. Lowland sheep and kine from the deep pastures were much discussed. The dragons pricked up their ears. They were hungry, and these rumours were attractive.

'So knights are mythical!' said the younger and less experienced dragons. 'We always thought so.'

'At least they may be getting rare,' thought the older and wiser worms; 'far and few and no longer to be feared.'

There was one dragon who was deeply moved. Chrysophylax Dives was his name, for he was of ancient and imperial lineage, and very rich. He was cunning, inquisitive, greedy, well-armoured, but not over bold. But at any rate he was not in the least afraid of flies or insects of any sort or size; and he was mortally hungry.

So one winter's day, about a week before Christmas, Chrysophylax spread his wings and took off. He landed quietly in the middle of the night plump in the heart of the midland realm of Augustus Bonifacius rex et basileus. He did a deal of damage in a short while, smashing and burning, and devouring sheep, cattle, and horses.

This was in a part of the land a long way from Ham, but Garm got the fright of his life. He had gone off on a long expedition, and taking advantage of his master's favour he had ventured to spend a night or two away from home. He was following an engaging scent along the eaves of a wood, when he turned a corner and came suddenly upon a new and alarming smell; he ran indeed slap into the tail of Chrysophylax Dives, who had just landed. Never did a dog turn his own tail round and bolt home swifter than Garm. The dragon, hearing his yelp, turned and snorted; but Garm was already far out of range. He ran all the rest of the night, and arrived home about breakfast-time.

'Help! help! help!' he cried outside the back door.

Giles heard, and did not like the sound of it. It reminded him that unexpected things may happen, when all seems to be going well.

'Wife, let that drafted dog in,' said he, 'and take a stick to him!'

Garm came bundling into the kitchen with his eyes starting and his tongue hanging out. 'Help!' he cried.

'Now what have you been a-doing this time?' said Giles, throwing a sausage at him.

'Nothing,' panted Garm, too flustered to give heed to the sausage.

'Well, stop doing it, or I'll skin you,' said the farmer.

'I've done no wrong. I didn't mean no harm,' said the dog. 'But I came on a dragon accidental-like, and it frightened me.'

The farmer choked in his beer. 'Dragon?' said he. 'Drat you for a good-for-nothing nosey-parker! What d'you want to go and find a dragon for at this time of the year, and me with my hands full? Where was it?'

'Oh! North over the hills and far away, beyond the Standing Stones and all,' said the dog.

'Oh, away there!' said Giles, mighty relieved. 'They're queer folk in those parts, I've heard tell, and aught might happen in their land. Let them get on with it! Don't come worriting me with such tales. Get out!'

Garm got out, and spread the news all over the village. He did forget to mention that his master was not scared in the least. 'Quite cool he was, and went on with his breakfast.'

People chatted about it pleasantly at their doors. 'How like old times!' they said. 'Just as Christmas is coming, too. So seasonable. How pleased the King will be! He will be able to have Real Tail this Christmas.'

But more news came in next day. The dragon, it appeared, was exceptionally large and ferocious. He was doing terrible damage.

'What about the King's knights?' people began to say.

*   *   *

Others had already asked the same question. Indeed, messengers were now reaching the King from the villages most afflicted by Chrysophylax, and they said to him as loudly and as often as they dared: 'Lord, what of your knights?'

But the knights did nothing; their knowledge of the dragon was still quite unofficial. So the King brought the matter to their notice, fully and formally, asking for necessary action at their early convenience. He was greatly displeased when he found that their convenience would not be early at all, and was indeed daily postponed.

Yet the excuses of the knights were undoubtedly sound. First of all, the Royal Cook had already made the Dragon's Tail for that Christmas, being a man who believed in getting things done in good time. It would not do at all to offend him by bringing in a real tail at the last minute. He was a very valuable servant.

'Never mind the Tail! Cut his head off and put an end to him!' cried the messengers from the villages most nearly affected.

But Christmas had arrived, and most unfortunately a grand tournament had been arranged for St John's Day: knights of many realms had been invited and were coming to compete for a valuable prize. It was obviously unreasonable to spoil the chances of the midland Knights by sending their best men off on a dragon-hunt before the tournament was over.

After that came the New Year Holiday.

But each night the dragon had moved; and each move had brought him nearer to Ham. On the night of New Year's Day people could see a blaze in the distance. The dragon had settled in a wood about ten miles away, and it was burning merrily. He was a hot dragon when he felt in the mood.

After that people began to look at Farmer Giles and whisper behind his back. It made him very uncomfortable; but he pretended not to notice it. The next day the dragon came several miles nearer. Then Farmer Giles himself began to talk loudly of the scandal of the King's knights.

'I should like to know what they do to earn their keep,' said he.

'So should we!' said everyone in Ham.

But the miller added: 'Some men still get knighthood by sheer merit, I am told. After all, our good Ægidius here is already a knight in a manner of speaking. Did not the King send him a red letter and a sword?'

'There's more to knighthood than a sword,' said Giles. 'There's dubbing and all that, or so I understand. Anyway I've my own business to attend to.'

'Oh! but the King would do the dubbing, I don't doubt, if he were asked,' said the miller. 'Let us ask him, before it is too late!'

'Nay!' said Giles. 'Dubbing is not for my sort. I am a farmer and proud of it: a plain honest man and honest men fare ill at court, they say. It is more in your line, Master Miller.'

The parson smiled: not at the farmer's retort, for Giles and the miller were always giving one another as good as they got, being bosom enemies, as the saying was in Ham. The parson had suddenly been struck with a notion that pleased him, but he said no more at that time. The miller was not so pleased, and he scowled.

'Plain certainly, and honest perhaps,' said he. 'But do you have to go to court and be a knight before you kill a dragon? Courage is all that is needed, as only yesterday I heard Master Ægidius declare. Surely he has as much courage as any knight?'

All the folk standing by shouted: 'Of course not!' and 'Yes indeed! Three cheers for the Hero of Ham!'

Then Farmer Giles went home feeling very uncomfortable. He was finding that a local reputation may require keeping up, and that may prove awkward. He kicked the dog, and hid the sword in a cupboard in the kitchen. Up till then it had hung over the fireplace.

The next day the dragon moved to the neighbouring village of Quercetum (Oakley in the vulgar tongue). He ate not only sheep and cows and one or two persons of tender age, but he ate the parson too. Rather rashly the parson had sought to dissuade him from his evil ways. Then there was a terrible commotion. All the people of Ham came up the hill headed by their own parson; and they waited on Farmer Giles.

'We look to you!' they said; and they remained standing

round and looking, until the farmer's face was redder than his beard.

'When are you going to start?' they asked.

'Well, I can't start today, and that's a fact,' said he.

'I've a lot on hand with my cowman sick and all. I'll see about it.'

They went away; but in the evening it was rumoured that the dragon had moved even nearer, so they all came back.

'We look to you Master Ægidius,' they said.

'Well,' said he, 'it's very awkward for me just now. My mare has gone lame, and the lambing has started. I'll see about it as soon as may be.'

So they went away once more, not without some grumbling and whispering. The miller was sniggering. The parson stayed behind, and could not be got rid of. He invited himself to supper, and made some pointed remarks. He even asked what had become of the sword and insisted on seeing it.

It was lying in a cupboard on a shelf hardly long enough for it, and as soon as Farmer Giles brought it out in a flash it leaped from the sheath, which the farmer dropped as if it had been hot. The parson sprang to his feet, upsetting his beer. He picked the sword up carefully and tried to put it back in the sheath; but it would not go so much as a foot in, and it jumped clean out again, as soon as he took his hand off the hilt.

'Dear me! This is very peculiar!' said the parson, and he took a good look at both scabbard and blade. He was a lettered man, but the farmer could only spell out large uncials with difficulty, and was none too sure of the reading even of his own name. That is why he had never given any heed to the strange letters that could dimly be seen on sheath and sword. As for the King's armourer, he was so accustomed to runes, names and other signs of power and significance upon swords and scabbards that he had not bothered his head about them; he thought them out of date, anyway.

But the parson looked long, and he frowned. He had expected to find some lettering on the sword or on the scabbard, and that was indeed the idea that had come to him the day before; but now he was surprised at what he saw, for letters and signs there were, to be sure but he could not make head or tail of them.

'There is an inscription on this sheath, and some, ah, epigraphical signs are visible also upon the sword,' he said.

'Indeed?' said Giles. 'And what may that amount to?'

'The characters are archaic and the language barbaric,' said the parson, to gain time. 'A little closer inspection will be required.' He begged the loan of the sword for the night, and the farmer let him have it with pleasure.

When the parson got home he took down many learned books from his shelves, and he sat up far into the night. Next morning it was discovered that the dragon had moved nearer still. All the people of Ham barred their doors and shuttered their windows; and those that had cellars went down into them and sat shivering in the candle-light.

But the parson stole out and went from door to door, and he told, to all who would listen through a crack or a keyhole, what he had discovered in his study.

'Our good Ægidius,' he said, 'by the King's grace is now the owner of Caudimordax, the famous sword that in popular romances is more vulgarly called Tailbiter.'

Those that heard this name usually opened the door.

They all knew the renown of Tailbiter, for that sword had belonged to Bellomarius, the greatest of all the dragon-slayers of the realm. Some accounts made him the maternal great-great-grandfather of the King. The song and tales of his deeds were many, and if forgotten at court, were still remembered in the villages.

'This sword,' said the parson, 'will not stay sheathed, if a dragon is within five miles; and without doubt in a brave man's hands no dragon can resist it.'

Then people began to take heart again; and some unshuttered the windows and put their heads out. In the end the parson persuaded a few to come and join him; but only the miller was really willing. To see Giles in a real fix seemed to him worth the risk.

They went up the hill, not without anxious looks north across the river. There was no sign of the dragon. Probably he was asleep; he had been feeding very well all the Christmastime.

The parson (and the miller) hammered on the farmer's door. There was no answer, so they hammered louder. At last Giles came out. His face was very red. He also had sat up far into the night, drinking a good deal of ale; and he had begun again as soon as he got up.

They all crowded round him, calling him Good Ægidius, Bold Ahenobarbus, Great Julius, Staunch Agricola, Pride of Ham, Hero of the Countryside. And they spoke of Caudimordax, Tailbiter, The Sword that would not be Sheathed, Death or Victory. The Glory of the Yeomanry, Backbone of the Country, and the Good of one's Fellow Men, until the farmer's head was hopelessly confused.

'Now then! One at a time!' he said, when he got a chance. 'What's all this, what's all this? It's my busy morning, you know.'

So they let the parson explain the situation. Then the miller had the pleasure of seeing the farmer in as tight a fix as he could wish. But things did not turn out quite as the miller expected. For one thing Giles had drunk a deal of strong ale. For another he had a queer feeling of pride and encouragement when he learned that his sword was actually Tailbiter. He had been very fond of tales about Bellomarius when he was a boy and before he had learned sense he had sometimes wished that he could have a marvellous and heroic sword of his own. So it came over him all of a sudden that he would take Tailbiter and go dragon-hunting. But he had been used to bargaining all his life, and he made one more effort to postpone the event.

'What!' said he. 'Me go dragon-hunting? In my old leggings and waistcoat? Dragon-fights need some kind of armour, from all I've heard tell. There isn't any armour in this house, and that's a fact,' said he.

That was a bit awkward, they all allowed; but they sent for the blacksmith. The blacksmith shook his head. He was a slow, gloomy man, vulgarly known as Sunny Sam, though his proper name was Fabricius Cunctator. He never whistled at his work, unless some disaster (such as frost in May) had duly occurred after he had foretold it. Since he was daily foretelling disasters of every kind, few happened that he had not foretold, and he was able to take credit of them. It was his chief pleasure; so naturally he was reluctant to do anything to avert them. He shook his head again.

'I can't make armour out of naught,' he said. 'And it's not in my line. You'd best get the carpenter to make you a wooden shield. Not that it will help you much. He's a hot dragon.'

Their faces fell; but the miller was not so easily to be turned from his plan of sending Giles to the dragon, if he would go; or of blowing the bubble of his local reputation, if he refused in the end. 'What about ring-mail?' he said. 'That would be a help; and it need not be very fine. It would be for business and not for showing off at court. What about your old leather jerkin, friend Ægidius? And there is a great pile of links and rings in the smithy. I don't suppose Master Fabricius himself knows what may be lying there.'

'You don't know what you are talking about,' said the smith, growing cheerful. 'If it's real ring-mail you mean, then you can't have it. It needs the skill of the dwarfs, with every little ring fitting into four others and all. Even if I had the craft, I should be working for weeks. And we shall all be in our graves before then,' said he, 'or leastways in the dragon.'

They all wrung their hands in dismay, and the black smith began to smile. But they were now so alarmed that they were unwilling to give up the miller's plan and they turned to him for counsel.

'Well,' said he, 'I've heard tell that in the old days those that could not buy bright hauberks out of the Southlands would stitch steel rings on a leather shirt and be content with that. Let's see what can be done in that line?'

So Giles had to bring out his old jerkin, and the smith was hurried back to his smithy. There they rummaged in every corner and turned over the pile of old metal, as had not been done for many a year. At the bottom they found, all dull with rust, a whole heap of small rings, fallen from some forgotten coat, such as the miller had spoken of. Sam, more unwilling and gloomy as the task seemed more hopeful, was set to work on the spot, gathering and sorting and cleaning the rings; and when (as he was pleased to point out) these were clearly insufficient for one so broad of back and breast as Master Ægidius, they made him split up old chains and hammer the links into rings as fine as his skill could contrive.

They took the smaller rings of steel and stitched them on to the breast of the jerkin, and the larger and clumsier rings they stitched on the back; and then, when still more rings were forthcoming, so hard was poor Sam driven, they took a pair of the farmer's breeches and stitched rings on to them. And up on a shelf in a dark nook of the smithy the miller found the old iron frame of a helmet, and he set the cobbler to work, covering it with leather as well as he could.

The work took them all the rest of the day, and all the next day – which was Twelfthnight and the eve of the Epiphany, but festivities were neglected. Farmer Giles celebrated the occasion with more ale than usual; but the dragon mercifully slept. For the moment he had forgotten all about hunger or swords.

Early on the Epiphany they went up the hill, carrying the strange result of their handiwork. Giles was expecting them. He had now no excuses left to offer; so he put on the mail jerkin and the breeches. The miller sniggered. Then Giles put on his topboots and an old pair of spurs; and also the leather-covered helmet. But at the last moment he clapped an old felt hat over the helmet, and over the mail coat he threw his big grey cloak.

'What is the purpose of that, Master?' they asked.

'Well,' said Giles, 'if it is your notion to go dragon-hunting jingling and dingling like Canterbury Bells, it ain't mine. It don't seem sense to me to let a dragon know that you are coming along the road sooner than need be.

And a helmet's a helmet, and a challenge to battle. Let the worm see only my old hat over the hedge, and maybe I'll get nearer before the trouble begins.'

They had stitched on the rings so that they overlapped, each hanging loose over the one below, and jingle they certainly did. The cloak did something to stop the noise of them, but Giles cut a queer figure in his gear. They did not tell him so. They girded the belt round his waist with difficulty, and they hung the scabbard upon it; but he had to carry the sword, for it would no longer stay sheathed, unless held with main strength.

The farmer called for Garm. He was a just man according to his lights. 'Dog,' he said, 'you are coming with me.'

The dog howled. 'Help! help!' he cried.

'Now stop it!' said Giles. 'Or I'll give you worse than any dragon could. You know the smell of this worm, and maybe you'll prove useful for once.'

Then Farmer Giles called for his grey mare. She gave him a queer look and sniffed at the spurs. But she let him get up; and then off they went, and none of them felt happy. They trotted through the village, and all the folk clapped and cheered, mostly from their windows. The farmer and his mare put as good a face on it as they could; but Garm had no sense of shame and slunk along with his tail down.

They crossed the bridge over the river at the end of the village. When at last they were well out of sight, they slowed to a walk. Yet all too soon they passed out of the lands belonging to Farmer Giles and to other folk of Ham and came to parts that the dragon had visited. There were broken trees, burned hedges and blackened grass, and a nasty uncanny silence.

The sun was shining bright, and Farmer Giles began to wish that he dared shed a garment or two; and he wondered if he had not taken a pint too many. 'A nice end to Christmas and all,' he thought. 'And I'll be lucky if it don't prove the end of me too.' He mopped his face with a large handkerchief – green, not red; for red rags infuriate dragons, or so he had heard tell.

But he did not find the dragon. He rode down many lanes, wide and narrow, and over other farmers' deserted fields, and still he did not find the dragon. Garm was, of course, of no use at all. He kept just behind the mare and refused to use his nose.

They came at last to a winding road that had suffered little damage and seemed quiet and peaceful. After following it for half a mile Giles began to wonder whether he had not done his duty and all that his reputation required. He had made up his mind that he had looked long and far enough, and he was just thinking of turning back, and of his dinner, and of telling his friends that the dragon had seen him coming and simply flown away, when he turned a sharp corner.

There was the dragon, lying half across a broken hedge with his horrible head in the middle of the road. 'Help!'

said Garm and bolted. The grey mare sat down plump, and Farmer Giles went off backwards into a ditch. When he put his head out, there was the dragon wide awake looking at him.

'Good morning!' said the dragon. 'You seem surprised.'

'Good morning!' said Giles. 'I am that.'

'Excuse me,' said the dragon. He had cocked a very suspicious ear when he caught the sound of rings jingling, as the farmer fell. 'Excuse my asking, but were you looking for me, by any chance?'

'No, indeed!' said the farmer. 'Who'd a'thought of seeing you here? I was just going for a ride.'

He scrambled out of the ditch in a hurry and backed away towards the grey mare. She was now on her feet again and was nibbling some grass at the wayside, seeming quite unconcerned.

'Then we meet by good luck,' said the dragon. The pleasure is mine. Those are your holiday clothes, I suppose. A new fashion, perhaps?' Farmer Giles's felt hat had fallen off and his grey cloak had slipped open; but he brazened it out.

'Aye,' said he, 'brand-new. But I must be after that dog of mine. He's gone after rabbits, I fancy.'

'I fancy not,' said Chrysophylax, licking his lips (a sign of amusement). 'He will get home a long time before you do, I expect. But pray proceed on your way, Master – let me see, I don't think I know your name?'

'Nor I yours,' said Giles; 'and we'll leave it at that.'

'As you like,' said Chrysophylax, licking his lips again, but pretending to close his eyes. He had a wicked heart (as dragons all have), but not a very bold one (as is not unusual). He preferred a meal that he did not have to fight for, but appetite had returned after a good long sleep. The parson of Oakley had been stringy, and it was years since he had tasted a large fat man. He had now made up his mind to try this easy meat, and he was only waiting until the old fool was off his guard.

But the old fool was not as foolish as he looked, and he kept his eye on the dragon, even while he was trying to mount. The mare, however, had other ideas, and she kicked and shied when Giles tried to get up. The dragon became impatient and made ready to spring.

'Excuse me!' said he. 'Haven't you dropped something?'

An ancient trick, but it succeeded; for Giles had indeed dropped something. When he fell he had dropped Caudimordax (or vulgarly Tailbiter), and there it lay by the wayside. He stooped to pick it up; and the dragon sprang. But not as quick as Tailbiter. As soon as it was in the farmer's hand, it leaped forward with a flash, straight at the dragon's eyes.

'Hey!' said the dragon, and stopped very short. 'What have you got there?'

'Only Tailbiter, that was given to me by the King,' said Giles.

'My mistake!' said the dragon. 'I beg your pardon.' He lay and grovelled, and Farmer Giles began to feel more comfortable. 'I don't think you have treated me fair.'

'How not?' said Giles. 'And anyway why should I?'

'You have concealed your honourable name and pretended that our meeting was by chance; yet you are plainly a knight of high lineage. It used, sir, to be the custom of knights to issue a challenge in such cases, after a proper exchange of titles and credentials.'

'Maybe it used, and maybe it still is,' said Giles, beginning to feel pleased with himself. A man who has a large and imperial dragon grovelling before him may be excused if he feels somewhat uplifted. 'But you are making more mistakes than one, old worm. I am no knight. I am Farmer Ægidius of Ham, I am; and I can't abide trespassers. I've shot giants with my blunderbuss before now, for doing less damage than you have. And I issued no challenge neither.'

The dragon was disturbed. 'Curse that giant for a liar!' he thought. 'I have been sadly misled. And now what on earth does one do with a bold farmer and a sword so bright and aggressive?' He could recall no precedent for such a situation. 'Chrysophylax is my name,' said he, 'Chrysophy-lax the Rich. What can I do for your honour?' he added ingratiatingly, with one eye on the sword, and hoping to escape battle.

'You can take yourself off, you horny old varmint,' said Giles, also hoping to escape battle. 'I only want to be shot of you. Go right away from here, and get back to your own dirty den!' He stepped towards Chrysophylax, waving his arms as if he was scaring crows.

That was quite enough for Tailbiter. It circled flashing the air; then down it came, smiting the dragon on the joint of the right wing, a ringing blow that shocked him exceedingly. Of course Giles knew very little about the right methods of killing a dragon, or the sword might have landed in a tenderer spot; but Tailbiter did the best it could in inexperienced hands. It was quite enough for Chrysophylax – he could not use his wing for days. Up he got and turned to fly, and found that he could not. The farmer sprang on the mare's back. The dragon began to run. So did the mare. The dragon galloped over a field puffing and blowing. So did the mare. The farmer bawled and shouted, as if he was watching a horse race; and all the while he waved Tailbiter. The faster the dragon ran the more bewildered he became; and all the while the grey mare put her best leg foremost and kept close behind him.

On they pounded down the lanes, and through the gaps in the fences, over many fields and across many brooks. The dragon was smoking and bellowing and losing all sense of direction. At last they came suddenly to the bridge of Ham, thundered over it, and came roaring down the village street. There Garm had the impudence to sneak out of an alley and join in the chase.

All the people were at their windows or on the roofs. Some laughed and some cheered; and some beat tins and pans and kettles; and others blew horns and pipes and

whistles; and the parson had the church bells rung. Such a
to-do and an ongoing had not been heard in Ham for a
hundred years.

Just outside the church the dragon gave up. He lay
down in the middle of the road and gasped. Garm came
and sniffed at his tail, but Chrysophylax was past all
shame.

'Good people, and gallant warrior,' he panted, as
Farmer Giles rode up, while the villagers gathered round
(at a reasonable distance) with hayforks, poles, and pokers
in their hands. 'Good people, don't kill me! I am very rich.
I will pay for all the damage I have done. I will pay for the
funerals of all the people I have killed, especially the
parson of Oakley; he shall have a noble cenotaph —
though he was rather lean. I will give you each a really
good present, if you will only let me go home and fetch it.'

'How much?' said the farmer.

'Well,' said the dragon, calculating quickly. He noticed
that the crowd was rather large. 'Thirteen and eightpence
each?'

'Nonsense!' said Giles. 'Rubbish!' said the people.
'Rot!' said the dog.

'Two golden guineas each, and children half price?' said
the dragon.

'What about dogs?' said Garm. 'Go on!' said the
farmer. 'We're listening.'

'Ten pounds and a purse of silver for every soul, and
gold collars for the dogs?' said Chrysophylax anxiously.

'Kill him!' shouted the people, getting impatient.

'A bag of gold for everybody, and diamonds for the ladies?' said Chrysophylax hurriedly.

'Now you're talking, but not good enough,' said Farmer Giles. 'You've left dogs out again,' said Garm. 'What size of bags?' said the men. 'How many diamonds?' said their wives.

'Dear me! dear me!' said the dragon. 'I shall be ruined.'

'You deserve it,' said Giles. 'You can choose between being ruined and being killed where you lie.' He brandished Tailbiter, and the dragon cowered. 'Make up your mind!' the people cried, getting bolder and drawing nearer.

Chrysophylax blinked; but deep down inside him he laughed: a silent quiver which they did not observe. Their bargaining had begun to amuse him. Evidently they expected to get something out of it. They knew very little of the ways of the wide and wicked world – indeed, there was no one now living in all the realm who had had any actual experience in dealing with dragons and their tricks. Chrysophylax was getting his breath back, and his wits as well. He licked his lips.

'Name your own price!' he said.

Then they all began to talk at once. Chrysophylax listened with interest. Only one voice disturbed him: that of the blacksmith.

'No good'll come of it, mark my words,' said he. 'A worm won't return, say what you like. But no good will come of it, either way.'

'You can stand out of the bargain, if that's your mind,' they said to him, and went on haggling, taking little further notice of the dragon.

Chrysophylax raised his head; but if he thought of springing on them, or of slipping off during the argument he was disappointed. Farmer Giles was standing by, chewing a straw and considering; but Tailbiter was in his hand, and his eye was on the dragon.

'You lie where you be!' said he, 'or you'll get what you deserve, gold or no gold.'

The dragon lay flat. At last the parson was made spokesman and he stepped up beside Giles. 'Vile Worm!' he said. 'You must bring back to this spot all your ill-gotten wealth; and after recompensing those whom you have injured we will share it fairly among ourselves. Then, if you make a solemn vow never to disturb our land again, nor to stir up any other monster to trouble us, we will let you depart with both your head and your tail to your own home. And now you shall take such strong oaths to return (with your ransom) as even the conscience of a worm must hold binding.'

Chrysophylax accepted, after a plausible show of hesitation. He even shed hot tears, lamenting his ruin, till there were steaming puddles in the road; but no one was moved by them. He swore many oaths, solemn and astonishing, that he would return with all his wealth on the feast of St Hilarius and St Felix. That gave him eight days, and far too short a time for the journey, as even those ignorant of geography might well have reflected. Nonetheless they let him go, and escorted him as far as the bridge.

'To our next meeting!' he said, as he passed over the river. 'I am sure we shall all look forward to it.'

'We shall indeed,' they said. They were, of course, very foolish. For though the oaths he had taken should have burdened his conscience with sorrow and a great fear of disaster, he had, alas! no conscience at all. And if this regrettable lack in one of imperial lineage was beyond the comprehension of the simple, at the least the parson with his booklearning might have guessed it. Maybe he did. He was a grammarian, and could doubtless see further into the future than others.

The blacksmith shook his head as he went back to his smithy. 'Ominous names,' he said. 'Hilarius and Felix! I don't like the sound of them.'

The King, of course, quickly heard the news. It ran through the realm like fire and lost nothing in the telling. The King was deeply moved, for various reasons, not the least being financial; and he made up his mind to ride at once in person to Ham, where such strange things seemed to happen.

He arrived four days after the dragon's departure, coming over the bridge on his white horse, with many knights and trumpeters, and a large baggage-train. All the people had put on their best clothes and lined the street to welcome him. The cavalcade came to a halt in the open space before the church gate. Farmer Giles knelt before the King, when he was presented; but the King told him to rise, and actually patted him on the back. The knights pretended not to observe this familiarity.

The King ordered the whole village to assemble in Farmer Giles's large pasture beside the river, and when they were all gathered together (including Garm, who felt that he was concerned), Augustus Bonifacius rex et basileus was graciously pleased to address them.

He explained carefully that the wealth of the miscreant Chrysophylax all belonged to himself as lord of the land. He passed rather lightly over his claim to be considered suzerain of the mountain-country (which was debatable); but 'we make no doubt in any case,' said he, 'that all the treasure of this worm was stolen from our ancestors. Yet we are, as all know, both just and generous, and our good liege Ægidius shall be suitably rewarded; nor shall any of our loyal subjects in this place go without some token of our esteem, from the parson to the youngest child. For we are well pleased with Ham. Here at least a sturdy and uncorrupted folk still retain the ancient courage of our race.' The knights were talking among themselves about the new fashion in hats.

The people bowed and curtsied, and thanked him humbly. But they wished now that they had closed with the dragon's offer of ten pounds all round, and kept the matter private. They knew enough, at any rate, to feel sure that the King's esteem would not rise to that. Garm noticed that there was no mention of dogs. Farmer Giles was the only one of them who was really content. He felt sure of some reward, and was mighty glad anyway to have come safely out of a nasty business with his local reputation higher than ever.

The King did not go away. He pitched his pavilions in Farmer Giles's field, and waited for January the fourteenth, making as merry as he could in a miserable village far from the capital. The royal retinue ate up nearly all the bread, butter, eggs, chickens, bacon and mutton, and drank up every drop of old ale there was in the place in the next three days. Then they began to grumble at short commons. But the King paid handsomely for everything (in tallies to be honoured later by the Exchequer, which he hoped would shortly be richly replenished); so the folk of Ham were well satisfied, not knowing the actual state of the Exchequer.

January the fourteenth came, the feast of Hilarius and of Felix, and everybody was up and about early. The knights put on their armour. The farmer put on his coat of home-made mail, and they smiled openly, until they caught the King's frown. The farmer also put on Tailbiter, and it went into its sheath as easy as butter, and stayed there. The parson looked hard at the sword, and nodded to himself. The blacksmith laughed.

Midday came. People were too anxious to eat much. The afternoon passed slowly. Still Tailbiter showed no sign of leaping from the scabbard. None of the watchers on the hill, nor any of the small boys who had climbed to the top of tall trees, could see anything by air or by land that might herald the return of the dragon.

The blacksmith walked about whistling; but it was not until evening fell and the stars came out that the other folk of the village began to suspect that the dragon did not mean to come back at all. Still they recalled his many solemn and astonishing oaths and kept on hoping. When, however, midnight struck and the appointed day was over, their disappointment was deep. The blacksmith was delighted.

'I told you so,' he said. But they were still not convinced.

'After all he was badly hurt,' said some.

'We did not give him enough time,' said others. 'It is a powerful long way to the mountains, and he would have a lot to carry. Maybe he has had to get help.'

But the next day passed and the next. Then they all gave up hope. The King was in a red rage. The victuals and drinks had run out, and the knights were grumbling loudly. They wished to go back to the merriments of court. But the King wanted money.

He took leave of his loyal subjects, but he was short and sharp about it; and he cancelled half the tallies on the Exchequer. He was quite cold to Farmer Giles and dismissed him with a nod.

'You will hear from us later,' he said, and rode off with his knights and his trumpeters.

* * *

141

The more hopeful and simple-minded thought that a message would soon come from the court to summon Master Ægidius to the King, to be knighted at the least. In a week the message came, but it was of different sort. It was written and signed in triplicate: one copy for Giles; one for the parson; and one to be nailed on the church door. Only the copy addressed to the parson was of any use, for the court-hand was peculiar and as dark to the folk of Ham as the Book-latin. But the parson rendered it into the vulgar tongue and read it from the pulpit. It was short and to the point (for a royal letter); the King was in a hurry.

'We Augustus B. A. A. P. and M. rex et cetera make known that we have determined, for the safety of our realm and for the keeping of our honour, that the worm or dragon styling himself Chrysophylax the Rich shall be sought out and condignly punished for his misdemeanours, torts, felonies, and foul perjury. All the knights of our Royal Household are hereby commanded to arm and make ready to ride upon this quest, so soon as Master Aegidius A. J. Agricola shall arrive at this our court. Inasmuch as the said Aegidius has proved himself a trusty man and well able to deal with giants, dragons, and other enemies of the King's peace, now therefore we command him to ride forth at once, and to join the company of our knights with all speed.'

People said this was a high honour and next door to being dubbed. The miller was envious. 'Friend Ægidius is rising in the world,' said he. 'I hope he will know us when he gets back.'

'Maybe he never will,' said the blacksmith.

'That's enough from you, old horse-face!' said the farmer, mighty put out. 'Honour be blowed! If I get back even the miller's company will be welcome. Still, it is some comfort to think that I shall be missing you both for a bit.' And with that he left them.

You cannot offer excuses to the King as you can to your neighbours; so lambs or no lambs, ploughing or none, milk or water, he had to get up on his grey mare and go. The parson saw him off.

'I hope you are taking some stout rope with you?' he said.

'What for?' said Giles. 'To hang myself?'

'Nay! Take heart, Master Ægidius!' said the parson. 'It seems to me that you have a luck that you can trust. But take also a long rope, for you may need it, unless my foresight deceives me. And now farewell, and return safely!'

'Aye! And come back and find all my house and land in a pickle. Blast dragons!' said Giles. Then, stuffing a great coil of rope in a bag by his saddle, he climbed up and rode off.

He did not take the dog, who had kept well out of sight all the morning. But when he was gone, Garm slunk home and stayed there, and howled all the night, and was beaten for it, and went on howling.

'Help, ow help!' he cried. 'I'll never see dear master

again, and he was so terrible and splendid. I wish I had gone with him, I do.'

'Shut up!' said the farmer's wife, 'or you'll never live to see if he comes back or he don't.'

The blacksmith heard the howls. 'A bad omen,' he said cheerfully.

Many days passed and no news came. 'No news is bad news,' he said, and burst into song.

When Farmer Giles got to court he was tired and dusty. But the knights, in polished mail and with shining helmets on their heads, were all standing by their horses. The King's summons and the inclusion of the farmer had annoyed them, and so they insisted on obeying orders literally, setting off the moment that Giles arrived. The poor farmer had barely time to swallow a sop in a draught of wine before he was off on the road again. The mare was offended. What she thought of the King was luckily unexpressed, as it was highly disloyal.

It was already late in the day. 'Too late in the day to start a dragon-hunt,' thought Giles. But they did not go far. The knights were in no hurry, once they had started. They rode along at their leisure, in a straggling line, knights, esquires, servants, and ponies trussed with baggage; and Farmer Giles jogging behind on his tired mare.

When evening came, they halted and pitched their tents. No provision had been made for Farmer Giles and he had to borrow what he could. The mare was indignant,

and she forswore her allegiance to the house of Augustus
Bonifacius.

The next day they rode on, and all the day after. On the
third day they descried in the distance the dim and inhos-
pitable mountains. Before long they were in regions
where the lordship of Augustus Bonifacius was not universally acknowledged. They rode then with more care
and kept closer together.

On the fourth day they reached the Wild Hills and the
borders of the dubious lands where legendary creatures
were reputed to dwell. Suddenly one of those riding ahead
came upon ominous footprints in the sand by a stream.
They called for the farmer.

'What are these, Master Ægidius?' they said.

'Dragon-marks,' said he.

'Lead on!' said they.

So now they rode west with Farmer Giles at their head,
and all the rings were jingling on his leather coat. That
mattered little; for all the knights were laughing and
talking, and a minstrel rode with them singing a lay. Every
now and again they took up the refrain of the song and
sang it all together, very loud and strong. It was encourag-
ing, for the song was good – it had been made long before
in days when battles were more common than tourna-
ments; but it was unwise. Their coming was now known to
all the creatures of that land, and the dragons were cocking
their ears in all the caves of the West. There was no longer
any chance of their catching old Chrysophylax napping.

As luck (or the grey mare herself) would have it, when at last they drew under the very shadow of the dark mountains, Farmer Giles's mare went lame. They had now begun to ride along steep and stony paths, climbing upwards with toil and ever-growing disquiet. Bit by bit she dropped back in line, stumbling and limping and looking so patient and sad that at last Farmer Giles was obliged to get off and walk. Soon they found themselves right at the back among the pack-ponies; but no one took any notice of them. The knights were discussing points of precedence and etiquette, and their attention was distracted. Otherwise they would have observed that dragon-marks were now obvious and numerous.

They had come, indeed, to the places where Chryso-phylax often roamed, or alighted after taking his daily exercise in the air. The lower hills, and the slopes on either side of the path, had a scorched and trampled look. There was little grass, and the twisted stumps of heather and gorse stood up black amid wide patches of ash and burned earth. The region had been a dragons' playground for many a year. A dark mountain-wall loomed up before them.

Farmer Giles was concerned about his mare; but he was glad of the excuse for no longer being so conspicuous. It had not pleased him to be riding at the head of such a cavalcade in these dreary and dubious places. A little later he was gladder still, and had reason to thank his fortune (and his mare). For just about midday – it being then the Feast of

Candlemas, and the seventh day of their riding – Tailbiter leaped out of its sheath, and the dragon out of his cave.

Without warning or formality he swooped out to give battle. Down he came upon them with a rush and a roar. Far from his home he had not shown himself over bold, in spite of his ancient and imperial lineage. But now he was filled with a great wrath; for he was fighting at his own gate, as it were, and with all his treasure to defend. He came round a shoulder of the mountain like a ton of thunderbolts, with a noise like a gale and a gust of red lightning.

The argument concerning precedence stopped short. All the horses shied to one side or the other, and some of the knights fell off. The ponies and the baggage and the servants turned and ran at once. They had no doubt as to the order of precedence.

Suddenly there came a rush of smoke that smothered them all, and right in the midst of it the dragon crashed into the head of the line. Several of the knights were killed before they could even issue their formal challenge to battle, and several others were bowled over, horses and all. As for the remainder, their steeds took charge of them, and turned round and fled, carrying their masters off, whether they wished it or no. Most of them wished it indeed.

But the old grey mare did not budge. Maybe she was afraid of breaking her legs on the steep stony path. Maybe she felt too tired to run away. She knew in her bones that dragons on the wing are worse behind you than before you, and you need more speed than a race-horse for flight to be useful. Besides, she had seen this Chrysophylax before, and remembered chasing him over field and brook in her own country, till he lay down tame in the village street. Anyway she stuck her legs out wide, and she snorted. Farmer Giles went as pale as his face could manage, but he stayed by her side; for there seemed nothing else to do.

And so it was that the dragon, charging down the line, suddenly saw straight in front of him his old enemy with Tailbiter in his hand. It was the last thing he expected. He swerved aside like a great bat and collapsed on the hillside close to the road. Up came the grey mare, quite forgetting to walk lame. Farmer Giles, much encouraged, had scrambled hastily on her back.

'Excuse me,' said he, 'but were you looking for me, by any chance?'

'No, indeed!' said Chrysophylax. 'Who would have thought of seeing you here? I was just flying about,'

'Then we meet by good luck,' said Giles, 'and the pleasure is mine; for I was looking for *you*. What's more, I have a bone to pick with you, several bones in a manner of speaking.'

The dragon snorted. Farmer Giles put up his arm to ward off the hot gust, and with a flash Tailbiter swept forward, dangerously near the dragon's nose.

'Hey!' said he, and stopped snorting. He began to tremble and backed away, and all the fire in him was chilled.

'You have not, I hope, come to kill me, good master?' he whined.

'Nay! nay!' said the farmer. 'I said naught about killing.' The grey mare sniffed.

'Then what, may I ask, are you doing with all these knights?' said Chrysophylax. 'Knights always kill dragons, if we don't kill them first.'

'I'm doing nothing with them at all. They're naught to me,' said Giles. 'And anyway, they are all dead now or gone. What about what you said last Epiphany?'

'What about it?' said the dragon anxiously.

'You're nigh on a month late,' said Giles, 'and payment is overdue. I've come to collect it. You should beg my pardon for all the bother I have been put to.'

'I do indeed!' said he. 'I wish you had not troubled to come.'

'It'll be every bit of your treasure this time, and no market-tricks,' said Giles, 'or dead you'll be, and I shall hang your skin from our church steeple as a warning.

'It's cruel hard!' said the dragon.

'A bargain's a bargain,' said Giles.

'Can't I keep just a ring or two, and a mite of gold, in consideration of cash payment?' said he.

'Not a brass button!' said Giles. And so they kept on for a while, chaffering and arguing like folk at a fair. Yet the end of it was as you might expect; for whatever else might be said, few had ever outlasted Farmer Giles at a bargaining.

149

The dragon had to walk all the way back to his cave, for Giles stuck to his side with Tailbiter held mighty close. There was a narrow path that wound up and round the mountain, and there was barely room for the two of them.

The mare came just behind and she looked rather thoughtful.

It was five miles, if it was a step, and stiff going; and Giles trudged along, puffing and blowing, but never taking his eye off the worm. At last on the west side of the mountain they came to the mouth of the cave. It was large and black and forbidding, and its brazen doors swung on great pillars of iron. Plainly it had been a place of strength and pride in days long forgotten; for dragons do not build such works nor delve such mines, but dwell rather, when they may, in the tombs and treasuries of mighty men and giants of old. The doors of this deep house were set wide, and in their shadow they halted. So far Chrysophylax had had no chance to escape, but coming now to his own gate he sprang forward and prepared to plunge in.

Farmer Giles hit him with the flat of the sword. 'Woa!' said he. 'Before you go in, I've something to say to you. If you ain't outside again in quick time with something worth bringing, I shall come in after you and cut off your tail to begin with.'

The mare sniffed. She could not imagine Farmer Giles going down alone into a dragon's den for any money on earth. But Chrysophylax was quite prepared to believe it, with Tailbiter looking so bright and sharp and all. And maybe he was right, and the mare, for all her wisdom, had not yet understood the change in her master. Farmer Giles was backing his luck, and after two encounters was beginning to fancy that no dragon could stand up to him.

Anyway, out came Chrysophylax again in mighty quick time, with twenty pounds (troy) of gold and silver, and a chest of rings and necklaces and other pretty stuff.

'There!' said he.

'Where?' said Giles. 'That's not half enough, if that's what you mean. Nor half what you've got, I'll be bound.'

'Of course not!' said the dragon, rather perturbed to find that the farmer's wits seemed to have become brighter since that day in the village. 'Of course not! But I can't bring it all out at once.'

'Nor at twice, I'll wager,' said Giles. 'In you go again, and out again double quick, or I'll give you a taste of Tailbiter!'

'No!' said the dragon, and in he popped and out again double quick. 'There!' said he, putting down an enormous load of gold and two chests of diamonds.

'Now try again!' said the farmer. 'And try harder!'

'It's hard, cruel hard,' said the dragon, as he went back in again.

But by this time the grey mare was getting a bit anxious on her own account. 'Who's going to carry all this heavy stuff home, I wonder?' thought she; and she gave such a long sad look at all the bags and boxes that the farmer guessed her mind.

'Never you worry, lass!' said he. 'We'll make the old worm do the carting.'

'Mercy on us!' said the dragon, who overheard these words as he came out of the cave for the third time with the biggest load of all, and a mort of rich jewels like green and red fire. 'Mercy on us! If I carry all this, it will be near the death of me, and a bag more I never could manage, not if you killed me for it.'

'Then there is more still, is there?' said the farmer.

'Yes,' said the dragon, 'enough to keep me respectable.' He spoke near the truth for a rare wonder, and wisely as it turned out. 'If you will leave me what remains,' said he very wily, 'I'll be your friend for ever. And I will carry all this treasure back to your honour's own house and not to the King's. And I will help you to keep it, what is more,' said he.

Then the farmer took out a toothpick with his left hand, and he thought very hard for a minute. Then 'Done with you!' he said, showing a laudable discretion. A knight would have stood out for the whole hoard and got a curse laid upon it. And as likely as not, if Giles had driven the worm to despair, he would have turned and fought in the end, Tailbiter or no Tailbiter. In which case Giles, if not slain himself, would have been obliged to slaughter his transport and leave the best part of his gains in the mountains.

Well, that was the end of it. The farmer stuffed his pockets with jewels, just in case anything went wrong;

and he gave the grey mare a small load to carry. All the rest he bound on the back of Chrysophylax in boxes and bags, till he looked like a royal pantechnicon. There was no chance of his flying, for his load was too great, and Giles had tied down his wings.

'Mighty handy this rope has turned out in the end!' he thought, and he remembered the parson with gratitude.

So off now the dragon trotted, puffing and blowing, with the mare at his tail, and the farmer holding out Caudimordax very bright and threatening. He dared try no tricks.

In spite of their burdens the mare and the dragon made better speed going back than the cavalcade had made coming. For Farmer Giles was in a hurry – not the least reason being that he had little food in his bags. Also he had no trust in Chrysophylax after his breaking of oaths so solemn and binding, and he wondered much how to get through a night without death or great loss. But before that night fell he ran again into luck; for they overtook half a dozen of the servants and ponies that had departed in haste and were now wandering at a loss in the Wild Hills. They scattered in fear and amazement, but Giles shouted after them.

'Hey, lads!' said he. 'Come back! I have a job for you, and good wages while this packet lasts.'

So they entered his service, being glad of a guide, and thinking that their wages might indeed come more regular now than had been usual. Then they rode on, seven men, six ponies, one mare, and a dragon; and Giles began to feel like a lord and stuck out his chest. They halted as seldom as they could. At night Farmer Giles roped the dragon to four pickets, one to each leg, with three men to watch him in turn. But the grey mare kept half an eye open, in case the men should try any tricks on their own account.

After three days they were back over the borders of their own country; and their arrival caused such wonder and uproar as had seldom been seen between the two seas before. In the first village that they stopped at food and drink was showered on them free, and half the young lads wanted to join in the procession. Giles chose out a dozen likely young fellows. He promised them good wages, and bought them such mounts as he could get. He was beginning to have ideas.

After resting a day he rode on again, with his new escort at his heels. They sang songs in his honour: rough and ready, but they sounded good in his ears. Some folk cheered and others laughed. It was a sight both merry and wonderful.

Soon Farmer Giles took a bend southward, and steered towards his own home, and never went near the court of the King nor sent any message. But the news of the return of Master Ægidius spread like fire from the West; and there was great astonishment and confusion. For he came hard on the heels of a royal proclamation bidding all the towns and villages to go into mourning for the fall of the brave knights in the pass of the mountains.

Wherever Giles went the mourning was cast aside, and bells were set ringing, and people thronged by the wayside shouting and waving their caps and their scarves. But they booed the poor dragon, till he began bitterly to regret the bargain he had made. It was most humiliating for one of ancient and imperial lineage. When they got back to Ham all the dogs barked at him scornfully. All except Garm: he had eyes, ears, and nose only for his master. Indeed, he went quite off his head, and turned somersaults all along the street.

Ham, of course, gave the farmer a wonderful welcome; but probably nothing pleased him more than finding the miller at a loss for a sneer and the blacksmith quite out of countenance.

'This is not the end of the affair, mark my words!' said he; but he could not think of anything worse to say and hung his head gloomily. Farmer Giles, with his six men and his dozen likely lads and the dragon and all, went on up the hill, and there they stayed quiet for a while. Only the parson was invited to the house.

The news soon reached the capital, and forgetting the official mourning, and their business as well, people gathered in the streets. There was much shouting and noise.

The King was in his great house, biting his nails and tugging his beard. Between grief and rage (and financial anxiety) his mood was so grim that no one dared speak to him. But at last the noise of the town came to his ears; it did not sound like mourning or weeping.

'What is all the noise about?' he demanded. 'Tell the people to go indoors and mourn decently! It sounds more like a goose-fair.'

'The dragon has come back, lord,' they answered.

'What!' said the King. 'Summon our knights, or what is left of them!'

'There is no need, lord,' they answered. 'With Master Ægidius behind him the dragon is tame as tame. Or so we are informed. The news has not long come in, and reports are conflicting.'

'Bless our Soul!' said the King, looking greatly relieved. 'And to think that we ordered a Dirge to be sung for the fellow the day after tomorrow! Cancel it! Is there any sign of our treasure?'

'Reports say that there is a veritable mountain of it, lord,' they answered.

'When will it arrive?' said the King eagerly. 'A good man this Ægidius – send him in to us as soon as he comes!'

There was some hesitation in replying to this. At last someone took courage and said: 'Your pardon, lord, but we hear that the farmer has turned aside towards his own home. But doubtless he will hasten here in suitable raiment at the earliest opportunity.'

'Doubtless,' said the King. 'But confound his raiment! He had no business to go home without reporting. We are much displeased!'

*   *   *

The earliest opportunity presented itself, and passed, and so did many later ones. In fact, Farmer Giles had been back for a good week or more, and still no word or news of him came to the court.

On the tenth day the King's rage exploded. 'Send for the fellow!' he said; and they sent. It was a day's hard riding to Ham, each way.

'He will not come, lord!' said a trembling messenger two days later.

'Lightning of Heaven!' said the King. 'Command him to come on Tuesday next, or he shall be cast into prison for life!'

'Your pardon, lord, but he still will not come,' said a truly miserable messenger returning alone on the Tuesday.

'Ten Thousand Thunders!' said the King. 'Take this fool to prison instead! Now send some men to fetch the churls in chains!' he bellowed to those that stood by.

'How many men?' they faltered. 'There's a dragon, and . . . and Tailbiter, and –'

'And broomstales and fiddlesticks!' said the King. Then he ordered his white horse, and summoned his knights (or what was left of them) and a company of men-at-arms, and he rode off in fiery anger. All the people ran out of their houses in surprise.

But Farmer Giles had now become more than the Hero of the Countryside: he was the Darling of the Land; and folk did not cheer the knights and men-at-arms as they went by, though they still took off their hats to the King.

As he drew nearer to Ham the looks grew more sullen; in some villages the people shut their doors and not a face could be seen.

Then the King changed from hot wrath to cold anger. He had a grim look as he rode up at last to the river beyond which lay Ham and the house of the farmer. He had a mind to burn the place down. But there was Farmer Giles on the bridge, sitting on the grey mare with Tailbiter in his hand. No one else was to be seen, except Garm, who was lying in the road.

'Good morning, lord!' said Giles, as cheerful as day, not waiting to be spoken to.

The King eyed him coldly. 'Your manners are unfit for our presence,' said he; 'but that does not excuse you from coming when sent for.'

'I had not thought of it, lord, and that's a fact,' said Giles. 'I had matters of my own to mind, and had wasted time enough on your errands.'

'Ten Thousand Thunders!' cried the King in a hot rage again. 'To the devil with you and your insolence! No reward will you get after this; and you will be lucky if you escape hanging. And hanged you shall be, unless you beg our pardon here and now, and give us back our sword.'

'Eh?' said Giles. 'I have got my reward, I reckon. Finding's keeping, and keeping's having, we say here, and I reckon Tailbiter is better with me than with your folk.

But what are all these knights and men for, by any chance?' he asked. 'If you've come on a visit, you'd be welcome with fewer. If you want to take me away you'll need a lot more.'

The King choked, and the knights went very red and looked down their noses. Some of the men-at-arms grinned, since the King's back was turned to them.

'Give me my sword!' shouted the King, finding his voice, but forgetting his plural.

'Give us your crown!' said Giles: a staggering remark, such as had never before been heard in all the days of the Middle Kingdom.

'Lightning of Heaven! Seize him and bind him!' cried the King, justly enraged beyond bearing. 'What do you hang back for? Seize him or slay him!'

The men-at-arms strode forward.

'Help! help! help!' cried Garm.

Just at that moment the dragon got up from the bridge. He had lain there concealed under the far bank, deep in the river. Now he let off a terrible steam, for he had drunk many gallons of water. At once there was a thick fog, and only the red eyes of the dragon to be seen in it.

'Go home, you fools!' he bellowed. 'Or I will tear you to pieces. There are knights lying cold in the mountain-pass, and soon there will be more in the river. All the King's horses and all the King's men!' he roared.

Then he sprang forward and struck a claw into the

King's white horse; and it galloped away like the ten thousand thunders that the King mentioned so often. The other horses followed as swiftly: some had met this dragon before and did not like the memory. The men-at-arms legged it as best they could in every direction save that of Ham.

The white horse was only scratched, and he was not allowed to go far. After a while the King brought him back. He was master of his own horse at any rate; and no one could say that he was afraid of any man or dragon on the face of the earth. The fog was gone when he got back, but so were all his knights and his men. Now things looked very different with the King all alone to talk to a stout farmer with Tailbiter and a dragon as well.

But talk did no good. Farmer Giles was obstinate. He would not yield, and he would not fight, though the King challenged him to single combat there and then.

'Nay, lord!' said he, laughing. 'Go home and get cool! I don't want to hurt you; but you had best be off, or I won't be answerable for the worm. Good day!'

And that was the end of the Battle of the Bridge of Ham. Never a penny of all the treasure did the King get, nor any word of apology from Farmer Giles, who was beginning to think mighty well of himself. What is more, from that day the power of the Middle Kingdom came to an end in that neighbourhood. For many a mile round about men took Giles for their lord. Never a man could

the King with all his titles get to ride against the rebel
Ægidius; for he had become the Darling of the Land, and
the matter of song; and it was impossible to suppress all
the lays that celebrated his deeds. The favourite one dealt
with the meeting on the bridge in a hundred mock-heroic
couplets.

Chrysophylax remained long in Ham, much to the
profit of Giles; for the man who has a tame dragon is naturally respected. He was housed in the tithe barn, with the
leave of the parson, and there he was guarded by the
twelve likely lads. In this way arose the first of the titles of
Giles: Dominus de Domito Serpente, which is in the
vulgar Lord of the Tame Worm, or shortly of Tame. As
such he was widely honoured; but he still paid a nominal
tribute to the King: six oxtails and a pint of bitter, deliv-
ered on St Matthias' Day, that being the date of the
meeting on the bridge. Before long, however, he advanced
the Lord to Earl, and the belt of the Earl of Tame was
indeed of great length.

After some years he became Prince Julius Ægidius
and the tribute ceased. For Giles, being fabulously rich,
had built himself a hall of great magnificence, and gathered great strength of men-at-arms. Very bright and gay
they were, for their gear was the best that money could
buy.

Each of the twelve likely lads became a captain. Garm
had a gold collar, and while he lived roamed at his will, a
proud and happy dog, insufferable to his fellows; for he

expected all other dogs to accord him the respect due to the terror and splendour of his master. The grey mare passed to her days' end in peace and gave no hint of her reflections.

In the end Giles became a king, of course, the King of the Little Kingdom. He was crowned in Ham in the name of Ægidius Draconarius; but he was more often known as Old Giles Worming. For the vulgar tongue came into fashion at his court, and none of his speeches were in the Book-latin. He wife made a queen of great size and majesty, and she kept a tight hand on the household accounts. There was no getting round Queen Agatha – at least it was a long walk.

Thus Giles became at length old and venerable and had a white beard down to this knees, and a very respectable court (in which merit was often rewarded), and an entirely new order of knighthood. These were the Wormwardens, and a dragon was their ensign: the twelve likely lads were the senior members.

It must be admitted that Giles owed his rise in a large measure to luck, though he showed some wits in the use of it. Both the luck and the wits remained with him to the end of his days, to the great benefit of his friends and his neighbours. He rewarded the parson very handsomely; and even the blacksmith and the miller had their bit. For Giles could afford to be generous. But after he became King he issued a strong law against unpleasant prophecy, and made milling a royal monopoly. The blacksmith changed to the trade of an undertaker; but the miller became an obsequious servant of the crown. The parson became a bishop, and set up his see in the church of Ham, which was suitably enlarged.

Now those who live still in the lands of the Little Kingdom will observe in this history the true explanation of the names that some of its towns and villages bear in our time. For the learned in such matters inform us that Ham, being made the chief town of the new realm, by a natural confusion between the Lord of Ham and the Lord of Tame became known by the latter name, which it retains to this day; for Thame with an *h* is folly without warrant. Whereas in memory of the dragon, upon whom their fame and fortune were founded, the Draconarii built themselves a great house, four miles north-west of Tame, upon the spot where Giles and Chrysophylax first made acquaintance. That place became known throughout the kingdom as Aula Draconaria, or in the vulgar Worminghall, after the king's name and his standard.

The face of the land has changed since that time, and kingdoms have come and gone; woods have fallen, and rivers have shifted, and only the hills remain, and they are worn down by the rain and the wind. But still that name endures; though men now call it Wunnle (or so I am told); for villages have fallen from their pride. But in the days of which this tale speaks Worminghall it was, and a Royal Seat, and the dragon-standard flew above the trees; and all things went well there and merrily, while Tailbiter was above ground.

Envoy

Chrysophylax begged often for his liberty; and he proved expensive to feed, since he continued to grow, as dragons will, like trees, as long as there is life in them. So it came to pass, after some years, when Giles felt himself securely established, that he let the poor worm go back home. They parted with many expressions of mutual esteem, and a pact of non-aggression upon either side. In his bad heart of hearts the dragon felt as kindly disposed towards Giles as a dragon can feel towards anyone. After all there was Tailbiter: his life might easily have been taken, and all his hoard too. As it was, he still had a mort of treasure at home in his cave (as indeed Giles suspected).

He flew back to the mountains, slowly and laboriously, for his wings were clumsy with long disuse, and his size and his armour were greatly increased. Arriving home, he at once routed out a young dragon who had had the temerity to take up residence in his cave while Chrysophylax was away. It is said that the noise of the battle was heard throughout Venedotia. When, with great satisfaction, he had devoured his defeated opponent, he felt better, and the scars of his humiliation were assuaged, and he slept for a long while. But at last, waking suddenly, he set off in search of that tallest and stupidest of the giants, who had started all the trouble one summer's night long before. He gave him a piece of his mind, and the poor fellow was very much crushed.

'A blunderbuss, was it?' said he, scratching his head. 'I thought it was horseflies!'

finis

or in the vulgar

THE END

THE ADVENTURES
OF TOM BOMBADIL

PREFACE

The Red Book contains a large number of verses. A few are included in the narrative of the *Downfall of the Lord of the Rings*, or in the attached stories and chronicles; many more are found on loose leaves, while some are written carelessly in margins and blank spaces. Of the last sort most are nonsense, now often unintelligible even when legible, or half-remembered fragments. From these marginalia are drawn Nos. 4, 12, 13; though a better example of their general character would be the scribble, on the page recording Bilbo's *When winter first begins to bite*:

> The wind so whirled a weathercock
> He could not hold his tail up;
> The frost so nipped a throstlecock
> He could not snap a snail up.
> 'My case is hard! the throstle cried,
> And 'All is vane' the cock replied;
> And so they set their wail up.

The present selection is taken from the older pieces, mainly concerned with legends and jests of the Shire at the end of the Third Age, that appear to have been made by Hobbits, especially by Bilbo and his friends, or their immediate descendants. Their authorship is, however, seldom indicated. Those outside the narratives are in various hands, and were probably written down from oral tradition.

In the Red Book it is said that No. 5 was made by Bilbo, and No. 7 by Sam Gamgee. No. 8 is marked SG, and the ascription may be accepted. No. 11 is also marked SG, though at most Sam can only have touched up an older piece of the comic bestiary lore of which Hobbits appear to have been fond. In *The Lord of the Rings* Sam stated that No. 10 was traditional in the Shire.

No. 3 is an example of another kind which seems to have amused Hobbits: a rhyme or story which returns to its own beginning, and so may be recited until the hearers revolt. Several specimens are found in the Red Book, but the others are simple and crude. No. 3 is much the longest and most elaborate. It was evidently made by Bilbo. This is indicated by its obvious relationship to the long poem recited by Bilbo, as his own composition, in the house of Elrond. In origin a 'nonsense rhyme', it is in the Rivendell version found transformed and applied, somewhat incongruously, to the High-elvish and Númenorean legends of Eärendil. Probably because Bilbo invented its metrical devices and was proud of them. They do not appear in other pieces in the Red Book. The older form, here given, must belong to the early days after Bilbo's return from his journey. Though the influence of Elvish traditions is seen, they are not seriously treated, and the names used (*Derrilyn, Thellamie, Belmarie, Aerie*) are mere inventions in the Elvish style, and are not in fact Elvish at all.

The influence of the events at the end of the Third Age, and the widening of the horizons of the Shire by contact with Rivendell and Gondor, is to be seen in other pieces. No. 6, though here placed next to Bilbo's Man-in-the-Moon rhyme, and the last item, No. 16, must be derived ultimately from Gondor. They are evidently based on the traditions of Men, living in shorelands and familiar with rivers running into the Sea. No. 6 actually mentions *Belfalas* (the windy bay of Bel), and the Sea-ward Tower, *Tirith Aear*, of Dol Amroth. No. 16 mentions the Seven Rivers[1] that flowed into the Sea in the South Kingdom, and uses the Gondorian name, of High-elvish form, *Fíriel*, mortal woman.[2] In the Langstrand and Dol Amroth there were many traditions of the ancient Elvish dwellings, and of the haven at the mouth of the Morthond from which 'westward ships' had sailed as far back as the fall of

---

[1] *Lefnui, Morthond-Kiril-Ringló, Gilrain-Sernui,* and *Anduin.*

[2] The name was borne by a princess of Gondor, through whom Aragorn claimed descent from the Southern line. It was also the name of a daughter of Elanor, daughter of Sam, but her name, if connected with the rhyme, must be derived from it; it could not have arisen in Westmarch.

Eregion in the Second Age. These two pieces, therefore, are only re-handlings of Southern matter, though this may have reached Bilbo by way of Rivendell. No. 14 also depends on the lore of Rivendell, Elvish and Númenorean, concerning the heroic days at the end of the First Age; it seems to contain echoes of the Númenorean tale of Túrin and Mim the Dwarf.

Nos. 1 and 2 evidently come from the Buckland. They show more knowledge of that country, and of the Dingle, the wooded valley of the Withywindle,[1] than any Hobbits west of the Marish were likely to possess. They also show that the Bucklanders knew Bombadil,[2] though, no doubt, they had as little understanding of his powers as the Shire-folk had of Gandalf's: both were regarded as benevolent persons, mysterious maybe and unpredictable but nonetheless comic. No. 1 is the earlier piece, and is made up of various hobbit-versions of legends concerning Bombadil. No. 2 uses similar traditions, though Tom's raillery is here turned in jest upon his friends, who treat it

1 *Grindwall* was a small hythe on the north bank of the Withywindle; it was outside the Hay, and so was well watched and protected by a *grind* or fence extended into the water. *Breredon* (Briar Hill) was a little village on rising ground behind the hythe, in the narrow tongue between the end of the High Hay and the Brandywine. At the *Mithe,* the outflow of the Shirebourn, was a landing-stage, from which a lane ran to Deephallow and so on to the Causeway road that went through Rushey and Stock.

2 Indeed they probably gave him this name (it is Bucklandish in form) to add to his many older ones.

with amusement (tinged with fear); but it was probably composed much later and after the visit of Frodo and his companions to the house of Bombadil.

The verses, of hobbit origin, here presented have generally two features in common. They are fond of strange words, and of rhyming and metrical tricks – in their simplicity Hobbits evidently regarded such things as virtues or graces, though they were, no doubt, mere imitations of Elvish practices. They are also, at least on the surface, lighthearted or frivolous, though sometimes one may uneasily suspect that more is meant than meets the ear. No. 15, certainly of hobbit origin, is an exception. It is the latest piece and belongs to the Fourth Age; but it is included here, because a hand has scrawled at its head *Frodos Dreme.* That is remarkable, and though the piece is most unlikely to have been written by Frodo himself, the title shows that it was associated with the dark and despairing dreams which visited him in March and October during his last three years. But there were certainly other traditions, concerning Hobbits that were taken by the 'wandering-madness', and if they ever returned, were afterwards queer and uncommunicable. The thought of the Sea was ever-present in the background of hobbit imagination; but fear of it and distrust of all Elvish lore, was the prevailing mood in the Shire at the end of the Third Age, and that mood was certainly not entirely dispelled by the events and changes with which that Age ended.

I

THE ADVENTURES OF TOM BOMBADIL

Old Tom Bombadil was a merry fellow;
bright blue his jacket was and his boots were yellow,
green were his girdle and his breeches all of leather;
he wore in his tall hat a swan-wing feather.
He lived up under Hill, where the Withywindle
ran from a grassy well down into the dingle.

Old Tom in summertime walked about the meadows
gathering the buttercups, running after shadows,
tickling the bumblebees that buzzed among the flowers,
sitting by the waterside for hours upon hours.

There his beard dangled long down into the water:
up came Goldberry, the River-woman's daughter;
pulled Tom's hanging hair. In he went a-wallowing
under the water-lilies, bubbling and a-swallowing.

'Hey, Tom Bombadil! Whither are you going?'
said fair Goldberry. 'Bubbles you are blowing,
frightening the finny fish and the brown water-rat,
startling the dabchicks, and drowning your feather-hat!'

'You bring it back again, there's a pretty maiden!'
said Tom Bombadil. 'I do not care for wading.
Go down! Sleep again where the pools are shady
far below willow-roots, little water-lady!'

Back to her mother's house in the deepest hollow
swam young Goldberry. But Tom, he would not follow;
on knotted willow-roots he sat in sunny weather,
drying his yellow boots and his draggled feather.

Up woke Willow-man, began upon his singing,
sang Tom fast asleep under branches swinging;
in a crack caught him tight: snick! it closed together,
trapped Tom Bombadil, coat and hat and feather.

'Ha, Tom Bombadil! What be you a-thinking,
peeping inside my tree, watching me a-drinking
deep in my wooden house, tickling me with feather,
dripping wet down my face like a rainy weather?'

'You let me out again, Old Man Willow!
I am stiff lying here; they're no sort of pillow,
your hard crooked roots. Drink your river-water!
Go back to sleep again like the River-daughter!'

Willow-man let him loose when he heard him speaking;
locked fast his wooden house, muttering and creaking,
whispering inside the tree. Out from willow-dingle
Tom went walking on up the Withywindle.
Under the forest-eaves he sat a while a-listening:
on the boughs piping birds were chirruping and whistling.
Butterflies about his head went quivering and winking,
until grey clouds came up, as the sun was sinking.

Then Tom hurried on. Rain began to shiver,
round rings spattering in the running river;
a wind blew, shaken leaves chilly drops were dripping;
into a sheltering hole Old Tom went skipping.

Out came Badger-brock with his snowy forehead
and his dark blinking eyes. In the hill he quarried
with his wife and many sons. By the coat they
    caught him,
pulled him inside their earth, down their tunnels
    brought him.

Inside their secret house, there they sat a-mumbling:
'Ho, Tom Bombadil! Where have you come tumbling,
bursting in the front-door? Badger-folk have caught you.
You'll never find it out, the way that we have brought you!'

'Now, old Badger-brock, do you hear me talking?
You show me out at once! I must be a-walking.
Show me to your backdoor under briar-roses;
then-clean grimy paws, wipe your earthy noses!
Go back to sleep again on your straw pillow,
like fair Goldberry and Old Man Willow!'

Then all the Badger-folk said: 'We beg your pardon!'
They showed Tom out again to their thorny garden,
went back and hid themselves, a-shivering and a-shaking,
blocked up all their doors, earth together raking.

Rain had passed. The sky was clear, and in the summer-
    gloaming
Old Tom Bombadil laughed as he came homing,
unlocked his door again, and opened up a shutter.
In the kitchen round the lamp moths began to flutter;
Tom through the window saw waking stars come
    winking,
and the new slender moon early westward sinking.

Dark came under Hill. Tom, he lit a candle;
upstairs creaking went, turned the door-handle.
'Hoo, Tom Bombadil! Look what night has brought you!
I'm here behind the door. Now at last I've caught you!
You'd forgotten Barrow-wight dwelling in the old
   mound
up there on hill-top with the ring of stones round.
He's got loose again. Under earth he'll take you.
Poor Tom Bombadil, pale and cold he'll make you!'

'Go out! Shut the door, and never come back after!
Take away gleaming eyes, take your hollow laughter!
Go back to grassy mound, on your stony pillow
lay down your bony head, like Old Man Willow,
like young Goldberry, and Badger-folk in burrow!
Go back to buried gold and forgotten sorrow!'

Out fled Barrow-wight through the window leaping,
through the yard, over wall like a shadow sweeping,
up hill wailing went back to leaning stone-rings,
back under lonely mound, rattling his bone-rings.

Old Tom Bombadil lay upon his pillow
sweeter than Goldberry, quieter than the Willow,
snugger than the Badger-folk or the Barrow-dwellers;
slept like a humming-top, snored like a bellows.

He woke in morning-light, whistled like a starling,
sang, 'Come, derry-dol, merry-dol, my darling!'
He clapped on his battered hat, boots, and coat and
    feather,
opened the window wide to the sunny weather.

Wise old Bombadil, he was a wary fellow;
bright blue his jacket was, and his boots were yellow.
None ever caught old Tom in upland or in dingle,
walking the forest-paths, or by the Withywindle,
or out on the lily-pools in boat upon the water.
But one day Tom, he went and caught the River-daughter,
in green gown, flowing hair, sitting in the rushes,
singing old water-songs to birds upon the bushes.

He caught her, held her fast! Water-rats went scuttering
reeds hissed, herons cried, and her heart was fluttering.
Said Tom Bombadil: 'Here's my pretty maiden!
You shall come home with me! The table is all laden:
yellow cream, honeycomb, white bread and butter;
roses at the window-sill and peeping round the shutter.
You shall come under Hill! Never mind your mother
in her deep weedy pool: there you'll find no lover!'

Old Tom Bombadil had a merry wedding,
crowned all with buttercups, hat and feather shedding;
his bride with forgetmenots and flag-lilies for garland
was robed all in silver-green. He sang like a starling,
hummed like a honey-bee, lilted to the fiddle,
clasping his river-maid round her slender middle.

Lamps gleamed within his house, and white was the
    bedding;
in the bright honey-moon Badger-folk came treading,
danced down under Hill, and Old Man Willow
tapped, tapped at window-pane, as they slept on the
    pillow,
on the bank in the reeds River-woman sighing
heard old Barrow-wight in his mound crying.

Old Tom Bombadil heeded not the voices,
taps, knocks, dancing feet, all the nightly noises;
slept till the sun arose, then sang like a starling:
'Hey! Come derry-dol, merry-dol, my darling!'
sitting on the door-step chopping sticks of willow,
while fair Goldberry combed her tresses yellow.

2

BOMBADIL GOES BOATING

The old year was turning brown; the West Wind was
  calling;
Tom caught a beechen leaf in the Forest falling.
'I've caught a happy day blown me by the breezes!
Why wait till morrow-year? I'll take it when me pleases.
This day I'll mend my boat and journey as it chances
west down the withy-stream, following my fancies!'

Little Bird sat on twig. 'Whillo, Tom! I heed you.
I've a guess, I've a guess where your fancies lead you.
Shall I go, shall I go, bring him word to meet you?'

'No names, you tell-tale, or I'll skin and eat you,
babbling in every ear things that don't concern you!
If you tell Willow-man where I've gone, I'll burn you,
roast you on a willow-spit. That'll end your prying!'

Willow-wren cocked her tail, piped as she went flying:
'Catch me first, catch me first! No names are needed.
I'll perch on his hither ear: the message will be heeded.
"Down by Mithe," I'll say, "just as sun is sinking."
Hurry up, hurry up! That's the time for drinking!'

Tom laughed to himself: 'Maybe then I'll go there.
I might go by other ways, but today I'll row there.'
He shaved oars, patched his boat; from hidden creek he
    hauled her
through reed and sallow-brake, under leaning alder,
then down the river went, singing: 'Silly-sallow,
Flow withy-willow-stream over deep and shallow!'

'Whee! Tom Bombadil! Whither be you going,
bobbing in a cockle-boat, down the river rowing?'

'Maybe to Brandywine along the Withywindle;
maybe friends of mind fire for me will kindle
down by the Hays-end. Little folk I know there,
kind at the day's end. Now and then I go there.'

'Take word to my kin, bring me back their tidings!
Tell me of diving pools and the fishes' hidings!'

'Nay then,' said Bombadil, 'I am only rowing
just to smell the water like, not on errands going.'

'Tee hee! Cocky Tom! Mind your tub don't founder!
Look out for willow-snags! I'd laugh to see you
    flounder.'

'Talk less, Fisher Blue! Keep your kindly wishes!
Fly off and preen yourself with the bones of fishes!
Gay lord on your bough, at home a dirty varlet
living in a sloven house, though your breast be scarlet.
I've heard of fisher-birds beak in air a-dangling
to show how the wind is set: that's an end of angling!'

The King's fisher shut his beak, winked his eye, as
    singing
Tom passed under bough. Flash! then he went winging;
dropped down jewel-blue a feather, and Tom caught it
gleaming in a sun-ray: a pretty gift he thought it.
He stuck it in his tall hat, the old feather casting:
'Blue now for Tom,' he said, 'a merry hue and lasting!'

Rings swirled round his boat, he saw the bubbles quiver.
Tom slapped his oar, smack! at a shadow in the river.
'Hoosh! Tom Bombadil! 'Tis long since last I met you.
Turned water-boatman, eh? What if I upset you?'

'What? Why, Whisker-lad, I'd ride you down the river.
My fingers on your back would set your hide a-shiver.'

'Pish, Tom Bombadil! I'll go and tell my mother;
"Call all our kin to come, father, sister, brother!
Tom's gone mad as a coot with wooden legs: he's paddling
down Withywindle stream, an old tub a-straddling!'

'I'll give your otter-fell to Barrow-wights. They'll taw
 you!
Then smother you in gold-rings! Your mother if she saw
 you,
she'd never know her son, unless 'twas by a whisker.
Nay, don't tease old Tom, until you be far brisker!'

'Whoosh!' said otter-lad, river-water spraying
over Tom's hat and all; set the boat a-swaying,
dived down under it, and by the bank lay peering,
till Tom's merry song faded out of hearing.

Old Swan of Elver-isle sailed past him proudly,
gave Tom a black look, snorted at him loudly.
Tom laughed: 'You old cob, do you miss your feather?
Give me a new one then! The old was worn by weather.
Could you speak a fair word, I would love you dearer:
long neck and dumb throat, but still a haughty sneerer!
If one day the King returns, in upping he may take you,
brand your yellow bill, and less lordly make you!'
Old Swan huffed his wings, hissed, and paddled faster;
in his wake bobbing on Tom went rowing after.

Tom came to Withy-weir. Down the river rushing
foamed into Windle-reach, a-bubbling and a-splashing;
bore Tom over stone spinning like a windfall,
bobbing like a bottle-cork, to the hythe at Grindwall.

'Hoy! Here's Woodman Tom with his billy-beard on!'
laughed all the little folk of Hays-end and Breredon.
'Ware, Tom! We'll shoot you dead with our bows and
     arrows!
We don't let Forest-folk nor bogies from the Barrows
cross over Brandywine by cockle-boat nor ferry.'
'Fie, little fatbellies! Don't ye make so merry!

I've seen hobbit-folk digging holes to hide 'em,
frightened if a horny goat or a badger eyed 'em,
afeared of the moony-beams, their old shadows shunning.
I'll call the orks on you: that'll send you running!'

'You may call, Woodman Tom. And you can talk your
     beard off.
Three arrows in your hat! You we're not afeared of!
Where would you go to now? If for beer you're making,
the barrels aint deep enough in Breredon for your slaking!'

'Away over Brandywine by Shirebourn I'd be going,
but too swift for cockle-boat the river now is flowing.
I'd bless little folk that took me in their wherry,
wish them evenings fair and many mornings merry.'

Red flowed the Brandywine; with flame the river kindled,
as sun sank beyond the Shire, and then to grey it dwindled.
Mithe Steps empty stood. None was there to greet him.
Silent the Causeway lay. Said Tom: 'A merry meeting!'

Tom stumped along the road, as the light was failing.
Rushey lamps gleamed ahead. He heard a voice him
    hailing.
'Whoa there!' Ponies stopped, wheels halted sliding.
Tom went plodding past, never looked beside him.

'Ho there! beggarman tramping in the Marish!
What's your business here? Hat all stuck with arrows!
Someone's warned you off, caught you at your sneaking?
Come here! Tell me now what it is you're seeking!
Shire-ale, I'll be bound, though you've not a penny.
I'll bid them lock their doors, and then you won't get any!'

'Well, well, Muddy-feet! From one that's late for meeting
away back by the Mithe that's a surly greeting!
You old farmer fat that cannot walk for wheezing,
cart-drawn like a sack, ought to be more pleasing.

Penny-wise tub-on-legs! A beggar can't be chooser,
or else I'd bid you go, and you would be the loser.
Come, Maggot! Help me up! A tankard now you owe me.
Even in cockshut light an old friend should know me!'

Laughing they drove away, in Rushey never halting,
though the inn open stood and they could smell the malting.
They turned down Maggot's Lane, rattling and bumping,
Tom in the farmer's cart dancing round and jumping.
Stars shone on Bamfurlong, and Maggot's house was
    lighted;
fire in the kitchen burned to welcome the benighted.

Maggot's sons bowed at door, his daughters did their
    curtsy,
his wife brought tankards out for those that might be
    thirsty.
Songs they had and merry tales, the supping and the
    dancing;
Goodman Maggot there for all his belt was prancing,
Tom did a hornpipe when he was not quaffing,
daughters did the Springle-ring, goodwife did the laughing.

When others went to bed in hay, fern, or feather,
close in the inglenook they laid their heads together,
old Tom and Muddy-feet, swapping all the tidings
from Barrow-downs to Tower Hills: of walkings and of
    ridings;
of wheat-ear and barley-corn, of sowing and of reaping;
queer tales from Bree, and talk at smithy, mill, and
    cheaping;
rumours in whispering trees, south-wind in the larches,
tall Watchers by the Ford, Shadows on the marches.

Old Maggot slept at last in chair beside the embers.
Ere dawn Tom was gone: as dreams one half remembers,
some merry, some sad, and some of hidden warning.
None heard the door unlocked; a shower of rain at
    morning
his footprints washed away, at Mithe he left no traces,
at Hays-end they heard no song nor sound of heavy paces.

Three days his boat lay by the hythe at Grindwall,
and then one morn was gone back up Withywindle.
Otter-folk, hobbits said, came by night and loosed her,
dragged her over weir, and up stream they pushed her.

Out from Elvet-isle Old Swan came sailing,
in beak took her painter up in the water trailing,
drew her proudly on; otters swam beside her
round old Willow-man's crooked roots to guide her;
the King's fisher perched on bow, on thwart the wren
    was singing,
merrily the cockle-boat homeward they were bringing.
To Tom's creek they came at last. Otter-lad said: 'Whish
    now!
What's a coot without his legs, or a finless fish now?'
O! silly-sallow-willow-stream! The oars they'd left
    behind them!
Long they lay at Grindwall hythe for Tom to come and
    find them.

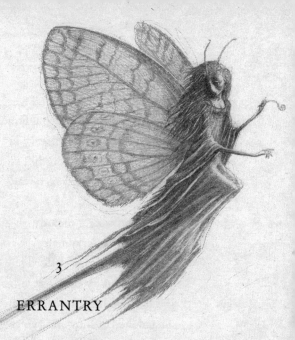

3

ERRANTRY

There was a merry passenger,
a messenger, a mariner:
he built a gilded gondola
to wander in, and had in her
a load of yellow oranges
and porridge for his provender;
he perfumed her with marjoram
and cardamon and lavender.

He called the winds of argosies
with cargoes in to carry him
across the rivers seventeen
that lay between to tarry him.
He landed all in loneliness
where stonily the pebbles on
the running river Derrilyn

goes merrily for ever on.
He journeyed then through meadow-lands
to Shadow-land that dreary lay,
and under hill and over hill
went roving still a weary way.

He sat and sang a melody,
his errantry a-tarrying;
he begged a pretty butterfly
that fluttered by to marry him.
She scorned him and she scoffed at him,
she laughed at him unpitying;
so long he studied wizardry
and sigaldry and smithying.

He wove a tissue airy-thin
to snare her in; to follow her
he made him beetle-leather wing
and feather wing of swallow-hair.
He caught her in bewilderment
with filament of spider-thread;
he made her soft pavilions
of lilies, and a bridal bed
of flowers and of thistle-down
to nestle down and rest her in;
and silken webs of filmy white
and silver light he dressed her in.

He threaded gems in necklaces,
but recklessly she squandered them
and fell to bitter quarrelling;
then sorrowing he wandered on,
and there he left her withering,
as shivering he fled away;
with windy weather following
on swallow-wing he sped away.

He passed the archipelagoes
where yellow grows the marigold,
where countless silver fountains are,
and mountains are of fairy-gold.
He took to war and foraying,
a-harrying beyond the sea,
and roaming over Belmarie
and Thellamie and Fantasie.

He made a shield and morion
of coral and of ivory,
a sword he made of emerald,
and terrible his rivalry
with elven-knights of Aerie
and Faerie, with paladins
that golden-haired and shining-eyed
came riding by and challenged him.

Of crystal was his habergeon,
his scabbard of chalcedony;
with silver tipped at plenilune
his spear was hewn of ebony.
His javelins were of malachite
and stalactite – he brandished them,
and went and fought the dragon-flies
of Paradise, and vanquished them.

He battled with the Dumbledors,
the Hummerhorns, and Honeybees,
and won the Golden Honeycomb;
and running home on sunny seas
in ship of leaves and gossamer
with blossom for a canopy,
he sat and sang, and furbished up
and burnished up his panoply.

He tarried for a little while
in little isles that lonely lay,
and found there naught but blowing grass;
and so at last the only way
he took, and turned, and coming home
with honeycomb, to memory
his message came, and errand too!
In derring-do and glamoury
he had forgot them, journeying
and tourneying, a wanderer.

So now he must depart again
and start again his gondola,
for ever still a messenger,
a passenger, a tarrier,
a-roving as a feather does,
a weather-driven mariner.

4

PRINCESS MEE

Little Princess Mee
  Lovely was she
As in elven-song is told:
  She had pearls in hair
  All threaded fair;
Of gossamer shot with gold
  Was her kerchief made,
  And a silver braid
Of stars about her throat.
  Of moth-web light
  All moonlit-white
She wore a woven coat,
  And round her kirtle
  Was bound a girdle
Sewn with diamond dew.

She walked by day
    Under mantle grey
And hood of clouded blue;
    But she went by night
    All glittering bright
Under the starlit sky,
    And her slippers frail
    Of fishes' mail
Flashed as she went by
    To her dancing-pool,
    And on mirror cool
Of windless water played.
    As a mist of light
    In whirling flight
A glint like glass she made
    Wherever her feet
    Of silver fleet
Flicked the dancing-floor.

    She looked on high
    To the roofless sky,
And she looked to the shadowy shore;
    Then round she went,
    And her eyes she bent
And saw beneath her go
    A Princess Shee
    As fair as Mee:
They were dancing toe to toe!

Shee was as light
As Mee, and as bright;
But Shee was, strange to tell,
Hanging down
With starry crown
Into a bottomless well!
Her gleaming eyes
In great surprise
Looked up to the eyes of Mee:
A marvellous thing,
Head-down to swing
Above a starry sea!

Only their feet
Could ever meet;
For where the ways might lie
To find a land
Where they do not stand
But hang down in the sky
No one could tell
Nor learn in spell
In all the elven-lore.

So still on her own
An elf alone
Dancing as before
With pearls in hair
And kirtle fair

And slippers frail
  Of fishes' mail went Mee:
  Of fishes' mail
And slippers frail
  And kirtle fair
  With pearls in hair went Shee!

THE MAN IN THE MOON
STAYED UP TOO LATE

There is an inn, a merry old inn
   beneath an old grey hill,
And there they brew a beer so brown
That the Man in the Moon himself came down
   one night to drink his fill.

The ostler has a tipsy cat
   that plays a five-stringed fiddle;
And up and down he runs his bow,
Now squeaking high, now purring low,
   now sawing in the middle.

The landlord keeps a little dog
   that is mighty fond of jokes;
When there's good cheer among the guests,

He cocks an ear at all the jests
  and laughs until he chokes.

They also keep a hornéd cow
  as proud as any queen;
But music turns her head like ale,
And makes her wave her tufted tail
  and dance upon the green.

And O! the row of silver dishes
  and the store of silver spoons!
For Sunday there's a special pair,
And these they polish up with care
  on Saturday afternoons.

The Man in the Moon was drinking deep,
  and the cat began to wail;
A dish and a spoon on the table danced,
The cow in the garden madly pranced,
  and the little dog chased his tail.

The Man in the Moon took another mug,
  and then rolled beneath his chair;
And there he dozed and dreamed of ale,
Till in the sky the stars were pale,
  and dawn was in the air.

The ostler said to his tipsy cat:
   'The white horses of the Moon,
They neigh and champ their silver bits;
But their master's been and drowned his wits,
   and the Sun'll be rising soon!'

So the cat on his fiddle played hey-diddle-diddle,
   a jig that would wake the dead:
He squeaked and sawed and quickened the tune,
While the landlord shook the Man in the Moon:
   'It's after three!' he said.

They rolled the Man slowly up the hill
   and bundled him into the Moon,
While his horses galloped up in rear,
And the cow came capering like a deer,
   and a dish ran up with a spoon.

Now quicker the fiddle went deedle-dum-diddle;
   the dog began to roar,
The cow and the horses stood on their heads;
The guests all bounded from their beds
   and danced upon the floor.

With a ping and a pong the fiddle-strings broke!
   the cow jumped over the Moon,
And the little dog laughed to see such fun,
And the Saturday dish went off at a run
   with the silver Sunday spoon.

The round Moon rolled behind the hill,
    as the Sun raised up her head.
She hardly believed her fiery eyes;
For though it was day, to her surprise
    they all went back to bed!

6

THE MAN IN THE MOON CAME
DOWN TOO SOON

The Man in the Moon had silver shoon,
    and his beard was of silver thread;
With opals crowned and pearls all bound
    about his girdlestead,
In his mantle grey he walked one day
    across a shining floor,
And with crystal key in secrecy
    he opened an ivory door.

On a filigree stair of glimmering hair
    then lightly down he went,
And merry was he at last to be free
    on a mad adventure bent.
In diamonds white he had lost delight;
    he was tired of his minaret

Of tall moonstone that towered alone
    on a lunar mountain set.

He would dare any peril for ruby and beryl
    to broider his pale attire,
For new diadems of lustrous gems,
    emerald and sapphire.
He was lonely too with nothing to do
    but stare at the world of gold
And heark to the hum that would distantly come
    as gaily round it rolled.

At plenilune in his argent moon
    in his heart he longed for Fire:
Not the limpid lights of wan selenites;
    for red was his desire,
For crimson and rose and ember-glows,
    for flame with burning tongue,
For the scarlet skies in a swift sunrise
    when a stormy day is young.

He'd have seas of blues, and the living hues
    of forest green and fen;
And he yearned for the mirth of the populous earth
    and the sanguine blood of men.
He coveted song, and laughter long,
    and viands hot, and wine,

Eating pearly cakes of light snowflakes
   and drinking thin moonshine.

He twinkled his feet, as he thought of the meat,
   of pepper, and punch galore;
And he tripped unaware on his slanting stair,
   and like a meteor,
A star in flight, ere Yule one night
   flickering down he fell
From his laddery path to a foaming bath
   in the windy Bay of Bel.

He began to think, lest he melt and sink,
   what in the moon to do,
When a fisherman's boat found him far afloat
   to the amazement of the crew,
Caught in their net all shimmering wet
   in a phosphorescent sheen
Of bluey whites and opal lights
   and delicate liquid green.

Against his wish with the morning fish
   they packed him back to land:
'You had best get a bed in an inn,' they said;
   'the town is near at hand.'
Only the knell of one slow bell
   high in the Seaward Tower

Announced the news of his moonsick cruise
    at that unseemly hour.

Not a hearth was laid, not a breakfast made,
    and dawn was cold and damp.
There were ashes for fire, and for grass the mire,
    for the sun a smoking lamp
In a dim back-street. Not a man did he meet,
    no voice was raised in song;
There were snores instead, for all folk were abed
    and still would slumber long.

He knocked as he passed on doors locked fast,
    and called and cried in vain,
Till he came to an inn that had light within,
    and he tapped at a window-pane.
A drowsy cook gave a surly look,
    and 'What do you want?' said he.
'I want fire and gold and songs of old
    and red wine flowing free!'

'You won't get them here,' said the cook with a leer,
    'but you may come inside.
Silver I lack and silk to my back –
    maybe I'll let you bide.'
A silver gift the latch to lift,
    a pearl to pass the door;

For a seat by the cook in the ingle-nook
　　it cost him twenty more.

For hunger or drouth naught passed his mouth
　　till he gave both crown and cloak;
And all that he got, in an earthen pot
　　broken and black with smoke,
Was porridge cold and two days old
　　to eat with a wooden spoon.
For puddings of Yule with plums, poor fool,
　　he arrived so much too soon:
An unwary guest on a lunatic quest
　　from the Mountains of the Moon.

7

THE STONE TROLL

Troll sat alone on his seat of stone,
And munched and mumbled a bare old bone;
   For many a year he had gnawed it near,
     For meat was hard to come by.
     Done by! Gum by!
In a cave in the hills he dwelt alone,
   And meat was hard to come by.

Up came Tom with his big boots on.
Said he to Troll: 'Pray, what is yon?
   For it looks like the shin o' my nuncle Tim,
     As should be a-lyin' in graveyard.
     Caveyard! Paveyard!
This many a year has Tim been gone,
   And I thought he were lyin' in graveyard.'

'My lad,' said Troll, 'this bone I stole.
But what be bones that lie in a hole?
 Thy nuncle was dead as a lump o' lead,
  Afore I found his shinbone.
   Tinbone! Thinbone!
He can spare a share for a poor old troll;
 For he don't need his shinbone.'

Said Tom: 'I don't see why the likes o' thee
Without axin' leave should go makin' free
 With the shank or the shin o' my father's kin;
 So hand the old bone over!
  Rover! Trover!
Though dead he be, it belongs to he;
 So hand the old bone over!'

'For a couple o' pins,' says Troll, and grins,
'I'll eat thee too, and gnaw thy shins.
 A bit o' fresh meat will go down sweet!
  I'll try my teeth on thee now.
   Hee now! See now!
I'm tired o' gnawing old bones and skins;
 I've a mind to dine on thee now.'

But just as he thought his dinner was caught,
He found his hands had hold of naught.
 Before he could mind, Tom slipped behind

And gave him the boot to larn him.
  Warn him! Darn him!
A bump o' the boot on the seat, Tom thought,
 Would be the way to larn him.

But harder than stone is the flesh and bone
Of a troll that sits in the hills alone.
 As well set your boot to the mountain's root,
  For the seat of a troll don't feel it.
   Peel it! Heal it!
Old Troll laughed, when he heard Tom groan,
 And he knew his toes could feel it.

Tom's leg is game, since home he came,
And his bootless foot is lasting lame;
 But Troll don't care, and he's still there
  With the bone he boned from its owner.
   Doner! Boner!
Troll's old seat is still the same,
 And the bone he boned from its owner!

8

PERRY-THE-WINKLE

The Lonely Troll he sat on a stone
   and sang a mournful lay:
'O why, O why must I live on my own
   in the hills of Faraway?
My folk are gone beyond recall
   and take no thought of me;
alone I'm left, the last of all
   from Weathertop to the Sea.'

'I steal no gold, I drink no beer,
   I eat no kind of meat;
but People slam their doors in fear,
   whenever they hear my feet.
O how I wish that they were neat,
   and my hands were not so rough!
Yet my heart is soft, my smile is sweet,
   and my cooking good enough.'

'Come, come!' he thought, 'this will not do!
   I must go and find a friend;
a-walking soft I'll wander through
   the Shire from end to end.'
Down he went, and he walked all night
   with his feet in boots of fur;
to Delving he came in the morning light,
   when folk were just astir.

He looked around, and who did he meet
   but old Mrs Bunce and all
with umbrella and basket walking the street;
   and he smiled and stopped to call:
'Good morning, ma'am! Good day to you!
   I hope I find you well?'
But she dropped umbrella and basket too,
   and yelled a frightful yell.

Old Pott the Mayor was strolling near;
   when he heard that awful sound,
he turned all purple and pink with fear,
   and dived down underground.
The Lonely Troll was hurt and sad:
   'Don't go!' he gently said,
but old Mrs Bunce ran home like mad
   and hid beneath her bed.

The Troll went on to the market-place
    and peeped above the stalls;
the sheep went wild when they saw his face,
    and the geese flew over the walls.
Old Farmer Hogg he spilled his ale,
    Bill Butcher threw a knife,
and Grip his dog, he turned his tail
    and ran to save his life.

The old Troll sadly sat and wept
    outside the Lockholes gate,
and Perry-the-Winkle up he crept
    and patted him on the pate.
'O why do you weep, you great big lump?
    You're better outside than in!'
He gave the Troll a friendly thump,
    and laughed to see him grin.

'O Perry-the-Winkle boy,' he cried,
    'come, you're the lad for me!
Now if you're willing to take a ride,
    I'll carry you home to tea.'
He jumped on his back and held on tight,
    and 'Off you go!' said he;
and the Winkle had a feast that night,
    and sat on the old Troll's knee.

There were pikelets, there was buttered toast,
    and jam, and cream, and cake,
and the Winkle strove to eat the most,
    though his buttons all should break.
The kettle sang, the fire was hot,
    the pot was large and brown,
and the Winkle tried to drink the lot,
    in tea though he should drown.

When full and tight were coat and skin,
    they rested without speech,
till the old Troll said: 'I'll now begin
    the baker's art to teach,
the making of beautiful cramsome bread,
    of bannocks light and brown;
and then you can sleep on a heather-bed
    with pillows of owlet's down.'

'Young Winkle, where've you been?' they said.
    'I've been to a fulsome tea,
and I feel so fat, for I have fed
    on cramsome bread,' said he.
'But where, my lad, in the Shire was that?
    Or out in Bree?' said they.
But Winkle he up and answered flat:
    'I aint a-going to say.'

'But I know where,' said Peeping Jack,
   'I watched him ride away:
he went upon the old Troll's back
   to the hills of Faraway.'
Then all the People went with a will,
   by pony, cart, or moke,
until they came to a house in a hill
   and saw a chimney smoke.

They hammered upon the old Troll's door.
   'A beautiful cramsome cake
O bake for us, please, or two, or more;
   O bake!' they cried, 'O bake!'
'Go home, go home!' the old Troll said.
   'I never invited you.
Only on Thursdays I bake my bread,
   and only for a few.'

'Go home! Go home! There's some mistake.
   My house is far too small;
and I've no pikelets, cream, or cake:
   the Winkle has eaten all!
You Jack, and Hogg, old Bunce and Pott
   I wish no more to see.
Be off! Be off now all the lot!
   The Winkle's the boy for me!'

Now Perry-the-Winkle grew so fat
    through eating of cramsome bread,
his weskit bust, and never a hat
    would sit upon his head;
for Every Thursday he went to tea,
    and sat on the kitchen floor,
and smaller the old Troll seemed to be,
    as he grew more and more.

The Winkle a Baker great became,
    as still is said in song;
from the Sea to Bree there went the fame
    of his bread both short and long.
But it weren't so good as the cramsome bread;
    no butter so rich and free,
as Every Thursday the old Troll spread
    for Perry-the-Winkle's tea.

9

THE MEWLIPS

The shadows where the Mewlips dwell
    Are dark and wet as ink,
And slow and softly rings their bell,
    As in the slime you sink.

You sink into the slime, who dare
    To knock upon their door,
While down the grinning gargoyles stare
    And noisome waters pour.

Beside the rotting river-strand
    The drooping willows weep,
And gloomily the gorcrows stand
    Croaking in their sleep.

Over the Merlock Mountains a long and weary way,
   In a mouldy valley where the trees are grey,
By a dark pool's borders without wind or tide,
   Moonless and sunless, the Mewlips hide.

      The cellars where the Mewlips sit
         Are deep and dank and cold
      With single sickly candle lit;
         And there they count their gold.

      Their walls are wet, their ceilings drip;
         Their feet upon the floor
      Go softly with a squish-flap-flip,
         As they sidle to the door.

      They peep out slyly; through a crack
         Their feeling fingers creep,
      And when they've finished, in a sack
         Your bones they take to keep.

Beyond the Merlock Mountains, a long and lonely road,
   Through the spider-shadows and the marsh of Tode,
And through the wood of hanging trees and the gallows-
      weed,
   You go to find the Mewlips – and the Mewlips feed.

10

OLIPHAUNT

Grey as a mouse,
Big as a house,
Nose like a snake,
I make the earth shake,
As I tramp through the grass;
Trees crack as I pass.
With horns in my mouth
I walk in the South,
Flapping big ears.
Beyond count of years
I stump round and round,
Never lie on the ground,
Not even to die.
Oliphaunt am I,
Biggest of all,
Huge, old, and tall.

If ever you'd met me,
You wouldn't forget me.
If you never do,
You won't think I'm true;
But old Oliphaunt am I,
And I never lie.

II

FASTITOCALON

Look, there is Fastitocalon!
An island good to land upon,
    Although 'tis rather bare.
Come, leave the sea! And let us run,
Or dance, or lie down in the sun!
    See, gulls are sitting there!
        Beware!
      Gulls do not sink.
There they may sit, or strut and prink:
Their part it is to tip the wink,
    If anyone should dare
    Upon that isle to settle,
Or only for a while to get
Relief from sickness or the wet,
    Or maybe boil a kettle.

Ah! foolish folk, who land on HIM,
And little fires proceed to trim
   And hope perhaps for tea!
It may be that His shell is thick,
He seems to sleep; but He is quick,
   And floats now in the sea
      With guile;
And when He hears their tapping feet,
Or faintly feels the sudden heat,
      With smile
    HE dives,
And promptly turning upside down
He tips them off, and deep they drown,
   And lose their silly lives
    To their surprise.
      Be wise!
There are many monsters in the Sea,
But none so perilous as HE,
Old horny Fastitocalon,
Whose mighty kindred all have gone,
The last of the old Turtle-fish.
So if to save your life you wish
   Then I advise:
Pay heed to sailors' ancient lore,
Set foot on no uncharted shore!
   Or better still,
Your days at peace on Middle-earth
   In mirth
   Fulfil!

12

CAT

The fat cat on the mat
   may seem to dream
of nice mice that suffice
   for him, or cream;
but he free, maybe,
   walks in thought
unbowed, proud, where loud
   roared and fought
his kin, lean and slim,
   or deep in den
in the East feasted on beasts
   and tender men.

The giant lion with iron
    claw in paw,
and huge ruthless tooth
    in gory jaw;
the pard dark-starred,
    fleet upon feet,
that oft soft from aloft
    leaps on his meat
where woods loom in gloom –
    far now they be,
    fierce and free,
    and tamed is he;
but fat cat on the mat
    kept as a pet,
    he does not forget.

13

SHADOW-BRIDE

There was a man who dwelt alone,
   as day and night went past
he sat as still as carven stone,
   and yet no shadow cast.
The white owls perched upon his head
   beneath the winter moon;
they wiped their beaks and thought him dead
   under the stars of June.

There came a lady clad in grey
   in the twilight shining:
one moment she would stand and stay,
   her hair with flowers entwining.
He woke, as had he sprung of stone,
   and broke the spell that bound him;
he clasped her fast, both flesh and bone,
   and wrapped her shadow round him.

There never more she walks her ways
    by sun or moon or star;
she dwells below where neither days
    nor any nights there are.
But once a year when caverns yawn
    and hidden things awake,
they dance together then till dawn
    and a single shadow make.

14

THE HOARD

When the moon was new and the sun young
of silver and gold the gods sung:
in the green grass they silver spilled,
and the white waters they with gold filled.
Ere the pit was dug or Hell yawned,
ere dwarf was bred or dragon spawned,
there were Elves of old, and strong spells
under green hills in hollow dells
they sang as they wrought many fair things,
and the bright crowns of the Elf-kings.
But their doom fell, and their song waned,
by iron hewn and by steel chained.
Greed that sang not, nor with mouth smiled,
in dark holes their wealth piled,
graven silver and carven gold:
over Elvenhome the shadow rolled.

There was an old dwarf in a dark cave,
to silver and gold his fingers clave;
with hammer and tongs and anvil-stone
he worked his hands to the hard bone,
and coins he made, and strings of rings,
and thought to buy the power of kings.
But his eyes grew dim and his ears dull
and the skin yellow on his old skull;
through his bony claw with a pale sheen
the stony jewels slipped unseen.
No feet he heard, though the earth quaked,
when the young dragon his thirst slaked,
and the stream smoked at his dark door,
The flames hissed on the dank floor,
and he died alone in the red fire;
his bones were ashes in the hot mire.

There was an old dragon under grey stone;
his red eyes blinked as he lay alone.
His joy was dead and his youth spent,
he was knobbed and wrinkled, and his limbs bent
in the long years to his gold chained;
in his heart's furnace the fire waned.
To his belly's slime gems stuck thick,
silver and gold he would snuff and lick:
he knew the place of the least ring
beneath the shadow of his black wing.
Of thieves he thought on his hard bed,

and dreamed that on their flesh he fed,
their bones crushed, and their blood drank:
his ears drooped and his breath sank.
Mail-rings rang. He heard them not.
A voice echoed in his deep grot:
a young warrior with a bright sword
called him forth to defend his hoard.
His teeth were knives, and of horn his hide,
but iron tore him, and his flame died.

There was an old king on a high throne:
his white beard lay on knees of bone;
his mouth savoured neither meat nor drink,
nor his ears song; he could only think
of his huge chest with carven lid
where pale gems and gold lay hid
in secret treasury in the dark ground;
its strong doors were iron-bound.

The swords of his thanes were dull with rust,
his glory fallen, his rule unjust,
his halls hollow, and his bowers cold,
but king he was of elvish gold.
He heard not the horns in the mountain-pass,
he smelt not the blood on the trodden grass,
but his halls were burned, his kingdom lost;
in a cold pit his bones were tossed.

There is an old hoard in a dark rock,
forgotten behind doors none can unlock;
that grim gate no man can pass.
On the mound grows the green grass;
there sheep feed and the larks soar,
and the wind blows from the sea-shore.
The old hoard the Night shall keep,
while earth waits and the Elves sleep.

15

THE SEA-BELL

I walked by the sea, and there came to me,
    as a star-beam on the wet sand,
a white shell like a sea-bell;
    trembling it lay in my wet hand.
In my fingers shaken I heard waken
    a ding within, by a harbour bar
a buoy swinging, a call ringing
    over endless seas, faint now and far.

Then I saw a boat silently float
    on the night-tide, empty and grey.
'It is later than late! Why do we wait?'
    I leapt in and cried: 'Bear me away!'

It bore me away, wetted with spray,
    wrapped in a mist, wound in a sleep,
to a forgotten strand in a strange land.
    In the twilight beyond the deep
I heard a sea-bell swing in the swell,
    dinging, dinging, and the breakers roar
on the hidden teeth of a perilous reef;
    and at last I came to a long shore.
White it glimmered, and the sea simmered
    with star-mirrors in a silver net;
cliffs of stone pale as ruel-bone
    in the moon-foam were gleaming wet.
Glittering sand slid through my hand,
    dust of pearl and jewel-grist,
trumpets of opal, roses of coral,
    flutes of green and amethyst.

But under cliff-eaves there were glooming caves,
    weed-curtained, dark and grey;
a cold air stirred in my hair,
    and the light waned, as I hurried away.

Down from a hill ran a green rill;
    its water I drank to my heart's ease.
Up its fountain-stair to a country fair
    of ever-eve I came, far from the seas,
climbing into meadows of fluttering shadows:
    flowers lay there like fallen stars,

and on a blue pool, glassy and cool,
    like floating moons the nenuphars.
Alders were sleeping, and willows weeping
    by a slow river of rippling weeds;
gladdon-swords guarded the fords,
    and green spears, and arrow-reeds.

There was echo of song all the evening long
    down in the valley; many a thing
running to and fro: hares white as snow,
    voles out of holes; moths on the wing
with lantern-eyes; in quiet surprise
    brocks were staring out of dark doors.
I heard dancing there, music in the air,
    feet going quick on the green floors.
But wherever I came it was ever the same:
    the feet fled, and all was still;
never a greeting, only the fleeting
    pipes, voices, horns on the hill.

Of river-leaves and the rush-sheaves
    I made me a mantle of jewel-green,
a tall wand to hold, and a flag of gold;
    my eyes shone like the star-sheen.
With flowers crowned I stood on a mound,
    and shrill as a call at cock-crow
proudly I cried: 'Why do you hide?
    Why do none speak, wherever I go?

Here now I stand, king of this land,
   with gladdon-sword and reed-mace.
Answer my call! Come forth all!
   Speak to me words! Show me a face!'

Black came a cloud as a night-shroud.
   Like a dark mole groping I went,
to the ground falling, on my hands crawling
   with eyes blind and my back bent.
I crept to a wood: silent it stood
   in its dead leaves; bare were its boughs.
There must I sit, wandering in wit,
   while owls snored in their hollow house.
For a year and a day there must I stay:
   beetles were tapping in the rotten trees,
spiders were weaving, in the mould heaving
   puffballs loomed about my knees.

At last there came light in my long night,
   and I saw my hair hanging grey.
'Bent though I be, I must find the sea!
   I have lost myself, and I know not the way,
but let me be gone!' Then I stumbled on;
   like a hunting bat shadow was over me;
in my ears dinned a withering wind,
   and with ragged briars I tried to cover me.
My hands were torn and my knees worn,
   and years were heavy upon my back.

when the rain in my face took a salt taste,
    and I smelled the smell of sea-wrack.

Birds came sailing, mewing, wailing;
    I heard voices in cold caves,
seals barking, and rocks snarling,
    and in spout-holes the gulping of waves.
Winter came fast; into a mist I passed,
    to land's end my years I bore;
snow was in the air, ice in my hair,
    darkness was lying on the last shore.

There still afloat waited the boat,
    in the tide lifting, its prow tossing.
Weary I lay, as it bore me away,
    the waves climbing, the seas crossing,
passing old hulls clustered with gulls
    and great ships laden with light,
coming to haven, dark as a raven,
    silent as snow, deep in the night.

Houses were shuttered, wind round them muttered,
    roads were empty. I sat by a door,
and where drizzling rain poured down a drain
    I cast away all that I bore:
in my clutching hand some grains of sand,
    and a sea-shell silent and dead.

Never will my ear that bell hear,
   never my feet that shore tread,
never again, as in sad lane,
   in blind alley and in long street
ragged I walk. To myself I talk;
   for still they speak not, men that I meet.

16

THE LAST SHIP

Fíriel looked out at three o'clock:
   the grey night was going;
far away a golden cock
   clear and shrill was crowing.
The trees were dark, and the dawn pale,
   waking birds were cheeping,
a wind moved cool and frail
   through dim leaves creeping,

She watched the gleam at window grow,
   till the long light was shimmering
on land and leaf; on grass below
   grey dew was glimmering.
Over the floor her white feet crept,
   down the stair they twinkled,
through the grass they dancing stepped
   all with dew besprinkled.

Her gown had jewels upon its hem,
    as she ran down to the river,
and leaned upon a willow-stem,
    and watched the water quiver.
A kingfisher plunged down like a stone
    in a blue flash falling,
bending reeds were softly blown,
    lily-leaves were sprawling.

A sudden music to her came,
    as she stood there gleaming
with free hair in the morning's flame
    on her shoulders streaming.
Flutes there were, and harps were wrung,
    and there was sound of singing,
like wind-voices keen and young
    and far bells ringing.

A ship with golden beak and oar
    and timbers white came gliding;
swans went sailing on before,
    her tall prow guiding.
Fair folk out of Elvenland
    in silver-grey were rowing,
and three with crowns she saw there stand
    with bright hair flowing.

With harp in hand they sang their song
    to the slow oars swinging:
'Green is the land, the leaves are long,
    and the birds are singing.
Many a day with dawn of gold
    this earth will lighten,
many a flower will yet unfold,
    ere the cornfields whiten.

'Then whither go ye, boatmen fair,
    down the river gliding?
To twilight and to secret lair
    in the great forest hiding?
To Northern isles and shores of stone
    on strong swans flying,
by cold waves to dwell alone
    with the white gulls crying?'

'Nay!' they answered. 'Far away
    on the last road faring,
leaving western havens grey,
    the seas of shadow daring,
we go back to Elvenhome,
    where the White Tree is growing,
and the Star shines upon the foam
    on the last shore flowing.

'To mortal fields say farewell,
  Middle-earth forsaking!
In Elvenhome a clear bell
  in the high tower is shaking.
Here grass fades and leaves fall,
  and sun and moon wither,
and we have heard the far call
  that bids us journey thither'.

The oars were stayed. They turned aside:
  'Do you hear the call, Earth-maiden?
Fíriel! Fíriel!' they cried.
  'Our ship is not full-laden.
One more only we may bear.
  Come! For your days are speeding.
Come! Earth-maiden elven-fair,
  our last call heeding.'

Fíriel looked from the river-bank,
  one step daring;
then deep in clay her feet sank,
  and she halted staring.
Slowly the elven-ship went by
  whispering through the water:
'I cannot come!' they heard her cry.
  'I was born Earth's daughter!'

No jewels bright her gown bore,
   as she walked back from the meadow
under roof and dark door,
   under the house-shadow.
She donned her smock of russet brown,
   her long hair braided,
and to her work came stepping down.
   Soon the sunlight faded.

Year still after year flows
   down the Seven Rivers;
cloud passes, sunlight glows,
   reed and willow quivers
as morn and eve, but never more
   westward ships have waded
in mortal waters as before,
   and their song has faded.

SMITH OF
WOOTTON MAJOR

SMITH OF WOOTTON MAJOR

There was a village once, not very long ago for those with long memories, not very far away for those with long legs. Wootton Major it was called because it was larger than Wootton Minor, a few miles away deep in the trees; but it was not very large, though it was at that time prosperous, and a fair number of folk lived in it, good, bad, and mixed, as is usual.

It was a remarkable village in its way, being well known in the country round about for the skill of its workers in various crafts, but most of all for its cooking. It had a large Kitchen which belonged to the Village Council, and the Master Cook was an important person. The Cook's House and the Kitchen adjoined the Great Hall, the largest and oldest building in the place and the most beautiful. It was built of good stone and good oak and was well tended, though it was no longer painted or gilded as it had been once upon a time. In the Hall the villagers held their meetings and debates, and their public feasts, and their family gatherings. So the Cook was kept busy, since for all these occasions he had to provide suitable fare. For the festivals, of which there were many in the course of a year, the fare that was thought suitable was plentiful and rich.

There was one festival to which all looked forward, for it was the only one held in winter. It went on for a week, and on its last day at sundown there was a merry-making called The Feast of Good Children, to which not many were invited. No doubt some who deserved to be asked were overlooked, and some who did not were invited by mistake; for that is the way of things, however careful those who arrange such matters may try to be. In any case it was largely by chance of birthday that any child came in for the Twenty-four Feast, since that was only held once in twenty-four years, and only twenty-four children were invited. For that occasion the Master Cook was expected to do his best, and in addition to many other good things it was the custom for him to make the Great Cake. By the excellence (or otherwise) of this his name was chiefly remembered, for a Master Cook seldom if ever lasted long enough in office to make a second Great Cake.

There came a time, however, when the reigning Master Cook, to everyone's surprise, since it had never happened before, suddenly announced that he needed a holiday; and he went away, no one knew where; and when he came back some months later he seemed rather changed. He had been a kind man who liked to see other people enjoying themselves, but he was himself serious, and said very little. Now he was merrier, and often said and did most laughable things; and at feasts he would himself sing gay songs, which was not expected of Master Cooks. Also he brought back with him an Apprentice; and that astonished the Village.

It was not astonishing for the Master Cook to have an apprentice. It was usual. The Master chose one in due time, and he taught him all that he could; and as they both grew older the apprentice took on more of the important work, so that when the Master retired or died there he was, ready to take over the office and become Master Cook in his turn. But this Master had never chosen an apprentice. He had always said 'time enough yet', or 'I'm keeping my eyes open and I'll choose, one when I find one to suit me'. But now he brought with him a mere boy, and not one from the village. He was more lithe than the Wootton lads and quicker, soft-spoken and very polite, but ridiculously young for the work, barely in his teens by the look of him. Still, choosing his apprentice was the Master Cook's affair, and no one had the right to interfere in it; so the boy remained and stayed in the Cook's House until he was old enough to find lodgings for himself. People soon became used to seeing him about, and he made a few friends. They and the Cook called him Alf, but to the rest he was just Prentice.

* * *

The next surprise came only three years later. One spring morning the Master Cook took off his tall white hat, folded up his clean aprons, hung up his white coat, took a stout ash stick and a small bag, and departed. He said goodbye to the apprentice. No one else was about.

'Goodbye for now, Alf,' he said. 'I leave you to manage things as best you can, which is always very well. I expect it will turn out all right. If we meet again, I hope to hear all about it. Tell them that I've gone on another holiday, but this time I shan't be coming back again.'

There was quite a stir in the village when Prentice gave this message to people who came to the Kitchen. 'What a thing to do!' they said. 'And without warning or farewell! What are we going to do without any Master Cook? He has left no one to take his place.' In all their discussions no one ever thought of making young Prentice into Cook. He had grown a bit taller but still looked like a boy, and he had only served for three years.

In the end for lack of anyone better they appointed a man of the village, who could cook well enough in a small way. When he was younger he had helped the Master at busy times, but the Master had never taken to him and would not have him as apprentice. He was now a solid sort of man with a wife and children, and careful with money. 'At any rate he won't go off without notice,' they said, 'and poor cooking is better than none. It is seven years till the next Great Cake, and by that time he should be able to manage it.'

Nokes, for that was his name, was very pleased with the turn things had taken. He had always wished to become Master Cook, and had never doubted that he could manage it. For some time, when he was alone in the Kitchen, he used to put on the tall white hat and look at himself in a polished frying pan and say: 'How do you do, Master. That hat suits you properly, might have been made for you. I hope things go well with you.'

Things went well enough; for at first Nokes did his best, and he had Prentice to help him. Indeed he learned a lot from him by watching him slyly, though that Nokes never admitted. But in due course the time for the Twenty-four Feast drew near, and Nokes had to think about making the Great Cake. Secretly he was worried about it, for although with seven years' practice he could turn out passable cakes and pastries for ordinary occasions, he knew that his Great Cake would be eagerly awaited, and would have to satisfy severe critics. Not only the children. A smaller cake of the same materials and baking had to be provided for those who came to help at the feast. Also it was expected that the Great Cake should have something novel and surprising about it and not be a mere repetition of the one before.

His chief notion was that it should be very sweet and rich; and he decided that it should be entirely covered in sugar-icing (at which Prentice had a clever hand). 'That will make it pretty and fairylike,' he thought. Fairies and sweets were two of the very few notions he had about the tastes of children. Fairies he thought one grew out of; but of sweets he remained very fond. 'Ah! fairylike,' he said, 'that gives me an idea'; and so it came into his head that he would stick a little doll on a pinnacle in the middle of the Cake, dressed all in white, with a little wand in her hand ending in a tinsel star, and *Fairy Queen* written in pink icing round her feet.

But when he began preparing the materials for the cake-making he found that he had only dim memories of what should go *inside* a Great Cake; so he looked in some old books of recipes left behind by previous cooks. They puzzled him, even when he could make out their handwriting, for they mentioned many things that he had not heard of, and some that he had forgotten and now had no time to get; but he thought he might try one or two of the spices that the books spoke of. He scratched his head and remembered an old black box with several different compartments in which the last Cook had once kept spices and other things for special cakes. He had not looked at it since he took over, but after a search he found it on a high shelf in the store-room.

He took it down and blew the dust off the lid; but when he opened it he found that very little of the spices were left, and they were dry and musty. But in one compartment in the corner he discovered a small star, hardly as big as one of our sixpences, black-looking as if it was made of silver but was tarnished. 'That's funny!' he said as he held it up to the light.

'No, it isn't!' said a voice behind him, so suddenly that he jumped. It was the voice of Prentice, and he had never spoken to the Master in that tone before. Indeed he seldom spoke to Nokes at all unless he was spoken to first. Very right and proper in a youngster; he might be clever with icing but he had a lot to learn yet: that was Nokes's opinion.

'What do you mean, young fellow?' he said, not much pleased. 'If it isn't funny what is it?'

'It is *fay,*' said Prentice. 'It comes from Faery.'

Then the Cook laughed. 'All right, all right,' he said. 'It means much the same; but call it that if you like. You'll grow up some day. Now you can get on with stoning the raisins. If you notice any funny fairy ones, tell me.'

'What are you going to do with the star, Master?' said Prentice.

'Put it into the Cake, of course,' said the Cook. 'Just the thing, especially if it's *fairy,*' he sniggered. 'I daresay you've been to children's parties yourself, and not so long ago either, where little trinkets like this were stirred into the mixture, and little coins and what not. Anyway we do that in this village: it amuses the children.'

'But this isn't a trinket, Master, it's a fay-star,' said Prentice.

'So you've said already,' snapped the Cook. 'Very well, I'll tell the children. It'll make them laugh.'

'I don't think it will, Master,' said Prentice. 'But it's the right thing to do, quite right.'

'Who do you think you're talking to?' said Nokes.

In time the Cake was made and baked and iced, mostly by Prentice. 'As you are so set on fairies, I'll let you make the Fairy Queen,' Nokes said to him.

'Very good, Master,' he answered. 'I'll do it if you are too busy. But it was your idea and not mine.'

'It's my place to have ideas, and not yours,' said Nokes.

At the Feast the Cake stood in the middle of the long table, inside a ring of twenty-four red candles. Its top rose into a small white mountain, up the sides of which grew little trees glittering as if with frost; on its summit stood a tiny white figure on one foot like a snow-maiden dancing, and in her hand was a minute wand of ice sparkling with light.

The children looked at it with wide eyes, and one or two clapped their hands, crying: 'Isn't it pretty and fairy-like!' That delighted the Cook, but the apprentice looked displeased. They were both present: the Master to cut up the Cake when the time came, and the apprentice to sharpen the knife and hand it to him.

At last the Cook took the knife and stepped up to the table. 'I should tell you, my dears,' he said, 'that inside this lovely icing there is a cake made of many nice things to eat; but also stirred well in there are many pretty little things, trinkets and little coins and what not, and I'm told that it is lucky to find one in your slice. There are twenty-four in the Cake, so there should be one for each of you, if the Fairy Queen plays fair. But she doesn't always do so: she's a tricky little creature. You ask Mr Prentice.' The apprentice turned away and studied the faces of the children.

'No! I'm forgetting,' said the Cook. 'There's twenty-five this evening. There's also a little silver star, a special magic one, or so Mr Prentice says. So be careful! If you break one of your pretty front teeth on it, the magic star won't mend it. But I expect it's a specially lucky thing to find, all the same.'

It was a good cake, and no one had any fault to find with it, except that it was no bigger than was needed. When it was all cut up there was a large slice for each of the children, but nothing left over: no coming again. The slices soon disappeared, and every now and then a trinket or a coin was discovered. Some found one, and some found two, and several found none; for that is the way luck goes, whether there is a doll with a wand on the cake or not. But when the Cake was all eaten, there was no sign of any magic star.

'Bless me!' said the Cook. 'Then it can't have been made of silver after all; it must have melted. Or perhaps Mr Prentice was right and it was really magical, and it's just vanished and gone back to Fairyland. Not a nice trick to play, I don't think.' He looked at Prentice with a smirk, and Prentice looked at him with dark eyes and did not smile at all.

* * *

All the same, the silver star was indeed a fay-star: the apprentice was not one to make mistakes about things of that sort. What had happened was that one of the boys at the Feast had swallowed it without ever noticing it, although he had found a silver coin in his slice and had given it to Nell, the little girl next to him: she looked so disappointed at finding nothing lucky in hers. He sometimes wondered what had really become of the star, and did not know that it had remained with him, tucked away in some place where it could not be felt; for that was what it was intended to do. There it waited for a long time, until its day came.

The Feast had been in mid-winter, but it was now June, and the night was hardly dark at all. The boy got up before dawn, for he did not wish to sleep: it was his tenth birthday. He looked out of the window, and the world seemed quiet and expectant. A little breeze, cool and fragrant, stirred the waking trees. Then the dawn came, and far away he heard the dawn-song of the birds beginning, growing as it came towards him, until it rushed over him, filling all the land round the house, and passed on like a wave of music into the West, as the sun rose above the rim of the world.

'It reminds me of Faery,' he heard himself say; 'but in Faery the people sing too.' Then he began to sing, high and clear, in strange words that he seemed to know by heart; and in that moment the star fell out of his mouth and he caught it on his open hand. It was bright silver now, glistening in the sunlight; but it quivered and rose a little, as if it was about to fly away. Without thinking he clapped his hand to his head, and there the star stayed in the middle of his forehead, and he wore it for many years.

Few people in the village noticed it though it was not invisible to attentive eyes; but it became part of his face, and it did not usually shine at all. Some of its light passed into his eyes; and his voice, which had begun to grow beautiful as soon as the star came to him, became ever more beautiful as he grew up. People liked to hear him speak, even if it was no more than a 'good morning'.

He became well known in his country, not only in his own village but in many others round about, for his good workmanship. His father was a smith, and he followed him in his craft and bettered it. Smithson he was called while his father was still alive, and then just Smith. For by that time he was the best smith between Far Easton and the Westwood, and he could make all kinds of things of iron in his smithy. Most of them, of course, were plain and useful, meant for daily needs: farm tools, carpenters' tools, kitchen tools and pots and pans, bars and bolts and hinges, pot-hooks, fire-dogs, and horse-shoes, and the like. They were strong and lasting, but they also had a grace about them, being shapely in their kinds, good to handle and to look at.

But some things, when he had time, he made for delight; and they were beautiful, for he could work iron into wonderful forms that looked as light and delicate as a spray of leaves and blossom, but kept the stern strength of iron, or seemed even stronger. Few could pass by one of the gates or lattices that he made without stopping to admire it; no one could pass through it once it was shut. He sang when he was making things of this sort; and when Smith began to sing those nearby stopped their own work and came to the smithy to listen.

That was all that most people knew about him. It was enough indeed and more than most men and women in the village achieved, even those who were skilled and hardworking. But there was more to know. For Smith became acquainted with Faery, and some regions of it he knew as well as any mortal can; though since too many had become like Nokes, he spoke of this to few people, except his wife and his children. His wife was Nell, to whom he gave the silver coin, and his daughter was Nan, and his son was Ned Smithson. From them it could not have been kept secret anyway, for they sometimes saw the star shining on his forehead, when he came back from one of the long walks he would take alone now and then in the evening, or when he returned from a journey.

From time to time he would go off, sometimes walking, sometimes riding, and it was generally supposed that it was on business; and sometimes it was, and sometimes it was not. At any rate not to get orders for work, or to buy pig-iron and charcoal and other supplies, though he attended to such things with care and knew how to turn an honest penny into twopence, as the saying went. But he had business of its own kind in Faery, and he was welcome there; for the star shone bright on his brow, and he was as safe as a mortal can be in that perilous country. The Lesser Evils avoided the star, and from the Greater Evils he was guarded.

For that he was grateful, for he soon became wise and understood that the marvels of Faery cannot be approached without danger, and that many of the Evils cannot be challenged without weapons of power too great for any mortal to wield. He remained a learner and explorer, not a warrior; and though in time he could have forged weapons that in his own world would have had power enough to become the matter of great tales and be worth a king's ransom, he knew that in Faery they would have been of small account. So among all the things that he made it is not remembered that he ever forged a sword or a spear or an arrow-head.

In Faery at first he walked for the most part quietly among the lesser folk and the gentler creatures in the woods and meads of fair valleys, and by the bright waters in which at night strange stars shone and at dawn the gleaming peaks of far mountains were mirrored. Some of his briefer visits he spent looking only at one tree or one flower; but later in longer journeys he had seen things of both beauty and terror that he could not clearly remember nor report to his friends, though he knew that they dwelt deep in his heart. But some things he did not forget, and they remained in his mind as wonders and mysteries that he often recalled.

When he first began to walk far without a guide he thought he would discover the further bounds of the land; but great mountains rose before him, and going by long ways round about them he came at last to a desolate shore. He stood beside the Sea of Windless Storm where the blue waves like snow-clad hills roll silently out of Unlight to the long strand, bearing the white ships that return from battles on the Dark Marches of which men know nothing. He saw a great ship cast high upon the land, and the waters fell back in foam without a sound. The elven mariners were tall and terrible; their swords shone and their spears glinted and a piercing light was in their eyes. Suddenly they lifted up their voices in a song of triumph, and his heart was shaken with fear, and he fell upon his face, and they passed over him and went away into the echoing hills.

Afterwards he went no more to that strand, believing that he was in an island realm beleaguered by the Sea, and he turned his mind towards the mountains, desiring to come to the heart of the kingdom. Once in these wanderings he was overtaken by a grey mist and strayed long at a loss, until the mist rolled away and he found that he was in a wide plain. Far off there was a great hill of shadow, and out of that shadow, which was its root, he saw the King's Tree springing up, tower upon tower, into the sky, and its light was like the sun at noon; and it bore at once leaves and flowers and fruits uncounted, and not one was the same as any other that grew on the Tree.

He never saw that Tree again, though he often sought for it. On one such journey climbing into the Outer Mountains he came to a deep dale among them, and at its bottom lay a lake, calm and unruffled though a breeze stirred the woods that surrounded it. In that dale the light was like a red sunset, but the light came up from the lake. From a low cliff that overhung it he looked down, and it seemed that he could see to an immeasurable depth; and there he beheld strange shapes of flame bending and branching and wavering like great weeds in a sea-dingle, and fiery creatures went to and fro among them. Filled with wonder he went down to the water's edge and tried it with his foot, but it was not water: it was harder than stone and sleeker than glass. He stepped on it and he fell heavily, and a ringing boom ran across the lake and echoed in its shores.

At once the breeze rose to a wild Wind, roaring like a great beast, and it swept him up and flung him on the shore, and it drove him up the slopes whirling and falling like a dead leaf. He put his arms about the stem of a young birch and clung to it, and the Wind wrestled fiercely with them, trying to tear him away; but the birth was bent down to the ground by the blast and enclosed him in its branches. When at last the Wind passed on he rose and saw that the birch was naked. It was stripped of every leaf, and it wept, and tears fell from its branches like rain. He set his hand upon its white bark, saying: 'Blessed be the birch! What can I do to make amends or give thanks?' He felt the answer of the tree pass up from his hand: 'Nothing,' it said. 'Go away! The Wind is hunting you. You do not belong here. Go away and never return!'

As he climbed back out of that dale he felt the tears of the birch trickle down his face and they were bitter on his lips. His heart was saddened as he went on his long road, and for some time he did not enter Faery again. But he could not forsake it, and when he returned his desire was still stronger to go deep into the land.

At last he found a road through the Outer Mountains, and he went on till he came to the Inner Mountains, and they were high and sheer and daunting. Yet in the end he found a pass that he could scale, and upon a day of days greatly daring he came through a narrow cleft and looked down, though he did not know it, into the Vale of Evermorn where the green surpasses the green of the meads of Outer Faery as they surpass ours in our springtime. There the air is so lucid that eyes can see the red tongues of birds as they sing on the trees upon the far side of the valley, though that is very wide and the birds are no greater than wrens.

On the inner side the mountains went down in long slopes filled with the sound of bubbling waterfalls, and in great delight he hastened on. As he set foot upon the grass of the Vale he heard elven voices singing, and on a lawn beside a river bright with lilies he came upon many maidens dancing. The speed and the grace and the ever-changing modes of their movements enchanted him, and he stepped forward towards their ring. Then suddenly they stood still, and a young maiden with flowing hair and kilted skirt came out to meet him.

She laughed as she spoke to him, saying: 'You are becoming bold, Starbrow, are you not? Have you no fear what the Queen might say, if she knew of this? Unless you have her leave.' He was abashed, for he became aware of his own thought and knew that she read it: that the star on his forehead was a passport to go wherever he wished; and now he knew that it was not. But she smiled as she spoke again: Come! Now that you are here you shall dance with me'; and she took his hand and led him into the ring.

There they danced together, and for a while he knew what it was to have the swiftness and the power and the joy to accompany her. For a while. But soon as it seemed they halted again, and she stooped and took up a white flower from before her feet, and she set it in his hair. 'Farewell now!' she said. 'Maybe we shall meet again, by the Queen's leave.'

*　*　*

He remembered nothing of the journey home from that meeting, until he found himself riding along the roads in his own country; and in some villages people stared at him in wonder and watched him till he rode out of sight. When he came to his own house his daughter ran out and greeted him with delight – he had returned sooner than was expected, but none too soon for those that awaited him. 'Daddy!' she cried. 'Where have you been? Your star is shining bright!'

When he crossed the threshold the star dimmed again; but Nell took him by the hand and led him to the hearth, and there she turned and looked at him. 'Dear Man,' she said, 'where have you been and what have you seen? There is a flower in your hair.' She lifted it gently from his head, and it lay on her hand. It seemed like a thing seen from a great distance, yet there it was, and a light came from it that cast shadows on the walls of the room, now growing dark in the evening. The shadow of the man before her loomed up and its great head was bowed over her. 'You look like a giant, Dad,' said his son, who had not spoken before.

The flower did not wither nor grow dim; and they kept it as a secret and a treasure. The smith made a little casket with a key for it, and there it lay and was handed down for many generations in his kin; and those who inherited the key would at times open the casket and look long at the Living Flower, till the casket closed again: the time of its shutting was not theirs to choose.

*   *   *

The years did not halt in the village. Many now had passed. At the Children's Feast when he received the star the smith was not yet ten years old. Then came another Twenty-four Feast, by which time Alf had become Master Cook and had chosen a new apprentice, Harper. Twelve years later the smith had returned with the Living Flower; and now another Children's Twenty-four Feast was due in the winter to come. One day in that year Smith was walking in the woods of Outer Faery, and it was autumn. Golden leaves were on the boughs and red leaves were on the ground. Footsteps came behind him, but he did not heed them or turn round, for he was deep in thought.

On that visit he had received a summons and had made a far journey. Longer it seemed to him than any he had yet made. He was guided and guarded, but he had little memory of the ways that he had taken; for often he had been blindfolded by mist or by shadow, until at last he came to a high place under a night-sky of innumerable stars. There he was brought before the Queen herself. She wore no crown and had no throne. She stood there in her majesty and her glory, and all about her was a great host shimmering and glittering like the stars above; but she was taller than the points of their great spears, and upon her head there burned a white flame. She made a sign for him to approach, and trembling he stepped forward. A high clear trumpet sounded, and behold! they were alone.

He stood before her, and he did not kneel in courtesy, for he was dismayed and felt that for one so lowly all gestures were in vain. At length he looked up and beheld her face and her eyes bent gravely upon him; and he was troubled and amazed, for in that moment he knew her again: the fair maid of the Green Vale, the dancer at whose feet the flowers sprang. She smiled seeing his memory, and drew towards him; and they spoke long together, for the most part without words, and he learned many things in her thought, some of which gave him joy, and others filled him with grief. Then his mind turned back retracing his life, until he came to the day of the Children's Feast and the coming of the star, and suddenly he saw again the little dancing figure with its wand, and in shame he lowered his eyes from the Queen's beauty.

But she laughed again as she had laughed in the Vale of Evermorn. 'Do not be grieved for me, Starbrow,' she said. 'Nor too much ashamed of your own folk. Better a little doll, maybe, than no memory of Faery at all. For some the only glimpse. For some the awaking. Ever since that day you have desired in your heart to see me, and I have granted your wish. But I can give you no more. Now at farewell I will make you my messenger. If you meet the King, say to him: *The time has come. Let him choose.*'

'But Lady of Faery,' he stammered, 'where then is the King?' For he had asked this question many times of the people of Faery, and they had all said the same: 'He has not told us.'

And the Queen answered: 'If he has not told you, Starbrow, then I may not. But he makes many journeys and may
be met in unlikely places. Now kneel of your courtesy.'

Then he knelt, and she stooped and laid her hand on his
head, and a great stillness came upon him; and he seemed
to be both in the World and in Faery, and also outside
them and surveying them, so that he was at once in
bereavement, and in ownership, and in peace. When after
a while the stillness passed he raised his head and stood
up. The dawn was in the sky and the stars were pale, and
the Queen was gone. Far off he heard the echo of a
trumpet in the mountains. The high field where he stood
was silent and empty: and he knew that his way now led
back to bereavement.

That meeting-place was now far behind him, and here
he was, walking among the fallen leaves, pondering all that
he had seen and learned. The footsteps came nearer. Then
suddenly a voice said at his side: 'Are you going my way,
Starbrow?'

He started and came out of his thoughts, and he saw a
man beside him. He was tall, and he walked lightly and
quickly; he was dressed all in dark green and wore a hood
that partly overshadowed his face. The smith was puzzled,
for only the people of Faery called him 'Starbrow', but he
could not remember ever having seen this man there before;
and yet he felt uneasily that he should know him. 'What
way are you going then?' he said.

'I am going back to your village now,' the man answered, 'and I hope that you are also returning.'

'I am indeed,' said the smith. 'Let us walk together. But now something has come back to my mind. Before I began my homeward journey a Great Lady gave me a message, but we shall soon be passing from Faery, and I do not think that I shall ever return. Will you?'

'Yes, I shall. You may give the message to me.'

'But the message was to the King. Do you know where to find him?'

'I do. What was the message?'

'The Lady only asked me to say to him: *The time has come. Let him choose.*'

'I understand. Trouble yourself no further.'

They went on then side by side in silence save for the rustle of the leaves about their feet; but after a few miles while they were still within the bounds of Faery the man halted. He turned towards the smith and threw back his hood. Then the smith knew him. He was Alf the Prentice, as the smith still called him in his own mind, remembering always the day when as a youth Alf had stood in the Hall, holding the bright knife for the cutting of the Cake, and his eyes had gleamed in the light of the candles. He must be an old man now, for he had been Master Cook for many years; but here standing under the eaves of the Outer Wood he looked like the apprentice of long ago, though more masterly: there was no grey in his hair nor line on his face, and his eyes gleamed as if they reflected a light.

'I should like to speak to you, Smith Smithson, before we go back to your country,' he said. The smith wondered at that, for he himself had often wished to talk to Alf, but had never been able to do so. Alf had always greeted him kindly and had looked at him with friendly eyes, but had seemed to avoid talking to him alone. He was looking now at the smith with friendly eyes; but he lifted his hand and with his forefinger touched the star on his brow. The gleam left his eyes, and then the smith knew that it had come from the star, and that it must have been shining brightly but now was dimmed. He was surprised and drew away angrily.

'Do you not think, Master Smith,' said Alf, 'that it is time for you to give this thing up?'

'What is that to you, Master Cook?' he answered. 'And why should I do so? Isn't it mine? It came to me, and may a man not keep things that come to him so, at the least as a remembrance?'

'Some things. Those that are free gifts and given for remembrance. But others are not so given. They cannot belong to a man for ever, nor be treasured as heirlooms. They are lent. You have not thought, perhaps, that someone else may need this thing. But it is so. Time is pressing.'

Then the smith was troubled, for he was a generous man, and he remembered with gratitude all that the star had brought to him. 'Then what should I do?' he asked. 'Should I give it to one of the Great in Faery? Should I give it to the King?' And as he said this a hope sprang in his heart that on such an errand he might once more enter Faery.

'You could give it to me,' said Alf, 'but you might find that too hard. Will you come with me to my storeroom and put it back in the box where your grandfather laid it?'

'I did not know that,' said the smith.

'No one knew but me. I was the only one with him.'

'Then I suppose that you know how he came by the star, and why he put it in the box?'

'He brought it from Faery: that you know without asking,' Alf answered. 'He left it behind in the hope that it might come to you, his only grandchild. So he told me, for he thought that I could arrange that. He was your mother's father. I do not know whether she told you much about him, if indeed she knew much to tell. Rider was his name, and he was a great traveller: he had seen many things and could do many things before he settled down and became Master Cook. But he went away when you were only two years old – and they could find no one better to follow him than Nokes, poor man. Still, as we expected, I became Master in time. This year I shall make another Great Cake: the only Cook, as far as is remembered, ever to make a second one. I wish to put the star in it.'

'Very well, you shall have it,' said the smith. He looked at Alf as if he was trying to read his thought. 'Do you know who will find it?'

'What is that to you, Master Smith?'

'I should like to know, if you do, Master Cook. It might make it easier for me to part with a thing so dear to me. My daughter's child is too young.'

'It might and it might not. We shall see,' said Alf.

They said no more, and they went on their way until they passed out of Faery and came back at last to the village. Then they walked to the Hall; and in the world the sun was now setting and a red light was in the windows. The gilded carvings on the great door glowed, and strange faces of many colours looked down from the water-sprouts under the roof. Not long ago the Hall had been re-glazed and re-painted, and there had been much debate on the Council about it. Some disliked it and called it 'new-fangled', but some with more knowledge knew that it was a return to old custom. Still, since it had cost no one a penny and the Master Cook must have paid for it himself, he was allowed to have his own way. But the smith had not seen it in such a light before, and he stood and looked at the Hall in wonder, forgetting his errand.

He felt a touch on his arm, and Alf led him round to a small door at the back. He opened it and led the smith down a dark passage into the store-room. There he lit a tall candle, and unlocking a cupboard he took down from a shelf the black box. It was polished now and adorned with silver scrolls.

He raised the lid and showed it to the smith. One small compartment was empty; the others were now filled with spices, fresh and pungent, and the smith's eyes began to water. He put his hand to his forehead, and the star came away readily, but he felt a sudden stab of pain, and tears ran down his face. Though the star shone brightly again as it lay in his hand, he could not see it, except as a blurred dazzle of light that seemed far away.

'I cannot see clearly,' he said. 'You must put it in for me.' He held out his hand, and Alf took the star and laid it in its place, and it went dark.

The smith turned away without another word and groped his way to the door. On the threshold he found that his sight had cleared again. It was evening and the Even-star was shining in a luminous sky close to the Moon. As he stood for a moment looking at their beauty, he felt a hand on his shoulder and turned.

'You gave me the star freely,' said Alf. 'If you still wish to know to which child it will go, I will tell you.'

'I do indeed.'

'It shall go to any one that you appoint.'

The smith was taken aback and did not answer at once. 'Well,' he said hesitating, 'I wonder what you may think of my choice. I believe you have little reason to love the name of Nokes, but, well, his little great-grandson, Nokes of Townsend's Tim, is coming to the Feast. Nokes of Townsend is quite different.'

'I have observed that,' said Alf. 'He had a wise mother.'

'Yes, my Nell's sister. But apart from the kinship I love little Tim. Though he's not an obvious choice.'

Alf smiled. 'Neither were you,' he said. 'But I agree. Indeed I had already chosen Tim.'

'Then why did you ask me to choose?'

'The Queen wished me to do so. If you had chosen differently I should have given way.'

The smith looked long at Alf. Then suddenly he bowed low. 'I understand at last, sir,' he said. 'You have done us too much honour.'

'I have been repaid,' said Alf. 'Go home now in peace!'

When the smith reached his own house on the western outskirts of the village he found his son by the door of the forge. He had just locked it, for the day's work was done, and now he stood looking up the white road by which his father used to return from his journeys. Hearing footsteps, he turned in surprise to see him coming from the village, and he ran forward to meet him. He put his arms about him in loving welcome.

'I've been hoping for you since yesterday, Dad,' he said. Then looking into his father's face he said anxiously: 'How tired you look! You have walked far, maybe?'

'Very far indeed, my son. All the way from Daybreak to Evening.'

They went into the house together, and it was dark except for the fire flickering on the hearth. His son lit candles, and for a while they sat by the fire without speaking; for a great weariness and bereavement was on the smith. At last he looked round, as if coming to himself, and he said: 'Why are we alone?'

His son looked hard at him. 'Why? Mother's over at Minor, at Nan's. It's the little lad's second birthday. They hoped you would be there too.'

'Ah yes. I ought to have been. I should have been, Ned, but I was delayed; and I have had matters to think of that put all else out of mind for a time. But I did not forget Tomling.'

He put his hand in his breast and drew out a little wallet of soft leather. 'I have brought him something. A trinket old Nokes maybe would call it – but it comes out of Faery, Ned.' Out of the wallet he took a little thing of silver. It was like the smooth stem of a tiny lily from the top of which came three delicate flowers, bending down like shapely bells. And bells they were, for when he shook them gently each flower rang with a small clear note. At the sweet sound the candles flickered and then for a moment shone with a white light.

Ned's eyes were wide with wonder. 'May I look at it, Dad?' he said. He took it with careful fingers and peered into the flowers. 'The work is a marvel!' he said. 'And, Dad, there is a scent in the bells: a scent that reminds me of, reminds me, well of something I've forgotten.'

'Yes, the scent comes for a little while after the bells have rung. But don't fear to handle it, Ned. It was made for a babe to play with. He can do it no harm, and he'll take none from it.'

The smith put the gift back in the wallet and stowed it away. 'I'll take it over to Wootton Minor myself tomorrow,' he said. 'Nan and her Tom, and Mother, will forgive me, maybe. As for Tomling, his time has not yet come for the counting of days . . . and of weeks, and of months, and of years.'

'That's right. You go, Dad. I'd be glad to go with you; but it will be some time before I can get over to Minor. I couldn't have gone today, even if I hadn't waited here for you. There's a lot of work in hand, and more coming in.'

'No, no, Smith's son! Make it a holiday! The name of grandfather hasn't weakened my arms yet a while. Let the work come! There'll be two pairs of hands to tackle it now, all working days. I shall not be going on journeys again, Ned: not on long ones, if you understand me.'

'It's that way is it, Dad? I wondered what had become of the star. That's hard.' He took his father's hand. 'I'm grieved for you; but there's good in it too, for this house. Do you know, Master Smith, there is much you can teach me yet, if you have the time. And I do not mean only the working of iron.'

They had supper together, and long after they had finished they still sat at the table, while the smith told his son of his last journey in Faery, and of other things that came to his mind – but about the choice of the next holder of the star he said nothing.

At last his son looked at him, and 'Father,' he said, 'do you remember the day when you came back with the Flower? And I said that you looked like a giant by your shadow. The shadow was the truth. So it was the Queen herself that you danced with. Yet you have given up the star. I hope it may go to someone as worthy. The child should be grateful.'

'The child won't know,' said the smith. 'That's the way with such gifts. Well, there it is. I have handed it on and come back to hammer and tongs.'

It is a strange thing, but old Nokes, who had scoffed at his apprentice, had never been able to put out of his mind the disappearance of the star in the Cake, although that event had happened so many years ago. He had grown fat and lazy, and retired from his office when he was sixty (no great age in the village). He was now near the end of his eighties, and was of enormous bulk, for he still ate heavily and doted on sugar. Most of his days, when not at table, he spent in a big chair by the window of his cottage, or by the door if it was fine weather. He liked talking, since he still had many opinions to air; but lately his talk mostly turned to the one Great Cake that he had made (as he was now firmly convinced), for whenever he fell asleep it came into his dreams. Prentice sometimes stopped for a word or two. So the old cook still called him, and he expected himself to be called Master. That Prentice was careful to do; which was a point in his favour, though there were others that Nokes was more fond of.

One afternoon Nokes was nodding in his chair by the door after his dinner. He woke with a start to find Prentice standing by and looking down at him. 'Hullo!' he said. 'I'm glad to see you, for that cake's been on my mind again. I was thinking of it just now in fact. It was the best cake I ever made, and that's saying something. But perhaps you have forgotten it.'

'No, Master. I remember it very well. But what is troubling you? It was a good cake, and it was enjoyed and praised.'

'Of course. I made it. But that doesn't trouble me. It's the little trinket, the star. I cannot make up my mind what became of it. Of course it wouldn't melt. I only said that to stop the children from being frightened. I have wondered if one of them did not swallow it. But is that likely? You might swallow one of those little coins and not notice it, but not that star. It was small but it had sharp points.'

'Yes, Master. But do you really know what the star was made of? Don't trouble your mind about it. Someone swallowed it, I assure you.'

'Then who? Well, I've a long memory, and that day sticks in it somehow. I can recall all the children's names. Let me think. It must have been Miller's Molly! She was greedy and bolted her food. She's as fat as a sack now.'

'Yes, there are some folk who get like that, Master. But Molly did not bolt her cake. She found two trinkets in her slice.'

'Oh, did she? Well, it was Cooper's Harry then. A barrel of a boy with a big mouth like a frog's.'

'I should have said, Master, that he was a nice boy with a large friendly grin. Anyway he was so careful that he took his slice to pieces before he ate it. He found nothing but cake.'

'Then it must have been that little pale girl, Draper's Lily. She used to swallow pins as a baby and came to no harm.'

'Not Lily, Master. She only ate the paste and the sugar, and gave the inside to the boy that sat next to her.'

'Then I give up. Who was it? You seem to have been watching very closely. If you're not making it all up.'

'It was the Smith's son, Master; and I think it was good for him.'

'Go on!' laughed old Nokes. 'I ought to have known you were having a game with me. Don't be ridiculous! Smith was a quiet slow boy then. He makes more noise now: a bit of a songster, I hear; but he's cautious. No risks for him. Chews twice before he swallows, and always did, if you take my meaning.'

'I do, Master. Well, if you won't believe it was Smith, I can't help you. Perhaps it doesn't matter much now. Will it ease your mind if I tell you that the star is back in the box now? Here it is!'

Prentice was wearing a dark green cloak, which Nokes now noticed for the first time. From its folds he produced the black box and opened it under the old cook's nose.

'There is the star, Master, down in the corner.'

Old Nokes began coughing and sneezing, but at last he looked into the box. 'So it is!' he said. 'At least it looks like it.'

'It is the same one, Master. I put it there myself a few days ago. It will go back in the Great Cake this winter.'

'A-ha!' said Nokes, leering at Prentice; and then he laughed till he shook like a jelly. 'I see, I see! Twenty-four children and twenty-four lucky bits, and the star was one extra. So you nipped it out before the baking and kept it for another time. You were always a tricky fellow: nimble one might say. And thrifty: wouldn't waste a bee's knee of butter. Ha, ha, ha! So that was the way of it. I might have guessed. Well, that's cleared up. Now I can have a nap in peace.' He settled down in his chair. 'Mind that prentice-man of yours plays you no tricks! The artful don't know all the arts, they say.' He closed his eyes.

'Goodbye, Master!' said Prentice, shutting the box with such a snap that the cook opened his eyes again. 'Nokes,' he said, 'your knowledge is so great that I have only twice ventured to tell you anything. I told you that the star came from Faery; and I have told you that it went to the smith. You laughed at me. Now at parting I will tell you one thing more. Don't laugh again! You are a vain old fraud, fat, idle and sly. I did most of your work. Without thanks you learned all that you could from me – except respect for Faery, and a little courtesy. You have not even enough to bid me good day.'

'If it comes to courtesy,' said Nokes, 'I see none in calling your elders and betters by ill names. Take your Fairy and your nonsense somewhere else! Good day to you, if that's what you're waiting for. Now go along with you!' He flapped his hand mockingly. 'If you've got one of your fairy friends hidden in the Kitchen, send him to me and I'll have a look at him. If he waves his little wand and makes me thin again, I'll think better of him,' he laughed.

'Would you spare a few moments for the King of Faery?' the other answered. To Nokes's dismay he grew taller as he spoke. He threw back his cloak. He was dressed like a Master Cook at a Feast, but his white garments shimmered and glinted, and on his forehead was a great jewel like a radiant star. His face was young but stern.

'Old man,' he said, 'you are at least not my elder. As to my better: you have often sneered at me behind my back. Do you challenge me now openly?' He stepped forward, and Nokes shrank from him, trembling. He tried to shout for help but found that he could hardly whisper.

'No, sir!' he croaked. 'Don't do me a harm! I'm only a poor old man.'

The King's face softened. 'Alas, yes! You speak the truth. Do not be afraid! Be at ease! But will you not expect the King of Faery to do something for you before he leaves you? I grant you your wish. Farewell! Now go to sleep!'

He wrapped his cloak about him again and went away towards the Hall; but before he was out of sight the old cook's goggling eyes had shut and he was snoring.

When the old cook woke again the sun was going down. He rubbed his eyes and shivered a little, for the autumn air was chilly. 'Ugh! What a dream!' he said. 'It must have been that pork at dinner.'

From that day he became so afraid of having more bad dreams of that sort that he hardly dared eat anything for fear that it might upset him, and his meals became very short and plain. He soon became lean, and his clothes and his skin hung on him in folds and creases. The children called him old Rag-and-Bones. Then for a time he found that he could get about the village again and walk with no more help than a stick; and he lived many years longer than he would otherwise have done. Indeed it is said that he just made his century: the only memorable thing he ever achieved. But till his last year he could be heard saying to any that would listen to his tale: 'Alarming, you might call it; but a silly dream, when you come to think of it. King o' Fairy! Why, he hadn't no wand. And if you stop eating you grow thinner. That's natural. Stands to reason. There ain't no magic in it.'

The time for the Twenty-four Feast came round. Smith was there to sing songs and his wife to help with the children. Smith looked at them as they sang and danced, and he thought that they were more beautiful and lively than they had been in his boyhood – for a moment it crossed his mind to wonder what Alf might have been doing in his spare time. Any one of them seemed fit to find the star. But his eyes were mostly on Tim: a rather plump little boy, clumsy in the dances, but with a sweet voice in the singing. At table he sat silent watching the sharpening of the knife and the cutting of the Cake. Suddenly, he piped up: 'Dear Mr Cook, only cut me a small slice please. I've eaten so much already, I feel rather full.'

'All right, Tim,' said Alf. 'I'll cut you a special slice. I think you'll find it go down easily.'

Smith watched as Tim ate his cake slowly, but with evident pleasure; though when he found no trinket or coin in it he looked disappointed. But soon a light began to shine in his eyes, and he laughed and became merry, and sang softly to himself. Then he got up and began to dance all alone with an odd grace that he had never shown before. The children all laughed and clapped.

'All is well then,' thought Smith. 'So you are my heir. I wonder what strange places the star will lead you to? Poor old Nokes. Still I suppose he will never know what a shocking thing has happened in his family.'

He never did. But one thing happened at that Feast that pleased him mightily. Before it was over the Master Cook took leave of the children and of all the others that were present.

'I will say goodbye now,' he said. 'In a day or two I shall be going away. Master Harper is quite ready to take over. He is a very good cook, and as you know he comes from your own village. I shall go back home. I do not think you will miss me.'

The children said goodbye cheerfully, and thanked the Cook prettily for his beautiful Cake. Only little Tim took his hand and said quietly, 'I'm sorry.'

In the village there were in fact several families that did miss Alf for some time. A few of his friends, especially Smith and Harper, grieved at his going, and they kept the Hall gilded and painted in memory of Alf. Most people, however, were content. They had had him for a very long time and were not sorry to have a change. But old Nokes thumped his stick on the floor and said roundly: 'He's gone at last! And I'm glad for one. I never liked him. He was artful. Too nimble, you might say.'

LEAF BY NIGGLE

LEAF BY NIGGLE

There was once a little man called Niggle, who had a long
journey to make. He did not want to go, indeed the whole
idea was distasteful to him; but he could not get out of it.
He knew he would have to start sometime, but he did not
hurry with his preparations.

Niggle was a painter. Not a very successful one, partly
because he had many other things to do. Most of these
things he thought were a nuisance; but he did them fairly
well, when he could not get out of them: which (in his
opinion) was far too often. The laws in his country were
rather strict. There were other hindrances, too. For one
thing, he was sometimes just idle, and did nothing at all.
For another, he was kindhearted, in a way. You know the
sort of kind heart: it made him uncomfortable more often
than it made him do anything; and even when he did anything, it did not prevent him from grumbling, losing his
temper and swearing (mostly to himself). All the same, it
did land him in a good many odd jobs for his neighbour,

Mr Parish, a man with a lame leg. Occasionally he even helped other people from further off, if they came and asked him to. Also, now and again, he remembered his journey, and began to pack a few things in an ineffectual way: at such times he did not paint very much.

He had a number of pictures on hand; most of them were too large and ambitious for his skill. He was the sort of painter who can paint leaves better than trees. He used to spend a long time on a single leaf, trying to catch its shape, and its sheen, and the glistening of dewdrops on its edges. Yet he wanted to paint a whole tree, with all of its leaves in the same style, and all of them different.

There was one picture in particular which bothered him. It had begun with a leaf caught in the wind, and it became a tree; and the tree grew, sending out innumerable branches, and thrusting out the most fantastic roots. Strange birds came and settled on the twigs and had to be attended to. Then all round the Tree, and behind it, through the gaps in the leaves and boughs, a country began to open out; and there were glimpses of a forest marching over the land, and of mountains tipped with snow. Niggle lost interest in his other pictures; or else he took them and tacked them on to the edges of his great picture. Soon the canvas became so large that he had to get a ladder, and he ran up and down it, putting in a touch here, and rubbing out a patch there. When people came to call, he seemed polite enough, though he fiddled a little with the pencils on his desk. He listened to what they said, but underneath he was thinking all the time about his big canvas, in the tall shed that had been built for it out in his garden (on a plot where once he had grown potatoes).

He could not get rid of his kind heart. 'I wish I was more strong-minded' he sometimes said to himself, meaning that he wished other people's troubles did not make him feel uncomfortable. But for a long time he was not seriously perturbed. 'At any rate, I shall get this one picture done, my real picture, before I have to go on that wretched journey,' he used to say. Yet he was beginning to see that he could not put off his start indefinitely. The picture would have to stop just growing and get finished.

One day, Niggle stood a little way off from his picture and considered it with unusual attention and detachment. He could not make up his mind what he thought about it, and wished he had some friend who would tell him what to think. Actually it seemed to him wholly unsatisfactory, and yet very lovely, the only really beautiful picture in the world. What he would have liked at that moment would have been to see himself walk in, and slap him on the back and say (with obvious sincerity): 'Absolutely magnificent! I see exactly what you are getting at. Do get on with it, and don't bother about anything else! We will arrange for a public pension, so that you need not.'

However, there was no public pension. And one thing he could see: it would need some concentration, some *work*, hard uninterrupted work, to finish the picture, even at its present size. He rolled up his sleeves, and began to concentrate. He tried for several days not to bother about other things. But there came a tremendous crop of inter-ruptions. Things went wrong in his house; he had to go and serve on a jury in the town; a distant friend felt ill; Mr Parish was laid up with lumbago; and visitors kept on coming. It was springtime, and they wanted a free tea in the country: Niggle lived in a pleasant little house, miles away from the town. He cursed them in his heart, but he could not deny that he had invited them himself, away back in the winter, when he had not thought it an 'inter-ruption' to visit the shops and have tea with acquaintances in the town. He tried to harden his heart; but it was not a success. There were many things that he had not the face to say *no* to, whether he thought them duties or not; and there were some things he was compelled to do, whatever he thought. Some of his visitors hinted that his garden was rather neglected, and that he might get a visit from an Inspector. Very few of them knew about his picture, of course; but if they had known, it would not have made much difference. I doubt if they would have thought that it mattered much. I dare say it was not really a very good picture, though it may have had some good passages. The Tree, at any rate, was curious. Quite unique in its way. So was Niggle; though he was also a very ordinary and rather silly little man.

At length Niggle's time became really precious. His acquaintances in the distant town began to remember that the little man had got to make a troublesome journey, and some began to calculate how long at the latest he could put off starting. They wondered who would take his house, and if the garden would be better kept.

The autumn came, very wet and windy. The little painter was in his shed. He was up on the ladder, trying to catch the gleam of the westering sun on the peak of a snow-mountain, which he had glimpsed just to the left of the leafy tip of one of the Tree's branches. He knew that he would have to be leaving soon: perhaps early next year. He could only just get the picture finished, and only so so, at that: there were some corners where he would not have time now to do more than hint at what he wanted.

There was a knock on the door. 'Come in!' he said sharply, and climbed down the ladder. He stood on the floor twiddling his brush. It was his neighbour, Parish: his only real neighbour, all other folk lived a long way off. Still, he did not like the man very much: partly because he was so often in trouble and in need of help; and also because he did not care about painting, but was very critical about gardening. When Parish looked at Niggle's garden (which was often) he saw mostly weeds; and when he looked at Niggle's pictures (which was seldom) he saw only green and grey patches and black lines, which seemed to him nonsensical. He did not mind mentioning the weeds (a neighbourly duty), but he refrained from giving any opinion of the pictures. He thought this was very kind, and he did not realise that, even if it was kind, it was not kind enough. Help with the weeds (and perhaps praise for the pictures) would have been better.

'Well, Parish, what is it?' said Niggle.

'I oughtn't to interrupt you, I know,' said Parish (without a glance at the picture). 'You are very busy, I'm sure.'

Niggle had meant to say something like that himself, but he had missed his chance. All he said was: 'Yes.'

'But I have no one else to turn to,' said Parish.

'Quite so,' said Niggle with a sigh: one of those sighs that are a private comment, but which are not made quite inaudible. 'What can I do for you?'

'My wife has been ill for some days, and I am getting worried,' said Parish. 'And the wind has blown half the tiles off my roof, and water is pouring into the bedroom. I think I ought to get the doctor. And the builders, too, only they take so long to come. I was wondering if you had any wood and canvas you could spare, just to patch me up and see me through for a day or two.' Now he did look at the picture.

'Dear, dear!' said Niggle. 'You *are* unlucky. I hope it is no more than a cold that your wife has got. I'll come round presently, and help you move the patient downstairs.'

'Thank you very much,' said Parish, rather coolly. 'But it is not a cold, it is a fever. I should not have bothered you for a cold. And my wife is in bed downstairs already. I can't get up and down with trays, not with my leg. But I see you are busy. Sorry to have troubled you. I had rather hoped you might have been able to spare the time to go for the doctor, seeing how I'm placed; and the builder too, if you really have no canvas you can spare.'

'Of course,' said Niggle; though other words were in his heart, which at the moment was merely soft without feeling at all kind. 'I could go. I'll go, if you are really worried.'

'I am worried, very worried. I wish I was not lame,' said Parish.

So Niggle went. You see, it was awkward. Parish was his neighbour, and everyone else a long way off. Niggle had a bicycle, and Parish had not, and could not ride one. Parish had a lame leg, a genuine lame leg which gave him a good deal of pain: that had to be remembered, as well as his sour expression and whining voice. Of course, Niggle had a picture and barely time to finish it. But it seemed that this was a thing that Parish had to reckon with and not Niggle. Parish, however, did not reckon with pictures; and Niggle could not alter that. 'Curse it!' he said to himself, as he got out his bicycle.

It was wet and windy, and daylight was waning. 'No more work for me today!' thought Niggle, and all the time that he was riding, he was either swearing to himself, or imagining the strokes of his brush on the mountain, and on the spray of leaves beside it, that he had first imagined in the spring. His fingers twitched on the handlebars. Now he was out of the shed, he saw exactly the way in which to treat that shining spray which framed the distant vision of the mountain. But he had a sinking feeling in his heart, a sort of fear that he would never now get a chance to try it out.

Niggle found the doctor, and he left a note at the builder's. The office was shut, and the builder had gone home to his fireside. Niggle got soaked to the skin, and caught a chill himself. The doctor did not set out as promptly as Niggle had done. He arrived next day, which was quite convenient for him, as by that time there were two patients to deal with, in neighbouring houses. Niggle was in bed, with a high temperature, and marvellous patterns of leaves and involved branches forming in his head and on the ceiling. It did not comfort him to learn that Mrs Parish had only had a cold, and was getting up. He turned his face to the wall and buried himself in leaves.

He remained in bed some time. The wind went on blowing. It took away a good many more of Parish's tiles, and some of Niggle's as well: his own roof began to leak. The builder did not come. Niggle did not care; not for a day or two. Then he crawled out to look for some food (Niggle had no wife). Parish did not come round: the rain had got into his leg and made it ache; and his wife was busy mopping up water, and wondering if 'that Mr Niggle' had forgotten to call at the builder's. Had she seen any chance of borrowing anything useful, she would have sent Parish round, leg or no leg; but she did not, so Niggle was left to himself.

At the end of a week or so Niggle tottered out to his shed again. He tried to climb the ladder, but it made his head giddy. He sat and looked at the picture, but there were no patterns of leaves or visions of mountains in his mind that day. He could have painted a far-off view of a sandy desert, but he had not the energy.

Next day he felt a good deal better. He climbed the ladder, and began to paint. He had just begun to get into it again, when there came a knock on the door.

'Damn!' said Niggle. But he might just as well have said 'Come in!' politely, for the door opened all the same. This time a very tall man came in, a total stranger.

'This is a private studio,' said Niggle. 'I am busy. Go away!'

'I am an Inspector of Houses,' said the man, holding up his appointment-card, so that Niggle on his ladder could see it.

'Oh!' he said.

'Your neighbour's house is not satisfactory at all,' said the Inspector.

'I know,' said Niggle. 'I took a note to the builder's a long time ago, but they have never come. Then I have been ill.'

'I see,' said the Inspector. 'But you are not ill now.'

'But I'm not a builder. Parish ought to make a complaint to the Town Council, and get help from the Emergency Service.'

'They are busy with worse damage than any up here,' said the Inspector. 'There has been a flood in the valley, and many families are homeless. You should have helped your neighbour to make temporary repairs and prevent the damage from getting more costly to mend than necessary. That is the law. There is plenty of material here: canvas, wood, waterproof paint.'

'Where?' asked Niggle indignantly.

'There!' said the Inspector, pointing to the picture.

'My picture!' exclaimed Niggle.

'I dare say it is,' said the Inspector. 'But houses come first. That is the law.'

'But I can't . . .' Niggle said no more, for at that moment another man came in. Very much like the Inspector he was, almost his double: tall, dressed all in black.

'Come along!' he said. 'I am the Driver.'

Niggle stumbled down from the ladder. His fever seemed to have come on again, and his head was swimming; he felt cold all over.

'Driver? Driver?' he chattered. 'Driver of what?'

'You, and your carriage,' said the man. 'The carriage was ordered long ago. It has come at last. It's waiting. You start today on your journey, you know.'

'There now!' said the Inspector. 'You'll have to go; but it's a bad way to start on your journey, leaving your jobs undone. Still, we can at least make some use of this canvas now.'

'Oh dear!' said poor Niggle, beginning to weep. 'And it's not even finished!'

'Not finished!' said the Driver. 'Well, it's finished with, as far as you're concerned, at any rate. Come along!'

Niggle went, quite quietly. The Driver gave him no time to pack, saying that he ought to have done that before, and they would miss the train; so all Niggle could do was to grab a little bag in the hall. He found that it contained only a paint-box and a small book of his own sketches: neither food nor clothes. They caught the train all right. Niggle was feeling very tired and sleepy; he was hardly aware of what was going on when they bundled him into his compartment. He did not care much: he had forgotten where he was supposed to be going, or what he was going for. The train ran almost at once into a dark tunnel.

Niggle woke up in a very large, dim railway station. A Porter went along the platform shouting, but he was not shouting the name of the place; he was shouting *Niggle!*

Niggle got out in a hurry, and found that he had left his little bag behind. He turned back, but the train had gone away.

'Ah, there you are!' said the Porter. 'This way! What! No luggage? You will have to go to the Workhouse.'

Niggle felt very ill, and fainted on the platform. They put him in an ambulance and took him to the Workhouse Infirmary.

He did not like the treatment at all. The medicine they gave him was bitter. The officials and attendants were unfriendly, silent, and strict; and he never saw anyone else, except a very severe doctor, who visited him occasionally. It was more like being in a prison than in a hospital. He had to work hard, at stated hours: at digging, carpentry, and painting bare boards all one plain colour. He was never allowed outside, and the windows all looked inwards. They kept him in the dark for hours at a stretch, 'to do some thinking,' they said. He lost count of time. He did not even begin to feel better, not if that could be judged by whether he felt any pleasure in doing anything. He did not, not even in getting into bed.

At first, during the first century or so (I am merely giving his impressions), he used to worry aimlessly about the past. One thing he kept on repeating to himself, as he lay in the dark: 'I wish I had called on Parish the first morning after the high winds began. I meant to. The first loose tiles would have been easy to fix. Then Mrs Parish might never have caught cold. Then I should not have caught cold either. Then I should have had a week longer.' But in time he forgot what it was that he had wanted a week longer for. If he worried at all after that, it was about his jobs in the hospital. He planned them out, thinking how quickly he could stop that board creaking, or rehang that door, or mend that table-leg. Probably he really became rather useful, though no one ever told him so. But that, of course, cannot have been the reason why they kept the poor little man so long. They may have been waiting for him to get better, and judging 'better' by some odd medical standard of their own.

At any rate, poor Niggle got no pleasure out of life, not what he had been used to call pleasure. He was certainly not amused. But it could not be denied that he began to have a feeling of – well satisfaction: bread rather than jam. He could take up a task the moment one bell rang, and lay it aside promptly the moment the next one went, all tidy and ready to be continued at the right time. He got through quite a lot in a day, now; he finished small things off neatly. He had no 'time of his own' (except alone in his bed-cell), and yet he was becoming master of his time; he began to know just what he could do with it. There was no sense of rush. He was quieter inside now, and at resting-time he could really rest.

Then suddenly they changed all his hours; they hardly let him go to bed at all; they took him off carpentry altogether and kept him at plain digging, day after day. He took it fairly well. It was a long while before he even began to grope in the back of his mind for the curses that he had practically forgotten. He went on digging, till his back seemed broken, his hands were raw, and he felt that he could not manage another spadeful. Nobody thanked him. But the doctor came and looked at him.

'Knock off!' he said. 'Complete rest – in the dark.'

Niggle was lying in the dark, resting completely; so that, as he had not been either feeling or thinking at all, he might have been lying there for hours or for years, as far as he could tell. But now he heard Voices: not voices that he had ever heard before. There seemed to be a Medical

Board, or perhaps a Court of Inquiry, going on close at hand, in an adjoining room with the door open, possibly, though he could not see any light.

'Now the Niggle case,' said a Voice, a severe voice, more severe than the doctor's.

'What was the matter with him?' said a Second Voice, a voice that you might have called gentle, though it was not soft – it was a voice of authority, and sounded at once hopeful and sad. 'What was the matter with Niggle? His heart was in the right place.'

'Yes, but it did not function properly,' said the First Voice. 'And his head was not screwed on tight enough: he hardly ever thought at all. Look at the time he wasted, not even amusing himself! He never got ready for his journey. He was moderately well-off, and yet he arrived here almost destitute, and had to be put in the paupers' wing. A bad case, I am afraid. I think he should stay some time yet.'

'It would not do him any harm, perhaps,' said the Second Voice. 'But, of course, he is only a little man. He was never meant to be anything very much; and he was never very strong. Let us look at the Records. Yes. There are some favourable points, you know.'

'Perhaps,' said the First Voice; 'but very few that will really bear examination.'

'Well,' said the Second Voice, 'there are these. He was a painter by nature. In a minor way, of course; still, a Leaf by Niggle has a charm of its own. He took a great deal of pains with leaves, just for their own sake. But he never thought that that made him important. There is no note in the Records of his pretending, even to himself, that it excused his neglect of things ordered by the law.'

'Then he should not have neglected so many,' said the First Voice.

'All the same, he did answer a good many Calls.'

'A small percentage, mostly of the easier sort, and he called those Interruptions. The Records are full of the word, together with a lot of complaints and silly imprecations.'

'True; but they looked like interruptions to him, of course, poor little man. And there is this: he never expected any Return, as so many of his sort call it. There is the Parish case, the one that came in later. He was Niggle's neighbour, never did a stroke for him, and seldom showed any gratitude at all. But there is no note in the Records that Niggle expected Parish's gratitude; he does not seem to have thought about it.'

'Yes, that is a point,' said the First Voice; 'but rather small. I think you will find Niggle often merely forgot. Things he had to do for Parish he put out of his mind as a nuisance he had done with.'

'Still, there is this last report,' said the Second Voice, 'that wet bicycle-ride. I rather lay stress on that. It seems plain that this was a genuine sacrifice: Niggle guessed that he was throwing away his last chance with his picture, and he guessed, too, that Parish was worrying unnecessarily.'

'I think you put it too strongly,' said the First Voice. 'But you have the last word. It is your task, of course, to put the best interpretation on the facts. Sometimes they will bear it. What do you propose?'

'I think it is a case for a little gentle treatment now,' said the Second Voice.

Niggle thought that he had never heard anything so generous as that Voice. It made Gentle Treatment sound like a load of rich gifts, and a summons to a King's feast. Then suddenly Niggle felt ashamed. To hear that he was considered a case for Gentle Treatment overwhelmed him, and made him blush in the dark. It was like being publicly praised, when you and all the audience knew that the praise was not deserved. Niggle hid his blushes in the rough blanket.

There was a silence. Then the First Voice spoke to Niggle, quite close. 'You have been listening,' it said.

'Yes,' said Niggle.

'Well, what have you to say?'

'Could you tell me about Parish?' said Niggle. 'I should like to see him again. I hope he is not very ill? Can you cure his leg? It used to give him a wretched time. And please don't worry about him and me. He was a very good neighbour, and let me have excellent potatoes, very cheap, which saved me a lot of time.'

'Did he?' said the First Voice. 'I am glad to hear it.'

There was another silence. Niggle heard the Voices receding. 'Well, I agree,' he heard the First Voice say in the distance. 'Let him go on to the next stage. Tomorrow, if you like.'

*　*　*

Niggle woke up to find that his blinds were drawn, and his little cell was full of sunshine. He got up, and found that some comfortable clothes had been put out for him, not hospital uniform. After breakfast the doctor treated his sore hands, putting some salve on them that healed them at once. He gave Niggle some good advice, and a bottle of tonic (in case he needed it). In the middle of the morning they gave Niggle a biscuit and a glass of wine; and then they gave him a ticket.

'You can go to the railway station now,' said the doctor. 'The Porter will look after you. Goodbye.'

Niggle slipped out of the main door, and blinked a little. The sun was very bright. Also he had expected to walk out into a large town, to match the size of the station; but he did not. He was on the top of a hill, green, bare, swept by a keen invigorating wind. Nobody else was about. Away down under the hill he could see the roof of the station shining.

He walked downhill to the station briskly, but without hurry. The Porter spotted him at once.

'This way!' he said, and led Niggle to a bay, in which there was a very pleasant little local train standing: one coach, and a small engine, both very bright, clean, and newly painted. It looked as if this was their first run. Even the track that lay in front of the engine looked new: the rails shone, the chairs were painted green, and the sleepers gave off a delicious smell of fresh tar in the warm sunshine. The coach was empty.

'Where does this train go, Porter?' asked Niggle.

'I don't think they have fixed its name yet,' said the Porter. 'But you'll find it all right.' He shut the door.

The train moved off at once. Niggle lay back in his seat. The little engine puffed along in a deep cutting with high green banks, roofed with blue sky. It did not seem very long before the engine gave a whistle, the brakes were put on, and the train stopped. There was no station, and no signboard, only a flight of steps up the green embankment. At the top of the steps there was a wicket-gate in a trim hedge. By the gate stood his bicycle; at least, it looked like his, and there was a yellow label tied to the bars with NIGGLE written on it in large black letters.

Niggle pushed open the gate, jumped on the bicycle, and went bowling downhill in the spring sunshine. Before long he found that the path on which he had started had disappeared, and the bicycle was rolling along over a marvellous turf. It was green and close; and yet he could see every blade distinctly. He seemed to remember having seen or dreamed of that sweep of grass somewhere or other. The curves of the land were familiar somehow. Yes: the ground was becoming level, as it should, and now, of course, it was beginning to rise again. A great green shadow came between him and the sun. Niggle looked up, and fell off his bicycle.

Before him stood the Tree, his Tree, finished. If you could say that of a Tree that was alive, its leaves opening, its branches growing and bending in the wind that Niggle had so often felt or guesses, and had so often failed to catch. He gazed at the Tree, and slowly he lifted his arms and opened them wide.

'It's a gift!' he said. He was referring to his art, and also to the result; but he was using the word quite literally.

He went on looking at the Tree. All the leaves he had ever laboured at were there, as he had imagined them rather than as he had made them; and there were others that had only budded in his mind, and many that might have budded, if only he had had time. Nothing was written on them, they were just exquisite leaves, yet they were dated as clear as a calendar. Some of the most beautiful – and the most characteristic, the most perfect examples of the Niggle style – were seen to have been produced in collaboration with Mr Parish: there was no other way of putting it.

The birds were building in the Tree. Astonishing birds: how they sang! They were mating, hatching, growing wings, and flying away singing into the Forest even while he looked at them. For now he saw that the Forest was there too, opening out on either side, and marching away into the distance. The Mountains were glimmering far away.

After a time Niggle turned towards the Forest. Not because he was tired of the Tree, but he seemed to have got it all clear in his mind now, and was aware of it, and of its growth, even when he was not looking at it. As he walked away, he discovered an odd thing: the Forest, of course, was a distant Forest, yet he could approach it, even enter it, without its losing that particular charm. He had never before been able to walk into the distance without turning it into mere surroundings. It really added a considerable attraction to walking in the country, because, as you walked, new distances opened out; so that you now had double, treble, and quadruple distances, doubly, trebly, and quadruply enchanting. You could go on and on, and have a whole country in a garden, or in a picture (if you preferred to call it that). You could go on and on, but not perhaps for ever. There were the Mountains in the background. They did get nearer, very slowly. They did not seem to belong to the picture, or only as a link to something else, a glimpse through the trees of something different, a further stage: another picture.

Niggle walked about, but he was not merely pottering. He was looking round carefully. The Tree was finished, though not finished with – 'Just the other way about to what it used to be,' he thought – but in the Forest there were a number of inconclusive regions, that still needed work and thought. Nothing needed altering any longer, nothing was wrong, as far as it had gone, but it needed continuing up to a definite point. Niggle saw the point precisely, in each case.

He sat down under a very beautiful distant tree – a variation of the Great Tree, but quite individual, or it would be with a little more attention – and he considered where to begin work, and where to end it, and how much time was required. He could not quite work out his scheme.

'Of course!' he said. 'What I need is Parish. There are lots of things about earth, plants, and trees that he knows and I don't. This place cannot be left just as my private park. I need help and advice: I ought to have got it sooner.'

He got up and walked to the place where he had decided to begin work. He took off his coat. Then, down in a little sheltered hollow hidden from a further view, he saw a man looking round rather bewildered. He was leaning on a spade, but plainly did not know what to do. Niggle hailed him. 'Parish!' he called.

Parish shouldered his spade and came up to him. He still limped a little. They did not speak, just nodded as they used to do, passing in the lane, but now they walked about together, arm in arm. Without talking, Niggle and Parish agreed exactly where to make the small house and garden, which seemed to be required.

As they worked together, it became plain that Niggle was now the better of the two at ordering his time and getting things done. Oddly enough, it was Niggle who became most absorbed in building and gardening, while Parish often wandered about looking at trees, and especially at the Tree.

One day Niggle was busy planting a quickset hedge, and Parish was lying on the grass near by, looking attentively at a beautiful and shapely little yellow flower growing in the green turf. Niggle had put a lot of them among the roots of his Tree long ago. Suddenly parish looked up: his face was glistening in the sun, and he was smiling.

'This is grand!' he said. 'I oughtn't to be here, really. Thank you for putting in a word for me.'

'Nonsense,' said Niggle. 'I don't remember what I said, but anyway it was not nearly enough.'

'Oh yes, it was,' said Parish. 'It got me out a lot sooner. That Second Voice, you know: he had me sent here; he said you had asked to see me. I owe it to you.'

'No. You owe it to the Second Voice,' said Niggle. 'We both do.'

They went on living and working together: I do not know how long. It is no use denying that at first they occasionally disagreed, especially when they got tired. For at first they did sometimes get tired. They found that they had both been provided with tonics. Each bottle had the same label: *A few drops to be taken in water from the Spring, before resting.*

They found the Spring in the heart of the Forest; only once long ago had Niggle imagined it, but he had never drawn it. Now he perceived that it was the source of the lake that glimmered, far away and the nourishment of all that grew in the country. The few drops made the water astringent, rather bitter, but invigorating; and it cleared the head. After drinking they rested alone; and then they got up again and things went on merrily. At such times Niggle would think of wonderful new flowers and plants, and

Parish always knew exactly how to set them and where they would do best. Long before the tonics were finished they had ceased to need them. Parish lost his limp.

As their work drew to an end they allowed themselves more and more time for walking about, looking at the trees, and the flowers, and the lights and shapes, and the lie of the land. Sometimes they sang together; but Niggle found that he was now beginning to turn his eyes, more and more often, towards the Mountains.

The time came when the house in the hollow, the garden, the grass, the forest, the lake, and all the country was nearly complete, in its own proper fashion. The Great Tree was in full blossom.

'We shall finish this evening,' said Parish one day. 'After that we will go for a really long walk.'

They set out next day, and they walked until they came right through the distances to the Edge. It was not visible, of course: there was no line, or fence, or wall; but they knew that they had come to the margin of that country. They saw a man, he looked like a shepherd; he was walking towards them, down the grass-slopes that led up into the Mountains.

'Do you want a guide?' he asked. 'Do you want to go on?'

For a moment a shadow fell between Niggle and Parish, for Niggle knew that he did now want to go on, and (in a sense) ought to go on; but Parish did not want to go on, and was not yet ready to go.

'I must wait for my wife,' said Parish to Niggle. 'She'd be lonely. I rather gathered that they would send her after me, some time or other, when she was ready, and when I had got things ready for her. The house is finished now, as well as we could make it; but I should like to show it to her. She'll be able to make it better, I expect: more homely. I hope she'll like this country, too.' He turned to the shepherd. 'Are you a guide?' he asked. 'Could you tell me the name of this country?'

'Don't you know?' said the man. 'It is Niggle's Country. It is Niggle's Picture, or most of it: a little of it is now Parish's Garden.'

'Niggle's Picture!' said Parish in astonishment. 'Did *you* think of all this, Niggle? I never knew you were so clever. Why didn't you tell me?'

'He tried to tell you long ago,' said the man, 'but you would not look. He had only got canvas and paint in those days, and you wanted to mend your roof with them. This is what you and your wife used to call Niggle's Nonsense, or That Daubing.'

'But it did not look like this then, not *real*,' said Parish.

'No, it was only a glimpse then,' said the man; 'but you might have caught the glimpse, if you had ever thought it worth while to try.'

'I did not give you much chance,' said Niggle. 'I never tried to explain. I used to call you Old Earthgrubber. But what does it matter? We have lived and worked together now. Things might have been different, but they could not have been better. All the same, I am afraid I shall have to be going on. We shall meet again, I expect: there must be many more things we can do together. Goodbye!' He shook Parish's hand warmly: a good, firm, honest hand it seemed. He turned and looked back for a moment. The blossom on the Great Tree was shining like flame. All the birds were flying in the air and singing. Then he smiled and nodded to Parish and went off with the shepherd.

He was going to learn about sheep, and the high pasturages, and look at a wider sky, and walk ever further and further towards the Mountains, always uphill. Beyond that I cannot guess what became of him. Even little Niggle in his old home could glimpse the Mountains far away, and they got into the borders of his picture; but what they are really like, and what lies beyond them only those can say who have climbed them.

'I think he was a silly little man,' said Councillor Tompkins. 'Worthless, in fact; no use to Society at all.'

'Oh, I don't know,' said Atkins, who was nobody of importance, just a schoolmaster. 'I am not so sure; it depends on what you mean by use.'

'No practical or economic use,' said Tompkins. 'I dare say he could have been made into a serviceable cog of some sort, if you schoolmasters knew your business. But you don't, and so we get useless people of his sort. If I ran this country I should put him and his like to some job that they're fit for, washing dishes in a communal kitchen or something, and I should see that they did it properly. Or I would put them away. I should have put *him* away long ago.'

'Put him away? You mean you'd have made him start on the journey before his time?'

'Yes, if you must use that meaningless old expression. Push him through the tunnel into the great Rubbish Heap: that's what I mean.'

'Then you don't think painting is worth anything, not worth preserving, or improving, or even making use of?'

'Of course, painting has uses,' said Tompkins. 'But you couldn't make use of his painting. There is plenty of scope for bold young men not afraid of new ideas and new methods. None for this old-fashioned stuff. Private daydreaming. He could not have designed a telling poster to save his life. Always fiddling with leaves and flowers. I asked him why, once. He said he thought they were pretty! Can you believe it? He said *pretty!* "What, digestive and genital organs of plants?" I said to him; and he had nothing to answer. Silly footler.'

'Footler,' sighed Atkins. 'Yes, poor little man, he never finished anything. Ah well, his canvases have been put to "better uses", since he went. But I am not so sure, Tompkins. You remember that large one, the one they used to patch the damaged house next door to his, after the gales and floods? I found a corner of it torn off, lying in a field. It was damaged, but legible: a mountain-peak and a spray of leaves. I can't get it out of my mind.'

'Out of your what?' said Tompkins.

'Who are you two talking about?' said Perkins, intervening in the cause of peace: Atkins had flushed rather red.

'The name's not worth repeating,' said Tompkins. 'I don't know why we are talking about him at all. He did not live in town.'

'No,' said Atkins; 'but you had your eye on his house, all the same. That is why you used to go and call, and sneer at him while drinking his tea. Well, you've got his house now, as well as the one in town, so you need not grudge him his name. We were talking about Niggle, if you want to know, Perkins.'

'Oh, poor little Niggle!' said Perkins. 'Never knew he painted.'

That was probably the last time Niggle's name ever came up in conversation. However, Atkins preserved the odd corner. Most of it crumbled; but one beautiful leaf remained intact. Atkins had it framed. Later he left it to the Town Museum, and for a long time while 'Leaf: by Niggle' hung there in a recess, and was noticed by a few eyes. But eventually the Museum was burnt down, and the leaf, and Niggle, were entirely forgotten in his old country.

'It is proving very useful indeed,' said the Second Voice. 'As a holiday, and a refreshment. It is splendid for convalescence; and not only for that, for many it is the best introduction to the Mountains. It works wonders in some cases. I am sending more and more there. They seldom have to come back.'

'No, that is so,' said the First Voice. 'I think we shall have to give the region a name. What do you propose?'

'The Porter settled that some time ago,' said the Second Voice. '*Train for Niggle's Parish in the bay:* he has shouted that for a long while now. Niggle's Parish. I sent a message to both of them to tell them.'

'What did they say?'

'They both laughed. Laughed – the Mountains rang with it!'

APPENDIX

ON FAIRY-STORIES

I propose to speak about fairy-stories, though I am aware that this is a rash adventure. Faërie is a perilous land, and in it are pitfalls for the unwary and dungeons for the over-bold. And overbold I may be accounted, for though I have been a lover of fairy-stories since I learned to read, and have at times thought about them, I have not studied them professionally. I have been hardly more than a wandering explorer (or trespasser) in the land, full of wonder but not of information.

The realm of fairy-story is wide and deep and high and filled with many things: all manner of beasts and birds are found there; shoreless seas and stars uncounted; beauty that is an enchantment, and an ever-present peril; both joy and sorrow as sharp as swords. In that realm a man may, perhaps, count himself fortunate to have wandered, but its very richness and strangeness tie the tongue of a traveller who would report them. And while he is there it is dangerous for him to ask too many questions, lest the gates should be shut and the keys be lost.

There are, however, some questions that one who is to speak about fairy-stories must expect to answer, or attempt to answer, whatever the folk of Faërie may think of his impertinence. For instance: What are fairy-stories? What is their origin? What is the use of them? I will try to give answers to these questions, or such hints of answers to them as I have gleaned – primarily from the stories themselves, the few of all their multitude that I know.

FAIRY-STORY

What is a fairy-story? In this case you will turn to the *Oxford English Dictionary* in vain. It contains no reference to the combination *fairy-story,* and is unhelpful on the subject of *fairies* generally. In the Supplement, *fairy-tale* is recorded since the year 1750, and its leading sense is said to be (*a*) a tale about fairies, or generally a fairy legend; with developed senses, (*b*) an unreal or incredible story, and (*c*) a falsehood.

The last two senses would obviously make my topic hopelessly vast. But the first sense is too narrow. Not too narrow for an essay; it is wide enough for many books, but too narrow to cover actual usage. Especially so, if we accept the lexicographer's definition of *fairies:* 'supernatural beings of diminutive size, in popular belief supposed to possess magical powers and to have great influence for good or evil over the affairs of man'.

Supernatural is a dangerous and difficult word in any of its senses, looser or stricter. But to fairies it can hardly be applied, unless *super* is taken merely as a superlative prefix. For it is man who is, in contrast to fairies, supernatural (and often of diminutive stature); whereas they are natural, far more natural than he. Such is their doom. The road to fairyland is not the road to Heaven; nor even to Hell, I believe, though some have held that it may lead thither indirectly by the Devil's tithe.

> O see ye not yon narrow road
> So thick beset wi' thorns and briers?
> That is the path of Righteousness,
> Though after it but few inquires.
>
> And see ye not yon braid, braid road
> That lies across the lily leven?
> That is the path of Wickedness,
> Though some call it the Road to Heaven.
>
> And see ye not yon bonny road
> That winds about yon fernie brae?
> That is the road to fair Elfland,
> Where thou and I this night maun gae.

As for *diminutive size:* I do not deny that the notion is a leading one in modern use. I have often thought that it would be interesting to try to find out how that has come to be so; but my knowledge is not sufficient for a certain answer. Of old there were indeed some inhabitants of Faërie that were small (though hardly diminutive), but smallness was not characteristic of that people as a whole. The diminutive being, elf or fairy, is (I guess) in England largely a sophisticated product of literary fancy.[1] It is perhaps not unnatural that in England, the land where the love of the delicate and fine has often reappeared in art, fancy should in this matter turn towards the dainty and diminutive, as in France it went to court and put on powder and diamonds. Yet I suspect that this flower-and-butterfly minuteness was also a product of 'rationalisation', which transformed the glamour of Elfland into mere finesse, and invisibility into a fragility that could hide in a cowslip or shrink behind a blade of grass. It seems to become fashionable soon after the great voyages had begun to make the world seem too narrow to hold both men and elves; when the magic land of Hy Breasail in the West had become the mere Brazils, the land of red-dye-wood.[2] In any case it was largely a literary business in which

---

[1] I am speaking of developments before the growth of interest in the folk-lore of other countries. The English words, such as *elf,* have long been influenced by French (from which *fay* and *faërie, fairy* are derived); but in later times, through their use in translation, both *fairy* and *elf* have acquired much of the atmosphere of German, Scandinavian, and Celtic tales, and many characteristics of the *huldu-fólk,* the *daoine-sithe,* and the *tylwyth teg.*

[2] For the probability that the Irish *Hy Breasail* played a part in the naming of Brazil see Nansen, *In Northern Mists,* ii, 223-30.

William Shakespeare and Michael Drayton played a part.[1] Drayton's *Nymphidia* is one ancestor of that long line of flower-fairies and fluttering sprites with antennae that I so disliked as a child, and which my children in their turn detested. Andrew Lang had similar feelings. In the preface to the *Lilac Fairy Book* he refers to the tales of tiresome contemporary authors: 'they always begin with a little boy or girl who goes out and meets the fairies of polyanthuses and gardenias and apple-blossom... These fairies try to be funny and fail; or they try to preach and succeed.'

But the business began, as I have said, long before the nineteenth century, and long ago achieved tiresomeness, certainly the tiresomeness of trying to be funny and failing. Drayton's *Nymphidia* is, considered as a fairy-story (a story about fairies), one of the worst ever written. The palace of Oberon has walls of spider's legs,

> And windows of the eyes of cats,
> And for the roof, instead of slats,
> Is covered with the wings of bats.

The knight Pigwiggen rides on a frisky earwig, and sends his love, Queen Mab, a bracelet of emmets' eyes, making an assignation in a cowslip-flower. But the tale that is told

---

[1] Their influence was not confined to England. German *Elf, Elfe* appears to be derived from *A Midsummer-night's Dream*, in Wieland's translation (1764).

amid all this prettiness is a dull story of intrigue and sly go-betweens; the gallant knight and angry husband fall into the mire, and their wrath is stilled by a draught of the waters of Lethe. It would have been better if Lethe had swallowed the whole affair. Oberon, Mab, and Pigwiggen may be diminutive elves or fairies, as Arthur, Guinevere, and Lancelot are not; but the good and evil story of Arthur's court is a 'fairy-story' rather than this tale of Oberon.

Fairy, as a noun more or less equivalent to *elf,* is a relatively modern word, hardly used until the Tudor period. The first quotation in the *Oxford Dictionary* (the only one before A.D. 1450) is significant. It is taken from the poet Gower: *as he were a faierie.* But this Gower did not say. He wrote *as he were of faierie,* 'as if he were come from Faërie'. Gower was describing a young gallant who seeks to bewitch the hearts of the maidens in church.

> His croket kembd and thereon set
> A Nouche with a chapelet,
> Or elles one of grene leves
> Which late com out of the greves,
> Al for he sholde seme freissh;
> And thus he loketh on the fleissh,
> Riht as an hauk which hath a sihte
> Upon the foul ther he schal lihte,
> And as he were of faierie
> He scheweth him tofore here yhe.[1]

[1] *Confessio Amantis,* v. 7065 ff.

This is a young man of mortal blood and bone; but he gives a much better picture of the inhabitants of Elfland than the definition of a 'fairy' under which he is, by a double error, placed. For the trouble with the real folk of Faërie is that they do not always look like what they are; and they put on the pride and beauty that we would fain wear ourselves. At least part of the magic that they wield for the good or evil of man is power to play on the desires of his body and his heart. The Queen of Elfland, who carried off Thomas the Rhymer upon her milk-white steed swifter than the wind, came riding by the Eildon Tree as a lady, if one of enchanting beauty. So that Spenser was in the true tradition when he called the knights of his Faërie by the name of Elfe. It belonged to such knights as Sir Guyon rather than to Pigwiggen armed with a hornet's sting.

Now, though I have only touched (wholly inadequately) on *elves* and *fairies,* I must turn back; for I have digressed from my proper theme: fairy-stories. I said the sense 'stories about fairies' was too narrow.[1] It is too narrow, even if we reject the diminutive size, for fairy-stories are not in normal English usage stories *about* fairies or elves, but stories about Fairy, that is *Faërie,* the

---

[1] Except in special cases such as collections of Welsh or Gaelic tales. In these the stories about the 'Fair Family' or the Shee-folk are sometimes distinguished as 'fairy-tales' from 'folk-tales' concerning other marvels. In this use 'fairytales' or 'fairy-lore' are usually short accounts of the appearances of 'fairies' or their intrusions upon the affairs of men. But this distinction is a product of translation.

realm or state in which fairies have their being. *Faërie* contains many things besides elves and fays, and besides dwarfs, witches, trolls, giants, or dragons: it holds the seas, the sun, the moon, the sky; and the earth, and all things that are in it: tree and bird, water and stone, wine and bread, and ourselves, mortal men, when we are enchanted.

Stories that are actually concerned primarily with 'fairies', that is with creatures that might also in modern English be called 'elves', are relatively rare, and as a rule not very interesting. Most good 'fairy-stories' are about the *aventures* of men in the Perilous Realm or upon its shadowy marches. Naturally so; for if elves are true, and really exist independently of our tales about them, then this also is certainly true: elves are not primarily concerned with us, nor we with them. Our fates are sundered, and our paths seldom meet. Even upon the borders of Faërie we encounter them only at some chance crossing of the ways.[1]

The definition of a fairy-story – what it is, or what it should be – does not, then, depend on any definition or historical account of elf or fairy, but upon the nature of *Faërie:* the Perilous Realm itself, and the air that blows in that country. I will not attempt to define that, nor to describe it directly. It cannot be done. Faërie cannot be

---

[1]   This is true also, even if they are only creations of Man's mind, 'true' only as reflecting in a particular way one of Man's visions of Truth.

caught in a net of words; for it is one of its qualities to be indescribable, though not imperceptible. It has many ingredients, but analysis will not necessarily discover the secret of the whole. Yet I hope that what I have later to say about the other questions will give some glimpses of my own imperfect vision of it. For the moment I will say only this: a 'fairy-story' is one which touches on or uses Faërie, whatever its own main purpose may be: satire, adventure, morality, fantasy. Faërie itself may perhaps most nearly be translated by Magic[I] – but it is magic of a peculiar mood and power, at the furthest pole from the vulgar devices of the laborious, scientific, magician. There is one proviso: if there is any satire present in the tale, one thing must not be made fun of, the magic itself. That must in that story be taken seriously, neither laughed at nor explained away. Of this seriousness the medieval *Sir Gawain and the Green Knight* is an admirable example.

But even if we apply only these vague and ill-defined limits, it becomes plain that many, even the learned in such matters, have used the term 'fairy-tale' very care-lessly. A glance at those books of recent times that claim to be collections of 'fairy-stories' is enough to show that tales about fairies, about the fair family in any of its houses, or even about dwarfs and goblins, are only a small part of their content. That, as we have seen, was to be expected. But these books also contain many tales that do

[I] See further below, p. 368.

not use, do not even touch upon, Faërie at all; that have in fact no business to be included.

I will give one or two examples of the expurgations I would perform. This will assist the negative side of definition. It will also be found to lead on to the second question: what are the origins of fairy-stories?

The number of collections of fairy-stories is now very great. In English none probably rival either the popularity, or the inclusiveness, or the general merits of the twelve books of twelve colours which we owe to Andrew Lang and to his wife. The first of these appeared more than fifty years ago (1889), and is still in print. Most of its contents pass the test, more or less clearly. I will not analyse them, though an analysis might be interesting, but I note in passing that of the stories in this *Blue Fairy Book* none are primarily about 'fairies', few refer to them. Most of the tales are taken from French sources: a just choice in some ways at that time, as perhaps it would be still (though not to my taste, now or in childhood). At any rate, so powerful has been the influence of Charles Perrault, since his *Contes de ma Mère l'Oye* were first Englished in the eighteenth century, and of such other excerpts from the vast storehouse of the *Cabinet des Fées* as have become well known, that still, I suppose, if you asked a man to name at random a typical 'fairy-story', he would be most likely to name one of these French things: such as *Puss-in-Boots, Cinderella,* or *Little Red Riding Hood.* With some people *Grimm's Fairy Tales* might come first to mind.

But what is to be said of the appearance in the *Blue Fairy Book* of *A Voyage to Lilliput?* I will say this: it is *not* a fairy-story, neither as its author made it, nor as it here appears 'condensed' by Miss May Kendall. It has no business in this place. I fear that it was included merely because Lilliputians are small, even diminutive – the only way in which they are at all remarkable. But smallness is in Faërie, as in our world, only an accident. Pygmies are no nearer to fairies than are Patagonians. I do not rule this story out because of its satirical intent: there is satire, sustained or intermittent, in undoubted fairy-stories, and satire may often have been intended in traditional tales where we do not now perceive it. I rule it out, because the vehicle of the satire, brilliant invention though it may be, belongs to the class of travellers' tales. Such tales report many marvels, but they are marvels to be seen in this mortal world in some region of our own time and space; distance alone conceals them. The tales of Gulliver have no more right of entry than the yarns of Baron Munchausen; or than, say, *The First Men in the Moon* or *The Time-Machine.* Indeed, for the Eloi and the Morlocks there would be a better claim than for the Lilliputians. Lilliputians are merely men peered down at, sardonically, from just above the house-tops. Eloi and Morlocks live far away in an abyss of time so deep as to work an enchantment upon them; and if they are descended from ourselves, it may be remembered that an ancient English thinker once derived the *ylfe,* the very elves, through Cain from Adam.[1] This enchantment of distance, especially of distant time, is weakened only by the preposterous and incredible Time Machine itself. But we see in this example one of the main reasons why the borders of fairy-story are inevitably dubious. The magic of Faërie is not an end in itself, its virtue is in its operations: among these are the satisfaction of certain primordial human desires. One of these desires is to survey the depths of space and time. Another is (as will be seen) to hold communion with other living things. A story may thus deal with the satisfaction of these desires, with or without the operation of either machine or magic, and in proportion as it succeeds it will approach the quality and have the flavour of fairy-story.

Next, after travellers' tales, I would also exclude, or rule out of order, any story that uses the machinery of Dream, the dreaming of actual human sleep, to explain the apparent occurrence of its marvels. At the least, even if the reported dream was in other respects in itself a fairy-story, I would condemn the whole as gravely defective: like a good picture in a disfiguring frame. It is true that Dream is not unconnected with Faërie. In dreams strange powers of the mind may be unlocked. In some of them a man may for a space wield the power of Faërie, that power which, even as it conceives the story, causes it to take living form and colour before the eyes. A real dream may indeed

[1] *Beowulf*, 111-12.

sometimes be a fairy-story of almost elvish ease and skill – while it is being dreamed. But if a waking writer tells you that his tale is only a thing imagined in his sleep, he cheats deliberately the primal desire at the heart of Faërie: the realization, independent of the conceiving mind, of imagined wonder. It is often reported of fairies (truly or lyingly, I do not know) that they are workers of illusion, that they are cheaters of men by 'fantasy'; but that is quite another matter. That is their affair. Such trickeries happen, at any rate, inside tales in which the fairies are not themselves illusions; behind the fantasy real wills and powers exist, independent of the minds and purposes of men.

It is at any rate essential to a genuine fairy-story, as distinct from the employment of this form for lesser or debased purposes, that it should be presented as 'true'. The meaning of 'true' in this connection I will consider in a moment. But since the fairy-story deals with 'marvels', it cannot tolerate any frame or machinery suggesting that the whole story in which they occur is a figment or illusion. The tale itself may, of course, be so good that one can ignore the frame. Or it may be successful and amusing as a dream-story. So are Lewis Carroll's *Alice* stories, with their dream-frame and dream-transitions. For this (and other reasons) they are not fairy-stories.[1]

There is another type of marvellous tale that I would exclude from the title 'fairy-story', again certainly not

[1] See Note A at the end (p. 389).

because I do not like it: namely pure 'Beast-fable'. I will choose an example from Lang's Fairy Books: *The Monkey's Heart*, a Swahili tale which is given in the *Lilac Fairy Book*. In this story a wicked shark tricked a monkey into riding on his back, and carried him half-way to his own land, before he revealed the fact that the sultan of that country was sick and needed a monkey's heart to cure his disease. But the monkey outwitted the shark, and induced him to return by convincing him that the heart had been left behind at home, hanging in a bag on a tree.

The beast-fable has, of course, a connection with fairy-stories. Beasts and birds and other creatures often talk like men in real fairy-stories. In some part (often small) this marvel derives from one of the primal 'desires' that lie near the heart of Faërie: the desire of men to hold communion with other living things. But the speech of beasts in the beast-fable, as developed into a separate branch, has little reference to that desire, and often wholly forgets it. The magical understanding by men of the proper languages of birds and beasts and trees, that is much nearer to the true purposes of Faërie. But in stories in which no human being is concerned; or in which the animals are the heroes and heroines, and men and women, if they appear, are mere adjuncts; and above all those in which the animal form is only a mask upon a human face, a device of the satirist or the preacher, in these we have beast-fable and not fairy-story: whether it be *Reynard the Fox*, or *The Nun's Priest's Tale*, or *Brer Rabbit*, or merely *The Three Little Pigs*. The stories of Beatrix Potter lie near the borders of Faërie, but outside it, I think, for the most part.[1] Their nearness is due largely to their strong moral element: by which I mean their inherent morality, not any allegorical *significatio*. But *Peter Rabbit*, though it contains a prohibition, and though there are prohibitions in fairyland (as, probably, there are throughout the universe on every plane and in every dimension), remains a beast-fable.

Now *The Monkey's Heart* is also plainly only a beast-fable. I suspect that its inclusion in a 'Fairy Book' is due not primarily to its entertaining quality, but precisely to the monkey's heart supposed to have been left behind in a bag. That was significant to Lang, the student of folk-lore, even though this curious idea is here used only as a joke; for, in this tale, the monkey's heart was in fact quite normal and in his breast. None the less this detail is plainly only a secondary use of an ancient and very widespread folk-lore notion, which does occur in fairy-stories;[2] the notion that the life or strength of a man or creature may reside in some other place or thing; or in

---

[1] *The Tailor of Gloucester* perhaps comes nearest. *Mrs. Tiggywinkle* would be as near, but for the hinted dream-explanation. I would also include *The Wind in the Willows* in Beast-fable.

[2] Such as, for instance: *The Giant that had no Heart* in Dasent's *Popular Tales from the Norse;* or *The Sea-Maiden* in Campbell's *Popular Tales of the West Highlands* (no. iv, cf. also no. i); or more remotely *Die Kristallkugel* in Grimm.

some part of the body (especially the heart) that can be detached and hidden in a bag, or under a stone, or in an egg. At one end of recorded folk-lore history this idea was used by George MacDonald in his fairy-story *The Giant's Heart*, which derives this central motive (as well as many other details) from well-known traditional tales. At the other end, indeed in what is probably one of the oldest stories in writing, it occurs in *The Tale of the Two Brothers* on the Egyptian D'Orsigny papyrus. There the younger brother says to the elder:

> 'I shall enchant my heart, and I shall place it upon the top of the flower of the cedar. Now the cedar will be cut down and my heart will fall to the ground, and thou shalt come to seek for it, even though thou pass seven years in seeking it; but when thou has found it, put it into a vase of cold water, and in very truth I shall live.'[1]

But that point of interest and such comparisons as these bring us to the brink of the second question: What are the origins of 'fairy-stories'? That must, of course, mean: the origin or origins of the fairy elements. To ask what is the origin of stories (however qualified) is to ask what is the origin of language and of the mind.

---

[1]   Budge, *Egyptian Reading Book*, p. xxi

ORIGINS

Actually the question: What is the origin of the fairy element? lands us ultimately in the same fundamental inquiry; but there are many elements in fairy-stories (such as this detachable heart, or swan-robes, magic rings, arbitrary prohibitions, wicked step-mothers, and even fairies themselves) that such can be studied without tackling this main question. Such studies are, however, scientific (at least in intent); they are the pursuit of folklorists or anthropologists: that is of people using the stories not as they were meant to be used, but as a quarry from which to dig evidence, or information, about matters in which they are interested. A perfectly legitimate procedure in itself – but ignorance or forgetfulness of the nature of a story (as a thing told in its entirety) has often led such inquirers into strange judgements. To investigators of this sort recurring similarities (such as this matter of the heart) seem specially important. So much so that students of folk-lore are apt to get off their own proper track, or to express themselves in a misleading 'shorthand': misleading in particular, if it gets out of their monographs into books about literature. They are inclined to say that any two stories that are built round the same folk-lore motive, or are made up of a generally similar combination of such motives, are 'the same stories'. We read that *Beowulf* 'is only a version of *Dat Erdmänneken*'; that '*The Black Bull of Norroway* is *Beauty and the Beast*', or 'is the same story as *Eros and Psyche*'; that the Norse *Mastermaid* (or the

Gaelic *Battle of the Birds*[1] and its many congeners and variants) is 'the same story as the Greek tale of Jason and Medea'.

Statements of that kind may express (in undue abbreviation) some element of truth; but they are not true in a fairy-story sense, they are not true in art or literature. It is precisely the colouring, the atmosphere, the unclassifiable individual details of a story, and above all the general purport that informs with life the undissected bones of the plot, that really count. Shakespeare's *King Lear* is not the same as Layamon's story in his *Brut.* Or to take the extreme case of *Red Riding Hood:* it is of merely secondary interest that the re-told versions of this story, in which the little girl is saved by wood-cutters, is directly derived from Perrault's story in which she was eaten by the wolf. The really important thing is that the later version has a happy ending (more or less, and if we do not mourn the grandmother overmuch), and that Perrault's version had not. And that is a very profound difference, to which I shall return.

Of course, I do not deny, for I feel strongly, the fascination of the desire to unravel the intricately knotted and ramified history of the branches on the Tree of Tales. It is closely connected with the philologists' study of the tangled skein of Language, of which I know some small pieces. But even with regard to language it seems to me

[1] See Campbell, op. cit., vol. i

that the essential quality and aptitudes of a given language in a living moment is both more important to seize and far more difficult to make explicit than its linear history. So with regard to fairy-stories, I feel that it is more interesting, and also in its way more difficult, to consider what they are, what they have become for us, and what values the long alchemic processes of time have produced in them. In Dasent's words I would say: 'We must be satisfied with the soup that is set before us, and not desire to see the bones of the ox out of which it has been boiled.'[1] Though, oddly enough, Dasent by 'the soup' meant a mishmash of bogus pre-history founded on the early surmises of Comparative Philology; and by 'desire to see the bones' he meant a demand to see the workings and the proofs that led to these theories. By 'the soup' I mean the story as it is served up by its author or teller, and by 'the bones' its sources or material – even when (by rare luck) those can be with certainty discovered. But I do not, of course, forbid criticism of the soup as soup.

I shall therefore pass lightly over the question of origins. I am too unlearned to deal with it in any other way; but it is the least important of the three questions for my purpose, and a few remarks will suffice. It is plain enough that fairy-stories (in wider or in narrower sense) are very ancient indeed. Related things appear in very

[1] *Popular Tales from the Norse*, p. xviii

early records; and they are found universally, wherever there is language. We are therefore obviously confronted with a variant of the problem that the archaeologist encounters, or the comparative philologist: with the debate between *independent evolution* (or rather *invention*) of the similar; *inheritance* from a common ancestry; and *diffusion* at various times from one or more centres. Most debates depend on an attempt (by one or both sides) at over-simplification; and I do not suppose that this debate is an exception. The history of fairy-stories is probably more complex than the physical history of the human race, and as complex as the history of human language. All three things: independent invention, inheritance, and diffusion, have evidently played their part in producing the intricate web of Story. It is now beyond all skill but that of the elves to unravel it.[1] Of these three *invention* is the most important and fundamental, and so (not surprisingly) also the most mysterious. To an inventor, that is to a story-maker, the other two must in the end lead back. *Diffusion* (borrowing in space) whether of an artefact or a story, only refers the problem of origin elsewhere. At the centre of the

---

[1] Except in particularly fortunate cases; or in a few occasional details. It is indeed easier to unravel a single *thread* – an incident, a name, a motive – than to trace the history of any *picture* defined by many threads. For with the picture in the tapestry a new element has come in: the picture is greater than, and not explained by, the sum of the component threads. Therein lies the inherent weakness of the analytic (or 'scientific') method: it finds out much about things that occur in stories, but little or nothing about their effect in any given story.

supposed diffusion there is a place where once an inventor lived. Similarly with *inheritance* (borrowing in time): in this way we arrive at last only at an ancestral inventor. While if we believe that sometimes there occurred the independent striking out of similar ideas and themes or devices, we simply multiply the ancestral inventor but do not in that way the more clearly understand his gift.

Philology has been dethroned from the high place it once had in this court of inquiry. Max Müller's view of mythology as a 'disease of language' can be abandoned without regret. Mythology is not a disease at all, though it may like all human things become diseased. You might as well say that thinking is a disease of the mind. It would be more near the truth to say that languages, especially modern European languages, are a disease of mythology. But Language cannot, all the same, be dismissed. The incarnate mind, the tongue, and the tale are in our world coeval. The human mind, endowed with the powers of generalisation and abstraction, sees not only *green-grass,* discriminating it from other things (and finding it fair to look upon), but sees that it is *green* as well as being *grass.* But how powerful, how stimulating to the very faculty that produced it, was the invention of the adjective: no spell or incantation in Faërie is more potent. And that is not surprising: such incantations might indeed be said to be only another view of adjectives, a part of speech in a mythical grammar. The mind that thought of *light, heavy, grey, yellow, still, swift,* also conceived of magic that would make heavy things light and able to fly, turn grey lead into yellow gold, and the still rock into a swift water. If it could do the one, it could do the other; it inevitably did both. When we can take green from grass, blue from heaven, and red from blood, we have already an enchanter's power – upon one plane; and the desire to wield that power in the world external to our minds awakes. It does not follow that we shall use that power well upon any plane. We may put a deadly green upon a man's face and produce a horror; we may make the rare and terrible blue moon to shine; or we may cause woods to spring with silver leaves and rams to wear fleeces of gold, and put hot fire into the belly of the cold worm. But in such 'fantasy', as it is called, new form is made; Faërie begins; Man becomes a sub-creator.

An essential power of Faërie is thus the power of making immediately effective by the will the visions of 'fantasy'. Not all are beautiful or even wholesome, not at any rate the fantasies of fallen Man. And he has stained the elves who have this power (in verity or fable) with his own stain. This aspect of 'mythology' – sub-creation, rather than either representation or symbolic interpretation of the beauties and terrors of the world – is, I think, too little considered. Is that because it is seen rather in Faërie than upon Olympus? Because it is thought to belong to the 'lower mythology' rather than to the 'higher'? There has been much debate concerning the relations of these things, of *folk-tale* and *myth;* but, even if there had been no debate, the question would require some notice in any consideration of origins, however brief.

At one time it was a dominant view that all such matter was derived from 'nature-myths'. The Olympians were *personifications* of the sun, of dawn, of night, and so on, and all the stories told about them were originally *myths* (*allegories* would have been a better word) of the greater elemental changes and processes of nature. Epic, heroic legend, saga, then localised these stories in real places and humanised them by attributing them to ancestral heroes, mightier than men and yet already men. And finally these legends, dwindling down, became folk-tales, *Märchen*, fairy-stories – nursery-tales.

That would seem to be the truth almost upside down. The nearer the so-called 'nature myth', or allegory of the large processes of nature, is to its supposed archetype, the less interesting it is, and indeed the less is it of a myth capable of throwing any illumination whatever on the world. Let us assume for the moment, as this theory assumes, that nothing actually exists corresponding to the 'gods' of mythology: no personalities, only astronomical or meteorological objects. Then these natural objects can only be arrayed with a personal significance and glory by a gift, the gift of a person, of a man. Personality can only be derived from a person. The gods may derive their colour and beauty from the high splendours of nature, but it was Man who obtained these for them, abstracted them from sun and moon and cloud; their personality they get direct from him; the shadow or flicker of divinity that is upon them they receive through him from the invisible world, the Supernatural. There is no fundamental distinction between the higher and lower mythologies. Their peoples live, if they live at all, by the same life, just as in the mortal world do kings and peasants.

Let us take what looks like a clear case of Olympian nature-myth: the Norse god Thórr. His name is Thunder, of which Thórr is the Norse form; and it is not difficult to interpret his hammer, Miöllnir, as lightning. Yet Thórr has (as far as our late records go) a very marked character, or personality, which cannot be found in thunder or in lightning, even though some details can, as it were, be related to these natural phenomena: for instance, his red beard, his loud voice and violent temper, his blundering and smashing strength. None the less it is asking a question without much meaning, if we inquire: Which came first, nature-allegories about personalized thunder in the mountains, splitting rocks and trees; or stories about an irascible, not very clever, red-beard farmer, of a strength beyond common measure, a person (in all but mere stature) very like the Northern farmers, the *bœndr* by whom Thórr was chiefly beloved? To a picture of such a man Thórr may be held to have 'dwindled', or from it the god may be held to have been enlarged. But I doubt whether either view is right – not by itself, not if you insist that one of these things must precede the other. It is more reasonable to suppose that the farmer popped up in the very moment when Thunder got a voice and face; that there was a distant growl of thunder in the hills every time a story-teller heard a farmer in a rage.

Thórr must, of course, be reckoned a member of the higher aristocracy of mythology: one of the rulers of the world. Yet the tale that is told of him in *Thrymskvitha* (in the Elder Edda) is certainly just a fairy-story. It is old, as far as Norse poems go, but that is not far back (say AD 900 or a little earlier, in this case). But there is no real reason for supposing that this tale is 'unprimitive', at any rate in quality: that is, because it is of folk-tale kind and not very dignified. If we could go backwards in time, the fairy-story might be found to change in details, or to give way to other tales. But there would always be a 'fairy-tale' as long as there was any Thórr. When the fairy-tale ceased, there would be just thunder, which no human ear had yet heard.

Something really 'higher' is occasionally glimpsed in mythology: Divinity, the right to power (as distinct from its possession), the due worship; in fact 'religion'. Andrew Lang said, and is by some still commended for saying,[1] that mythology and religion (in the strict sense of that word) are two distinct things that have become inextricably entangled, though mythology is in itself almost devoid of religious significance.[2]

---

[1] For example, by Christopher Dawson in *Progress and Religion*.

[2] This is borne out by the more careful and sympathetic study of 'primitive' peoples: that is, peoples still living in an inherited paganism, who are not, as we say, civilised. The hasty survey finds only their wilder tales; a closer examination finds their cosmological myths; only patience and inner knowledge discovers their philosophy and religion: the truly worshipful, of which the 'gods' are not necessarily an embodiment at all, or only in a variable measure (often decided by the individual).

Yet these things have in fact become entangled – or maybe they were sundered long ago and have since groped slowly, through a labyrinth of error, through confusion, back towards re-fusion. Even fairy-stories as a whole have three faces: the Mystical towards the Supernatural; the Magical towards Nature; and the Mirror of scorn and pity towards Man. The essential face of Faërie is the middle one, the Magical. But the degree in which the others appear (if at all) is variable, and may be decided by the individual story-teller. The Magical, the fairy-story, may be used as a *Mirour de l'Omme;* and it may (but not so easily) be made a vehicle of Mystery. This at least is what George MacDonald attempted, achieving stories of power and beauty when he succeeded, as in *The Golden Key* (which he called a fairy-tale); and even when he partly failed, as in *Lilith* (which he called a romance).

For a moment let us return to the 'Soup' that I mentioned above. Speaking of the history of stories and especially of fairy-stories we may say that the Pot of Soup, the Cauldron of Story, has always been boiling, and to it have continually been added new bits, dainty and undainty. For this reason, to take a casual example, the fact that a story resembling the one known as *The Goosegirl* (*Die Gänsemagd* in Grimm) is told in the thirteenth century of Bertha Broadfoot, mother of Charlemagne, really proves nothing either way: neither that the story was (in the thirteenth century) descending from Olympus or Asgard by way of an already legendary king of old, on its way to become a *Hausmärchen;* nor that it was on its way up. The story is found to be widespread, unattached to the mother of Charlemagne or to any historical character. From this fact by itself we certainly cannot deduce that it is not true of Charlemagne's mother, though that is the kind of deduction that is most frequently made from that kind of evidence. The opinion that the story is not true of Bertha Broadfoot must be founded on something else: on features in the story which the critic's philosophy does not allow to be possible in 'real life', so that he would actually disbelieve the tale, even if it were found nowhere else; or on the existence of good historical evidence that Bertha's actual life was quite different, so that he would disbelieve the tale, even if his philosophy allowed that it was perfectly possible in 'real life'. No one, I fancy, would discredit a story that the Archbishop of Canterbury slipped on a banana skin merely because he found that a similar comic mishap had been reported of many people, and especially of elderly gentlemen of dignity. He might disbelieve the story, if he discovered that in it an angel (or even a fairy) had warned the Archbishop that he would slip if he wore gaiters on a Friday. He might also disbelieve the story, if it was stated to have occurred in the period between, say, 1940 and 1945. So much for that. It is an obvious point, and it has been made before; but I venture to make it again (although it is a little beside my present purpose), for it is constantly neglected by those who concern themselves with the origins of tales.

But what of the banana skin? Our business with it really only begins when it has been rejected by historians. It is more useful when it has been thrown away. The historian would be likely to say that the banana-skin story 'became attached to the Archbishop', as he does say on fair evidence that 'the Goosegirl *Märchen* became attached to Bertha'. That way of putting it is harmless enough, in what is commonly known as 'history'. But is it really a good description of what is going on and has gone on in the history of story-making? I do not think so. I think it would be nearer the truth to say that the Archbishop became attached to the banana skin, or that Bertha was turned into the Goosegirl. Better still: I would say that Charlemagne's mother and the Archbishop were put into the Pot, in fact got into the Soup. They were just new bits added to the stock. A considerable honour, for in that soup were many things older, more potent, more beautiful, comic, or terrible than they were in themselves (considered simply as figures of history).

It seems fairly plain that Arthur, once historical (but perhaps as such not of great importance), was also put into the Pot. There he was boiled for a long time, together with many other older figures and devices, of mythology and Faërie, and even some other stray bones of history (such as Alfred's defence against the Danes), until he emerged as a King of Faërie. The situation is similar in the great Northern 'Arthurian' court of the Shield-Kings of Denmark, the *Scyldingas* of ancient English tradition.

King Hrothgar and his family have many manifest marks of true history, far more than Arthur; yet even in the older (English) accounts of them they are associated with many figures and events of fairy-story: they have been in the Pot. But I refer now to the remnants of the oldest recorded English tales of Faërie (or its borders), in spite of the fact that they are little known in England, not to discuss the turning of the bear-boy into the knight Beowulf, or to explain the intrusion of the ogre Grendel into the royal hall of Hrothgar. I wish to point to something else that these traditions contain: a singularly suggestive example of the relation of the 'fairy-tale element' to gods and kings and nameless men, illustrating (I believe) the view that this element does not rise or fall, but is there, in the Cauldron of Story, waiting for the great figures of Myth and History, and for the yet nameless He or She, waiting for the moment when they are cast into the simmering stew, one by one or all together, without consideration of rank or precedence.

The great enemy of King Hrothgar was Froda, King of the Heathobards. Yet of Hrothgar's daughter Freawaru we hear echoes of a strange tale – not a usual one in Northern heroic legend: the son of the enemy of her house, Ingeld son of Froda, fell in love with her and wedded her, disastrously. But that is extremely interesting and significant. In the background of the ancient feud looms the figure of that god whom the Norsemen called Frey (the Lord) or Yngvi-frey, and the Angles called Ing: a god of the ancient Northern mythology (and religion) of Fertility and Corn. The enmity of the royal houses was connected with the sacred site of a cult of that religion. Ingeld and his father bear names belonging to it. Freawaru herself is named 'Protection of the Lord (of Frey)'. Yet one of the chief things told later (in Old Icelandic) about Frey is the story in which he falls in love from afar with the daughter of the enemies of the gods, Gerdr, daughter of the giant Gymir, and weds her. Does this prove that Ingeld and Freawaru, or their love, are 'merely mythical'? I think not. History often resembles 'Myth', because they are both ultimately of the same stuff. If indeed Ingeld and Freawaru never lived, or at least never loved, then it is ultimately from nameless man and woman that they get their tale, or rather into whose tale they have entered. They have been put into the Cauldron, where so many potent things lie simmering agelong on the fire, among them Love-at-first-sight. So too of the god. If no young man had ever fallen in love by chance meeting with a maiden, and found old enmities to stand between him and his love, then the god Frey would never have seen Gerdr the giant's daughter from the high-seat of Odin. But if we speak of a Cauldron, we must not wholly forget the Cooks. There are many things in the Cauldron, but the Cooks do not dip in the ladle quite blindly. Their selection is important. The gods are after all gods, and it is a matter of some moment what stories are told of them. So we must freely admit that a tale of love is more likely to be told of a prince in history, indeed is more likely actually to happen in an historical family whose traditions are those of golden Frey and the Vanir, rather than those of Odin the Goth, the Necromancer, glutter of the crows, Lord of the Slain. Small wonder that *spell* means both a story told, and a formula of power over living men.

But when we have done all that research – collection and comparison of the tales of many lands – can do; when we have explained many of the elements commonly found embedded in fairy-stories (such as stepmothers, enchanted bears and bulls, cannibal witches, taboos on names, and the like) as relics of ancient customs once practised in daily life, or of beliefs once held as beliefs and not as 'fancies' – there remains still a point too often forgotten: that is the effect produced *now* by these old things in the stories as they are.

For one thing they are now *old*, and antiquity has an appeal in itself. The beauty and horror of *The Juniper Tree* (*Von dem Machandelboom*), with its exquisite and tragic beginning, the abominable cannibal stew, the gruesome bones, the gay and vengeful bird-spirit coming out of a mist that rose from the tree, has remained with me since childhood; and yet always the chief flavour of that tale lingering in the memory was not beauty or horror, but distance and a great abyss of time, not measurable even by *twe tusend Johr*. Without the stew and the bones – which children are now too often spared in mollified versions of Grimm[1] – that vision would largely have been lost. I do

---

[1] They should not be spared it – unless they are spared the whole story until their digestions are stronger.

not think I was harmed by the horror *in the fairytale setting*, out of whatever dark beliefs and practices of the past it may have come. Such stories have now a mythical or total (unanalysable) effect, an effect quite independent of the findings of Comparative Folk-lore, and one which it cannot spoil or explain; they open a door on Other Time, and if we pass through, though only for a moment, we stand outside our own time, outside Time itself, maybe.

If we pause, not merely to note that such old elements have been preserved, but to think *how* they have been preserved, we must conclude, I think, that it has happened, often if not always, precisely because of this literary effect. It cannot have been we, or even the brothers Grimm, that first felt it. Fairy-stories are by no means rocky matrices out of which the fossils cannot be prised except by an expert geologist. The ancient elements can be knocked out, or forgotten and dropped out, or replaced by other ingredients with the greatest ease: as any comparison of a story with closely related variants will show. The things that are there must often have been retained (or inserted) because the oral narrators, instinctively or consciously, felt their literary 'significance'.[1] Even where a prohibition in a fairy-story is guessed to be derived from some taboo once practised long ago, it has probably been preserved in the later stages of the tale's history because of the great mythical significance of prohibition. A sense of that significance

[1] See Note B at end (p. 390).

may indeed have lain behind some of the taboos themselves. Thou shalt not – or else thou shall depart beggared into endless regret. The gentlest 'nursery-tales' know it. Even Peter Rabbit was forbidden a garden, lost his blue coat, and took sick. The Locked Door stands as an eternal Temptation.

CHILDREN

I will now turn to children, and so come to the last and most important of the three questions: what, if any, are the values and functions of fairy-stories *now*? It is usually assumed that children are the natural or the specially appropriate audience for fairy-stories. In describing a fairy-story which they think adults might possibly read for their own entertainment, reviewers frequently indulge in such waggeries as: 'this book is for children from the ages of six to sixty'. But I have never yet seen the puff of a new motor-model that began thus: 'this toy will amuse infants from seventeen to seventy'; though that to my mind would be much more appropriate. Is there any *essential* connection between children and fairy-stories? Is there any call for comment, if an adult reads them for himself? *Reads* them as tales, that is, not *studies* them as curios. Adults are allowed to collect and study anything, even old theatre programmes or paper bags.

Among those who still have enough wisdom not to think fairy-stories pernicious, the common opinion seems to be that there is a natural connection between the minds

of children and fairy-stories, of the same order as the connection between children's bodies and milk. I think this is
an error; at best an error of false sentiment, and one that
is therefore most often made by those who, for whatever
private reason (such as childlessness), tend to think of
children as a special kind of creature, almost a different
race, rather than as normal, if immature, members of a
particular family, and of the human family at large.

Actually, the association of children and fairy-stories is
an accident of our domestic history. Fairy-stories have in
the modern lettered world been relegated to the 'nursery',
as shabby or old-fashioned furniture is relegated to the
play-room, primarily because the adults do not want it,
and do not mind if it is misused.[1] It is not the choice of the
children which decides this. Children as a class – except in
a common lack of experience they are not one – neither
like fairy-stories more, nor understand them better than
adults do; and no more than they like many other things.
They are young and growing, and normally have keen
appetites, so the fairy-stories as a rule go down well
enough. But in fact only some children, and some adults,

---

[1] In the case of stories and other nursery lore, there is also another
factor. Wealthier families employed women to look after their
children, and the stories were provided by these nurses, who were
sometimes in touch with rustic and traditional lore forgotten by
their 'betters'. It is long since this source dried up, at any rate in
England; but it once had some importance. But again there is no
proof of the special fitness of children as the recipients of this
vanishing 'folk-lore'. The nurses might just as well (or better)
have been left to choose the pictures and furniture.

have any special taste for them; and when they have it, it is not exclusive, nor even necessarily dominant.[1] It is a taste, too, that would not appear, I think, very early in childhood without artificial stimulus; it is certainly one that does not decrease but increases with age, if it is innate.

It is true that in recent times fairy-stories have usually been written or 'adapted' for children. But so may music be, or verse, or novels, or history, or scientific manuals. It is a dangerous process, even when it is necessary. It is indeed only saved from disaster by the fact that the arts and sciences are not as a whole relegated to the nursery; the nursery and schoolroom are merely given such tastes and glimpses of the adult thing as seem fit for them in adult opinion (often much mistaken). Any one of these things would, if left altogether in the nursery, become gravely impaired. So would a beautiful table, a good picture, or a useful machine (such as a microscope), be defaced or broken, if it were left long unregarded in a schoolroom. Fairy-stories banished in this way, cut off from a full adult art, would in the end be ruined; indeed in so far as they have been so banished, they have been ruined.

The value of fairy-stories is thus not, in my opinion, to be found by considering children in particular. Collections of fairy-stories are, in fact, by nature attics and lumber-rooms, only by temporary and local custom playrooms. Their contents are disordered, and often battered,

[1] See Note C at end (p. 392).

a jumble of different dates, purposes, and tastes; but among them may occasionally be found a thing of permanent virtue: an old work of art, not too much damaged, that only stupidity would ever have stuffed away.

Andrew Lang's *Fairy Books* are not, perhaps, lumber-rooms. They are more like stalls in a rummage-sale. Someone with a duster and a fair eye for things that retain some value has been round the attics and box-rooms. His collections are largely a by-product of his adult study of mythology and folk-lore; but they were made into and presented as books for children.[1] Some of the reasons that Lang gave are worth considering.

The introduction to the first of the series speaks of 'children to whom and for whom they are told'. 'They represent', he says, 'the young age of man true to his early loves, and have his unblunted edge of belief, a fresh appetite for marvels'. '"Is it true?"' he says, 'is the great question children ask.'

I suspect that *belief* and *appetite for marvels* are here regarded as identical or as closely related. They are radically different, though the appetite for marvels is not at once or at first differentiated by a growing human mind from its general appetite. It seems fairly clear that Lang was using *belief* in its ordinary sense: belief that a thing exists or can happen in the real (primary) world. If so, then I fear that Lang's words, stripped of sentiment, can

---

[1]   By Lang and his helpers. It is not true of the majority of the contents in their original (or oldest surviving) forms.

only imply that the teller of marvellous tales to children must, or may, or at any rate does trade on their *credulity,* on the lack of experience which makes it less easy for children to distinguish fact from fiction in particular cases, though the distinction in itself is fundamental to the sane human mind, and to fairy-stories.

Children are capable, of course, of *literary belief,* when the story-maker's art is good enough to produce it. That state of mind has been called 'willing suspension of disbelief'. But this does not seem to me a good description of what happens. What really happens is that the story-maker proves a successful 'sub-creator'. He makes a Secondary World which your mind can enter. Inside it, what he relates is 'true': it accords with the laws of that world. You therefore believe it, while you are, as it were, inside. The moment disbelief arises, the spell is broken; the magic, or rather art, has failed. You are then out in the Primary World again, looking at the little abortive Secondary World from outside. If you are obliged, by kindliness or circumstance, to stay, then disbelief must be suspended (or stifled), otherwise listening and looking would become intolerable. But this suspension of disbelief is a substitute for the genuine thing, a subterfuge we use when condescending to games or make-believe, or when trying (more or less willingly) to find what virtue we can in the work of an art that has for us failed.

A real enthusiast for cricket is in the enchanted state: Secondary Belief. I, when I watch a match, am on the lower level. I can achieve (more or less) willing suspension of disbelief, when I am held there and supported by some other motive that will keep away boredom: for instance, a wild, heraldic, preference for dark blue rather than light. This suspension of disbelief may thus be a somewhat tired, shabby, or sentimental state of mind, and so lean to the 'adult'. I fancy it is often the state of adults in the presence of a fairy-story. They are held there and supported by sentiment (memories of childhood, or notions of what childhood ought to be like); they think they ought to like the tale. But if they really liked it, for itself, they would not have to suspend disbelief: they would believe – in this sense.

Now if Lang had meant anything like this there might have been some truth in his words. It may be argued that it is easier to work the spell with children. Perhaps it is, though I am not sure of this. The appearance that it is so is often, I think, an adult illusion produced by children's humility, their lack of critical experience and vocabulary, and their voracity (proper to their rapid growth). They like or try to like what is given to them: if they do not like it, they cannot well express their dislike or give reasons for it (and so may conceal it); and they like a great mass of different things indiscriminately, without troubling to analyse the planes of their belief. In any case I doubt if this potion – the enchantment of the effective fairy-story – is really one of the kind that becomes 'blunted' by use, less potent after repeated draughts.

'"Is it true?" is the great question children ask', Lang said. They do ask that question, I know; and it is not one to be rashly or idly answered.[1] But that question is hardly evidence of 'unblunted belief', or even of the desire for it. Most often it proceeds from the child's desire to know which kind of literature he is faced with. Children's knowledge of the world is often so small that they cannot judge, off-hand and without help, between the fantastic, the strange (that is rare or remote facts), the nonsensical, and the merely 'grown-up' (that is ordinary things of their parents' world, much of which still remains unexplored). But they recognise the different classes, and may like all of them at times. Of course the borders between them are often fluctuating or confused; but that is not only true for children. We all know the differences in kind, but we are not always sure how to place anything that we hear. A child may well believe a report that there are ogres in the next county; many grown-up persons find it easy to believe of another country; and as for another planet, very few adults seem able to imagine it as peopled, if at all, by anything but monsters of iniquity.

Now I was one of the children whom Andrew Lang was addressing – I was born at about the same time as the *Green Fairy Book* – the children for whom he seemed to

---

[1] Far more often they have asked me: 'Was he good? Was he wicked?' That is, they were more concerned to get the Right side and the Wrong side clear. For that is a question equally important in History and in Faërie.

think that fairy-stories were the equivalent of the adult novel, and of whom he said: 'Their taste remains like the taste of their naked ancestors thousands of years ago; and they seem to like fairy-tales better than history, poetry, geography, or arithmetic.'[1] But do we really know much about these 'naked ancestors', except that they were certainly not naked? Our fairy-stories, however old certain elements in them may be, are certainly not the same as theirs. Yet if it is assumed that we have fairy-stories because they did, then probably we have history, geography, poetry, and arithmetic because they liked these things too, as far as they could get them, and in so far as they had yet separated the many branches of their general interest in everything.

And as for children of the present day, Lang's description does not fit my own memories, or my experience of children. Lang may have been mistaken about the children he knew, but if he was not, then at any rate children differ considerably, even within the narrow borders of Britain, and such generalizations which treat them as a class (disregarding their individual talents, and the influences of the countryside they live in, and their upbringing) are delusory. I had no special childish 'wish to believe'. I wanted to know. Belief depended on the way in which stories were presented to me, by older people, or by the authors, or on the inherent tone and quality of the tale. But at no

[1]   Preface to the *Violet Fairy Book*.

time can I remember that the enjoyment of a story was dependent on belief that such things could happen, or had happened, in 'real life'. Fairy-stories were plainly not primarily concerned with possibility, but with desirability. If they awakened *desire*, satisfying it while often whetting it unbearably, they succeeded. It is not necessary to be more explicit here, for I hope to say something later about this desire, a complex of many ingredients, some universal, some particular to modern men (including modern children), or even to certain kinds of men. I had no desire to have either dreams or adventures like *Alice*, and the account of them merely amused me. I had very little desire to look for buried treasure or fight pirates, and *Treasure Island* left me cool. Red Indians were better: there were bows and arrows (I had and have a wholly unsatisfied desire to shoot well with a bow), and strange languages, and glimpses of an archaic mode of life, and, above all, forests in such stories. But the land of Merlin and Arthur was better than these, and best of all the nameless North of Sigurd of the Völsungs, and the prince of all dragons. Such lands were pre-eminently desirable. I never imagined that the dragon was of the same order as the horse. And that was not solely because I saw horses daily, but never even the footprint of a worm.[1] The dragon had the trademark *Of Faërie* written plain upon him. In whatever world he had his being it was an Other-world. Fantasy,

[1] See Note D at end (p. 393).

the making or glimpsing of Other-worlds, was the heart of the desire of Faërie. I desired dragons with a profound desire. Of course, I in my timid body did not wish to have them in the neighbourhood, intruding into my relatively safe world, in which it was, for instance, possible to read stories in peace of mind, free from fear.[1] But the world that contained even the imagination of Fáfnir was richer and more beautiful, at whatever cost of peril. The dweller in the quiet and fertile plains may hear of the tormented hills and the unharvested sea and long for them in his heart. For the heart is hard though the body be soft.

All the same, important as I now perceive the fairy-story element in early reading to have been, speaking for myself as a child, I can only say that a liking for fairy-stories was not a dominant characteristic of early taste. A real taste for them awoke after 'nursery' days, and after the years, few but long-seeming, between learning to read and going to school. In that (I nearly wrote 'happy' or 'golden', it was really a sad and troublous) time I liked many other things as well, or better: such as history, astronomy, botany, grammar, and etymology. I agreed with Lang's generalised 'children' not at all in principle, and only in some points by accident: I was, for instance, insensitive to poetry, and skipped it if it came in tales.

---

[1] This is, naturally, often enough what children mean when they ask: 'Is it true?' They mean: 'I like this, but is it contemporary? Am I safe in my bed?' The answer: 'There is certainly no dragon in England today', is all that they want to hear.

Poetry I discovered much later in Latin and Greek, and especially through being made to try and translate English verse into classical verse. A real taste for fairy-stories was wakened by philology on the threshold of manhood, and quickened to full life by war.

I have said, perhaps, more than enough on this point. At least it will be plain that in my opinion fairy-stories should not be *specially* associated with children. They are associated with them: naturally, because children are human and fairy-stories are a natural human taste (though not necessarily a universal one); accidentally, because fairy-stories are a large part of the literary lumber that in latter-day Europe has been stuffed away in attics; unnaturally, because of erroneous sentiment about children, a sentiment that seems to increase with the decline in children.

It is true that the age of childhood-sentiment has produced some delightful books (especially charming, however, to adults) of the fairy kind or near to it; but it has also produced a dreadful undergrowth of stories written or adapted to what was or is conceived to be the measure of children's minds and needs. The old stories are mollified or bowdlerised, instead of being reserved; the imitations are often merely silly, Pigwiggenry without even the intrigue; or patronizing; or (deadliest of all) covertly sniggering, with an eye on the other grown-ups present. I will not accuse Andrew Lang of sniggering, but certainly he smiled to himself, and certainly too often he had an eye on the faces of other clever people over the heads of his child-audience – to the very grave detriment of the *Chronicles of Pantouflia*.

Dasent replied with vigour and justice to the prudish critics of his translations from Norse popular tales. Yet he committed the astonishing folly of particularly *forbidding* children to read the last two in his collection. That a man could study fairy-stories and not learn better than that seems almost incredible. But neither criticism, rejoinder, nor prohibition would have been necessary if children had not unnecessarily been regarded as the inevitable readers of the book.

I do not deny that there is a truth in Andrew Lang's words (sentimental though they may sound): 'He who would enter into the Kingdom of Faërie should have the heart of a little child.' For that possession is necessary to all high adventure, into kingdoms both less and far greater than Faërie. But humility and innocence – these things 'the heart of a child' must mean in such a context – do not necessarily imply an uncritical wonder, nor indeed an uncritical tenderness. Chesterton once remarked that the children in whose company he saw Maeterlinck's *Blue Bird* were dissatisfied 'because it did not end with a Day of Judgement, and it was not revealed to the hero and the heroine that the Dog had been faithful and the Cat faithless'. 'For children', he says, 'are innocent and love justice; while most of us are wicked and naturally prefer mercy.'

Andrew Lang was confused on this point. He was at pains to defend the slaying of the Yellow Dwarf by

Prince Ricardo in one of his own fairy-stories. 'I hate cruelty', he said, '. . . but that was in fair fight, sword in hand, and the dwarf, peace to his ashes! died in harness.' Yet it is not clear that 'fair fight' is less cruel than 'fair judgement'; or that piercing a dwarf with a sword is more just than the execution of wicked kings and evil step-mothers – which Lang abjures: he sends the criminals (as he boasts) to retirement on ample pensions. That is mercy untempered by justice. It is true that this plea was not addressed to children but to parents and guardians, to whom Lang was recommending his own *Prince Prigio* and *Prince Ricardo* as suitable for their charges.[1] It is parents and guardians who have classified fairy-stories as *Juvenilia*. And this is a small sample of the falsification of values that results.

If we use *child* in a good sense (it has also legitimately a bad one) we must not allow that to push us into the senti-mentality of only using *adult* or *grown-up* in a bad sense (it has also legitimately a good one). The process of growing older is not necessarily allied to growing wickeder, though the two do often happen together. Children are meant to grow up, and not to become Peter Pans. Not to lose inno-cence and wonder, but to proceed on the appointed journey: that journey upon which it is certainly not better to travel hopefully than to arrive, though we must travel hopefully if we are to arrive. But it is one of the lessons of

[1] Preface to the *Lilac Fairy Book*.

fairy-stories (if we can speak of the lessons of things that do not lecture) that on callow, lumpish, and selfish youth peril, sorrow, and the shadow of death can bestow dignity, and even sometimes wisdom.

Let us not divide the human race into Eloi and Morlocks: pretty children – 'elves' as the eighteenth century often idiotically called them – with their fairytales (carefully pruned), and dark Morlocks tending their machines. If fairy-story as a kind is worth reading at all it is worthy to be written for and read by adults. They will, of course, put more in and get more out than children can. Then, as a branch of a genuine art, children may hope to get fairy-stories fit for them to read and yet within their measure; as they may hope to get suitable introductions to poetry, history, and the sciences. Though it may be better for them to read some things, especially fairy-stories, that are beyond their measure rather than short of it. Their books like their clothes should allow for growth, and their books at any rate should encourage it.

Very well, then. If adults are to read fairy-stories as a natural branch of literature – neither playing at being children, nor pretending to be choosing for children, nor being boys who would not grow up – what are the values and functions of this kind? That is, I think, the last and most important question. I have already hinted at some of my answers. First of all: if written with art, the prime value of fairy-stories will simply be that value which, as literature, they share with other literary forms. But fairy-stories offer also, in a peculiar degree or mode, these things: Fantasy, Recovery, Escape, Consolation, all things of which children have, as a rule, less need than older people. Most of them are nowadays very commonly considered to be bad for anybody. I will consider them briefly, and will begin with *Fantasy*.

FANTASY

The human mind is capable of forming mental images of things not actually present. The faculty of conceiving the images is (or was) naturally called Imagination. But in recent times, in technical not normal language, Imagination has often been held to be something higher than the mere image-making, ascribed to the operations of Fancy (a reduced and depreciatory form of the older word Fantasy); an attempt is thus made to restrict, I should say misapply, Imagination to 'the power of giving to ideal creations the inner consistency of reality'.

Ridiculous though it may be for one so ill-instructed to have an opinion on this critical matter, I venture to think the verbal distinction philologically inappropriate, and the analysis inaccurate. The mental power of image-making is one thing, or aspect; and it should appropriately be called Imagination. The perception of the image, the grasp of its implications, and the control, which are necessary to a successful expression, may vary in vividness and strength: but this is a difference of degree in Imagination, not a difference in kind. The achievement of the expression, which gives (or seems to give) 'the inner consistency of reality',[1] is indeed another thing, or aspect, needing another name: Art, the operative link between Imagination and the final result, Sub-creation. For my present purpose I require a word which shall embrace both the Sub-creative Art in itself and a quality of strangeness and wonder in the Expression, derived from the Image: a quality essential to fairy-story. I propose, therefore, to arrogate to myself the powers of Humpty-Dumpty, and to use Fantasy for this purpose: in a sense, that is, which combines with its older and higher use as an equivalent of Imagination the derived notions of 'unreality' (that is, of unlikeness to the Primary World), of freedom from the domination of observed 'fact', in short of the fantastic. I am thus not only aware but glad of the etymological and semantic connections of *fantasy* with *fantastic:* with images of things that are not only 'not actually present', but which are indeed not to be found in our primary world at all, or are generally believed not to be found there. But while admitting that, I do not assent to the depreciative tone. That the images are of things not in the primary world (if that indeed is possible) is a virtue not a vice. Fantasy (in this sense) is, I think, not a lower but a higher form of Art, indeed the most nearly pure form, and so (when achieved) the most potent.

Fantasy, of course, starts out with an advantage: arresting strangeness. But that advantage has been turned

---

[1]   That is: which commands or induces Secondary Belief.

against it, and has contributed to its disrepute. Many people dislike being 'arrested'. They dislike any meddling with the Primary World, or such small glimpses of it as are familiar to them. They, therefore, stupidly and even maliciously confound Fantasy with Dreaming, in which there is no Art;[1] and with mental disorders, in which there is not even control: with delusion and hallucination.

But the error or malice, engendered by disquiet and consequent dislike, is not the only cause of this confusion. Fantasy has also an essential drawback: it is difficult to achieve. Fantasy may be, as I think, not less but more sub-creative; but at any rate it is found in practice that 'the inner consistency of reality' is more difficult to produce, the more unlike are the images and the rearrangements of primary material to the actual arrangements of the Primary World. It is easier to produce this kind of 'reality' with more 'sober' material. Fantasy thus, too often, remains undeveloped; it is and has been used frivolously, or only half-seriously, or merely for decoration: it remains merely 'fanciful'. Anyone inheriting the fantastic device of human language can say *the green sun*. Many can then imagine or picture it. But that is not enough – though it may already be a more potent thing than many a 'thumbnail sketch' or 'transcript of life' that receives literary praise.

[1]   This is not true of all dreams. In some Fantasy seems to take a part. But this is exceptional. Fantasy is a rational, not an irrational, activity.

To make a Secondary World inside which the green sun will be credible, commanding Secondary Belief, will probably require labour and thought, and will certainly demand a special skill, a kind of elvish craft. Few attempt such difficult tasks. But when they are attempted and in any degree accomplished then we have a rare achievement of Art: indeed narrative art, story-making in its primary and most potent mode.

In human art Fantasy is a thing best left to words, to true literature. In painting, for instance, the visible presentation of the fantastic image is technically too easy; the hand tends to outrun the mind, even to overthrow it.[1] Silliness or morbidity are frequent results. It is a misfortune that Drama, an art fundamentally distinct from Literature, should so commonly be considered together with it, or as a branch of it. Among these misfortunes we may reckon the depreciation of Fantasy. For in part at least this depreciation is due to the natural desire of critics to cry up the forms of literature or 'imagination' that they themselves, innately or by training, prefer. And criticism in a country that has produced so great a Drama, and possesses the works of William Shakespeare, tends to be far too dramatic. But Drama is naturally hostile to Fantasy. Fantasy, even of the simplest kind, hardly ever succeeds in Drama, when that is presented as it should be, visibly and audibly acted. Fantastic forms are not to be counterfeited.

[1]   See Note E at end (p. 394).

Men dressed up as talking animals may achieve buffoonery or mimicry, but they do not achieve Fantasy. This is, I think, well illustrated by the failure of the bastard form, pantomime. The nearer it is to 'dramatised fairy-story' the worse it is. It is only tolerable when the plot and its fantasy are reduced to a mere vestigiary framework for farce, and no 'belief' of any kind in any part of the performance is required or expected of anybody. This is, of course, partly due to the fact that the producers of drama have to, or try to, work with mechanism to represent either Fantasy or Magic. I once saw a so-called 'children's pantomime', the straight story of *Puss-in-Boots,* with even the metamorphosis of the ogre into a mouse. Had this been mechanically successful it would either have terrified the spectators or else have been just a turn of high-class conjuring. As it was, though done with some ingenuity of lighting, disbelief had not so much to be suspended as hung, drawn, and quartered.

In *Macbeth,* when it is read, I find the witches tolerable: they have a narrative function and some hint of dark significance; though they are vulgarised, poor things of their kind. They are almost intolerable in the play. They would be quite intolerable, if I were not fortified by some memory of them as they are in the story as read. I am told that I should feel differently if I had the mind of the period, with its witch-hunts and witch-trials. But that is to say: if I regarded the witches as possible, indeed likely, in the Primary World; in other words, if they ceased to be

'Fantasy'. That argument concedes the point. To be dissolved, or to be degraded, is the likely fate of Fantasy when a dramatist tries to use it, even such a dramatist as Shakespeare. *Macbeth* is indeed a work by a playwright who ought, at least on this occasion, to have written a story, if he had the skill or patience for that art.

A reason, more important, I think, than the inadequacy of stage-effects, is this: Drama has, of its very nature, already attempted a kind of bogus, or shall I say at least substitute, magic: *the visible and audible presentation of imaginary men in a story.* That is in itself an attempt to counterfeit the magician's wand. To introduce, even with mechanical success, into this quasi-magical secondary world a further fantasy or magic is to demand, as it were, an inner or tertiary world. It is a world too much. To make such a thing may not be impossible. I have never seen it done with success. But at least it cannot be claimed as the proper mode of Drama, in which walking and talking people have been found to be the natural instruments of Art and illusion.[1]

For this precise reason – that the characters, and even the scenes, are in Drama not imagined but actually beheld – Drama is, even though it uses a similar material (words, verse, plot), an art fundamentally different from narrative art. Thus, if you prefer Drama to Literature (as many literary critics plainly do), or form your critical theories primarily from dramatic critics, or even from Drama, you

[1]   See Note F at end (p. 396).

are apt to misunderstand pure story-making, and to constrain it to the limitations of stage-plays. You are, for instance, likely to prefer characters, even the basest and dullest, to things. Very little about trees as trees can be got into a play.

Now 'Faërian Drama' – those plays which according to abundant records the elves have often presented to men – can produce Fantasy with a realism and immediacy beyond the compass of any human mechanism. As a result their usual effect (upon a man) is to go beyond Secondary Belief. If you are present at a Faërian drama you yourself are, or think that you are, bodily inside its Secondary World. The experience may be very similar to Dreaming and has (it would seem) sometimes (by men) been confounded with it. But in Faërian drama you are in a dream that some other mind is weaving, and the knowledge of that alarming fact may slip from your grasp. To experience *directly* a Secondary World: the potion is too strong, and you give to it Primary Belief, however marvellous the events. You are deluded – whether that is the intention of the elves (always or at any time) is another question. They at any rate are not themselves deluded. This is for them a form of Art, and distinct from Wizardry or Magic, properly so called. They do not live in it, though they can, perhaps, afford to spend more time at it than human artists can. The Primary World, Reality, of elves and men is the same, if differently valued and perceived.

We need a word for this elvish craft, but all the words that have been applied to it have been blurred and confused with other things. Magic is ready to hand, and I have used it above (p. 323), but I should not have done so: Magic should be reserved for the operations of the Magician. Art is the human process that produces by the way (it is not its only or ultimate object) Secondary Belief. Art of the same sort, if more skilled and effortless, the elves can also use, or so the reports seem to show; but the more potent and specially elvish craft I will, for lack of a less debatable word, call Enchantment. Enchantment produces a Secondary World into which both designer and spectator can enter, to the satisfaction of their senses while they are inside; but in its purity it is artistic in desire and purpose. Magic produces, or pretends to produce, an alteration in the Primary World. It does not matter by whom it is said to be practised, fay or mortal, it remains distinct from the other two; it is not an art but a technique; its desire is *power* in this world, domination of things and wills.

To the elvish craft, Enchantment, Fantasy aspires, and when it is successful of all forms of human art most nearly approaches. At the heart of many man-made stories of the elves lies, open or concealed, pure or alloyed, the desire for a living, realised sub-creative art, which (however much it may outwardly resemble it) is inwardly wholly different from the greed for self-centred power which is the mark of the mere Magician. Of this desire the elves, in their better (but still perilous) part, are largely made; and it is from them that we may learn what is the central desire and aspiration of human Fantasy – even if the elves are, all the more in so far as they are, only a product of Fantasy itself. That creative desire is only cheated by counterfeits, whether the innocent but clumsy devices of the human dramatist, or the malevolent frauds of the magicians. In this world it is for men unsatisfiable, and so imperishable. Uncorrupted, it does not seek delusion, nor bewitchment and domination; it seeks shared enrichment, partners in making and delight, not slaves.

To many, Fantasy, this sub-creative art which plays strange tricks with the world and all that is in it, combining nouns and redistributing adjectives, has seemed suspect, if not illegitimate. To some it has seemed at least a childish folly, a thing only for peoples or for persons in their youth. As for its legitimacy I will say no more than to quote a brief passage from a letter I once wrote to a man who described myth and fairy-story as 'lies'; though to do him justice he was kind enough and confused enough to call fairy-story making 'Breathing a lie through Silver'.

'Dear Sir,' I said – 'Although now long estranged,
Man is not wholly lost nor wholly changed.
Dis-graced he may be, yet is not de-throned,
and keeps the rags of lordship once he owned:
Man, Sub-creator, the refracted Light
through whom is splintered from a single White
to many hues, and endlessly combined
in living shapes that move from mind to mind.
Though all the crannies of the world we filled

with Elves and Goblins, though we dared to build
Gods and their houses out of dark and light,
and sowed the seed of dragons – 'twas our right
(used or misused). That right has not decayed:
we make still by the law in which we're made.'

Fantasy is a natural human activity. It certainly does
not destroy or even insult Reason; and it does not either
blunt the appetite for, nor obscure the perception of, scientific verity. On the contrary. The keener and the clearer
is the reason, the better fantasy will it make. If men were
ever in a state in which they did not want to know or
could not perceive truth (facts or evidence), then Fantasy
would languish until they were cured. If they ever get into
that state (it would not seem at all impossible), Fantasy
will perish, and become Morbid Delusion.

For creative Fantasy is founded upon the hard recognition that things are so in the world as it appears under the
sun; on a recognition of fact, but not a slavery to it. So
upon logic was founded the nonsense that displays itself
in the tales and rhymes of Lewis Carroll. If men really
could not distinguish between frogs and men, fairy-stories
about frog-kings would not have arisen.

Fantasy can, of course, be carried to excess. It can be ill
done. It can be put to evil uses. It may even delude the
minds out of which it came. But of what human thing in
this fallen world is that not true? Men have conceived not
only of elves, but they have imagined gods, and worshipped

them, even worshipped those most deformed by their authors' own evil. But they have made false gods out of other materials: their notions, their banners, their monies; even their sciences and their social and economic theories have demanded human sacrifice. *Abusus non tollit usum.* Fantasy remains a human right: we make in our measure and in our derivative mode, because we are made: and not only made, but made in the image and likeness of a Maker.

RECOVERY, ESCAPE, CONSOLATION

As for old age, whether personal or belonging to the times in which we live, it may be true, as is often supposed, that this imposes disabilities (cf. p. 350). But it is in the main an idea produced by the mere *study* of fairy-stories. The analytic study of fairy-stories is as bad a preparation for the enjoying or the writing of them as would be the historical study of the drama of all lands and times for the enjoyment or writing of stage-plays. The study may indeed become depressing. It is easy for the student to feel that with all his labour he is collecting only a few leaves, many of them now torn or decayed, from the countless foliage of the Tree of Tales, with which the Forest of Days is carpeted. It seems vain to add to the litter. Who can design a new leaf? The patterns from bud to unfolding, and the colours from spring to autumn were all discovered by men long ago. But that is not true. The seed of the tree can be replanted in almost any soil, even in one so smoke-ridden (as Lang said) as that of England. Spring is, of course, not really less beautiful because we have seen or heard of other like events: like events, never from world's beginning to world's end the same event. Each leaf, of oak and ash and thorn, is a unique embodiment of the pattern, and for some eye this very year may be *the* embodiment, the first ever seen and recognised, though oaks have put forth leaves for countless generations of men.

We do not, or need not, despair of drawing because all lines must be either curved or straight, nor of painting because there are only three 'primary' colours. We may indeed be older now, in so far as we are heirs in enjoyment or in practice of many generations of ancestors in the arts. In this inheritance of wealth there may be a danger of boredom or of anxiety to be original, and that may lead to a distaste for fine drawing, delicate pattern, and 'pretty' colours, or else to mere manipulation and over-elaboration of old material, clever and heartless. But the true road of escape from such weariness is not to be found in the wilfully awkward, clumsy, or misshapen, not in making all things dark or unremittingly violent; nor in the mixing of colours on through subtlety to drabness, and the fantastical complication of shapes to the point of silliness and on towards delirium. Before we reach such states we need recovery. We should look at green again, and be startled anew (but not blinded) by blue and yellow and red. We should meet the centaur and the dragon, and then perhaps suddenly behold, like the ancient shepherds, sheep, and dogs, and horses – and wolves. This recovery fairy-stories help us to make. In that sense only a taste for them may make us, or keep us, childish.

Recovery (which includes return and renewal of health) is a re-gaining – regaining of a clear view. I do not say 'seeing things as they are' and involve myself with the philosophers, though I might venture to say 'seeing things as we are (or were) meant to see them' – as things apart from ourselves. We need, in any case, to clean our windows; so that the things seen clearly may be freed from the drab blur of triteness or familiarity – from possessiveness. Of all faces those of our *familiares* are the ones both most difficult to play fantastic tricks with, and most difficult really to see with fresh attention, perceiving their likeness and unlikeness: that they are faces, and yet unique faces. This triteness is really the penalty of 'appropriation': the things that are trite, or (in a bad sense) familiar, are the things that we have appropriated, legally or mentally. We say we know them. They have become like the things which once attracted us by their glitter, or their colour, or their shape, and we laid hands on them, and then locked them in our hoard, acquired them, and acquiring ceased to look at them.

Of course, fairy-stories are not the only means of recovery, or prophylactic against loss. Humility is enough. And there is (especially for the humble) *Mooreeffoc,* or Chestertonian Fantasy. *Mooreeffoc* is a fantastic word, but it could be seen written up in every town in this land. It is Coffee-room, viewed from the inside through a glass door, as it was seen by Dickens on a dark London day; and it was used by Chesterton to denote the queerness of things that have become trite, when they are seen suddenly from a new angle. That kind of 'fantasy' most people would allow to be wholesome enough; and it can never lack for material. But it has, I think, only a limited power; for the reason that recovery of freshness of vision is its only virtue. The word *Mooreeffoc* may cause you suddenly to realise that England is an utterly alien land, lost either in some remote past age glimpsed by history, or in some strange dim future to be reached only by a time-machine; to see the amazing oddity and interest of its inhabitants and their customs and feeding-habits; but it cannot do more than that: act as a time-telescope focused on one spot. Creative fantasy, because it is mainly trying to do something else (make something new), may open your hoard and let all the locked things fly away like cage-birds. The gems all turn into flowers or flames, and you will be warned that all you had (or knew) was dangerous and potent, not really effectively chained, free and wild; no more yours than they were you.

The 'fantastic' elements in verse and prose of other kinds, even when only decorative or occasional, help in this release. But not so thoroughly as a fairy-story, a thing built on or about Fantasy, of which Fantasy is the core. Fantasy is made out of the Primary World, but a good craftsman loves his material, and has a knowledge and feeling for clay, stone and wood which only the art of making can give. By the forging of Gram cold iron was revealed; by the making of Pegasus horses were ennobled; in the Trees of the Sun and Moon root and stock, flower and fruit are manifested in glory.

And actually fairy-stories deal largely, or (the better ones) mainly, with simple or fundamental things, untouched by Fantasy, but these simplicities are made all the more luminous by their setting. For the story-maker who allows himself to be 'free with' Nature can be her lover not her slave. It was in fairy-stories that I first divined the potency of the words, and the wonder of the things, such as stone, and wood, and iron; tree and grass; house and fire; bread and wine.

I will now conclude by considering Escape and Consolation, which are naturally closely connected. Though fairy-stories are of course by no means the only medium of Escape, they are today one of the most obvious and (to some) outrageous forms of 'escapist' literature; and it is thus reasonable to attach to a consideration of them some considerations of this term 'escape' in criticism generally.

I have claimed that Escape is one of the main functions of fairy-stories, and since I do not disapprove of them, it is plain that I do not accept the tone of scorn or pity with which 'Escape' is now so often used: a tone for which the uses of the word outside literary criticism give no warrant at all. In what the misusers of Escape are fond of calling Real Life, Escape is evidently as a rule very practical, and may even be heroic. In real life it is difficult to blame it, unless it fails; in criticism it would seem to be the worse the better it succeeds. Evidently we are faced by a misuse of words, and also by a confusion of thought. Why should a man be scorned, if, finding himself in prison, he tries to get out and go home? Or if, when he cannot do so, he thinks and talks about other topics than jailers and prison-walls? The world outside has not become less real because the prisoner cannot see it. In using Escape in this way the critics have chosen the wrong word, and, what is more, they are confusing, not always by sincere error, the Escape of the Prisoner with the Flight of the Deserter. Just so a Party-spokesman might have labelled departure from the misery of the Führer's or any other Reich and even criticism of it as treachery. In the same way these critics, to make confusion worse, and so to bring into contempt their opponents, stick their label of scorn not only on to Desertion, but on to real Escape, and what are often its companions, Disgust, Anger, Condemnation, and Revolt. Not only do they confound the escape of the prisoner with the flight of the deserter; but they would seem to prefer the acquiescence of the 'quisling' to the resistance of the patriot. To such thinking you have only to say 'the land you loved is doomed' to excuse any treachery, indeed to glorify it.

For a trifling instance: not to mention (indeed not to parade) electric street-lamps of mass-produced pattern in your tale is Escape (in that sense). But it may, almost certainly does, proceed from a considered disgust for so typical a product of the Robot Age, that combines elaboration and ingenuity of means with ugliness, and (often) with inferiority of result. These lamps may be excluded from the tale simply because they are bad lamps; and it is possible that one of the lessons to be learnt from the story is the realization of this fact. But out comes the big stick: 'Electric lamps have come to stay', they say. Long ago Chesterton truly remarked that, as soon as he heard that anything 'had come to stay', he knew that it would be very soon replaced – indeed regarded as pitiably obsolete and shabby. 'The march of Science, its tempo quickened by the needs of war, goes inexorably on . . . making some things obsolete, and foreshadowing new developments in the utilization of electricity': an advertisement. This says the same thing only more menacingly. The electric street-lamp may indeed be ignored, simply because it is so insignificant and transient. Fairy-stories, at any rate, have many more permanent and fundamental things to talk about. Lightning, for example. The escapist is not so subservient to the whims of evanescent fashion as these opponents. He does not make things (which it may be quite rational to regard as bad) his masters or his gods by worshipping them as inevitable, even 'inexorable'. And his opponents, so easily contemptuous, have no guarantee that he will stop there: he might rouse men to pull down the street-lamps. Escapism has another and even wickeder face: Reaction.

Not long ago – incredible though it may seem – I heard a clerk of Oxenford declare that he 'welcomed' the proximity of mass-production robot factories, and the roar of self-obstructive mechanical traffic, because it brought his university into 'contact with real life'. He may have meant that the way men were living and working in the twentieth century was increasing in barbarity at an alarming rate, and that the loud demonstration of this in the streets of Oxford might serve as a warning that it is not possible to preserve for long an oasis of sanity in a desert of unreason by mere fences, without actual offensive action (practical and intellectual). I fear he did not. In any case the expression 'real life' in this context seems to fall short of academic standards. The notion that motor-cars are more 'alive' than, say, centaurs or dragons is curious; that they are more 'real' than, say, horses is pathetically absurd. How real, how startlingly alive is a factory chimney compared with an elm tree: poor obsolete thing, insubstantial dream of an escapist!

For my part, I cannot convince myself that the roof of Bletchley station is more 'real' than the clouds. And as an artefact I find it less inspiring than the legendary dome of heaven. The bridge to platform 4 is to me less interesting than Bifröst guarded by Heimdall with the Gjallarhorn. From the wildness of my heart I cannot exclude the question whether railway-engineers, if they had been brought up on more fantasy, might not have done better with all their abundant means than they commonly do. Fairy-stories might be, I guess, better Masters of Arts than the academic person I have referred to.

Much that he (I must suppose) and others (certainly) would call 'serious' literature is no more than play under a glass roof by the side of a municipal swimming-bath. Fairy-stories may invent monsters that fly the air or dwell in the deep, but at least they do not try to escape from heaven or the sea.

And if we leave aside for a moment 'fantasy', I do not think that the reader or the maker of fairy-stories need even be ashamed of the 'escape' of archaism: of preferring not dragons but horses, castles, sailing-ships, bows and arrows; not only elves, but knights and kings and priests. For it is after all possible for a rational man, after reflection (quite unconnected with fairy-story or romance), to arrive at the condemnation, implicit at least in the mere silence of 'escapist' literature, of progressive things like factories, or the machine-guns and bombs that appear to be their most natural and inevitable, dare we say 'inexorable', products.

'The rawness and ugliness of modern European life' – that real life whose contact we should welcome – 'is the sign of a biological inferiority, of an insufficient or false reaction to environment.'[1] The maddest castle that ever

---

[1] Christopher Dawson, *Progress and Religion,* pp. 58, 59. Later he adds: 'The full Victorian panoply of top-hat and frock-coat undoubtedly expressed something essential in the nineteenth-century culture, and hence it has with that culture spread all over the world, as no fashion of clothing has ever done before. It is possible that our descendants will recognise in it a kind of grim Assyrian beauty, fit emblem of the ruthless and great age that created it; but however that may be, it misses the direct and inevitable beauty that all clothing should have, because like its parent culture it was out of touch with the life of nature and of human nature as well.'

came out of a giant's bag in a wild Gaelic story is not only much less ugly than a robot-factory, it is also (to use a very modern phrase) 'in a very real sense' a great deal more real. Why should we not escape from or condemn the 'grim Assyrian' absurdity of top-hats, or the Morlockian horror of factories? They are condemned even by the writers of that most escapist form of all literature, stories of Science fiction. These prophets often foretell (and many seem to yearn for) a world like one big glass-roofed railway-station. But from them it is as a rule very hard to gather what men in such a world-town will *do*. They may abandon the 'full Victorian panoply' for loose garments (with zip-fasteners), but will use this freedom mainly, it would appear, in order to play with mechanical toys in the soon-cloying game of moving at high speed. To judge by some of these tales they will still be as lustful, vengeful, and greedy as ever; and the ideals of their idealists hardly reach farther than the splendid notion of building more towns of the same sort on other planets. It is indeed an age of 'improved means to deteriorated ends'. It is part of the essential malady of such days – producing the desire to escape, not indeed from life, but from our present time and self-made misery – that we are acutely conscious both of the ugliness of our works, and of their evil. So that to us evil and ugliness seem indissolubly allied. We find it difficult to conceive of evil and beauty together. The fear of the beautiful fay that ran through the elder ages almost eludes our grasp. Even more alarming: goodness is itself bereft of its proper beauty. In Faërie one can indeed conceive of an ogre who possesses a castle hideous as a nightmare (for the evil of the ogre wills it so), but one cannot conceive of a house built with a good purpose – an inn, a hostel for travellers, the hall of a virtuous and noble king – that is yet sickeningly ugly. At the present day it would be rash to hope to see one that was not – unless it was built before our time.

This, however, is the modern and special (or accidental) 'escapist' aspect of fairy-stories, which they share with romances, and other stories out of or about the past. Many stories out of the past have only become 'escapist' in their appeal through surviving from a time when men were as a rule delighted with the work of their hands into our time when many men feel disgust with man-made things.

But there are also other and more profound 'escapisms' that have always appeared in fairy-tale and legend. There are other things more grim and terrible to fly from than the noise, stench, ruthlessness, and extravagance of the internal-combustion engine. There are hunger, thirst, poverty, pain, sorrow, injustice, death. And even when men are not facing hard things such as these, there are ancient limitations from which fairy-stories offer a sort of escape, and old ambitions and desires (touching the very roots of fantasy) to which they offer a kind of satisfaction and consolation. Some are pardonable weaknesses or curiosities: such as the desire to visit, free as a fish, the deep sea; or the longing for the noiseless, gracious, economical flight of a bird, that longing which the aeroplane cheats, except in rare moments, seen high and by wind and distance noiseless, turning in the sun: that is, precisely when imagined and not used. There are profounder wishes: such as the desire to converse with other living things. On this desire, as ancient as the Fall, is largely founded the talking of beasts and creatures in fairy-tales, and especially the magical understanding of their proper speech. This is the root, and not the 'confusion' attributed to the minds of men of the unrecorded past, an alleged 'absence of the sense of separation of ourselves from beasts'.[1] A vivid sense of that separation is very ancient; but also a sense that it was a severance: a strange fate and a guilt lies on us. Other creatures are like other realms with which Man has broken off relations, and sees now only from the outside at a distance, being at war with them, or on the terms of an uneasy armistice. There are a few men who are privileged to travel abroad a little; others must be content with travellers' tales. Even about frogs. In speaking of that rather odd but widespread fairy-story *The Frog-King* Max Müller asked in his prim way: 'How came such a story ever to be invented? Human beings were, we may hope, at all times sufficiently enlightened to know that a marriage between a frog and the daughter of a queen was absurd.' Indeed we may hope so! For if not, there would be no point in this story at all, depending as it does essentially on the sense of the absurdity. Folk-lore origins (or guesses about them) are here quite

[1]   See Note G at end (p. 397).

beside the point. It is of little avail to consider totemism. For certainly, whatever customs or beliefs about frogs and wells lie behind this story, the frog-shape was and is preserved in the fairy-story[1] precisely because it was so queer and the marriage absurd, indeed abominable. Though, of course, in the versions which concern us, Gaelic, German, English,[2] there is in fact no wedding between a princess and a frog: the frog was an enchanted prince. And the point of the story lies not in thinking frogs possible mates, but in the necessity of keeping promises (even those with intolerable consequences) that, together with observing prohibitions, runs through all Fairyland. This is one of the notes of the horns of Elfland, and not a dim note.

And lastly there is the oldest and deepest desire, the Great Escape: the Escape from Death. Fairy-stories provide many examples and modes of this – which might be called the genuine *escapist*, or (I would say) *fugitive* spirit. But so do other stories (notably those of scientific inspiration), and so do other studies. Fairy-stories are made by men not by fairies. The Human-stories of the elves are doubtless full of the Escape from Deathlessness. But our stories cannot be expected always to rise above our common level. They often do. Few lessons are taught more clearly in them than the burden of that kind of immortality, or rather endless serial living, to which the

[1] Or group of similar stories.
[2] The Queen who sought drink from a certain Well and the Lorgann (Campbell, xxiii); Der Froschkönig; The Maid and the Frog

'fugitive' would fly. For the fairy-story is specially apt to teach such things, of old and still today. Death is the theme that most inspired George MacDonald.

But the 'consolation' of fairy-tales has another aspect than the imaginative satisfaction of ancient desires. Far more important is the Consolation of the Happy Ending. Almost I would venture to assert that all complete fairy-stories must have it. At least I would say that Tragedy is the true form of Drama, its highest function; but the opposite is true of Fairy-story. Since we do not appear to possess a word that expresses this opposite – I will call it *Eucatastrophe.* The *eucatastrophic* tale is the true form of fairy-tale, and its highest function.

The consolation of fairy-stories, the joy of the happy ending: or more correctly of the good catastrophe, the sudden joyous 'turn' (for there is no true end to any fairy-tale):[1] this joy, which is one of the things which fairy-stories can produce supremely well, is not essentially 'escapist', nor 'fugitive'. In its fairy-tale – or otherworld – setting, it is a sudden and miraculous grace: never to be counted on to recur. It does not deny the existence of *dyscatastrophe,* of sorrow and failure: the possibility of these is necessary to the joy of deliverance; it denies (in the face of much evidence, if you will) universal final defeat and in so far is *evangelium,* giving a fleeting glimpse of Joy, Joy beyond the walls of the world, poignant as grief.

[1] See Note H at end (p. 398).

It is the mark of a good fairy-story, of the higher or more complete kind, that however wild its events, however fantastic or terrible the adventures, it can give to child or man that hears it, when the 'turn' comes, a catch of the breath, a beat and lifting of the heart, near to (or indeed accompanied by) tears, as keen as that given by any form of literary art, and having a peculiar quality.

Even modern fairy-stories can produce this effect sometimes. It is not an easy thing to do; it depends on the whole story which is the setting of the turn, and yet it reflects a glory backwards. A tale that in any measure succeeds in this point has not wholly failed, whatever flaws it may possess, and whatever mixture or confusion of purpose. It happens even in Andrew Lang's own fairy-story, *Prince Prigio,* unsatisfactory in many ways as that is. When 'each knight came alive and lifted his sword and shouted "long live Prince Prigio"', the joy has a little of that strange mythical fairy-story quality, greater than the event described. It would have none in Lang's tale, if the event described were not a piece of more serious fairy-story 'fantasy' than the main bulk of the story, which is in general more frivolous, having the half-mocking smile of the courtly, sophisticated *Conte.*[1] Far more powerful and

---

[1] This is characteristic of Lang's wavering balance. On the surface the story is a follower of the 'courtly' French *conte* with a satirical twist, and of Thackeray's *Rose and the Ring* in particular – a kind which being superficial, even frivolous, by nature, does not produce or aim at producing anything so profound; but underneath lies the deeper spirit of the romantic Lang.

poignant is the effect in a serious tale of Faërie.[1] In such stories when the sudden 'turn' comes we get a piercing glimpse of joy, and heart's desire, that for a moment passes outside the frame, rends indeed the very web of story, and lets a gleam come through.

> Seven long years I served for thee,
> The glassy hill I clamb for thee,
> The bluidy shirt I wrang for thee,
> And wilt thou not wauken and turn to me?

He heard and turned to her.[2]

EPILOGUE

This 'joy' which I have selected as the mark of the true fairy-story (or romance), or as the seal upon it, merits more consideration.

Probably every writer making a secondary world, a fantasy, every sub-creator, wishes in some measure to be a real maker, or hopes that he is drawing on reality: hopes that the peculiar quality of this secondary world (if not all the details)[3] are derived from Reality, or are flowing into it. If he indeed achieves a quality that can fairly be described by the dictionary definition: 'inner consistency of reality',

---

[1] Of the kind which Lang called 'traditional', and really preferred.
[2] *The Black Bull of Norroway.*
[3] For all the details may not be 'true': it is seldom that the 'inspiration' is so strong and lasting that it leavens all the lump, and does not leave much that is mere uninspired 'invention'.

it is difficult to conceive how this can be, if the work does not in some way partake of reality. The peculiar quality of the 'joy' in successful Fantasy can thus be explained as a sudden glimpse of the underlying reality or truth. It is not only a 'consolation' for the sorrow of this world, but a satisfaction, and an answer to that question, 'Is it true?' The answer to this question that I gave at first was (quite rightly): 'If you have built your little world well, yes: it is true in that world.' That is enough for the artist (or the artist part of the artist). But in the 'eucatastrophe' we see in a brief vision that the answer may be greater – it may be a far-off gleam or echo of *evangelium* in the real world. The use of this word gives a hint of my epilogue. It is a serious and dangerous matter. It is presumptuous of me to touch upon such a theme; but if by grace what I say has in any respect any validity, it is, of course, only one facet of a truth incalculably rich: finite only because the capacity of Man for whom this was done is finite.

I would venture to say that approaching the Christian Story from this direction, it has long been my feeling (a joyous feeling) that God redeemed the corrupt making-creatures, men, in a way fitting to this aspect, as to others, of their strange nature. The Gospels contain a fairy-story, or a story of a larger kind which embraces all the essence of fairy-stories. They contain many marvels – peculiarly artistic,[1] beautiful, and moving: 'mythical' in their perfect,

---

[1] The Art is here in the story itself rather than in the telling; for the Author of the story was not the evangelists.

self-contained significance; and among the marvels is the greatest and most complete conceivable eucatastrophe. But this story has entered History and the primary world; the desire and aspiration of sub-creation has been raised to the fulfillment of Creation. The Birth of Christ is the eucatastrophe of Man's history. The Resurrection is the eucatastrophe of the story of the Incarnation. This story begins and ends in joy. It has pre-eminently the 'inner consistency of reality'. There is no tale ever told that men would rather find was true, and none which so many sceptical men have accepted as true on its own merits. For the Art of it has the supremely convincing tone of Primary Art, that is, of Creation. To reject it leads either to sadness or to wrath.

It is not difficult to imagine the peculiar excitement and joy that one would feel, if any specially beautiful fairy-story were found to be 'primarily' true, its narrative to be history, without thereby necessarily losing the mythical or allegorical significance that it had possessed. It is not difficult, for one is not called upon to try and conceive anything of a quality unknown. The joy would have exactly the same quality, if not the same degree, as the joy which the 'turn' in a fairy-story gives: such joy has the very taste of primary truth. (Otherwise its name would not be joy.) It looks forward (or backward: the direction in this regard is unimportant) to the Great Eucatastrophe. The Christian joy, the *Gloria*, is of the same kind; but it is pre-eminently (infinitely, if our capacity were not finite) high and joyous.

Because this story is supreme; and it is true. Art has been verified. God is the Lord, of angels, and of men – and of elves. Legend and History have met and fused.

But in God's kingdom the presence of the greatest does not depress the small. Redeemed Man is still man. Story, fantasy, still go on, and should go on. The Evangelium has not abrogated legends; it has hallowed them, especially the 'happy ending'. The Christian has still to work, with mind as well as body, to suffer, hope, and die; but he may now perceive that all his bents and faculties have a purpose, which can be redeemed. So great is the bounty with which he has been treated that he may now, perhaps, fairly dare to guess that in Fantasy he may actually assist in the effoliation and multiple enrichment of creation. All tales may come true; and yet, at the last, redeemed, they may be as like and as unlike the forms that we give them as Man, finally redeemed, will be like and unlike the fallen that we know.

NOTES

A (page 327)
The very root (not only the use) of their 'marvels' is satiric, a mockery of unreason; and the 'dream' element is not a mere machinery of introduction and ending, but inherent in the action and transitions. These things children can perceive and appreciate, if left to themselves. But to many, as it was to me, *Alice* is presented as a fairy-story and while this misunderstanding lasts, the distaste for the

dream-machinery is felt. There is no suggestion of dream in *The Wind in the Willows.* 'The Mole had been working very hard all the morning, spring-cleaning his little house.' So it begins, and that correct tone is maintained. It is all the more remarkable that A. A. Milne, so great an admirer of this excellent book, should have prefaced to his dramatised version a 'whimsical' opening in which a child is seen telephoning with a daffodil. Or perhaps it is not very remarkable, for a perceptive admirer (as distinct from a great admirer) of the book would never have attempted to dramatise it. Naturally only the simpler ingredients, the pantomime, and the satiric beast-fable elements, are capable of presentation in this form. The play is, on the lower level of drama, tolerably good fun, especially for those who have not read the book; but some children that I took to see *Toad of Toad Hall,* brought away as their chief memory nausea at the opening. For the rest they preferred their rec-ollections of the book.

B (page 346)
Of course, these details, as a rule, got into the tales, *even in the days when they were real practices,* because they had a story-making value. If I were to write a story in which it happened that a man was hanged, that *might* show in later ages, if the story survived – in itself a sign that the story possessed some permanent, and more than local or tempo-rary, value – that it was written at a period when men were really hanged, as a legal practice. *Might:* the inference

would not, of course, in that future time be certain. For certainty on that point the future inquirer would have to know definitely when hanging was practised and when I lived. I could have borrowed the incident from other times and places, from other stories; I could simply have invented it. But even if this inference happened to be correct, the hanging-scene would only occur in the story, (a) because I was aware of the dramatic, tragic, or macabre force of this incident in my tale, and (b) because those who handed it down felt this force enough to make them keep the incident in. Distance of time, sheer antiquity and alienness, might later sharpen the edge of the tragedy or the horror; but the edge must be there even for the elvish hone of antiquity to whet it. The least useful question, therefore, for literary critics at any rate, to ask or to answer about Iphigeneia, daughter of Agamemnon, is: Does the legend of her sacrifice at Aulis come down from a time when human-sacrifice was commonly practised?

I say only 'as a rule', because it is conceivable that what is now regarded as a 'story' was once something different in intent: e.g. a record of fact or ritual. I mean 'record' strictly. A story invented to explain a ritual (a process that is sometimes supposed to have frequently occurred) remains primarily a story. It takes form as such, and will survive (long after the ritual evidently) only because of its story-values. In some cases details that now are notable merely because they are strange may have once been so everyday and unregarded that they were slipped in casually: like mentioning that a man 'raised his hat', or 'caught a train'. But such casual details will not long survive change in everyday habits. Not in a period of oral transmission. In a period of writing (and of rapid changes in habits) a story may remain unchanged long enough for even its casual details to acquire the value of quaintness or queerness. Much of Dickens now has this air. One can open today an edition of a novel of his that was bought and first read when things were so in everyday life as they are in the story, though these everyday details are now already as remote from our daily habits as the Elizabethan period. But that is a special modern situation. The anthropologists and folk-lorists do not imagine any conditions of that kind. But if they are dealing with unlettered oral transmission, then they should all the more reflect that in that case they are dealing with items whose primary object was story-building, and whose primary reason for survival was the same. The Frog-King (see p. 382) is not a *Credo*, nor a manual of totem-law: it is a queer tale with a plain moral.

C (page 349)

As far as my knowledge goes, children who have an early bent for writing have no special inclination to attempt the writing of fairy-stories, unless that has been almost the sole form of literature presented to them; and they fail most markedly when they try. It is not an easy form. If children have any special leaning it is to Beast-fable, which adults often confuse with Fairy-story. The best stories by children that I have seen have been either 'realistic' (in intent), or have had as their characters animals and birds, who were in the main the zoomorphic human beings usual in Beast-fable. I imagine that this form is so often adopted principally because it allows a large measure of realism: the representation of domestic events and talk that children really know. The form itself is, however, as a rule, suggested or imposed by adults. It has a curious preponderance in the literature, good and bad, that is nowadays commonly presented to young children: I suppose it is felt to go with 'Natural History', semi-scientific books about beasts and birds that are also considered to be proper pabulum for the young. And it is reinforced by the bears and rabbits that seem in recent times almost to have ousted human dolls from the playrooms even of little girls. Children make up sagas, often long and elaborate, about their dolls. If these are shaped like bears, bears will be the characters of the sagas; but they will talk like people.

D (page 355)

I was introduced to zoology and palaeontology ('for children') quite as early as to Faërie. I saw pictures of living beasts and of true (so I was told) prehistoric animals. I liked the 'prehistoric' animals best: they had at least lived long ago, and hypothesis (based on somewhat slender evidence) cannot avoid a gleam of fantasy. But I did not like being told that these creatures were 'dragons'. I can still re-feel the irritation that I felt in childhood at assertions of instructive relatives (or their gift-books) such as these: 'snowflakes are fairy jewels', or 'are more beautiful than fairy jewels'; 'the marvels of the ocean depths are more wonderful than fairyland'. Children expect the differences they feel but cannot analyse to be explained by their elders, or at least recognised, not to be ignored or denied. I was keenly alive to the beauty of 'Real things', but it seemed to me quibbling to confuse this with the wonder of 'Other things'. I was eager to study Nature, actually more eager than I was to read most fairy-stories; but I did not want to be quibbled into Science and cheated out of Faërie by people who seemed to assume that by some kind of original sin I should prefer fairy-tales, but according to some kind of new religion I ought to be induced to like science. Nature is no doubt a life-study, or a study for eternity (for those so gifted); but there is a part of man which is not 'Nature', and which therefore is not obliged to study it, and is, in fact, wholly unsatisfied by it.

E (page 364)

There is, for example, in surrealism commonly present a morbidity or un-ease very rarely found in literary fantasy. The mind that produced the depicted images may often be suspected to have been in fact already morbid; yet this is not a necessary explanation in all cases. A curious disturbance of the mind is often set up by the very act of drawing things of this kind, a state similar in quality and consciousness of morbidity to the sensations in a high fever, when the mind develops a distressing fecundity and facility in figure-making, seeing forms sinister or grotesque in all visible objects about it.

I am speaking here, of course, of the primary expression of Fantasy in 'pictorial' arts, not of 'illustrations'; nor of the cinematograph. However good in themselves, illustrations do little good to fairy-stories. The radical distinction between all art (including drama) that offers a *visible* presentation and true literature is that it imposes one visible form. Literature works from mind to mind and is thus more progenitive. It is at once more universal and more poignantly particular. If it speaks of *bread* or *wine* or *stone* or *tree,* it appeals to the whole of these things, to their ideas; yet each hearer will give to them a peculiar personal embodiment in his imagination. Should the story say 'he ate bread', the dramatic producer or painter can only show 'a piece of bread' according to his taste or fancy, but the hearer of the story will think of bread in general and picture it in some form of his own. If a story says 'he climbed a hill and saw a river in the valley below', the illustrator may catch, or nearly catch, his own vision of such a scene; but every hearer of the words will have his own picture, and it will be made out of all the hills and rivers and dales he has ever seen, but specially out of The Hill, The River, The Valley which were for him the first embodiment of the word.

F (page 366)

I am referring, of course, primarily to fantasy of forms and visible shapes. Drama can be made out of the impact upon human characters of some event of Fantasy, or Faërie, that requires no machinery, or that can be assumed or reported to have happened. But that is not fantasy in dramatic result; the human characters hold the stage and upon them attention is concentrated. Drama of this sort (exemplified by some of Barrie's plays) can be used frivolously, or it can be used for satire, or for conveying such 'messages' as the playwright may have in his mind – for men. Drama is anthropocentric. Fairy-story and Fantasy need not be. There are, for instance, many stories telling how men and women have disappeared and spent years among the fairies, without noticing the passage of time, or appearing to grow older. In *Mary Rose* Barrie wrote a play on this theme. No fairy is seen. The cruelly tormented human beings are there all the time. In spite of the sentimental star and the angelic voices at the end (in the printed version) it is a painful play, and can easily be made diabolic: by substituting (as I have seen it done) the elvish call for 'angel voices' at the end. The non-dramatic fairy-stories, in so far as they are concerned with the human victims, can also be pathetic or horrible. But they need not be. In most of them the fairies are also there, on equal terms. In some stories they are the real interest. Many of the short folk-lore accounts of such incidents purport to be just pieces of 'evidence' about fairies, items in an agelong accumulation of 'lore' concerning them and the modes of their existence. The sufferings of human beings who come into contact with them (often enough, wilfully) are thus seen in quite a different perspective. A drama could be made about the sufferings of a victim of research in radiology, but hardly about radium itself. But it is possible to be primarily interested in radium (not radiologists) – or primarily interested in Faërie, not tortured mortals. One interest will produce a scientific book, the other a fairy-story. Drama cannot well cope with either.

G (page 382)

The absence of this sense is a mere hypothesis concerning men of the lost past, whatever wild confusions men of today, degraded or deluded, may suffer. It is just as legitimate an hypothesis, and one more in agreement with what little is recorded concerning the thoughts of men of old on this subject, that this sense was once stronger. That fantasies which blended the human form with animal and vegetable forms, or gave human faculties to beasts, are ancient is, of course, no evidence for confusion at all. It is, if anything, evidence to the contrary. Fantasy does not blur the sharp outlines of the real world; for it depends on them. As far as our western, European, world is concerned, this 'sense of separation' has in fact been attacked and weakened in modern times not by fantasy but by scientific theory. Not by stories of centaurs or werewolves or enchanted bears, but by the hypotheses (or dogmatic guesses) of scientific writers who classed Man not only as 'an animal' – that correct classification is ancient – but as 'only an animal'. There has been a consequent distortion of sentiment. The natural love of men not wholly corrupt for beasts, and the human desire to 'get inside the skin' of living things, has run riot. We now get men who love animals more than men; who pity sheep so much that they curse shepherds as wolves; who weep over a slain warhorse and vilify dead soldiers. It is now, not in the days when fairy-stories were begotten, that we get 'an absence of the sense of separation'.

H (page 384)

The verbal ending – usually held to be as typical of the end of fairy-stories as 'once upon a time' is of the beginning – 'and they lived happily ever after' is an artificial device. It does not deceive anybody. End-phrases of this kind are to be compared to the margins and frames of pictures, and are no more to be thought of as the real end of any particular fragment of the seamless Web of Story than the frame is of the visionary scene, or the casement of the Outer World. These phrases may be plain or elaborate, simple or extravagant, as artificial and as necessary as frames plain, or carved, or gilded. 'And if they have not gone away they are there still.' 'My story is done – see there is a little mouse; anyone who catches it may make himself a fine fur cap of it.' 'And they lived happily ever after.' 'And when the wedding was over, they sent me home with little paper shoes on a causeway of pieces of glass.'

Endings of this sort suit fairy-stories, because such tales have a greater sense and grasp of the endlessness of the World of Story than most modern 'realistic' stories, already hemmed within the narrow confines of their own small time. A sharp cut in the endless tapestry is not unfittingly marked by a formula, even a grotesque or comic one. It was an irresistible development of modern illustration (so largely photographic) that borders should be abandoned and the 'picture' end only with the paper. This method may be suitable for photographs; but it is altogether inappropriate for the pictures that illustrate or are inspired by fairy-stories. An enchanted forest requires a margin, even an elaborate border. To print it conterminous with the page, like a 'shot' of the Rockies in *Picture Post*, as if it were indeed a 'snap' of fairyland or a 'sketch by our artist on the spot', is a folly and an abuse.

As for the beginnings of fairy-stories: one can scarcely improve on the formula *Once upon a time*. It has an immediate effect. This effect can be appreciated by reading, for instance, the fairy-story *The Terrible Head* in the *Blue Fairy Book*. It is Andrew Lang's own adaptation of the story of Perseus and the Gorgon. It begins 'once upon a time', and it does not name any year or land or person. Now this treatment does something which could be called 'turning mythology into fairy-story'. I should prefer to say that it turns high fairy-story (for such is the Greek tale) into a particular form that is at present familiar in our land: a nursery or 'old wives' form. Namelessness is not a virtue but an accident, and should not have been imitated; for vagueness in this regard is a debasement, a corruption due to forgetfulness and lack of skill. But not so, I think, the timelessness. That beginning is not poverty-stricken but significant. It produces at a stroke the sense of a great uncharted world of time.

AFTERWORD

One of the great rewards of being a book illustrator is the incentive and opportunity to return to stories that I had read many years before, and to engage with them again – often with more attention to detail – as well as find pleasure in works that are new to me. I read some of the stories in this volume for the first time just a few months ago, and regretted that I hadn't had it to hand when my children were expecting bedtime stories every evening.

Many of the most popular children's stories have their roots in tales invented for particular children, and this casual, often serendipitous, approach produces a stream of ideas which are later refined into great literature. With Tolkien's shorter stories and poems, I am even more aware of the presence of the author, and his children. There are elements and events that are so strikingly original that they could only arise as a result of observations and conversations ignited by two or more lively minds. In my mind, I see the mariner in "Errantry" brought into being as the author showed his children an insect floating, or flying across a pool on a summer's day, and speculated on the adventures it was embarking upon. For me it conjures up – even more strongly than the surreal and wonderful imagery – that magical moment of transmission, when an idea from one mind takes root in another, and a new story or creature is born.

Some of the other poems and tales have a more subtle, personal and elegiac tone, and I can imagine these being composed in the professor's study, between lectures and tutorials, in moments of relaxation or of boredom, like those of the scribes whose haiku-like musings have survived on the borders of the manuscripts they were copying. Whatever their genesis, I feel that much closer to the author, and value his story-telling skills even more for the lightness of touch and invention that he brings to some of his less consequential work.

I believe that we need good tale-tellers now, as much as we did when the oral tradition was the only way that they were passed on; that the active transmission of stories plays a vital role in the development of the brain. The quality of the stories that surround us as we grow up is vitally important to our well-being, in the same way as the quality of our food and our environment. The most beautiful aspect of this shared story-telling – and we have great examples of this in *Tales from the Perilous Realm* – is that the collaboration and engagement between teller and audience means that they are embarking on a journey together, which can lead to the most unexpected and wondrous of places.

ALAN LEE